Praise for *The Chords of War*

"In a meaningless war, the soldier must find meaning from within—this is the crux and conflict of *The Chords of War*, a must-read contemporary war novel by Christopher Meeks and Samuel Gonzalez, Jr., inspired by the real-life story of Gonzalez. An ex-rocker, Max, enlists as a military policeman in the Army after a series of bad decisions cause him to reconsider his life."
—**Dario DiBattista,** Editor of
Retire the Colors: Veterans and Civilians on Iraq and Afghanistan

"*The Chords of War* should be labeled memoir. It's real, it's honest, and it paints the Iraq War, and those who fought in it, in a realistic and truthful light. It reminds me of the saying that 'sometimes we can be more honest with fiction than we can with non-fiction.' It's not your usual war-novel, and that's good; that's why it should be read."
—**Michael Anthony, U.S. Army,** author of
Mass Casualties, and Civilianized: A Young Veteran's Memoir

"It's not your father's or grandfather's war novel. *The Chords of War*, about a young rock-and-roller who only thinks he is leaving music behind when he joins the Army to fight in Iraq, is realistically and movingly true to the voice, thought, and emotions of twenty-first century American soldiers on deployment. *The Chords of War* breaks clean of Vietnam and World War II war-writing traditions by incisively portraying the war experience of millennial-era men and women agonizingly stalled between adolescence and adulthood."
—**Professor and Lt. Col. (Ret.) Peter Molin,**
U.S. Army, Rutgers University

"*The Chords of War* brilliantly shows that the chaos, destruction, and terror of war can spawn primal desires, not only to survive, but also to love, to create, and, if you've got a guitar and the chops, to rock the hell out."
—**Graham Yost,** acclaimed writer and television showrunner
Justified, The Americans, The Pacific, Speed

Other Books by Christopher Meeks

A Death in Vegas

Blood Drama

Love at Absolute Zero

The Brightest Moon of the Century

Months & Seasons

The Middle-Aged Man and the Sea

Who Lives (A Drama)

Feature Film by Samuel Gonzalez, Jr.

Railway Spine

THE CHORDS OF WAR

*Inspired by a True Story of
Adolescence, War, and Rock'n'Roll*

CHRISTOPHER MEEKS

SAMUEL GONZALEZ, JR.

White Whisker Books
Los Angeles

ISBN: 978-0986326530
Library of Congress Control Number: 2017913704
Copyright © 2017 by Christopher Meeks

First edition

Associate Editor: Carol Fuchs
Book and cover design: Deborah Daly
Cover image: Jeff Joseph

To the men and women who have served their country and haven't been heard. May this book be your music.

Prologue

Music filled his mind. Specifically, seventeen-year-old Max Rivera dreamed of his last great gig with the Mad Suburbans. They played at a sleazy little bar in Orlando's Milk District where dollar beers flowed, the lighting came from strings of white Christmas lights, and cigarette smoke filled the place as if a mosquito fogger had plowed through. Nonetheless, Max glowed, his fingers ripping the chords on his white Fender Stratocaster. He had the greatest job in the world, just like J.R.'s ice cream truck when Max was a kid. They both gave out treats.

In the tightly packed lounge, men tried to hit on the women rather than focus on the band, the band's crazy hair, their ripped clothes, but Max nonetheless got people dancing with his songs "Now Comes Tomorrow" and "Ruby-Throated Sparrow." Max yelled into his mike, laughing, feeling the electricity beneath his fingers travel all the way into his amp. The crowd blasted with a cheer. Max, of course, didn't attach any meaning to this, meaning to life. He didn't know anything about philosophy—didn't know that it was a thing to know. Didn't know most people didn't. Didn't know whether he had choice or not. Did he have choice to dream this dream? Did that relate to his purpose? Was he like Galvani's frog leg—a dead leg that would move if electricity tickled it? Were we all just frog legs?

The dream was ruined only when his girlfriend, Lynette, in her dumpy Disneyland sweatshirt, glared at him, glared as if to remind him he was nothing.

A hammering started. No, it was the phone. Phone? Everyone in the bar stopped to look at him.

Max struggled awake to find the phone ringing. His head pounded. He rolled over in bed, and his hand and arm whacked around the nightstand. He finally touched the phone, an old-fashioned kind, one with a handset and a cord. Where was he?

"Hello?" he mumbled, and a happy up-and-down computer voice said, "Good morning, Mr. Rivera. This is your wake-up call. You wanted me to remind you, too, of the duck march at nine a.m."

"Fuckin' duck march?" he blurted and hung up the phone.

He jammed an extra pillow under his head and opened his eyes, trying to remember where he was. The throb in his head could be a metronome. He seemed to be in a hotel room with a high view. Duck march?

Now he remembered. When he'd checked in, the young woman at the front desk had explained that every morning at nine, five mallard ducks came down a special elevator from the roof, and a duck master led them down the carpet to the fountain. People lined up on either side to watch.

"That's what rich people call fun?" he had said.

"It's a tradition. And, yeah, kind of fun," replied the young woman, a clerk only a few years older than he.

"Sounds interesting," he said about the ducks, but he had meant it as "like needles in the eye."

And now he remembered why he'd come. Florida was for dead people, and he'd decided to join them. He booked a room at the elegant Peabody Hotel, which was the second tallest building in Orlando. The tallest was an exclusive office building, but there was no way he could get in there.

His plan would have worked, too, if his friend Claire hadn't called, having heard about his breakup with Lynette, and she weaseled out of him that he was at the Peabody. She assumed he was partying and asked if she could join him. Hot, red-headed Claire. She'd told her parents she would be studying with a girlfriend, but she got naked with him instead.

He turned his head to the side. Claire wasn't there. She had left the bed. "Claire?" he said as loudly as his weak voice would allow. No answer. He reached for what looked to be a note on her pillow.

It read, "Fuck you, Max. You said mean things."

Mean things? They were just true things.

"We're not losers—at least I'm not. You're a doosh."

He was a better speller than that. It was "douche."

"P.S. I took your money for a cab."

He held his poor, aching head. He saw all the empty mini-bottles and beer cans on the floor. He wondered if he'd be charged beyond the one hundred dollars he left as deposit.

The TV was on, but the sound was off. It showed a single tall building with smoke coming out of it. He vaguely remembered turning on the TV at night, but he didn't remember watching it. He'd been too tired to do anything, including killing himself. Maybe now he could do it.

He lumbered to the dresser to grab a cigarette. Maybe it'd stop the headache. He lit a match, which made his eyes blink and water. Christ. The lit cigarette slipped from his fingers, and the cherry popped off and burrowed into the Berber. Smoke rose, and he hammered it out with his bare heel, then yelped at the pain. He was doing nothing right.

First his girlfriend, then the band, now Claire. Everything he touched turned to shit. He looked down again, thirty stories. All he had to do was fly, and it'd be over. He needed to be brave and fly. He smashed his fist against the window, but it just boomed and didn't break. How to get through? It was time to fly.

A voice on the TV said, "We have word in that perhaps a small plane had gone off course." The sound was on, after all.

Max moved closer and could see it was a boxy skyscraper against a cobalt blue sky. There was no context, but clearly it wasn't Florida. The building was on fire. Why?

A wide shot from another angle had the Empire State Building in close, and in the distance, the building on fire had a matching tower, both far taller than the many buildings nearby. Beyond that gleamed a bay. The screen went back to a closer view of just the one tower burning. Max rubbed his lightly tattooed arms, suddenly cold, and he just stared. The same smooth male voice said, "We're told a number of firefighting companies have been called in. There are no ladders that can go that high. This is the north tower. We're trying to get an FDNY spokesperson to tell us how this fire will be fought. Buildings like this, I understand, are designed with automatic sprinklers as well as fire hose couplings on every floor. All should be well."

As Max stared, something came from the right side of the screen—a jet? It flew behind the tower on fire, and a huge orange smoky blast burst from either side of the building. "Oh, my God," he said in chorus with a man and woman's voice on TV. The announcer said, "I think a second plane has just hit the second tower."

"I didn't see a plane go in," said another male voice. "The building just exploded."

"We saw a plane come in from the side, from the right," said the woman.

Max felt as if he were hallucinating. Did a jet just crash into a building? Or was this just a strange movie? He turned the channel. The next channel, though, showed the same thing from a different angle where both towers were shown. Both were on fire. Max was about to shout for Claire, but he remembered she was gone. Maybe the front desk had answers. Maybe that woman at the front desk knew what's going on now.

When the doors opened to the lobby, no one stood behind the long check-in counter. As he walked through the vast space, his black Chuck Taylors squeaked on the white marble floor and the occasional black inlay. Because of how quiet the place was, it was as if he were in church—or the depths of outer space. He looked for the staff past the modern art, the areas with cushy chairs, the impressive pillars and curvy white walls. He found them around the corner at the mirrored bar. At least twenty people, half of them wearing Peabody Hotel uniforms, quietly watched the TV above the bar. Max joined them, and as the TV gave a slow-motion replay of the plane going in and exploding, everyone there gasped at the fireball. "Definitely a large jetliner," said a different announcer on the TV. "We may look back on this eleventh day in September as a turning point."

"I think it's terrorists," an old man in tennis whites next to Max said. "It's going to mean war." Max didn't think about who would fight it or where. He didn't think whether this would change his life. He didn't think if he could find choice or meaning.

The TV showed the plane yet again, and Max's headache reasserted itself. He really should get some aspirin or something for it. A bottle of Jack Daniels caught his eye, that would work, but he'd never be served. An older woman on his other side, silver-haired, a bit chunky, madly pressed numbers on her cell phone. She wore baggy beige shorts and a stiff blouse as if she were lost on a safari. Anxiety cut across her face. Apparently no one answered.

She looked at Max, worried. "Do you know someone there?" she asked, touching his shoulder as if expecting a yes. He said nothing.

She frantically punched in another phone number. He realized he'd been ready to kill himself today, and now in these two buildings on TV, people who surely wanted to live had been crushed and incinerated. They had families, hopes, goals, but some sick fucks decided to kill innocent people.

"My God," the woman gasped, and her shoulders shook. She stood, isolated, apart from the others, and closed her small Ericsson cell phone, a model Max had thought about getting because it was so small and had something new called Blue Tooth. He didn't know what to do for her.

"I take it you know someone there," Max said.

"My son works high up in one of those buildings," she said between sobs. "He won't answer his phone. I can't reach him."

He nodded.

"Why would two planes crash into those buildings?" she asked him. "What does this get anyone?"

He shook his head. "It's a strange world." He didn't know then, but his world in a few years would become stranger, the way heat could feel like ice, the way blood could look like sweet Hershey's syrup in the right fire light and sand. He would look back on today and think, "Yes, it started there."

She looked right in his eyes as if he might have more answers.

He said, "My girlfriend, the first girl I loved, slept with everyone in the band just to get back at me. The world doesn't make sense."

The woman shook her head, taking his hand. "You're a good boy."

He shook his head, not believing it.

Her phone rang. She looked hopeful. "Charles?" she said into her phone, and then she beamed and spoke quickly, stepping away.

Some ducks quacked. Max looked over to the red carpet. Apparently no one had told the duck master about the burning towers, and the red-jacketed man guided his five ducks down the empty red runway. The man looked around, confused, and then peered at Max as if Max had the answer to why everyone was at the bar instead of the duck march. No matter. The man guided his charges forward. Each duck faithfully followed the one in front. As if they now knew it was a solemn time, they did not quack. They just marched.

Kuwait and Iraq, November 2006

As we cleaned our barracks for the final time in Fort Lewis before our deployment, I felt excited. I swept around my bunk, tightened my duffle, and smiled in anticipation. God knows, I'm no thinker, but it occurred to me that few people loved where they were in life, and I did. Physically, I'd never been better. My small paunch had hardened into washboard abs. My arms could be Popeye's, my legs, more powerful than a locomotive. Mentally, too, I felt confident, and my parents were proud. Add to that, I was headed off with my two best friends, Hitch and Styles. I had purpose, helping my country. What more could a person want?

Sure, somewhere inside I knew Iraq wouldn't be easy, yet after all the training, I felt ready. Everyone in the platoon, men and women, watched my back, and I covered theirs. To be a part of something—that's special. Add to that, I'd be leaving the country for my first time ever. Ah, to travel! I'd see things beyond my dreams. I hadn't felt this eager since Christmas as a kid.

A hundred Army soldiers and I headed to Kuwait City in a C-17 military aircraft. We would be deployed to Iraq after extra training. The seats were arranged lengthwise against the plane's sidewalls with conventional rows in the middle.

With its vast space and fluorescent lighting, the C-17 felt like a moving Greyhound bus station. Two car-sized shipping containers, lashed down in the middle, did not add any elegance. With little to do, I fell asleep.

As if someone had shoved me, I awoke to a falling sensation and a huge creaking sound. Screams erupted. My right hand pressed against my chest. My uniformed comrades around me look startled, and one guy yelled "Shit!" Then we leveled off. The plane became steady. I laughed as I had on Disney World's Space Mountain.

I stood and moved to one of few windows on the plane. The clouds below me looked like the top of a brain, and the flashes of light going off in the ridges could be nerve endings sparking out electricity. *Synapse.* I remembered the term from high school biology. I'd never made it beyond a single semester of community college. I'd played in a few punk rock bands instead.

Soon, the plane started shaking. We must have been entering a storm, which was what probably had awakened me. I focused on the beauty of those flashes. "Wow," I blurted without thinking. A soldier near me seated on the sidewall stood to look out the same window, and then the captain sitting on the other side of the cavernous tube stepped over to see. Trying to make a good impression on the captain, I said, "Isn't nature amazing?"

After looking at my name on my uniform, then staring out the window at the clouds several seconds, he said, "Yes, Private Rivera, but that's not lightning. Those are bombs going off. We're over Baghdad—over hell." He sat down, grinning.

The short soldier next to me gasped, and only then did I realize the soldier was a woman—stocky, sturdy, but a feminine face. After other young faces jammed into the window, my skinny friend Hitch pushed on his tiptoes to look and said, "Shit. We're the mole in Whack-a-Mole." Whispers and groans erupted as fast as lit gasoline. The plane shook harder, and while it was probably from simple turbulence, we all surely assumed anti-aircraft missiles. The fasten seatbelt sign blinked on. I sat and clutched my seat as if we were already careening in a ball of flame. All the motivational films we'd witnessed in recruitment centers and in training—the "Be All You Can Be" and "Army Strong" stuff—did not prepare us for this moment.

Forty-five minutes later, we landed safely in Kuwait City. When I stepped out the rear into the sauna air, the hot tarmac nonetheless felt wonderfully solid. Adrenaline rushed through me as the words of our LT came back: "Every minute in Iraq can be filled with danger—snipers, car bombs, suicide bombers, IEDs, or an ambush. You'll have a lot of boredom, punctuated by terror. It's okay to be afraid. We all need a healthy dose of fright."

Heat waves made the green trees that edged the field and the brown mountains in the distance waver. It reminded me of when a film got stuck in a projector, and the single projected image would melt.

This would be home for ten days. After desert training and acclimatization, we would drive into Iraq. Our superiors wanted to see that we could perform in the heat and hoped to boost our confidence in our skills and equipment. We drove different vehicles and were reminded again and again of the rules of engagement. Near the end, we practiced fighting in a training village of two-story buildings, abandoned cars, and dirt roads with real IEDs. The bombs weren't powerful or filled with nails, but strong enough to show that, in a real situation, we could be dead.

Our company, the 571st Military Police Company based out of Fort Lewis in Tacoma, had 15% women, 85% men. We were a crazy parfait of people, like Hoogerheide, a thin woman from backwoods Georgia with an acne-covered face and fast feet, or Tracewski, a former lobsterman from Maine with fingers like thick ropes. None of us were particularly handsome, beautiful, or educated, and we came from poor families. If we had been to college, we could've been officers. We joined in a time of war in both Iraq and Afghanistan. I entered the Army for a few reasons: it was a job, it would give me discipline, and it would get me the hell out of fucking Florida.

We'd spent nearly a year getting ready for our deployment. Before I'd been a black-haired punk rocker whose only talents were writing teen-angst lyrics in a half-torn journal and playing a killer guitar—none of which translated to the Army, a place where music was banned in boot camp except for the cadences we barked out as we marched.

Now, we were one of five companies in the 42nd Military Police Brigade coming over to aid the infantry in forward operating bases north of Baghdad. In theory, at least, we military police would secure an area before the infantry went in to search for or fight insurgent groups. Before basic training, none of us knew where Iraq was, and no one knew that Arabic was the main language spoken there. Then again, I doubt any of us knew where North Dakota was, either.

Each day in Kuwait, to my surprise, made me anxious. I didn't have an appetite, and I didn't sleep well—perhaps because a number of soldiers didn't take the training seriously. One guy learning to be a sniper bragged, "I want to kill five hundred hajis, one bullet at a time!" The record by an American sniper was just over a hundred for an American sniper. Others laughed when someone came too close to a practice IED that blew off. One guy shouted, "You're fucking dead, man. You're a sweet potato pie!"

I also worried that my mother fretted about me, so I sent her an email from one of the computers in the Kuwaiti camp. I wrote her and cc'd Dad that I'd arrived, that it was hot, and I'd spotted a McDonald's here with its name in an Arabic scrawl. I said Kuwait City was on the sea, and we'd be in the desert. I tried to sound sure and untroubled, even if I felt the complete opposite. They divorced after I'd left high school, so I tried to be nice to them equally.

My mom had been born in Panama, where my father had been stationed in the U.S. Army. He wooed her right, always with one of her family members present, until they let him take her disco dancing. She didn't know much English, and my father, despite being a Rivera, didn't know much Spanish. He asked for her hand in marriage, and after a small ceremony, they moved to the Bronx, where he'd grown up poor. I'm told their first year was tough.

In those days, my father zipped off to work as a UPS driver, leaving my mother and me in a tough neighborhood. I didn't know it then, but my mother was scared, what with gang violence and neighbors robbed. She left the apartment only when she had to. I remember those years fondly, though, with my mother turning up the stereo loudly to block out the sounds of the neighborhood. "Oye Coma Va" remains one of my favorites.

I thought of Carlos Santana's lyrical guitar the day we had to leave Kuwait for Iraq, and the whoop whoop of a helicopter swept over our heads. Two platoons of just over twenty soldiers each drove north from Kuwait City toward Iraq's border. My stomach gurgled, empty, as I couldn't make myself eat. Some platoons got to fly into Baghdad, but ours just received reconditioned Humvees, our High-Mobility Multipurpose Wheeled Vehicles, ready to return to the theatre of war. The Hummers on American roads were variations of these wide-stanced Jeep-like vehicles. Ours were painted in camouflage. All were dented like hell, old and beat, but many had the latest armor added. They all once had working air conditioning, but as the LT explained, "The AC stops functioning in the Iraqi dust."

I was a gunner on top. I had the ability to swivel using my feet with some steel armor in front and, lower, around me. I felt exposed. There were newer models where a gunner could stand in the Humvee through a hole in the roof. Here I could certainly get hit from above or the side. I needed to remain vigilant. The enemy could hide in a mere indentation in the desert.

The air from above rushed in like exhaust from a jet engine. Florida had been hot, but not this hot, oven hot. None of the trucks followed closely because if an IED buried in the road went off, only one truck would get it. The whole platoon was split up into many Humvees. Each Humvee held three or four soldiers, and each Humvee was a team with a team leader: a specialist or corporal. That's how the Army worked, always with a clear chain of command. Every four Humvees were a squad, which had a squad leader, a specialist like Styles or a sergeant like the monster guy in my Humvee, Sergeant Gasparyan. Together, we were two squads, one platoon, with a platoon leader.

Our platoon leader was a first lieutenant named Graver. He was a beefy guy with a friendly smile but also at times a sharp stare. He must have worked with weights because of his broad shoulders. Just a few years older than me, he'd gone to the U.S. Military Academy at West Point. He'd grown up on a ranch in Wyoming and knew how to talk like he was one of us.

"Listen to me, and I'll keep you alive," he told us when we stopped at a pull-off near the Iraq border—a small gas-refill depot behind concertina wire and blast walls. It had blue porta-potties and a handful of trees sticking out of the sand. The whole area was so flat and bleak, with only hair-plugs of vegetation here and there, that I wondered how the trees grew. "This is your last place besides our camps where you can relax outside your vehicles. Think of this spot like a fucking rest stop on an American freeway. We're going to wait for sunset. Once we cross the border, all of damn Iraq is the war zone. While most of the highway is paved and wide like in Nevada, there can be enemy, ambushes, and IEDs. Even in the middle of nowhere, we're not safe. Stay in your Humvees once we cross."

The idea was we'd travel to Baghdad under the cover of darkness. I went for a porta-potty. Once we crossed the border, we'd have to piss into empty Gatorade bottles, so I took advantage. I can't say that a porta-potty in a hundred-degree heat is pleasant. The stink alone could curl your hair. Add flies, and you wanted out of there as fast as possible. I occupied my mind by reading the graffiti. Why Chuck Norris jokes appeared on porta-potty walls across Kuwait, I don't know, other than maybe soldiers wanted to channel him. ("Chuck Norris has already been to Mars—that's why there're no signs of life.")

I had the squirts. I can't lie. I was fucking nervous. I looked down into the stinking hole, imagining maybe I could jump in and just end it here. How the hell did I let myself in for this nightmare?

After I wiped and stepped back outside, I quickly lit up. Ever since I'd left America, my cigarette habit doubled.

Whit Hitchcock and Blake Styles, my two best friends, joined me at my Humvee. We rode in different trucks. Thin-boned Hitch didn't smoke but Styles did, and I offered Styles one. Hitch, from Texas, short and only eighteen, reminded me of Peter Pan, more kid than adult who tried to seem worldly and Southern, forever pushing his Texas drawl like he was George W. Bush—not my favorite president. Still, Hitch was so gosh-darn innocent, always asking questions like "You think if you burped and farted at the same time, part of your colon collapses?" you had to like him.

Styles, in contrast, a New Yorker, seemed out-of-place in this yokel Army, like a movie star among the masses. He listened to people and nodded. He'd give his George Clooney grin and often answer with something so smart, we didn't know what the hell he was saying. He talked about some German who liked to live in the moment. "Present in the moment," Styles said. Seems to me with someone shooting at you, you're living present in the moment—unless the bullet connects, and then you don't.

"Isn't this place a trip?" Hitch said. "It's like we're aliens on a whole new planet."

"Yeah," said Styles. "Or it's like we're on a tour of an amazing cave, and soon we'll see stalagmites."

"There's another of them big words," said Hitch.

"It's more like we're inside an Easy Bake Oven, and we're fucked," I said. "And we're still in the safe zone."

"We're going to have a year of this shit," said Styles. "Heat with bullets coming at us."

"As long as there're strip joints, I don't care," said Hitch.

Styles laughed. "Didn't you even Google this place? Haven't you noticed the women covered head to toe? No strip joints, no alcohol. Just Allah."

"Why do you have to be so negative?" said Hitch.

We stood stone-like for a while as we watched Private Jenny Brown, one of our fellow MPs, rush out of a john and gasp for air, laughing. A light-skinned African-American, she spoke giddily to Wilhelm, a husky guy my height, quiet but earnest. He was more a listener than a talker. I didn't even know where he was from. He looked down and kicked the dirt as she spoke. He must have been even more at a loss of words with her.

Out of the blue, Hitch said, "You ever think about dying?"

"Heidegger thought a lot about death," said Styles. "Said it colors every moment of our existence. It's not the physical death that's important, but one's attitude toward mortality."

Hitch's face screwed up as if a kangaroo just hopped from behind a bush. "I'm talking about God," said Hitch.

"Don't start getting into that God shit," said Styles. "When we joined, we each balanced certain risk factors."

"Balanced risk?" I said. "I said sign me up."

"Me, too," said Hitch.

Styles put his hand on my shoulder. "In your case, making a living as a musician was riskier."

"I just wasn't ready for nine-to-five shit," said Hitch. "This seemed a lot more fun."

"This is fun?" I asked.

"Isn't everything we do just pushing a boulder up a mountain, only to have it roll down again?" asked Styles.

"Stop it," I said to Styles. "You always say weird shit like that."

"I'm trying to say life is a bit absurd, no?"

"All I know," said Hitch," is that I didn't want no job at Staples."

"So you're willing to take risks," Styles said to Hitch. "Good. Here you are, not part of the domesticated, comfort-loving masses—no accident."

"Whatever," said Hitch. "God is a factor. I'm not ashamed to believe."

"That you'll be protected?" I said.

"Yeah, protected," said Hitch. "And if I'm not, God will have his reasons to bring me back."

For the last few days, Hitch had been parading God as if he'd had emails from the deity. We usually let it go.

"You don't think the other side has a God?" said Styles. "Why do you think they blow themselves up?" He slapped dust off his sleeve.

"Their belief system says to kill innocent people," said Hitch. "We're after the bad guys."

"Aren't we the bad guys to them?" I said jumping in. "And what about Ireland? Christian against Christian there. Was it the wrong Christ?"

"You too, Rivera?" said Hitch.

"For you, killing other people is God's work?" said Styles to Hitch, incredulous.

"Hopefully we don't have to kill a lot," said Hitch. "I think of it more as a missionary's mission. We're here to show them freedom and democracy is the best way to live."

"Dressed as soldiers?" said Styles. Turning to me, he said, "What do you believe in, Mad Max?"

"I think we'll do just fine. Just be careful."

Wilhelm strutted over.

"Hey, I saw you chatting up Private Brown," said Styles with a wink, teasing him. "Good going, man."

"Not really," he said. "Now that we're here, how're the women still with us?" He thumbed back to Jenny Brown. "How isn't this combat?"

"My guess is we'll be in trucks more often than not," said Styles.

"And trucks don't blow up? It just doesn't seem right they're here. We're supposed to protect our women."

"Yeah," I said. "It makes us look weird, like we're not so strong." The fact that women could be military police and serve in the Middle East just seemed odd to me. And why did the military insist women weren't in combat?

"You were in the training," said Styles. "We need women to talk to and inspect Iraqi females. Men and women don't mix in this society."

"That's crazy," Wilhelm said.

"Jenny's sweet," said Styles.

Hitch's mouth dropped as if he disagreed. I knew her as rough—in a street-smart way.

Wilhelm stared at Styles, then smiled shyly.

"Go on back and talk with her," said Styles. "Better she humps you than any of us. We're spoken for."

"I'm not," said Hitch.

"You just have to say the right things," said Styles to Wilhelm. "Women like to talk about their periods. It shows you're in touch with their feminine side."

"Their periods?"

"Ask her which brand of tampon she prefers."

Wilhelm nodded, taking it seriously. I could only laugh.

"I'm fuckin' with you, Wilhelm," said Styles. "The point is just to talk with her. Be friendly."

Wilhelm gave a thumbs up and walked back to Private Brown.

"I don't know," I said once Wilhelm was out of earshot. "That guy's too literal. I don't think he can make small talk."

"Everyone's got to learn," said Styles.

Hitch shook his head. "She's tough. She'll eat him up."

"He'll be fine."

Soon Brown shouted at Wilhelm, "What the fuck's wrong with you! What brand? What brand cream do you use to jerk off with?" She gave him the finger and walked off.

"Well, now I feel bad," said Styles. We all laughed.

Knowing we were going to move into Iraq soon, anxiety reached a recurring high C on my insides, and I pulled out my iPod to calm me down. As I fit one earbud in, someone touched my shoulder, and I turned around to see the LT.

"You don't want that in your ears right now, guy," he said. "You need your ears to save you—such as for incoming rockets, shooting going on, or hundreds of other deadly things."

Of course, my stomach did a few new somersaults. At this point, the horizon had nearly swallowed the cherry lozenge of the sun, giving the strata of clouds above us a parfait quality. Some people might have thought this worthy of painting, watercolor by God, but inside I was screaming.

The LT shouted for everyone to hear, "Everyone on point. Get your thumbs out of your asses. Let's move out."

These were my last minutes of this particular life.

Soon, we crossed the Kuwait-Iraq Barrier, which was the 120-mile border fence extending six miles into Iraq and three miles into Kuwait, bolstered with a berm and deep trench, electrified fence, and concertina wire. The United Nations Security Council approved it after Iraq invaded Kuwait in the 1990-91 Gulf War.

The first little town we passed through felt like the desert sand had somehow morphed into sand-colored buildings, cracked and broken. Many of the shops looked long abandoned, and it made me feel we were in a time warp, a place from a thousand years ago—no electric wires, no paving, not a lot of people. The women we saw often strolled in long dark cloaks and head scarves. Some covered their faces. How did they cope with the heat? The men appeared more Western—shirts or T-shirts and pants. Some of them, though, wore turbans and cloaks, and they scared me as an assault weapon could be under that.

"That guy looks badass!" said Hitch on the radio, speaking about a grim-faced man in white and a turban that my truck had passed and his truck was approaching.

"Stay sharp, soldiers," said the LT. "Careful. And no unnecessary comments."

The citizens looked at us with suspicion, as if we were the invaders rather than the ones protecting them. Now that I thought of it, we must appear alien to them. We had to wear much protective gear including Kevlar vests over T-shirts, and jackets and gloves over that. Add a backpack, canteen, a helmet with a light attached, a communications radio with earphone and mike, protective goggles, and kneepads. Each of us was the Michelin Man meets the Terminator.

We'd learned the rules of engagement as if it were a mantra. We had to hold our hand out and say "stop." If they did not, then we had to point our rifle at them. If they still did not stop, we needed to shoot in the air. If they still did not, we had to kill them—man, woman, child, or even dog. We'd never know who or what would blow up.

Once we made it through the town with no incident, I breathed relief. How was I going to get through a year of this?

"Just over three hundred miles to go," said the LT over the radio. I twisted my head in small movements back and forth, noticing the wind made different sounds as I did so—almost like music.

We were headed to what would be our base, Forward Operating Base Warhorse—Camp Warhorse—in Baqubah, just north of Baghdad. Our first stop would be Camp Victory in Baghdad, which included the Al Faw palace, Saddam Hussein's home before he was captured. He'd been found guilty just weeks earlier of killing 148 Shiites in what was called the Dujail Massacre, a reprisal for Hussein's attempted assassination in 1982. Up to a dozen gunman had fired on his motorcade after he gave a speech in Dujail, and he arrested nearly 400 men and another nearly 400 women and children, sending them to Abu Graib prison where they were tortured. Some of them died there while others were later executed. It wasn't a U.S. military court that found him guilty but an Iraqi court in the interim Iraq government. It was their choice to do with Hussein what they wanted, and they planned to hang him.

The highway along the way did not go through any more towns but went on the outside of them. While the road was paved, sections of it were blown up, and other sections were gravel. I wasn't sure if the gravel filled in bomb holes or if the road was simply exhausted, as weary as the people occasionally walking on the road. Abandoned cars, Fiats and Seats and rusted Fords, blown-up cars, burned and upside down, littered the highway like the discarded shells of cicadas. Once in a while, a car would still be burning, and in the distance, bombs exploded. My finger constantly wavered above the trigger. I could not relax.

Once it was dark, the side of the highway held a green glow stick every now and then.

I said in to my headset, "What are these glow sticks along the road? Are they ours? I don't remember this in training."

Sergeant Gasparyan, who'd been on two previous tours and was my team leader, said, "A convoy ahead of us dropped them. Shows everything's okay. You don't want to see a red stick." Big like an offensive lineman, I pictured him shaking his big head on his thick neck, and I listened.

Soon, we came across a few red ones together, and we stopped. "Stay in your vehicles," the LT said over our headsets. "Stay vigilant. We gotta wait."

Ahead of us were two other trucks, which I knew from our classes was an EOD team—Explosive Ordinance Disposal—and they may have been alerted from either a drone or another convoy reporting something suspicious. A bomb-sniffing dog was walking to the side of the road. I was stepping out of my turret when the LT in our vehicle shouted into the radio, "Guns up at all times, Rivera! No one is to get out until we're at Camp Victory."

"Yes, sir," I said. We were in the middle of nowhere, and there were no trees. Still, I didn't argue. He knew this place better than I, starting his second tour.

Soon the EOD was done and their two trucks moved off—no bombs— and we were back on the road. The air was getting chilly, actually, but I was still sweating because I was so nervous. My fear kept me awake. I kept my hands on my gun as otherwise they shook. I couldn't see the stars. I couldn't see much of anything. It's what I imagined driving on the moon might be like.

Styles' question came back to me—what did I believe? I believed this was going to be a hard year, and without a lot of music, it was going to be harder. Yet I chose this. I suppose I thought not only would I get a firm handshake on self-control here, but if I could survive this and the utter chaos, I could survive anything, maybe even touring again with a new band someday.

That's what I told myself. Yet I was having huge second thoughts about how prepared I was. Much of our combat training was on computers where "war" was played. It tested our thinking, yet most of us simply had fun playing those computer simulations. It wasn't real. This felt too real. I'd heard Vietnam vets had trained a lot more with real weapons. Now I was thinking it would have been a good idea. I felt like saying that I was outta here. Sorry, I made a mistake. I'd book a flight home. Yet I knew I couldn't.

At that moment, a Beatles' song came to mind, specifically Ringo's punchy drumming in "The End." Just before that, Paul would have sung, "Oh, yeah. All right. Are you going to be in my dreams tonight?" After the drumming came the guitar solo that I had learned so well. I could feel my fingers go up and down an imaginary guitar neck there in the Humvee. If we believed in the end lyric, we wouldn't be here in Iraq: "And in the end, the love you take is equal to the love you make."

I was humming the song to myself when what seemed the world's fastest rock slammed into the steel near my ass, and then ping-ping-ping bullets against the side of the truck. I swiveled my machine gun and pulled the trigger, but only one shot went off as smoke burst out the sides. I pulled the trigger again. One shot. More smoke. I hadn't set it to automatic, and as bullets were firing against us, and the LT was shouting, "What the fuck, Rivera," I fumbled to change over, but the swiveling, the shouting, the noise, I couldn't do it, and out there in the desert flats, I saw little flashes like bats' eyes in the dark. "Wilhelm!" the LT shouted. Wilhelm, the gunner in the truck ahead, started firing rapidly toward those flashes. Soon all shouting stopped. I smelled the gunpowder. I shook.

"Move ahead," the LT shouted into the radio, and soon we were out of there. I pictured his thick, beefy neck as red. "What happened, you guys?" he said back on the road.

"Sorry, Lieutenant," I said. It was the first time someone ever shot at me. I'd fumbled.

"You weren't paying attention."

"I'm so sorry," I said.

"This isn't training. It's real."

"I know."

"Sorry, too," said Wilhelm, the gunner in the truck ahead of us who fired back. "I was a little slow on the uptake. Won't happen again."

"I know it won't," said the LT.

Near an orange-pumpkin dawn, as the sun rose over an approaching line of sand dunes, we entered the outskirts of Baghdad. We stopped at what appeared to be a vast park of burned and ruined cars and busses. A double-decker bus, the vintage kind that Disney World had, was there, standing on its axels. Huge round wooden spools lay there, too. Perhaps they held overhead electrical wire once.

"Why're we stopping?" shouted the LT. "Keep moving!"

I could see why. The lead Humvee stopped for a cute if dirty collie dog that had wandered into the road. That's an American dog. What's it doing here? The dog stood as if confused. In training, we were told to run over dogs because they were sometimes used to stop a convoy—as we just did. If I were the driver, I wouldn't be able to run over Lassie, either.

I was still couched in my turret, and in the Humvee ahead of me, Wilhelm stood. Perhaps he just needed to stretch because the turret was cramped or perhaps he wanted to see the collie better. There was just the sound of a single firecracker, which also resounded in my headset, and Wilhelm made a perfect arc off the top of the Humvee on the driver's side, landed right on his head in the dirt, and crumpled. At first, I was so surprised, the image didn't make sense. Then I realized there had to be a sniper somewhere on the opposite side from where he fell. I swiveled and, machine gun blasting, I aimed at the only tall thing around, a tree.

The LT shouted, "What the—"

A figure with a rifle fell out of the tree.

Styles, the driver in Wilhelm's Humvee, burst out and rushed next to Wilhelm, shaking him. "Wilhelm is hit. He's hit!" he said into the radio.

"Does he need CPR?" the LT said in response.

"No, he's hit in the head. He's dead."

My Humvee moved forward and angled next to Wilhelm and Styles, and the LTs Humvee came next at another angle. I realized we were circling up like the stage coaches did in the Westerns during an Indian attack. I think I got the only shooter, but to be sure, our vehicles protected Styles and Wilhelm.

Styles pumped Wilhelm's chest quickly and madly—perhaps too hard as I heard bones breaking, and I grimaced. Wilhelm's eyes, open, showed no life. Styles, frantic, said, "Live, damn it! Wilhelm!" Every thirty pumps, he'd pinch Wilhelm's nose and give him two breaths, as we were trained.

The LT rushed in looking bear-like but in command, saying, "Off-load." We did, facing outward with our rifles out. No one else shot at us. The LT held out his hand for Styles to stop and then listened to Wilhelm's chest. Wilhelm's helmet had a little hole in the front, and when the LT moved Wilhelm's helmet up, I saw a bullet lodged in Wilhelm's forehead, the bullet slowed by his helmet. I wondered whether the bullet killed him or the fall did. I threw up near our rear tire. It didn't seem like we should be doing this stuff.

When I was done, Hitch still stared at Wilhelm. I thought Hitch might cry. The collie barked. Hitch stepped out, pulled out a handgun, and faced the dog, which now sat on the road, tail wagging, as if Hitch might feed him. Hitch shot the dog several times, blood spraying. The dog fell over.

"Hitchcock, enough of that," said the LT through our headsets and stepping over. "This isn't going to be the only time something like this happens. You each need to be prepared for this. I'm sorry it happened. Let's load Wilhelm into the back of my Humvee." A woman and three men, not Styles or Hitch or I, grabbed Wilhelm by an arm or leg and lifted.

The rest of us followed the LT to the sniper, a teenage boy whose chest was an open meat pie. In contrast, his untouched face, caught in a grimace, reminded me of a Pakistani boy I knew from the 7-11 near my mother's house in Orlando. I felt bad. I stepped away, toward where they were setting Wilhelm.

How was it possible Wilhelm died? I'd been talking to him earlier. It wasn't like I knew him well, but still, he'd been walking and talking, and now he wasn't, and it didn't make sense. I then remembered my dog Buster, a golden retriever who got hit by a car running to me as I got off a school bus. The driver could have hit a kid, but he hit my dog then took off. Buster was in deep pain, and his back legs didn't work. We raced him to the vet. "We've got to put him to sleep," my Dad had said, and I didn't fully understand what that meant. I thought he'd just sleep till he got better. The vet gave Buster two shots. The first made Buster close his eyes, out of his pain, and he was breathing steadily. Good, I'd thought. The next shot made him stop breathing within a second before the hypodermic needle was finished plunging. "Help him," I shouted. "He's not breathing!"

"Buster had to go," said my father. "He was in too much pain."

How could something work that fast? Buster was still warm, limp with his eyes opened. The vet must have heard me because he said, "For a dog to keep his eyes closed takes muscles. Dogs die with their eyes open."

Wilhelm's eyes were now closed. They'd crossed his arms over his chest. With Buster, I liked to believe he zipped off to heaven, but now with Wilhelm, I suspected there's no such place. He was just dead.

The LT stepped over to me. "Rivera. You were fast this time. You made up for earlier."

I nodded.

"You were defending us," said the LT, as if reading my mind. "Stay tight. You'll be all right."

"Okay." I didn't want to tell him I was ashamed that I killed someone. I was a guitar player, not a murderer.

Florida, July 2005

It had come to a head. At the Central Florida Fairgrounds in Orlando in the summer of 2005, my stomach lurched. Three guys in my band, Same Old Story, seemed to shoot tired looks at me while our newest member, Ralph Webber, offered a fuck-you glare using his thick arched eyebrows. Our star had been rising. We were about to step onto one of eight stages in this major stop of the Vans Warped Tour, which offered the best in punk and rock bands.

I looked behind the curtain at the audience of a thousand, who seemed full of anticipation, drugs, and rain water. The muddy scrappy-clothed misfits looked restless. Their energy crackled. On that drizzling July late afternoon, they chanted, "Same Old Story! Same Old Story!"

We needed the go-ahead—right after I finished throwing up into a tall, plastic-lined trashcan. I could get so nervous before a show. As I wiped my mouth, Ralph approached me. He had quickly proven himself in singing, writing, and playing rhythm and lead. While he didn't have the piercings or tattoos of punk—and had long hair like old-time Southern rocker Gregg Allman—I'd accepted him because the guy was an amazing musician. However, as he walked toward me, my stomach sank more because lately he was acting like the leader, suggesting songs we use in our show. He always drained me, and I hoped I wouldn't puke again. I drank from a bottle of water, and, for reassurance, fingered the tiny vial of coke in my pocket that had its own built-in spoon.

"I thought we'd start with 'Darkness and Hell,'" said Ralph, "then move into our new one, 'Shout at an Empire.'"

"No way," I said. "I don't even know why we do 'Shout at an Empire.' That's not our style. We're doing my song, 'Afterglow'."

"You don't get it, asshole," said Ralph. "We're a crossover band now— more metal core than punk."

It's as if Ralph were poison in a pond. I clenched my fists, telling myself to stay cool. My friends waited out in the audience. This was our hometown.

"Fucker, just go with the songs in this order," said Ralph, smacking me in my chest with his hand-written set list. "Be a good boy tonight, will you?"

"Whose band is this anyway?" I said, ready for the fight.

"If you don't want to play tonight," said Ralph, "we'll adapt."

That's when the stage manager gave us the go. Ralph moved on stage with the rest of the group, leaving me momentarily with my mouth open. I'd lost control of my own band. Did I have pussy written on my forehead? Why didn't the other guys defend me? Fuckers.

I strapped on my guitar, hurried on stage to a number of cheers, and plugged into my Marshall half-stack. My fingers innocently hit some strings, a sound which reverberated from the speakers across the stage— a moment of honest euphoric rush. I smiled. Okay. Okay. I can do this.

Ralph already stood at a microphone. "Thank you," he said. "We're thrilled to be here with so many fans and friends. Hope you like this one," and he hit the first chords of "Darkness and Hell." I took my spot. My momentary wave of adrenaline turned into anger. Fucking backstabber. After all, it'd taken years and a lot of energy to get here. I didn't want all this to collapse on me now. I started to feel panicked. I concentrated and held on.

Ralph sang this one—screeched it, I should say—as if he were the anti-Christ.

Darkness and Hell
I've got a bell
Come with me.
Fuck it.

Why're we stuck?
I'm in the corporate muck
Ain't got no luck
Follow me.

I joined the rising tide, energized by the audience's response. Ralph's songs were much darker than mine. My songs sometimes centered on girlfriends, hanging out at the beach, hating our parents. No matter—I loved performing. When I played, I became completely free. It's the most high I could ever feel. Drugs didn't match it. Sex didn't. I connected with everyone. I'd heard that Bruce Springsteen's legendary concerts went over four hours, and I completely understood why. He was the best "him" when playing.

The people dancing in front of me were my people. Like me, they'd never found a place to be until they found this music and each other. Punk music was an escape for musicians and audience alike. It was about being a rebel, not falling into step with society. We were unrestricted, like the hippies used to be. This was our family.

As we zoomed into the second song, my song, "Afterglow," we were awesome. I smiled. I focused on a girl in the front row with blue hair as Ralph and I sang:

The way you dance,
Any place at all.
Why do I stare?
You make me crazy down there.
I'm stuck on the ground.
Can't take any more.

That girl and others raised their arms in the air and mouthed my lyrics as we sang them. My stuff worked better. Ralph's songs sucked. I had to take control of this band again.

Throughout the second song, the audience danced, slipped in the mud, and shouted. Then I spotted Lynette, my old girlfriend, with her new boyfriend whose last name was Schmelder or something. I called him Smuckers. They'd make little baby jams soon, no doubt. God. Fucking slut. Last time I saw her was with my earlier band when we all stayed in someone's apartment on a tour. Lynette and I were having problems, so she was sleeping on another couch after taking too many pills. I awoke with her moaning. She was letting our former drummer finger her under the blanket, and she grinned, catching my eyes as I awoke. She stuck her tongue out at me as if to say *take that, asshole*. It was then I'd discovered what was going on with her and my band mates.

Thinking about that there on stage made me angry, and I played harder. Fucker Smucker. To think I'd almost killed myself over her, though—sad. That's one thing about life: if you could survive it, you grew stronger.

Six songs in, Ralph introduced the members, but he'd skipped me. Shithead. It was on purpose, and before he started the next song, I cleared my throat into the microphone. Ralph said, "Oh, yes. Max Rivera on rhythm and vocal."

As people clapped, I added, "And I also play lead, and I started this whole band. Maybe you remember this one, 'Don't Let Him Jump.'" I immediately started playing the guitar-lick intro. It wasn't a song on the list that Ralph had handed me, and I knew he'd be pissed. So what? From the corner of my eye, I caught sight of our drummer frowning. The others reluctantly joined in. Follow me, fuckers. Ralph joined in, playing the same solo—but it was no longer a solo. We now had a competitive duet. That's fine. I held my own, grinning. He couldn't get me. The other members knew the song well, and soon everyone played hard. For the moment, I was back in the saddle. This music was what had saved my life. It's what our followers wanted, not this new metal-core shit, which had more distorted guitar noise and lyrics of no consequence. My stuff, in contrast, showed anger with society and an openness to love. The best part was now watching people dancing, moving as one, to music I'd created.

After that song, I said, "This next one I wrote just after high school graduation, called, 'What Did We Expect?'"

Ralph blurted into the microphone. "We ain't playin' that."

"People want to hear it, right?" I said. Some people cheered. The other band members looked at me with surprise. Ralph laid his guitar down, walked up to my amplifier, yanked out my guitar's cable, and threw the end into the crowd, telling me, "You're outta here."

I couldn't believe it. In the front row, people held their mouths open. My complete and utter fury grew in seconds. I ran over to Ralph's Telecaster guitar and lifted it high in the air. As Ralph came running over, I channeled Pete Townsend and slammed the guitar hard on the stage. A piece of it flew and hit Ralph in the ear. Oops. But shouts of ecstasy flew from the audience. Ralph cupped his ear and then saw blood on his hands. He asked for it, right?

Ralph leaped in the air, and when I saw him launched, I didn't run. Rather I welcomed him with my arms out. The universe was testing me. After all, this was like the problem I had in high school when Lynette slept with all the members of my first band. This time what would I do? I'd embrace the problems—embrace Ralph—and meet the bullshit head on.

I caught him, and it's as if the audience thought it was a choreographed show. They burst out in applause. Ralph and I fell to the ground punching. Ralph embodied the worst of everything going wrong in my life then. If I punched him hard, he'd go away. The audience shouted and cheered while buffalo men wearing polo shirts that said "Security" on the front ran toward us. The other members rushed over first and pulled us apart.

"We never want to see you again!" shouted Ralph.

"You can't do that—right guys?" I said to my friends in the group. The audience looked as if they'd just watched a car accident, completely speechless.

"We took a vote earlier," said Ralph. "We feel you don't get us anymore."

Impossible! I looked at each one of my friends. Each one sheepishly said, "Sorry." One added, "Max, you always think music is going to save you, but you need people."

A security guy grabbed me. "That's it, guys. Everyone get *off*!" he said.

Some people booed the security guys, but most of the audience drifted off to one of the other stages. I caught my ex-girlfriend's snickering smile as she hopped away in her bright red Chucks. I'd hit another abyss. As I gathered my guitar and cord, I realized of course it wasn't as simple as just Ralph. I'd been betrayed again. It was part of the test.

"You owe me a Telecaster," shouted Ralph backstage.

"Bite it," I said, rushing at him, but security men kept us apart.

Later, I dragged myself and guitar back to the fairgrounds entrance, and I stood and watched all the bands load up their trucks in the rain. It was more than a drizzle now, and, as usual, I forgot an umbrella. In Florida, you can expect rain. Still, I didn't care. Getting wet felt like who-gives-a-fuck.

Roadies for the big-name bands were arranging their amps and instruments into large moving trucks, and the band members, holding newspapers over their heads, hopped onto their luxury buses. Then there were the small bands like mine stuffing a rented U-Haul trailer behind an underpowered Econoline van like Ralph's. I owned a beat-up funky green 1996 Geo Metro, but it was parked on the street near my apartment. We'd been staying in a motel near the fairgrounds because we'd just come from Tampa the day before. They were going on to Pompano Beach without me. I had my backpack and guitar. As I wondered how I'd get to my apartment, and when would I get my amps back, a voice shouted, "Max, hey Max!"

Right then it felt like being saved. Little did I know how I wrong I'd be.

Iraq, November-December 2006

In late 2006, our platoon drove our Humvees into Baghdad from the outskirts, where we'd lost Wilhelm. Still on top of the Humvee as gunner, I felt like a Martian or something, trying to understand what I was seeing. The city looked surprisingly modern. We took a highway with exits, found orderly city streets, and many of the buildings looked right out of the Lower East Side Bronx. The mosques, blown-up buildings, and trashy side streets made it different.

We approached the gates of Camp Victory, the headquarters for the U.S. Military in Iraq and one of more than seventy-five major U.S. bases in Iraq. General Petreus slept in the main palace, Styles told me, in a bed that was French Provincial with two doves kissing carved into the wood. Camp Victory used a complex of nine gaudy palaces for Saddam Hussein, with a giant lake in the middle and encircled with twenty-seven miles of concrete walls. Over twenty thousand U.S. troops were stationed there.

After we entered the camp through the gates, Camp Victory, for the most part, was just flat, with beige flat buildings on tan ground. Like viruses enveloping healthy cells, the Jersey barriers and blast walls had swallowed sections of Baghdad. Inside the camp, modular buildings popped up everywhere, including trailers for Cinnabon, Pizza Hut, Subway, Taco Bell, and other familiar fast-food stops. We'd brought in America. On one edge of the camp, surrounded by the lake and standing on an island, was the Al Faw Palace. I suppose I expected something like the Greek-like Metropolitan Museum of Art in New York, which I'd gone to as a kid before we moved to Florida, but the architecture was far different. Beige, two tall stories high, it had a flat roof, and its inset windows took the shape of Scud missiles. Inside, marble shined and chandeliers sparkled.

For a week, we had no other orders other than to wait for new orders. We would swim in the palace's marble pool. We would go bowling. We would spend our latest paychecks at the fast-food places or blow our cash on DVDs or music at a PX. The PX that I used was inside a large steel shipping container. Some guys would attempt to sweet-talk some of the female privates. Perhaps a few got lucky. I wasn't ready, still feeling wary after my breakup with my last girlfriend, Sophie, while I was in boot camp.

"Chow hall?" Styles asked Hitch and me around 5 p.m., our third day there. We'd had no mission work that day, and it just felt odd, like a toothache that had disappeared, and you missed it. That afternoon, we'd saluted off Wilhelm's transfer casket at the airport as we stood in formation.

"Let's get some real food," said Hitch. "Taco Bell."

"Subway," I said. "Better for you."

"Why you fucks spending money?" said Styles. "The chow hall is free, and you can eat all you want."

"Don't you miss home?" I asked him.

"I never eat fast food," he said. "Do you know about trans-fat?"

"What are you, fifty?" said Hitch to Styles. "Eat like normal people."

"No trans-fat at Subway," I said. "That Subway guy lost all that weight eating their subs. It's good for you."

"All right," said Styles.

"Taco Bell tomorrow," I assured Hitch.

"Do you think Wilhelm liked Subway?" Hitch asked me.

"Now why would you bring him up?"

"He was on the chubby side. I don't think he ate at Subway," he said. As I later thought about that statement, it occurred to me that Hitch focused on that instead of Wilhelm's death. We knew nothing about death. We were just kids. That's just the way things were over there. One day, alive. Next day, dead.

After lunch, I wanted to be alone. I didn't want any more conversations, feeling lonely even with my friends. I had my iPod, which I always carried with me. I listened to an acoustic musician named Dave Melillo, to his song "For the Sake of Remembering." It was for Wilhelm, especially the line, "You're taking a breath / and you never expect that the answer is death." My portable player had over 3,700 songs, and I knew this one would be just right.

On the second floor of the palace, I came across some books in English. Someone had set up a small lending library. I had not been a reader except what I was forced to read in high school, but I nonetheless looked at what the library had. One cover in purple appealed to me. It had a drawing of nearly naked women, veiled only by what looked to be wide silk scarves across their voluptuous bodies. One naked woman wore angel wings, and another, merely a toga across her back. A well-muscled guy with a loincloth tried touching one woman. The title was *The Sirens of Titan* by Kurt Vonnegut, Jr. I'd never heard of the author. The back cover said, "Why should the richest, most depraved man in America blast off in his private space ship for parts unknown with the one beautiful woman capable of resisting him? How can Salo, shipwrecked envoy from Tralfamadore, complete his vital mission?"

It looked so bizarre, this felt like my kind of story. I discovered a quiet nook just outside the palace in the shade near the lake, parked myself, and read. I had to laugh when the author opened saying, "All persons, places, and events in this book are real," and then the story takes place in the twenty-second century, a time after "Gimcrack religions were big business." It was a time when "Everyone now knows how to find the meaning of life within himself. But mankind wasn't always so lucky."

In the story, Earth is ready to battle with Martians on Mars, which has really been set up by a rich New Englander, Winston Niles Rumfoord, who wants to start his own religion that teaches that God is completely indifferent to people and that luck is not an actual force. The story was a crazy thing that had space travel, an alien robot, a dog named Kazak, and a warped space phenomenon called the chrono-synclastic infundibulum, which had Rumfoord materialize on different planets at different times. Rumfoord's home base is on one of Saturn's moons called Titan. I gobbled the book up as if it were a Thanksgiving feast, and I breathed pure oxygen. It made me forget I was in Iraq. I felt I didn't find the book, but the book found me. I went back to the library to find another Vonnegut book, but there weren't any. Still, it stayed on my mind.

One morning, as I was in a porta-potty before the heat of the day hit, I clicked on "Canadian Idiot" by Weird Al Yankovic, a parody of Green Day's "American Idiot" song. Hitch gave me Yankovic. "It's to cheer you up, buddy."

"Cheer up? I'm not depressed," I said.

"You could've fooled me. Where'd your laugh go?"

"Ha ha ha ha ha," I said sarcastically. "How's that?"

He didn't buy it. Frankly, I didn't think anything could make me laugh, even though I saw myself as a laughing guy. I could laugh with the best of them. I laughed when I got into the Army.

So there I was in the porta-potty, my pants down, and I pushed play.

The rhythm was exactly like Green Day, and Yankovik didn't want to be a Canadian idiot, a "beer swillin' hockey nut." When he sang that Canadians "all live on donuts and moose meat / and leave the house without packin' heat," my laugh erupted like the farts that filled the place, and the iPod slipped from my hand—right into the shithole, Yankoviking the earbuds right out of my ears. The device made a polite little splat.

"No!" I screamed, and I stood, looking down, but it was so dark down there. I yanked up my pants and flung open the door. "Shit!" I yelled.

A few soldiers about twenty yards away, walking down the path, paused, waved me off, and I yelled at them, "Shit, shit, shit!" now realizing the irony. They moved on. Just beyond them, in an open bay of a garage, with a Humvee up on a hydraulic rack, I could see mechanics working on it. One was shooting air at the butt of another guy using the air hose. The mechanics!

I ran over, shouting, "Hey, guys! Emergency! I need you!"

They watched me approach the way moose must watch hunters in orange jackets raise their funny sticks. They looked wary.

I ran in. "Who's in charge here?" No one volunteered. "See those porta-potties over there? I dropped my iPod down in the poop."

The guy nearest to me laughed and said, "That's it? You gotta be kiddin' me."

Another much older guy, balding with gray sides, said, "Whatever an iPod is."

"It's my music machine. It has all my songs on it. It has all my hope, my love, my everything on it."

"How's that an emergency?" said another, younger guy.

"I was thinking maybe you had a scooper of some sort or something," I blurted with hope.

"Oh, you mean a Humvee pooper scooper," said a guy with a heavy beard who didn't have the same grooming standards I had to keep.

I paused. "Is there such a thing?"

They all laughed.

"Isn't there anything you have here?" I asked. "I can't live here without my music—my iPod."

"Music? Don't you have friends to talk to?" said the guy with the beard. I must have looked or sounded desperate enough because he then said, "I imagine it's dark down there. We'd need a light on the end of a grabber thing."

"Yeah," said another guy, "And we'd need a little camera on the end to really see that shit." More laughter until the bearded guy came to me, clapped my shoulder and said, "This is the best job we've been asked to do yet."

He turned to the guy who suggested the camera and said, "You know that gizmo we used for the FMTV trucks?" He then turned to me, "Those FMTVs are motherfuckers to fix—so many variations and the engines in tight little spaces."

"The thing with the little ratchet on the end?" the guy said.

"Yeah. We could put clampers on the end instead."

Before I knew it, four guys had come together to adapt their tool for the shitter. It had a pole, a light, a camera, a grabber, and a little scope to look into.

The five of us ran over with a few of the guys giggling like this was the greatest thing. When we opened the door to the potty, a young female second lieutenant was sitting on the crapper, and I blurted, "I'm sorry, but I lost my iPod down in there. We're here to get it."

She slammed the door shut and said through the door, "Give me a minute."

"Yes, ma'am," we said in unison. Some guy blurted something about a new bomb on my iPod.

In short order, the young woman opened the door, and, dressed impeccably, cool and collected, looked at us. We saluted. She said, "Carry on" and left.

"Phew!" said one guy stepping in, holding his nose. "Whoever said women aren't the same as men is wrong."

The bearded guy took charge. He inserted the pole down the hole. At first, as he looked through the scope, he said, "I don't know, man."

"You gotta find it," I said. I clenched onto hope like a father watching the birth of his first child.

Within a minute he shouted, "Aha!" and squeezing on the scissor-like handles, he soon said, "Success!" What he pulled out was a shit-covered square with the earbuds like some strange dark, drippy appendage. It could have been the weirdest creature from deep in the sea where the sun don't shine. There was only the tiniest glint of its aluminum casing.

"Thank you, guys!"

"It's why we're the best," said the old guy, and all of them gave a cheer. One of the mechanics pulled on blue latex gloves and grabbed the iPod/earbuds from the end and handed it to me. I started reaching for it, pulled back, and then just grabbed it. "Eww!" said the bearded guy.

"I guess I should wash it, huh?" I said.

"I wouldn't." He said.

I pressed play. Nothing happened. I cleared my throat, shook it hard, and tried again. Nothing. Shit.

So I lost everything. At first, I only thought how everything I had was gone. Then when I looked from face to face, I realized we had a damn good Army. Strangers were there for me. "Thank you, guys. This really meant a lot to me—maybe even more than the music itself."

"Really?" said the bearded guy.

I laughed before saying, "No, but this was still fun, right?"

"Fucking A," said the bearded guy.

|. | |

The second week, we started training for our deployment, but we still didn't know what that was. Sometimes we met in newly built Quonset huts for lectures—air conditioned. A warehouse they took us to had ten big machines that almost looked like concrete mixers, but they were Humvee rollover simulators. There were the four doors of the Humvee that you'd get into, and the machine could put you in a variety of angles including upside down. It reminded me of the *Back to the Future* simulation ride at Universal Studios Orlando, but this thing had no IMAX screen or Doc Brown telling you shit. Rather, we learned what it felt like to lurch from an IED, how to help each other, and how to get out. It prepared us for the worst—maybe even save our lives.

Another room had computerized combat simulations. We would hold a specially designed assault rifle that, when you pulled the trigger, would fire air to give your gun a kick. The floor to ceiling in front of you had projections of a variety of situations. For instance, you might be walking into a haji house to clear the family inside. The family would speak to you in Arabic and appear friendly. If you fired your gun, red dots would appear onscreen to show where you shot. One family member might pull out a gun. Would you shoot? Another time, a boy might yank out a flashlight or the Koran. Would you shoot? You had to be smart and follow the rules of engagement but not get yourself killed or kill someone needlessly. It was like a giant video game. The simulations would change for each person. This was all more intense than what we had in Kuwait. It seemed more real to us now. This was not an easy time.

We could use the Internet to write home. Most living quarters were small concrete single-wides with sandbags halfway up. Some were large modular barracks. Our platoon, though, was divided into two big tents and a smaller one, all with bunk beds—women in the small tent, the guys in the other two. Military helicopters were forever flying overhead. Bombs randomly exploded outside the perimeter with a large enough force that dust shook from the top of our tent onto us and made us anxious. Camp Victory was the resort in hell.

One of our sergeants—a thin, muscled guy named Cunningham, on his third tour, with a deep tan and creases on his face—told us to "call home, tell them you're safe, and say that the food and chow hall kick ass." He was right about that, even if I liked the occasional fast food. We were always extremely well fed, meat at every meal, and such extras as a pasta bar, killer onion rings, and fresh fruit and salads. I guessed all the food was shipped in at great expense from the U.S.—our tax dollars at work.

We also went on patrols of the city where we were fully dressed in Kevlar, gloves, and all, ready with our weapons. In the heat, it felt heavy and awkward—all to get us used to being protected and on our toes. I was always surprised with the contrasts in Baghdad. Modern buildings with green lawns stood right next to desert plots of land with dead weeds, and rubble-like confetti seemed to exist everywhere, thanks to our initial bombing, our "shock and awe." Almost every street featured concrete barriers, the moveable kind often on American highways when construction was being done. Baghdad pod malls had the smaller barriers on the edge of the parking lot. Other barriers, bomb barriers, were fifteen feet high. Otherwise, it was a normal city with Hondas, Volvos, Fiats and more, just like any place in America. Some cars looked as if they'd met many a baseball bat, but others surprised me for being so new. There was money here, and it probably leaked from American government fingers.

I fell into the rhythms of Camp Victory. Our patrols and classes became a normal job. However, while the Iraqi citizens did not treat us hostilely, the men eyed us warily in our uniforms, and Iraqi women, all covered up except for their dark eyes, always hurried away from us.

The one odd thing about waiting for our orders and just finding things to do to "relax" was that I felt anxious about the future, even restless. It was like my night in jail: I didn't know what would happen next, and it probably wouldn't be good. While I didn't want to leave Camp Victory for somewhere more dangerous—which was anywhere else in Iraq—I couldn't enjoy the calm. Once a week, a few mortar shells would explode nearby. We'd run to the nearest shelter, a kind of modular on-ground concrete tunnel, and once in there, we'd all laugh as if it were funny how we could almost be killed. In contrast, Hitch rose early and out the door each day before any of us got up. I guess he simply explored.

One day, when I was on my bunk reading *Rolling Stone,* which I'd picked up in the PX, I blurted out, "Holy shit." I'd come across a "Best Local Bands" article, which happened to spotlight Orlando, Florida, and there was a fucking picture of Ralph with his black caterpillar eyebrows and his stupid brown boots. He stood with our old drummer and a couple of new guys in a new band called Living Now. They were signed by Sit

Down Records, a large independent label out of New York. Fucking shit. I was over in Iraq, protecting America for the likes of fucking Ralph. That's when I felt a hand on my shoulder, and I screamed.

"Sorry, Dude," said Hitch, standing next to me.

"What?" I said.

"You gotta come see. It's so cool, but if I tell you, it'll spoil the surprise."

"Tell me," I said.

He looked me in the eyes, and I could see this was important to him. He put his hand on my shoulder. "Follow me."

We walked many blocks, and though he seemed giddy, I just got more and more grumpy. "Fuck it, Hitch. Tell me already."

"We're almost there."

"This better be a brothel," I said.

"Better than that."

Soon, a large, empty parking lot approached, and beyond it, a wide building rose tall in concrete with French windows. Some windows were missing and blackened on the outside. One big chunk of the building was also missing as if a giant dinosaur had eaten a bite out of it. I guessed it had been hit by one of our bombs when we aimed for Saddam's palaces. "Is that it?" I asked.

"Yeah."

"What is it?"

"We gotta get closer."

Soon, I noticed it had a movie theater marquee with the huge word "Gladiator" on it. "A gladiator pit?" I said, confused.

"No, the movie! It's playing tonight. Want to go?"

"Are you kidding me?" I was hot, ready to whack him up upside the head. He wanted to see a war movie here?

"It's a story from two thousand years ago—about a Roman general whose family is murdered by an emperor's son. The general becomes a gladiator. He wants revenge."

"I saw it five years ago."

"Lots of swords and arrows and cool stuff. What else have you got to do?"

Really—what else did I have to do other than go over in my head for the thousandth time memories of Sophie—times at the movies, times at the beach, or times of just talking? We went back to the tent and roped Styles to come with us that night.

That evening as we approached, Styles frowned when he saw the bombed-out part and said, "This place is still open, and they're showing movies?"

"Yeah," said Hitch. "Other than a hole in its ceiling, it's still perfect inside."

A huge line had already formed, a double line of guys our age in their camo uniforms with their ever-present rifles—we had to carry our rifles everywhere. There were few women, despite the generous numbers around the swimming pools and in the mess hall. The ones in line seemed to be someone's girlfriend from the way the girls looked at their guys.

Hitch whispered in my ear, "Those two are holding hands. Isn't that against Army regulations? Saturnization, isn't it?" He pointed to a short guy and a taller woman toward the front.

Styles heard and said, "You mean *fraternization*?"

"Yeah. Right in front of our faces."

"As long as you're not caught making out in uniform and don't show favoritism—and you're not an officer dating an enlisted person—then things are technically cool. There's no Army regulation that prohibits dating."

Hitch smiled wide. "Good. Gives me a goal."

Inside the theater, you could see the place used to be luxurious: red velvet seats, ornate details on columns, private boxes on the edges. Now, a bombed hole in the ceiling and dust and rubble defiled it. We grabbed seats in the middle. When the lights dimmed, my stomach twisted. Maybe I was anxious in being with so many U.S. soldiers close together. It'd be a suicide bomber's delight. While the security was high everywhere in the camp, was I really up for witnessing violence when it could happen to us here?

I can't explain fully the magic of the place, though. When the lights went down, part of me felt ready to just let go.

One of the best fight scenes was when the freed slave, Proximus, played by Oliver Reed, reminds our gladiator, Maximus, Russell Crowe, that he needs to win the crowd, "entertain." With just one sword, Maximus enters the arena to face seven well-armed gladiators. Quick as anything, he disposes each one, and with each death, everyone in our theater, like the audience in the Roman stands, shouted. Men around me raised their guns. When Maximus grabs a second sword and swings at his last opponent's head with swords from either side, the man's head leaps off. Our theater cheered.

Arr! To battle!

Maximus throws one sword off in disgust and screams to the crowd, "Are you not entertained? Is that why you're here?"

We lifted our rifles and shouted "Yes!" We were entertained.

I left the movie exhausted, yet Hitch was keyed up and walked backwards to face Styles and me. "I loved the sister," he said. "Wasn't she hot? Do you think her brother forced himself on her?"

Styles laughed. "You got to get yourself to one of the pools and meet women. I'm telling you. It's better than always jerking off."

Hitch looked offended. "I don't jerk off."

"I can hear you," I said. "You think I'm invisible? We're all in that big tent, and with all the groaning each night from everyone, it's like a synchronized philharmonic."

Hitch laughed. "Awesome."

I said, "Can't you watch porn on a laptop in the porta-potty like the rest of us?"

"Hot and smelly in there," said Hitch. "Where's the romance?"

We laughed.

"The women need it as much as us," said Styles. "Help them out. Give them some of what they need."

"Girls aren't the same as guys," said Hitch firmly. "And they should save themselves for marriage."

Styles and I looked at each other and shook our heads. Hitch would never get it. Right then, Sergeant Gasparyan, who'd been in front of us, walking big as a redwood, came running over. We froze. Was he going to fucking tackle us or what? He laughed and said, "Hey, you guys want to help me do something funny?" Gasparyan had been my team leader on the ride from Kuwait to Baghdad.

"What kind of funny, Sergeant?" said Styles.

"Fuck the sergeant shit. This isn't about my rank."

"Gasparyan?" said Hitch, reading his nametag. "You're Armenian? My brother-in-law has a last name almost like yours."

"My great grandparents were from Armenia. My grandmother's Mexican. I'm one hundred percent American."

"Do people call you Gassy?" said Styles with a straight face.

If eyes could be laser beams, Styles would be dust. Without flinching, however, Gasparyan said, "Call me Yanni."

"Like the Greek musician?" I asked.

"I play keyboards, too," he said, "but not new-age shit like that Yanni."

"Call me Hitch," said Hitch and shook his hand.

In that moment, it occurred to me all of us liked music. Hitch could sing and, I'd later find out, he played drums. Styles said he played a mean bass and would buy one over here. I sang and played lead guitar, and now a keyboardist walked into our life. This shit didn't matter to the Army, though. It's not like we had instruments or could jam once we were given our orders. The thought of playing left me like the smoke of the bombs we could see in the distance. It was a strange world where complete strangers, our enemy, would happily kill any or all of us if given a chance. So what if at heart you wanted to harmonize and sing, "Don't Let Me Down."

"Nice to meet you, Yanni," said Styles and shook his hand. "What's the funny thing you want to do?"

Yanni smiled.

It was nearing sunset as we followed Yanni first to a PX larger than the one I'd found, and there he bought a few gallon-size plastic boxes with lids, like Tupperware. "What are these for?" I asked.

"To hold stuff—a couple for each of you."

"What'd you do before the Army, Yanni?" I asked, thinking he might have been a chef, knowing about Tupperware. Big guys were sometimes chefs.

"Police. Fucking Seattle. When 9/11 happened, I joined right up."

"So you been in five years?" said Hitch.

"Yep. Maybe I'll be a lifer."

He brought us to a large flat desolate area away from any buildings to a bunch of concrete rubble, perhaps left over from some razed building. "Ready?" he said. We had boxes open with their lids in our other hand as he'd shown us.

"Sure," I agreed, not really wanting to know. I didn't like the feel of this.

"Get closer," said Yanni, and when we circled the rubble, he kicked the concrete bits. From several open spaces, large tan scorpion-looking creatures with eight legs ran out. One had what looked like red puffy jaws. I saw its teeth and screamed.

Yanni laughed loudly.

"What the hell are they?" I shouted.

"Camel spiders," he said.

"There's one big as a bull terrier," said Styles.

"I think I saw teeth on one!" yelled Hitch.

"Yeah, they have teeth," said Yanni. "Harmless. Catch them. All of you, put them in your boxes."

"Why?" I asked.

"You'll see."

Hitch was grinning. I picked up a small one and threw it at Hitch, who screamed. Now I was into it. Styles ran after one enthusiastically.

"Herd them into your boxes," shouted Yanni, and now I chased a few. Fuck the red-jawed one. I aimed for a smaller one, scooped him in and slipped my top on so fast, that sucker didn't know what happened.

Styles captured the red-jawed one and said, "I'd shit a brick if I saw this on top of me."

Yanni smiled.

We stashed our spiders behind the Green Beans coffee shop, which was built like a mobile home and stood on a concrete pad, and we scrambled up front and treated ourselves to cappuccinos.

We killed some more time at the Speedway, a place Yanni showed us where we raced remote-controlled model cars. When it was nearly time for taps, we grabbed the spiders and hid them outside behind the sandbag wall to our tent. We agreed to meet there twenty minutes after lights out.

The time came, and all four of us slipped out of our beds, grabbed T-shirts and pants, and met outside.

"It's time," said Yanni, grinning in anticipation. From his backpack, he handed each of us night vision goggles, which were expensive and usually kept stored by the LT. "We gotta get the full benefit, right?" said Yanni. I still didn't know what we were doing, but I was in. I thought of the trouble we could get into if we were caught with these, but he was a sergeant, so who was I to argue? Donning our goggles, we crept to the opening of the tent. Yanni quietly opened the door, yanked the top off of one Tupperware, and launched the spiders in. He indicated to us to do the same thing, and we did. With the goggles, I could see the creatures scamper ahead toward the sleeping, unaware soldiers. I couldn't help myself: I laughed. My friends looked at me sharply.

Yanni motioned for us to pull back. We followed him to a wall about a hundred feet away. It was low enough that we could hide behind it and peer over. I looked toward the tent with my night-vision goggles still on. The door remained closed, and the tent, quiet.

Yanni pulled out a pack of cigarettes, appropriately Camels, and offered it to us. Styles and I took one each. Nearly every soldier smoked. If you never had before Iraq, you soon did—except Hitch, who remained a clean-cut all-American type. He didn't understand cigarettes were calming. The live ember always reminded me I was still here, burning like the tobacco. I felt perfect, sitting with those guys against a wall. By the time our embers neared the filters, nothing in the tent had happened.

"What if everyone is so sound asleep, they don't notice?" said Hitch.

"It only takes one person," said Yanni.

"Have you heard anyone else doing this?" asked Styles.

"No," said Yanni. "The spiders like the dark. I thought they'd crawl up on the beds."

"What if the spiders are scared of everyone and are hiding?" I said as if I knew spider psychology.

"Hmm," said Yanni. "Maybe it won't work. Maybe we should just go back to bed."

"No way am I going in there," said Hitch.

"They won't bite you," he replied. "You know what they are."

"I can't stand looking at them," I said.

"I'm going in," said Styles.

"Me, too," said Yanni.

We handed Yanni back our night vision goggles, which he returned to his backpack. Just as Styles squeezed the cherry off his cigarette onto the ground, we heard the first scream, and "Shit! Christ!" Then there were two other screams and "Fuckin' alien thing!" More shouts came as we heard feet running, and we leaped back and to the side. People streamed out in their underwear. One guy had a spider in his hand and threw it at another guy. The four of us, of course, couldn't contain our laughter, and another sergeant in his boxer shorts stormed over.

"Gasparyan!" he shouted.

Soon, we were all back in our beds. As I lay in the dark, the snoring, and a groan of someone jerking off or having a nightmare, was interrupted by bombs in the distance. I wondered what I might do if I made it out alive. I should have a goal. Originally, I thought the discipline of the Army would make me better in life. Now I realized we're all here for a few laughs and horrors and then we're gone. I wouldn't mind creating something important, though, whether it was an album or something else. I wanted to do more than protect people in a country I knew nothing about, and they couldn't give a shit about me. I just wanted to live and make something good.

| | | |

A week later, our orders arrived. We were told that Saddam Hussein and his cousin Ali Hassan al-Majeed, known as Chemical Ali, were imprisoned on an island in an artificial lake in the center of the base. It was separated by a causeway with a drawbridge. They had small windowless cells built with reinforced walls inside a former villa. The site, called Building 114, was top secret. Our platoon was to protect Hussein when he was to be moved to Camp Justice in a northeast suburb of Baghdad on the day he was to be hanged by the Iraq government.

On a Saturday at the end of December, we woke up at 3 a.m. and dressed for battle. After breakfast, Lieutenant Graver spoke to us. His sidekick now was Sergeant Ichisada, an Asian guy about fifteen years older, who carried out his orders.

The LT explained that Saddam was being officially turned over to Iraqi officials at the same camp where Saddam had had his military intelligence headquarters and where Iraqi civilians had been tortured and hanged on the same gallows. He said, "Our job is to prevent trouble or riots happening outside the camp. As you may know, Saddam and his Baath party are Sunni. They're only twenty percent of the population that's otherwise mostly Shiite. There will be Shiites there who'll want to get their hands on him and rip him apart. There will be Sunnis there wanting to save him, feeling today is an outrage. Don't let anything happen. Don't kill any Iraqis. Stop problems before they happen. We want the world to see we had absolutely nothing to do with his execution other than keep peace."

Thus, our first job was to protect Saddam—so he could be killed. Hitch raised his hand. The LT pointed to him and said, "Yeah?"

"I heard from one of Saddam's American guards, an MP like us," said Hitch, "that Saddam was a nice guy, very respectful. Saddam even gave him marriage advice—to find a woman who cooks and cleans. Should Saddam really be executed?"

Hitch had the balls to ask that? The LT looked surprised. Another LT might rip him apart for such a thing, but our LT said, "He's being executed by his own countrymen. Saddam's one of the worst despots of the last century, oppressing Iraq for more than thirty years, killing thousands of its citizens monthly on whatever whim or paranoid fantasy he had. He gassed a Kurdish village, killing five thousand and wounding ten thousand more. He killed his own sons-in-law and many of his ministers whom he didn't consider loyal. Then he'd smoke a cigar. Point is, the world'll be better off. You won't see him—you'll be on the outside. Once he's dead and the crowd disperses, you'll convoy to Baqubah, our new F.O.B.," our forward operating base.

Shortly thereafter, we hopped the transport to Camp Justice. On the way, the streets appeared dark and eerie. It was still the middle of the night, after all, and only the occasional dog or rat would run by, visible in a lonely streetlight. As we approached the prison, a swarm of people already congregated on a grassy area under palm trees, lit by spotlights on top of the prison walls. With our goggles, full battle gear, and our hands on our guns, we spread out, blocking the prison entrance and two sides of the grassy area by standing on the bricked circular driveway. The sergeant separated me from Styles, Hitch, and Yanni—I didn't know where they were but hoped they'd be okay. A wide gap stood between each soldier. If there were a riot, we could be swarmed and killed. Maybe we could let our assault rifles rip, but we knew we weren't supposed to be in the news for shooting into a crowd.

I couldn't pretend I was happy with this assignment. As I looked from face to Iraqi face, I imagined which one of these people would blow up or start a riot or otherwise kill me. I heard a shout, and my heart thumped, but it was a woman rejoicing and kissing her boyfriend—the first time I'd seen such affection here.

An hour later, with the first streaks of dawn and everyone quiet, awaiting word that he was dead, a funny kind of sound caught my attention. It came from the small parking area behind me, which had seven-foot concrete blast walls around it except for the entrance. A water dish for perhaps a dog sat on top of a Humvee, and on the dish chirped a bird. I couldn't tell what type, but it was white, and below it on the ground was a gray cat, built like a panther, slowly moving closer until sitting on its haunches, making funny bird-like noises in response. I didn't know cats, so this situation surprised me. In the sky behind them, a tinge of orange emerged on a paint-brush-stroke of clouds. The cat meowed, and the bird danced on the edge of the dish. That cat knew exactly what it wanted, how to try for it, and only looked at one thing, that bird. For a second there, I thought the cat would get it, but the bird flew up, and I expected away. In seconds, though, the bird dive-bombed the cat, again and again. The cat kept backing away. It was the funniest thing. At the soft clump of boots, the cat ran away. I saw the bird fly up to the nearest tree and a nest. That's why the bird dive-bombed the cat. The bird's family was there. Still, I felt like that cat.

The continuing bootsteps made me glance to my right, and another soldier approached. I couldn't see his face beneath his goggles because it was in shadow, but I could tell he was as fascinated by the cat and bird as I was. In a soft voice, he said, "I once had me a gray cat like that one—best birder I ever saw. It's like my cat reincarnated to Iraq."

We laughed. Moments later, shouts of joy went up into the park, and my radio crackled to life in my headphone. "Saddam is dead. His neck snapped at the end of a rope around six a.m. local time," said the LT.

Iraqis near me hugged each other. I guess none of them were Sunni like Saddam.

The crowd dispersed quickly—perhaps they had breakfast to make—and the other soldier and I looked at each other. The sky had lightened, and we removed our goggles. He had a friendly face, the kind you see on posters for the Army—mixed ethnicity: tan, maybe Asian, maybe Russian or something. We were all mutts.

"I'm Rivera," I told the guy and held out my hand.

"Tracewski," he said. "Ricky, but people here call me Trace." He had an accent that wasn't familiar.

"Where did you have that cat?" I asked.

"Up in Maine," he said. "That's where I'm from. I was aimin' to be a lobster man, but it didn't work out—almost drowned. My joining the Army seemed like a good idea at the time."

"Tracewski. Polish?" I said.

"Partly. Mom's black Japanese, and my Dad's all fisherman," he said with a laugh. He must be asked it a lot.

Our transport truck began filling with our platoon, and I turned to Trace. "Hey, good to meet you. See you in Warhorse."

"Like I want to be on the front lines."

Right. Everything we'd experienced until now was just a preamble for the fucking front lines.

Florida, July 2005

As I stood at the front entrance of the Orlando Fairgrounds in the rain with my guitar, having just been kicked out of my band, I heard, "Max, hey Max!"

Jeez, Billy Wagonkenect, a geeky guy from high school who used to get teased—never from me—ran over in a stupid plaid shirt, jeans, and a leather jacket with a fringe. It was as if his knees and elbows had an extra hinge as he had such a goofy way of running. He was smoking a joint. This guy?

"Hey," Wagonkenect said. "Your band really rocked tonight, loved it. I really like the new harder songs. You guys connect."

Could the guy make me more depressed?

"I guess you didn't see the finale," I said.

"No," he said in his stoner Floridian accent. "Sorry, Dude. New Found Glory was playing on Stage Five. I couldn't miss them this year. I heard, though, you had an amazing staged fight." He took another hit.

"It wasn't staged. It was real. I'm out of the band."

He looked aghast, then slowly said, as he exhaled a big blue cloud of smoke, "That's too bad."

"Whatever," I said. I glanced around at others leaving the venue. I hoped to recognize someone else and excuse myself.

"Wanna hit?"

Not with him. "No, thanks. Listen, I gotta go find my way home."

"Need a ride?"

I considered for a second. I really did. I didn't think I could be around him, as friendly as he was. "Thanks, but I'm waiting. For a friend."

"Okay, then." He started walking off, smoking his jay. Lightning flashed right then, and I guessed it would be raining harder soon. Damn. Leave it to me to choose the wrong option. I watched Wagonkenect amble away.

"Hey, Wagonkenect!" I shouted.

He turned and looked at me, a question on his face.

"Can you drop me near UCF?" I said, referring to the University of Central Florida. "My apartment's there."

"That's about twenty miles. I live the other direction," he said, tapping his chin.

"Never mind. Nice seeing you again, though," and I waved him off.

"No, I'm happy to do it," said Wagonkenect. "We can catch up on old times."

Like we had any old times. He handed me his joint. It was small now, I could barely hold it. After I took a hit, it slipped from my fingers and fell into a mud puddle and spit itself out.

On the ride home, Wagonkenect joyfully spoke about every song I hated. Wasn't he seeing I wasn't talking? I got away with a lot of "uh-huhs," and I was thinking there's no such thing as a free ride.

"I'm learning the steel guitar," Wagonkenect said. "Maybe when I get really good, you guys can use me." Did he forget I'd told him I wasn't in the band? "Wanna jam sometime, maybe even tonight?" he said.

Maybe the storm outside could become a hurricane, shove us into a tree, and put me out of my misery.

"I've got the guitar in my trunk," he said.

"Shit, Wagonkenect. You don't get it!" My hands became balls of anger. "I quit the band tonight. I don't want to talk music, play music, think music, okay?"

"You quit?"

"It wasn't my band anymore!"

"But it's the Vans Warped Tour. You made it, man. Why—"

"It's a stupid band and a stupid town where all it ever does is rain. Maybe you're like the tourist droids and think Orlando is fun, but this place is the armpit of the universe. This place is like being born in a cemetery. Fuck you if you want to stay in this shithole. I mean, don't you get what a droid you're becoming?"

Wagonkenect looked hurt.

Fuck. I realized what a scumbag thing I just did. A gust of rain slammed into the car. "I didn't mean to, you know—" I said. "Okay. How to explain?"

"You don't have to explain," he said, staring straight ahead. I know that look—the look of being mocked and teased.

"I'm sorry. As you see, I don't like Orlando. Don't you ever feel trapped—like all the things that school was supposed to teach us, they skipped? We're supposed to be like everyone else. We're supposed to stick around, get a dull, fucking job, marry, have kids, and die."

"You don't have a dull job," he said. "You have a band, and you shouldn't quit."

"But the band doesn't get it, either. It's like they think who cares what the words say? Just make music that will sell. Get rich, marry, have kids, die."

"You write good songs."

"Thanks, but that Ralph that you so adore is just doing what he thinks is popular. He can't write from his heart because he doesn't have one."

Wagonkenect nodded as if I got him doing something he wasn't used to doing: thinking.

"I'm sorry," I said. "I appreciate the ride."

"Okay," said Wagonkenect.

We said nothing more until we reached my apartment. I pulled out my guitar from the back. "Thank you," I blurted, holding out my hand. He shook it.

"Maybe the next band will be better," said Wagonkenect. "More feeling."

"Yeah. Exactly."

The rain, now intense, slashed into me, and my head pounded. I ran quickly into the courtyard of my apartment house where the pool was, surrounded on three sides by two levels of apartments. It was a good deal for me because I rented from a rich kid, Jack Derby, who was only going to college because his dad wanted him to. When I'd asked him what he wanted to be, he said, "I don't know. Maybe I'll be an entrepreneur." With the amazing growth of Napster, the music service, and then more recently, MySpace, I'm sure he saw himself as a future multimillionaire.

"Doing what?" I'd asked.

"Maybe into fashion—create my own onsite fashion service."

"You design or sew?" I'd asked.

"Whatever for? Or maybe I'll buy a juice store. I like smoothies. I'll just hire people to run it. "

"With your dad's money?"

"Fuck, no. I can do it on my own."

"How?"

"When I sell smoothies, I make money and then I pay them, duh," he told me—like I didn't know anything.

The thing was, for being a rich kid, Derby didn't have much of an allowance—his dad thought he'd use it up on drugs—so Derby had found an apprentice hair dresser, Michaela, to pay rent to sleep on a futon in a funny nook in the living room. With the extra money, Derby bought drugs. Sometimes he shared them with Michaela, who then would sleep with Derby. A couple of times, she'd slept with me when I had drugs. I didn't get her—she stayed up for days at time—but she could be fun.

Now someone was playing the Rolling Stone's "Sympathy for the Devil" loudly, accompanied by shouts. That's the kind of stuff that brings police. How parents let their kids go here, I never knew. It was a party school, and almost every party I'd been to had an ambulance or cop car scream in because someone drank too much and was barely breathing or there was a fight.

With the rain like needles hitting my face, I realized then that this place was just another of my bad decisions in a line of them. It was as if I were in one of those original *Star Trek* episodes where shitty pancake creatures lived on the ceiling of an alien apartment. One of those pancake creatures had flown onto Spock's face and fucked him up, and that's exactly what I wanted to do to someone's face the way I was feeling. As I approached my apartment, not only was the music getting louder, but there seemed to be a garage sale going on in the open-air landing.

Before I got to it, a young woman with pink hair who I vaguely remember visiting the apartment to score some meth from Derby was standing in front of a card table with orange crates full of someone's crap and clothes and said, "Hey, back from the show? I thought you were on tour."

I said nothing. I should be on tour. What the fuck? Those were my CDs and DVDs, my clothes just in a pile, and my posters rolled up the wrong way. A tall Midwestern-type girl in overalls was thumbing through my CDs. "Hey!" I shouted. "Get your hands off that stuff!"

She looked surprised, and then Derby, bong in hand, popped his head out. "Did you shout at her?"

"What's my stuff doing out here!"

"You don't pay the rent, you don't live here."

"You knew I was on tour! I said I'd send you a check this week."

"That's not what's known as a timely manner."

What a dick. From the ground, I seized a portrait of my mom and dad and me when I was young, just three, taken at one of those Sears studios, and now the glass was cracked.

I grabbed an armful of my clothes and a box of my CDs and marched past Derby, past the people inside the door, and through others dancing in the living room to the Stones. I found my door locked. Normally, it didn't even have a lock.

"Where's the fucking key?" I shouted.

I didn't wait. I kicked the door open. A half-naked couple was fucking on my mattress. I recognized Michaela. "Off of there," I shouted. "It's my room."

I looked at Derby, who was too stoned to look worried. "You gotta be fucking kidding me," I said.

"It's Michaela's room now. Sorry, Michaela. I wasn't expecting Max tonight."

The guy underneath her scrambled from the bed, but Michaela, also very stoned, said to Derby, "You didn't tell him?"

I was probably just like one of those frog legs in my high school bio class where we shocked the leg and it moved. I was just a charge of electricity, and when I twisted around, I punched Derby hard, right in the nose. Derby screamed and fell to the floor, and then Michaela and the boy jumped on me. The music was so loud, most people didn't know there was a fight until I, so fucking pissed off and full of adrenaline, barged into the living room with the couple on my back, and we crashed onto the glass coffee table, shattering it.

"Cops!" someone shouted.

I was still punching when two black-uniformed officers, a young man and an African-American woman, yanked Michaela and the guy off me.

Derby had a cloth on his bleeding nose and shouted, "He started it! I'm pressing charges!"

"You started it?" the male officer asked me.

"No, he put all my stuff out into the hallway!"

"He didn't pay his rent," shouted Derby. "Book him for assault."

"All right, you two," said the male cop, letting me go. "Let's just calm down. I'll have you turn down the music, and we'll call it a night." The female cop stepped away from Derby, who was glaring at me, now pointing and saying, "My nose, my glass table!"

I saw my opening and shouted, "And your nuts," which is where I kicked him. In hindsight, I should have waited for the cops to go, but I was so focused on Derby and all the things coming at me that day, I couldn't stand another second. Before I could get another punch in, the two cops grabbed me, yanking my arms behind me. I then felt the handcuffs.

Everyone at the party was staring at me, and the sound was way low. Some Pink Floyd eerie shit with squeals was playing, but that's the only thing I heard besides my deep, animal breathing. I told myself to get it together.

"I'm sorry," I said. "How about if I call my dad, and I'll just leave this place?"

"You'll call your dad from jail," said the male cop, now pissed off and shoving me forward. "I give you a break, and look what you do. Maybe this will teach you."

They led me handcuffed down to the cruiser. I could now hear someone in the party had put on a John Denver song, "Take Me Home, Country Roads." For that alone, I should beat someone up.

As we drove off, I looked out the rear window, passing one light pole after another and feeling utterly diminished, like a lake after a long drought. I was just a puddle.

Iraq, February 2007

As dirty and dusty as the moon, Camp Warhorse was a grimy flat camp with Quonset huts, shipping container housing, some air conditioned tents, and gatherings of porta-potties, the whole place surrounded by blast walls and festooned with sharp coils of concertina wire. The camp's tallest structure, our guard tower, overlooked a lot more dust as well as the local scrub growth.

The M2 gunners atop our platoon's eight Humvees attached barrels to their machine guns, adjusted the headspace and timing with tiny metal gauges on a keychain to make sure their weapons wouldn't jam or explode, and inserted their ammunition belts into the feed trays until the belt-holding pawl engaged the first round, ready to fire. I no longer had to do that. I'd been switched to a driver. The soldier I was replacing had become too nervous—"cold feet" as they say. That's because in battle, the driver was the prime target. Take out the driver, and the Humvee stops. Even so, I felt more protected inside than outside as a gunner.

As the the gunners prepared, I connected my new iPod—fresh from the PX—to the Humvee's communication system. I searched for the song I wanted and pressed play. At this point, I only had a hundred songs, but they were my favorites, including the hard-pounding "Monsters" from Matchbook Romance, a band of four guys from New York. The LT had said go for it. Like all of us—young, energetic, and music-loving—he punched the air with his stocky arm and shouted, "We are the monsters underneath your bed."

Each of us stepped out of our Humvees and drew our weapons, facing the test range. We always stopped here before we went beyond the wire to make sure our weapons worked. With the music still blasting, Sergeant Ichisada shouted, "Test fire!" and we all started shooting into the sandy bank at the far end. The gunners atop the Humvees unloaded their .50-caliber M2 machine guns in a searing staccato. I blasted my handgun and snapped off a few rounds of my M4, a magazine-fed assault rifle, the next generation after the Vietnam-era M16. All around me, hot brass—our used shell casings—dropped to the ground like metal confetti. All of us, men and women, shouted like gladiators as we shot up the range.

I wondered if God were amused at such things. In *The Sirens of Titan,* Kurt Vonnegut wrote how the alien robot, Salo, had been amused by Earthlings, who always acted as if there were a big eye in the sky always watching, and the eye was hungry for entertainment. Thus, Earthlings did funny and sad and often dramatic things, performing night and day and even in their dreams, as if the big eye was their only audience. Would the eye be amused by our shenanigans in Iraq? As Vonnegut suggested, it didn't matter. God was indifferent. That was okay. Then I could be myself.

As we departed, we all sang in harmony, "We are the monsters, yeah, yeah, yeah, yeah, yeah!"

We were actually two groups of four Humvees. Normally, we each went to two different police stations, with a sergeant overseeing each group. The LT would go with one group one day, and the other group the next, so he knew both stations. There were many platoons just like us so that we were covering Baqubah twenty-four hours a day. It's why the chow hall was open past midnight—for the platoons coming back or just going out.

In the lead, I drove out of Camp Warhorse. I was the driver in the only air conditioned Humvee. The fine dust here killed the air conditioners on the others quickly. Lieutenant Graver, sitting shotgun next to me, said, "Turn right at the next intersection, and I'm going to give you a new route."

"We always take a new route, sir," I said. We did so to reduce the chance of an ambush. We didn't want to be predictable.

"No, I mean we're not going to the police station today. Captain gave me new orders."

Our company commander, Captain Senbeef, whom we nicknamed Beef Jerky, wasn't the in-your-face type. He never visited the platoon or more-rare company formations, never ate in the chow hall with us. We'd only catch him at a distance—as I did this morning talking to the LT. I guessed then it was bad. Now the LT looked lost in thought. When I'd heard the LT had grown up on a ranch in Colorado, I'd expected him to be easygoing like a cowboy. Most of the time he was, but now I sensed the situation was beyond the usual. My stomach always knotted up when we left camp because we were always waiting for the boom, and now my stomach was doing somersaults. I had a bad feeling about this.

"New orders?" said Private Paulino from the back. She sounded as wary as me. We often had at least one woman each in a few Humvees in case we needed to search people. Our women would search the Iraqi women. Paulino was the gunner when we needed one, and she could slip up through the now-closed hole in the roof.

"Yeah," said the LT. "I'm about to explain on the radio. Cut the music, Rivera."

I did. I glanced at our interpreter, Ali, who sat next to Paulino, and he didn't look happy about this either. Ali, a thin young guy who had learned English from the University of Baghdad for a year before his parents called him back, was pro-American, so he signed on as an interpreter, which paid well. The insurgents were always out to kill our interpreters.

"This is Lieutenant Graver," said the LT into the radio. "Captain Senbeef this morning changed our plans. He'd learned that Al Queda has been leaving Baghdad and setting up shop here in Baqubah. Al Queda has declared Baqubah the capital of the Islamic state. I'm guessing our higher-ups are forming new plans now, but today we're supposed to secure a particular neighborhood for the 5-20 Battalion to go through. They're coming in their Strykers. I can't say what'll happen, boys and girls, but our job is just to stop anyone going or coming into the area until the 5-20 can be more thorough."

As military police, we were not infantry. Our mission in Baqubah was to patrol the roads and teach the local police stations how to maintain order. We would train them how to shoot and how to be better at their jobs. Today we'd be supporting the infantry—also part of our jobs.

"Each Humvee," said the LT, "will be positioned at key points around the neighborhood. You'll be having to talk with people, and we only have our one interpreter, Ali, today. Just keep people in the neighborhood. If someone is coming in, and they have papers to prove they live there, they can go in. No one goes out. It shouldn't take more than a couple of hours."

The thing about Iraq that I didn't expect is that many of the neighborhoods, like the one we were passing now, could almost be suburban America. There were houses and driveways and telephone poles and fences. The stucco houses, though, were generally flat-roofed, and all were the same beige as if the neighborhood paint store only sold one color. If the house were made of brick, as I often saw up close, the bricks were orange and rust-colored and laid by people generous with the mortar and not particularly strict with their levels. The subdivisions I grew up in Florida had much better craftsmanship, yet they weren't much different in terms of an overall look. Some had very strict rules, such as black mailboxes, red tile roofs, and earth-colored stucco—no variance allowed.

Here, while some neighborhoods had asphalted roads and green front lawns, others like the one we soon stopped at had dirt roads and dirt front yards, and rubble was spread generously about as if construction crews dumped off busted-up freeways. Some of the houses here had been bombed, mere shells and blackened—by us or insurgents, I didn't know.

"Stop here," said the LT at a corner where a wall started for a neighborhood. He spoke into the radio. "When we stop at a particular place, I want the vehicle behind us to stay there. The gunner will stay atop the Humvee to look out and be ready, and everyone else will maintain a checkpoint. The 5-20 should be here within a half hour."

We soon circled the neighborhood. The LT made Ali, Paulino, and me stop people. Now outside the truck, a hot wind blew in my face, along with dust. It had to be way over a hundred. We'd be here for hours in the hot sun, no place to piss except into a bottle—for Paulino and all women. Jittery from all the Rip It energy drinks we drank from the chow hall, we'd kick rocks, shoo away flies, and simply endure, punctuated by the occasional car trying to get in or out.

I took off my gloves and threw them in the Humvee, just as a shiny white Volvo approached us. Paulino, a short woman encumbered with full gear as we all were, held out her hand for them to stop. "Out," she shouted, using her thumb to show what she wanted.

Ali shouted something in Arabic, and a family of three emerged—a man in jeans and a black T-shirt that said in silver letters, "Top of the Pops." His wife was covered head to toe in white, and their son, about seven, came out in shorts and a yellow button-down shirt.

"Hello, hello," Ali said in Arabic, or at least that's what I figured he said. Ali explained to her husband that he had to keep his arms raised while I patted him down. Paulino inspected the woman, who was upset as Ali explained to her what Paulino was going to do. I know somewhere in his explanation was that Paulino was a woman. It was hard to tell with the gear. I'd seen her in a bikini at Camp Victory and with her hair down at Camp Warhorse. She was good looking, a brunette with a smile that could pull the birds out of the sky, but she was all business. Someone said she was engaged to some computer hack in Minnesota.

I was instantly anxious because of this family. Were they a family or terrorists? The wife could most easily conceal many explosives. They wouldn't kill the kid too, would they? Crazy thoughts. I doubted any suicide bombers were expecting us, considering this was even a surprise to us, but maybe we interrupted someone today.

The family proved fine, concealing nothing, and Ali sent them back home. They gave us wary looks but didn't utter a word as they passed us.

More than a half-hour later, gunfire came from a distance. Still fairly new to this life, we hadn't yet known when we were in danger or not, so we ducked behind the Humvee.

"That gunfire," said the LT into his radio. "Is it any of you?"

"Negative," came a response. "But we hear it close by and we're back in the truck. We have a problem."

"What's that?" said the LT.

"Hitch fell down. It's so fucking hot, we think it's heat stroke. He's fucking hallucinating. He's telling us it's Saddam's nerve gas or Anthrax, and we're going to die."

"Let me give you our position, then drive here. We'll get Hitch in the air conditioning. Give him water."

"Affirmative. We are."

A half hour later, Hitch looked fine inside our truck, apologizing for being a wimp. He never had heat stroke in Texas, so why here?

"You're not a wimp," I said. "Heat stroke can happen to any of us. It happened to Yanni last week."

After I said that, clouds of dust approached in the distance—the 5-20 in their Strykers.

A Stryker was built almost like a tank but with eight monster wheels, and the driver and vehicle commander had periscopes to see. There were no windows. Besides its two-man crew, it could carry up to nine infantry soldiers. It's akin to one of those small boats that stormed Normandy Beach in World War II. The Stryker had a panel that came down to off-load the men inside. The only real differences between the infantry and us in the military police was the way they were equipped and the way they were all men. We had women.

One Stryker stopped near us. The back opened up, and the men emerged, goggles on, guns ready. Three groups of three rushed toward houses and knocked on doors. If no one answered, they bashed the door in. Each home was inspected.

It took over two hours to go through the neighborhood. I heard machine gun fire again at one point. One house had put up resistance. I later learned a cache of guns and homemade bombs were found inside, and two Iraqis, both young men, killed. I never heard a report about what else was discovered. It was just so fucking hot there, I was happy when we could go.

As we approached Camp Warhorse, the LT said it was okay to broadcast music again. I'm not a Southern hick—even if Florida is the South—but I blasted a song my father would probably play: "Proud to Be an American" by Lee Greenwood. After all the tension and heat, it felt right in a fun, odd way. I could tell the others loved it, too, because they sang along, shouting, "And I'd gladly *stand up* next to you and defend her still today."

From the moment we arrived at Camp Warhorse, I had dived into my music, which I'd kept dormant until now. I'd been worried that music might distract me from keeping me alive. Now I realized it's what kept me going. Music reminded me there were better things than throwing fifty pounds of clothes and supplies on: always sweltering in the hundred-plus temperatures; driving in Humvees; marching; shooting; taking on mortars, RPGs, and gunfire; hoping to avoid IEDs; and worrying that even though the last five hundred corners I've turned had no enemy, the next corner might.

Music elevated me, reminded me there's sun in sunlight, bark in a terrier, and that doves could fly in a formation. My emotions rose and fell with the right music the way a seagull could glide and dive with the wind. The right voice, like Jeff Buckley or k.d. lang singing "Hallelujah," told me there's magic on earth. Music showed me we were meant to move.

Of course, music in war movies, which could be fuckin' awesome, could also be disturbing—violence and beauty slammed together. Francis Ford Coppola did it so well in *Apocalypse Now* as did Ridley Scott in *Black Hawk Down*.

We moved into the camp, back under the wire. Completely exhausted, we made it to the chow hall, which was a pre-fab building serving food four times a day, and lots of it. I was eating many cheese-and-bacon croissant sandwiches in those days. The smoothies were great, as were the pork chops—and, of course, Rip It energy drinks more than water. When people later asked me why the war was so expensive, I said the food had to always be shipped in. If each soldier ate $10 per meal, and we had 4,500 on base, that made for at least $135,000 in costs per day or close to a million dollars a week to feed us.

As I was in mid-bite, the LT shouted, "Atten hut!" We stopped and stood. Captain Beef Jerky approached us, looking mad. He reminded me of that old-time actor, Humphrey Bogart, in the film *The Caine Mutiny*, who swore he could run the ship. His two lackey assistants strode at his side.

"Lieutenant, may I have a word with you?" said the captain.

"Yes, sir," and the LT strode over, saying, "I'm proud of my soldiers today." I couldn't hear the specifics after that, but I could see the LT get a dressing down. After the captain turned sharply back for his office, the LT gathered us around him.

"I got the captain to allow a quick meal, but a squad of four trucks has to go back out there."

"Sir, whatever for?" said Styles, who had watched the captain retreat.

"Apparently a pair of night-vision binoculars are missing after our mission to the police stations yesterday, and we have to go back to our station and look for them."

"He's putting our fucking lives on the line for a pair of binoculars?" said Styles without regard to consequences.

The LT looked at Styles, and nodded. "I wish I could have told him as bluntly, but I did get the point across. He explained the camp was under review, and he needed them back.

"The guy's a pencil pusher," said Styles. "I can't fucking believe this."

"Language," said the LT. "And I can't believe it either. Any volunteers?"

"Me," said Hitch right away. "I want to redeem myself."

"Why aren't you getting checked by the doc? Off with you—and you don't need any redeeming," said the LT.

"I'm in," said Yanni.

"Me, too," said Styles.

"I'll drive," I said.

A couple women joined in, as did Ali, and soon we had twelve. The LT gave us thirty minutes to go back to our tents to freshen up. The camp was still being built, and we were new, so we once again bunked in two giant tents, and a smaller one for women, each surrounded with sandbags. Smaller concrete pads were being made for three-man CHUs—containerized housing units referred to as "chews"—which were basically box-like aluminum shipping containers with linoleum on the floor. Flat-roofed, they felt more substantial than tents, and if one could have come in thick steel like a bank vault, I would have taken that. The LT had said we'd move into those CHUs ASAP.

I drove out, seeing in my mirror the other Humvee following behind. Styles, the LT, and Private Paulino, rounded out my Humvee. The first place we headed for was the station that Styles, Hitch, and I normally worked at, a grim building not far from the open air marketplace. The problem with Baqubah was that it was between Baghdad and the border with Iran. Iran had been supporting the Shiite militias with weapons and foreign fighters, so a lot a sectarian violence had gripped the city long before we got there. The main market square had been used for executions by Islamic fundamentalists.

The sun was setting, and as we neared the police station, the streets were deserted as if the city had a curfew, but it didn't. The citizens knew if they wanted to stay alive, stay indoors most nights. It's when the insurgents liked to attack the most.

This was a fucking crazy place, and I was still trying to understand why we were in the middle. Yes, I understood our goal was to train the Iraqi police and army so that they could do it all, but I had my doubts. For instance, the place we were headed originally had a green Shiite militia flag waving out front. The station captain, a little man named Salih, built like a boxer, assured us it was a mistake, that some kid had probably placed it there. I doubted it as Ali, our translator, later told me he overheard the captain say something about a Sunni mongrel bastard, and others laughed. Also, the officers moved slowly at each exercise we offered. Still, who'd want such a job? Iraqi police were the first ones picked off by Sunni insurgents—perhaps why this station seemed to be with the Shiite majority of the population.

What took me a while to understand was that Shiites were a minority of worldwide Islamic population. Shiites were the bulk of the population in Iran and Iraq. The Sunnis ran all the other Arab states, including Saudi Arabia, Kuwait, Syria, and Jordan. Saddam was Sunni, a minority in Iraq. He didn't like Iran. His minority ruled through ruthlessness. When we overthrew Saddam, the Shiites swept into power. The U.S. didn't seem to fully understand this part. We seemed to feel with "bad guy" Saddam gone, all would be well.

The Sunni, however, became fundamentalist and soon tried to make Baqubah the capital of the Islamic State in Iraq, where Sharia law would be in force. This is Islamic law where thieves might have their hands or feet amputated or adulterers could be stoned to death. Baqubah became the hot spot just as my fellow Fort Lewis soldiers and I had arrived.

Of course, the political situation was not all this simple as a third group, the Kurds, based in Northern Iraq, Turkey, and Syria, wanted power, too, if not their own Kurdish state. Add to this, intermarriages among the three, and it was complex. We were fighting a uniformless enemy, and they didn't give a fuck about playing fair.

When we taught the police at the station the rules of engagement, only a few seemed to understand. What I first thought was resistance on their part, though, I later came to see they just didn't care.

As I approached the market area, we drove past buildings whose front walls were missing from various blasts. There had been a U.S.-led offensive in December before we arrived, and in this part of the city, even many of the sidewalks were rubble.

"I'm thinking," said the LT, "that what we did today in that neighborhood is a sign things are getting worse, not better."

"And don't you think Captain Beef Jerky is going to get us killed?" said Styles.

The LT turned sharply. "While I've encouraged candor, Styles, you need to hold your mouth more. As soldiers, we have to follow orders, and we can't be questioning our superiors."

Paulino spoke up. "Sir, he's not saying anything that the rest of us aren't thinking."

"Believe me, the generals aren't blind—or so I'm told." The LT turned back.

"And yet we're on this stupid mission," said Styles.

"You didn't have to volunteer," I said, thinking it'd help relieve the tension.

"Why'd you volunteer?" he shot back.

"To keep you around."

I drove past a wall with a lot of graffiti on it, but Arabic graffiti wasn't like ours. It looked like a scratch pad of squiggles for testing pens. A painting of an Arab with a white headscarf stared at us, proud, defiant.

We arrived at the station, built like a bunker—thick concrete walls and only tiny windows with bars on them. Unfortunately, police stations attracted suicide bombers. When we stopped in front of the station—normally no cars could be there—it was as if we whacked a bee hive. The young blue-shirted police in the doorway ran in shouting something, which I knew to be about us, and there seemed to be a lot of people running around in there. Normally, they knew when we were coming, but this time, no. As we got out of the car, two men with black turbans ran out. "Stop!" I shouted, raising my gun. My comrades did the same.

The two men smiled and raised their hands. They were Shiite. The black turban showed that they were clerks from the bloodline of the prophet called Sayyid. Ali had explained this to me once. Ali himself was Shiite, but he wanted his country to be whole, Sunni and Shiite together as friends, and he thought he was helping.

We patted the men down. They were clean. Ali said they'd been there to complain about noise in their building. We doubted it, but let them go.

Once we walked inside, Captain Salih swooped in from his office, saying, "Good evening, gentlemen." He must have heard that from a movie. "How can I help you?" He was the only one there that spoke English. He reminded me of the short little captain played by Claude Rains in one of those old movies I love, *Casablanca*. This guy was darker than Rains but had the same thin mustache, the same sense of entitlement.

"One of my men apparently left behind a pair of night vision binoculars," said the LT. "We need them back."

The captain looked hurt. "I thought they were a loan."

"Nope. We need accountability of all equipment." Some accountant on our base had probably pointed out to our captain how expensive they were.

The Iraqi captain quickly spoke in Arabic to a few young men nearby, boys, really, who could barely grow mustaches, who then laughed.

"All right. Let me get it," said the captain.

"We'll go with you."

He shrugged and led us out back to the gated parking lot. The captain strode to a white Mercedes S-class sedan—not a spot on it. How did a police captain own what was probably a $100,000 car? He opened the trunk, reached in, and then searched among a pile of AK47s. Where were those going?

"Nice car," said the LT.

"I get a deal," said the captain.

The man kept searching, then snapped his finger as if remembering. "I know where they are. I let my friend at another nearby station try them out."

The LT sighed. "Call him, then. We'll go there and get them."

"But—" The captain paused.

"Do you know how much we've spent on you guys to keep you alive?" asked the LT.

"No problem. I will arrange it."

We returned inside, and the Iraqi captain went to his office. None of us sat. Most of the Iraq police officers in the room found a reason to go elsewhere. If the anger on the LT's face were rope, he'd have enough for a hanging. I knew the LT. I'd overheard him talk to Sergeant Ichisada once about how corrupt the police were, and that in no way was our training at police stations going to help the country. It was the U.S.'s idea to train the police. The Iraqis didn't ask for it or accept it. The Iraqi citizens were ready to split into factions under the name of democracy.

In less than five minutes, the captain returned with a city map in his hands. He waved the LT over to the nearest desk. "It's right here, not very far away," said the captain, pointing to the map.

"It's on the edge of the city," said the LT. "Just the one road to it?"

"Yes. Very easy."

"You're coming with us," said the LT.

The captain's face looked surprised as if Saddam himself was going to torture him. "I can't," said the captain, pulling on his smile again. "Too much to do here."

"You're coming," said the LT, not giving him any more reason.

"May I make one phone call first?"

"No. We're leaving. Use your cell phone in the car if you want."

The captain nodded, reached in his desk for a revolver, and slipped it into his pocket. I moved my finger toward the safety switch of my rifle. I didn't trust this guy.

The LT then snapped his fingers to get Ali's attention. "You and the captain will ride in Rivera's Humvee. I'll go with Jordan." Jordan Frank was the new guy, twenty-six, who I barely knew. His first name made a better last name, so everyone called him Jordan. His cot was near mine. He showed some interest in my still camera when I showed him it could do video. He said he had iMovie on his MacBook, that we should make some videos sometime, to which I said, "Sure."

I realized the LT didn't trust the Iraqi captain. Maybe there would be no binoculars at the station, and I started wondering if the LT wanted Ali in my vehicle for Ali to hear and understand anything the captain said on his phone.

We hurried down to the Humvees. The LT gave me the map, said I'd be in the lead and be the team leader. He whispered in my ear to be careful. He whispered something in Paulino's ear, too, then told me, "She's the gunner. Going up top."

Before we started out, I decided we could all use some mellow music, so I brought up on my iPod a gentle piece called "Lake Tahoe" by the band Sherwood, out of San Luis Obispo in California. I'd rebuilt my list of tunes on this new iPod after I lost my last one in the shitter. The song "Lake Tahoe" has a single voice remembering not only special spots in Lake Tahoe, but also a girl. When it came down to it, a lot of my songs were about girls.

We drove through the city to the outskirts. As I listened to the song, I thought about how amazing it was that someone could think up notes and words and write them on paper—even though it's what I did. It's just ink on a page, yet it created energy. It made people feel something. Music notation could bend the universe.

We passed shuttered stores, which were merely stalls in a bazaar setting with their garage doors down. A few were open, but with all the rubble and only remnants of some buildings, it wasn't a teeming metropolis. Everyone and everything seemed displaced.

In the back, the captain and Ali were speaking with each other quietly, though I got the sense from the captain's tone, he was angry. Ali sounded patient, reassuring, which seemed to piss off the captain more. I turned up the music slightly. "I miss home and I miss you," went the sweet song, "when there's no one around and nothing to do...."

"Left here," the captain told me.

"No," I said, following the route given to me by the LT. Left would take us out of the city, not to the station.

"Left, driver," said the captain more emphatically.

I shook my head. This guy didn't even know his own city. We turned right.

"This is a stupid mission," said Ali to me.

At that moment, the radio crackled on, interrupting the music. Jordan in the car behind me yelled, "Rivera, veer left! Veer—"

I yanked the wheel. A moment later, I saw a flash and felt our truck lift in the air, leaping as if it were a kid's toy clawed by a cat. A terrible heat enveloped me, searing my face, before the sound of the explosion roared, deafening.

6

Florida, July 2005

After I was arrested in Florida, I was taken to the modern beige-brick-and-glass Orange County Booking and Release Center on John Young Parkway. The male officer who arrested me took my fingerprints and then brought me to a wall where my mug photo was taken, front and side. Soon he guided me into a holding cell by myself. "Do I get a call?" I asked.

"You'll get it when you get it. In the bigger holding tank later, there's a pay phone," said the officer.

"I don't have money."

"Then call collect."

In a little while, a new officer came for me. He was a thin old guy who reminded me of a school cop—thinner, wrinklier, but something friendly about him. In a green uniform and a black vest with the letters OCCD on the front, he took me to a shower area where my clothes were put in a box and labeled. The place smelled like the New York subway, which made me breathe only through my mouth. The old guy handed me a hotel-bar-size of soap. As I stood there, naked, covering my genitals, he said, "Go on, in. I don't have all night." Three other cops, much younger, chatted to themselves much farther down.

To the sounds of running water, I stepped into the tiled area. The shower room was similar to the one in my old high school, one shower head after another—more than a dozen. Here, however, two tall, massive black guys were laughing as they soaped up near each other, and on the other side, two shorter well-muscled Latino guys eyed me. I almost shit right there. But, hey, I was Latino, right? Maybe the Latinos would protect me. I didn't feel "Latino," though. I never thought much about race mainly because I felt inadequate all on my own. Their chests had ugly blue tattoos, the prison kind with a lot of lines, words, and fists. They had their own culture. Would this old cop really be able to stop these monsters from beating me to a pulp?

Fuck.

Why did I do impulsive things? The pleasure of smashing Derby hadn't lasted more than a few seconds. Now I was here, not quite twenty. I was the quintessential skinny suburban kid who'd thought he was a tough, angry kid. I'd been angry—suburban angry—which didn't measure up with these guys. I had loving parents who'd given me a hard time. Compared to where these guys had probably grown up, I'd had it easy— an only child who got the movies and CDs I'd asked for, as well as a car, guitar, and amp. My rage wasn't about material things but about what I was expected to do, to be part of some whole that was so fuzzy, I couldn't be specific. In one song, I said we were all mindless money-making monkeys for the big companies to sell shit to. But here I had nothing—was that better?

As the black guys laughed more, I turned and considered the shower the farthest from them, but that would put me in a corner and away from the entrance. I stepped back and took the shower closest to where I'd come in. The black guys now whispered something. Scared, I dropped my soap. The little bar slipped into the trough leading to the drain at my feet, into the stream of their soap scum. The bar was soon hidden underneath it.

I powered my shower on, spun once in it to get wet, then rushed back the way I came in.

The old guy said, "That was fast. Did you get your pits?"

"I'm fine."

He handed me a towel and an orange jump suit.

"To my own cell?" I asked, ready to be alone and away from these criminals.

"No, the holding tank—until we can find you something for the night."

Soon he directed me to a big cell with a lot of other men in orange jumpsuits, mean-looking ugly guys with terrible teeth out of a Scorcese movie, or so I imagined. Two bald thugs with thick, muscled arms glared at me with a smirk, as if I would be their night's entertainment. I remembered how my father, in teaching me how to fight, always said don't look afraid.

A toilet was on one side, and a three-hundred-pound white guy was on it, pants down, belly fat rolling onto his legs like icing off a donut. I'd rather shit in my pants than use the toilet in front of these guys. I then saw the pay phone.

I hadn't spoken to my parents in weeks—not that I hated them, but since they divorced, they had their own lives, and I had mine. Also, Dad and I had argued before I went on tour. I'd given him my CD fresh from the recording studio. He listened to perhaps thirty seconds of the first track, "Crack Pipe with Carla," grimaced, pulled out the CD and cracked it in half right in front of me. "You're wasting your life."

"I'm good, Dad."

"Then you're wasting mine. If this is talent, I'm fucking Santa Claus."

I imagined him fucking Santa, with the reindeer watching, but I said nothing. I'd been staying with him and his new wife, Carlita. He'd found another immigrant spouse. No matter how much I tried liking her, she never felt like my family. He couldn't do better than my mother, who had such heart and drive. I left then and there, which was when I found my apartment with Derby.

Dad answered after the first ring. I didn't like how the operator said, "This is a collect call. Will you accept charges from Max in the county jail?"

"Jail!" he blurted. "Yes," he added with a sigh. "I'll accept."

"Dad," I said quietly as I could into the receiver.

"What the hell did you do now?" he said loudly. I looked at the bald guy closest to me, who was smiling as if he could hear.

"Why do you say it that way?" I asked.

"You think I'm some old fart who doesn't know anything, especially about your life. I've tried to steer you away from trouble, and now you're in jail? Whatever for?"

"Hey, buddy," the bald guy said to me. "Don't hog the phone. I'm expecting a call."

I turned my back on Kojak, hoping it was the right move. "They say assault," I told my father. "Can you believe that? You always wanted me to be more of a fighter."

"So it's my fault, you're saying?" I pictured my dad standing tall like the Army sergeant he once was.

"My roommate and I got into a scuffle. Now he's pressing charges, "I said.

"What am I supposed to do?"

"Bail?"

"Max, I had to pay for that expensive car accident a couple years ago because you were drunk."

"And I thanked you." I was sensing where this was going.

"Hey, phone hog," the bald guy said. I held up one finger.

"Then there was the time you were so lost," my father said, "you lived with your mother and me for a few months. Before the divorce. Best I could tell, you spent money on drugs, women, and tattoos. Nothing I said mattered."

"Dad, you want me to apologize for my life? I'm doing the best I can."

"Dad-dee!" the bald guy bellowed. The other added in a high voice, "Dad-dee, come save me."

"Max, I know you have a talent—a talent for trouble," said my father. "I'll let you stay in that place tonight so you can think about how you got there."

"Dad!" I imagined him going to bed with Carlita that night, saying nothing about me in jail. "Dad!"

I could hear Carlita asking who it was. Dad said, "Nobody. Wrong number. "

Click.

Dialtone.

I slammed the phone down hard, then picked it up again, ready to bash in the head of Kojak if he kept coming at me. He backed up, surprised. "Fuck it," he said, turning back to his friends.

I stepped away, moving to the middle where I took a stand. Don't get me wrong, I was scared deep to my core, but I was also pissed at my father. Maybe that was good.

I remembered another fight I had with him, right after high school, when I told him about my new band. "Look at your choice of lifestyles," he had said then.

"What, you thought I'd be a banker? I'm following my dream."

"Your dream looks like a nightmare from my angle."

I'd have said his life was a nightmare, but that wouldn't have been respectful. After he and Mom had married, he'd worked in a steel warehouse in the Bronx that carried different gauges of rolled steel, and when he'd come home at night with blistering eyes from irritants in the air, my mother would place cold cucumber slices on his eyelids.

When I was a teenager, he always looked for ways to toughen me up. He had me try sports, which I hated, until I found roller hockey. Until then, I had liked art, music, and movies—and movies that brimmed with art and music were the best. No matter—my mother loved me openly, even as she moved her way up in the banking system and became a head banker at Citibank. After he went on Workers Comp, he had affairs. Maybe it made him feel strong. I'd had a lot of anger over that.

I shook my head. My being in jail wasn't just because of my roommate, but a deeper realization that I wasn't the happiest bunny rabbit. I managed to turn a number of people against me. Today alone there was Ralph and the whole band, Wagonkenect, Derby, Michaela, a couple cops, and, in the wings, a battalion of street criminals. I'd heard of the word *karma* before and wondered if that's what I had. What had I done wrong that I had to work through? This wasn't the usual thinking for someone raised Catholic as I had been. I'd been an altar boy, too, but since leaving home, I'd followed more spiritual things, such as music. Yet I had more challenges than anyone else I knew. Then again, most of my non-musician friends didn't want much. If they got a job at a hardware store, that's what they did for the last three years, that and party on the two days off during the week they got. I'd tried that for a while in a UPS warehouse,where I loaded trucks off a conveyor belt—scan, lift, and stack—during the graveyard shift. It sucked. It's like floating with the tide rather than swimming for a goal—yet my working friends seemed happier than me. I'd been swimming in a riptide, and at that moment, I was drowning.

The old cop returned for me. I couldn't move fast enough to the cell door.

"I got you a regular cell," the old cop said.

"Before these other guys?"

"They're making bail."

We entered another building.

"This is my first time arrested," I said to the officer. "I don't have money for bail, and I don't get how things work. Don't I have to go to court?"

"That'll happen in the morning when you're arraigned."

"Do I get a lawyer?"

"We're not supposed to chitchat," he said. After several more steps, he sighed and said, "Kid, if you can't afford a lawyer, one will be appointed. Someone was supposed to tell you this earlier. Didn't you get that?"

"I guess I couldn't concentrate."

The man guided me through two sets of doors. We were mysteriously buzzed in each time, but I saw small cameras near the ceiling after the first set. After the second set, we stepped into an open concrete courtyard of sorts. On either side of the open area stood jail cells. The cells featured floor-to-ceiling bars. I shouldn't be here, I thought. This is wrong.

Each cell had a bunk bed and a pair of prisoners in each, wearing the same orange jumpsuit I had. Two more levels of jail cells rose up—nothing warm or fuzzy about the place.

"Am I going to have a roommate?" I asked.

"Yeah," said the old cop, pointing to the stairs.

We walked up the set of metal stairs to the second level, and as we walked its corridor, a door slid open as we approached. He motioned for me to enter, and as I did, a man, maybe thirty-five, short and mean-looking with a scar that went from his nose to near his ear, sat up from the bottom bunk with a book in his hand. Great, I thought. I get the Mafia man. I felt the lump you get when the roller coaster makes it to the top of the first hill, and you know this was going to be far worse than you expected. Maybe I wouldn't make it to the morning.

The officer watched me as the barred door closed, and I faced the brutal looking man whose tattoos I now noticed. One featured a skull wearing a beret and eating a knife. A banner below proclaimed, "Saudi – Iraq – Kuwait." The other arm showed a rifle jammed into the ground with a helmet resting on top of the stock.

The man lay back down on his back, lifting up his book, reading a small paperback with the title *Being and Nothingness*. He was no more interested in me than a bug crawling on the gray concrete floor.

I stepped to the thin mattress of the top bunk, ran my hand over the top, looking for anything crawling. Nothing. I looked around for a clock, but there wasn't one—just a sink, an open-bowl toilet, and the bunk bed.

"Good book?" I asked, trying to figure out if I was to step on his bed to get up or what. There was no extra bar or ladder on the sides. This made no sense.

"Let me give you the rules," said the con. "No talkin' to me. No talkin' period. Don't get in my way. If you have to fucking fart, face outward. Got it? Otherwise, no noise from you."

"Sorry," I said. I tried a small jump to push myself up, but I fell back down. I tried it again.

"Fuck!" he said, stood, and eyed me hard. I stepped back, but he grabbed two fistfuls of my jumpsuit and threw me up on the bed.

"Stay up there till morning!" he commanded.

I laid down, staring at the spider webs on the ceiling. The smell of a raw, raunchy fart wafted my way, and from another level the sounds of fists against skin with muffled groans rose in tandem. Someone was raping or punishing someone else, and soon it'd be me.

Just then, I heard, "Come and get it" at our door. I looked, and a man in an orange jumpsuit with a cart held out two plastic meal trays, shoving one through a slot in the door. My cellmate grabbed the first, sat on his bunk, and began unwrapping his food. I jumped down and got the other tray.

"Didn't you hear what I said?" he said.

"But it's food."

He said nothing. I held my tray. Where was I supposed to sit? Up on my bunk? I looked at the white tray, which had what looked to be a turkey sandwich in cellophane, an ice cream scoop of maybe potato salad in a Styrofoam square under plastic, a small carton of two-percent milk, and a lame fucking apple.

Only then did I realize I was crying. I was so angry at myself, I threw the whole tray down onto the floor, and my cellmate shouted, "Hey!"

"Fuck you," I said, and stepping on his bed, I leaped up on top of my bunk, turning to the wall, waiting for the beating of my life in a second. I must have had a death wish.

I could hear the man pick up my tray and things. A few seconds later, he touched my shoulder, and I smashed myself against the wall as if my beating would be less severe.

"Boy, what's going on?" he said. If he weren't a criminal, his D.J. voice might be soothing.

"Nothing," I said as firmly as I could muster.

"Come down here," he said.

So he was going to beat me standing? "Okay," I replied. I gathered my strength, preparing myself the best I could for the fight to come.

When I stood in front of him, he said, "Sit down." He pointed to the end of his bed.

Was he going to beat me senseless on the bed, was that it? I said, "I'd rather not."

"Stand, then. This your first time in jail?"

"Yeah."

"After a couple of times, it's not so bad." His voice seemed strangely friendly. He held out his hand with an apple. It was his because I could still see mine in the corner.

"Eat something," he said, "so I don't have to listen to your fuckin' gurgling stomach all night."

I took a bite. It tasted surprisingly good.

"Why the tattoos?" he asked.

"You have tattoos."

"Mine were earned." He pointed to the knife-eating skull. "Desert Storm," he said. Then another with an anchor and a rope. "This one's from my time as a Merchant Marine delivering ammo to the Middle East. This one," he said, pointing to a parachute, "was the time I was a paratrooper in the reserves. You and kids your age don't earn shit. Look at all the color on your arms. You went to so-called tattoo artists, right?"

"They're my friends."

"You think you're tough or worldly because you have them? Fuck that."

"Each one of my tats is earned, too," I said. Sometimes I say things before thinking, like now, but it pissed me off he didn't get me, either. I pointed to the stars near my elbows. "These I got first after my band had its first paying gig."

"So you thought you were a star?"

I pointed to a small beautiful face of Lynette. "This was my first girlfriend who then slept with everyone in my band."

"Enough," he said firmly. "I don't want to hear about your pathetic life. Have the next artist paint you jail bars down your back because—mark my words—this is where you're going to spend a lot of your time. You'll get out tomorrow, but you'll be back."

"No, I won't." Part of me thought he might be right, but I wished for everything he was wrong.

He only gave a knowing grin. "I've spent a lot of my adult life here. You remind me of me. I bet we even have the same last names."

"I'm Rivera."

"Rheingold. Close enough. See what I'm saying? You have a choice: either do something different in your life, or you'll be back here. I've seen it with plenty of people in this place." He pointed to the cells on the other side like Vanna White on *Wheel of Fortune* revealing that there was a new vowel. When I didn't say anything, he said, "You can go back to your bunk."

I jumped up, then laid down. I wondered was he right? I couldn't say my life was going well lately. I did stupid things. Maybe I should read more, like this guy. "*Being and Nothingness*?" I said, referring to his book.

"We'll be dead before we know it. Then we'll be nothing."

"I know about nothingness. Nine-Eleven showed us that."

"Nine-eleven was just an excuse to pounce on Iraq. The war I was in, Desert Storm, was an honest one." He cleared his throat. "I don't want to see you in this system again. I don't want to see me here, again, either, but I've got a lot of shit to work out."

"Such as what?"

A voice from a speaker announced, "Lights out in one minute."

He didn't reply, and soon the lights snapped to a quarter-brightness. In the semi-darkness, he said just above a whisper, "I was trained as a soldier, and I never learned anything else. War was a lot more intense than anyone ever said. The guys you fight with become brothers. Somehow that led to robbing houses. Find your way, kid. I didn't find mine."

"You still can," I said. "If I can change, so can you."

The next morning, I was arraigned and released. As I left the cell, Rheingold and I nodded to each other. If it weren't for him, maybe I wouldn't have done what I did next.

Iraq, February 2007

After the IED, I awoke surrounded by white curtains. An IV ran into my arm. In a hospital gown, I uncovered the white sheet over me. I still had my arms and legs, and they moved. I flashed on images of what had happened, such as waking up on the ground outside the Humvee, which was on its side and burning. I had felt on fire, and my mouth, dry and gritty, held dirt and dust. I'd tried to spit. Ali lay next to me, bleeding, and his foot and leg looked bent at strange angles. Paulino sat on the ground, protesting something—I couldn't hear her—and then a wave of intense pain had swept up my limbs, and I'd screamed. A medic landed next to me, gave me a shot, which made me go out again.

Now, the curtain swung open, and I sat up. A nurse in a brown T-shirt, blue latex gloves, and ACU pants entered. She looked only a little older than I, her dark hair tight in a bun.

"Am I in Warhorse?" I asked.

"You are, and you're one lucky soldier. We removed some shrapnel from your legs and an arm, but nothing bad beyond a severe concussion. You're okay." I figured I was if this were Warhorse. Our medical facility was M*A*S*H, and if you needed much of anything after they initially worked on you, you'd be out by medevac.

"Paulino?"

"She's a couple rooms down. She's fine, too—a pretty nasty concussion. The blast was very focused, and most of it was absorbed by the police captain. He didn't make it."

Later I'd learn the captain had arranged the whole attack but hadn't expected to be on the mission. While the bottom of our Humvees were armored and could deflect all or part of a blast, it usually wasn't enough. We were lucky that the blast was so specific. I was told the captain's body absorbed so much of the blast, he became dog meat from the shrapnel. Some people might call it karma. I saw it as coincidence—but a lucky one with Jordan having me turn at the last second. "And Ali?" I asked.

"Medevacked to Balad," said the nurse. That must mean he was really bad. I could picture the medevac guys in the pair of Black Hawk helicopters—always two because if one bird was shot down or had mechanical problems, the other could provide cover until help arrived.

"But is he okay?"

"I'm guessing his leg will be amputated. I haven't heard officially, though. Ask your platoon sergeant."

"What time is it?"

"Evening."

I still felt groggy, and my ears were ringing. "Why am I so...out of it if I'm okay?"

"You had a severe concussion. Plus the anesthetic can leave you feeling this way. We're keeping you here at least until tomorrow.

"Do I really need an IV?"

"Not anymore," she said, and she pulled it out.

Soon I was feeling less fuzzy but my thoughts started to zoom around like a speed-freak on a motorcycle. Did we really have a God, and what was he anyway—galactic dust with thoughts? Did he float around, a million miles wide like a giant satellite dish, or was he fishing at a stream with over six billion people's thoughts banging around? If God could see everyone, what was he doing to me? Was he toughening me up, was that it? Giving me what I wanted? Was I tough now?

My brain did wheelies on these things until I thought maybe I was really going insane, and then I remembered my iPod. It was still in my pocket. There was a God. An hour with my music helped, especially drowning out the ringing. I went through most of a whole single album of The Early November, *The Room's Too Cold*. Normally I didn't listen to a whole album, but it felt like walking on an abandoned railroad track at sunset. Beautiful. I got to thinking more and more how lucky Paulino and I had been. I wasn't sure about Ali. I yanked out my earbuds, went to my door, and yelled down the clinic hallway, "Paulino—can you hear me?"

"Rivera?"

I stretched a little bit to make sure all systems were go, walked dizzily down the hall until I felt less dizzy, and I found her bed. Her face appeared red from crying. "You okay?"

She patted the bed. When I sat, she said, "Lay down." It was a damn narrow bed, but I squished next to her.

"So, you okay?" I asked again.

"I can't help thinking we almost died," she said in a cracking voice. I turned my head, just inches from hers. A tear slipped from her eye, and I wiped the drop off.

"But we didn't die. We'll probably even get some time off. Won't that be good?" Where I'd been so doubtful and confused an hour earlier, next to Paulino, I felt positive.

"I can't believe I joined up for something this stupid," she said.

"Why'd you join?"

"My boyfriend wanted to get married. I then pictured my life, moving from my parents' house to my husband's house and never really living, you know? I'd have kids and do all the right things, but I just wanted out of the usual."

"This isn't the usual."

"Yep. Except I see how hard families have it here. Most people aren't educated. Most have simple jobs, like selling carrots or bootleg DVDs. If they go to the market, a suicide bomber might kill them. In America, I had it good. I've been throwing it away."

"Maybe, just maybe, we can make a difference here. We're doing a positive thing." I'd never said this before, but she needed something good to hang onto, and it seemed to me this was it.

"To what end? What the fuck is the point?"

I nodded. "I'm not sure anymore."

She looked at me. "We're killing ourselves for nothing. All this shit's in the name of religion. If Mohammed and Jesus returned and saw Iraq, they'd shoot themselves in the head."

I shook my head. "I don't know. Maybe Styles is right, that everything here is in the name of power," I replied. "Like everywhere, the rich and corrupt have the power. But aren't we giving power back to the people?"

"No way," she said.

She needed something, and I realized I had my iPod with me. "Listen to this," I said and gave her one of the earbuds. I took the other, and I pushed play. The Early November's "Fluxy" started with its solo acoustic guitar, melding into dual guitars searing into our souls. Her head close to mine, she smiled. With her so close, I could feel a stiffy starting. Shit. I didn't mean for this. We didn't have that kind of relationship.

I smiled awkwardly—hoped she didn't see something growing under my gown in my underpants.

She smiled again. I tried to pretend I was thinking about the music, but now I was thinking about her. I better not kiss her, I thought. I better not kiss her. Don't kiss her.

She leaned in and kissed me, as simply as a leaf falling from the sky. I hadn't expected it, but the moment she started, I felt consumed, and my woody drove full bore ahead, no stopping for red lights.

Our faces pressed hard against each other. I'm dying, I'm dying, I thought. She opened her mouth wider, and her tongue played with mine. My fingers gently played with the line of her panties when the curtains yanked open.

It startled me so, I fell out of the bed. Our tight-bunned nurse grabbed my arm and pulled me up. "What the hell?" she said as if I were some errant puppy. She looked down at my gown with its teepee pole. Paulino probably saw it too. "Get back in your bed," the nurse said.

I zagged to the door, paused for Paulino and said, "Thank you, PFC. You'll be fine. You'll see." And I left.

In the hallway, I ran into the LT.

"Ah!" he said. "I came to see you." His sergeant, Ichisada, wasn't with him. He was doing this on his own. The LT must have noticed my state of arousal because he said, "You're looking better." He glanced at the doorway I just left. The nurse tucked the sheets around Paulino.

"My room's down here," I said, pointing, and soon we stepped into it. His muscular mass looked cramped in the small room. He sat in the folding chair, while I slipped back into my bed.

"I want you to know, Rivera, I did not expect that IED."

"I'm not blaming you."

"You're my driver. I entrust my life with you."

"And I, you, sir."

He cringed at that as if I'd said the wrong thing.

"Will I be out tomorrow, sir, back on a mission?" I asked with as much zest as I could, even if I wished to be shipped home. I didn't want him to feel bad.

"You've had a concussion. You have to take things easy. In fact, I want you to go to the stress unit."

"I don't need to talk with anyone, sir."

"And you'll have at least a few days off. I worry about you and Paulino."

"We'll be fine, sir."

"Your brain's been shaken," he said. "You need to get back to normal. I need you thinking well out there."

"Okay. And what's happening to Ali?"

"He'll recover, minus a leg."

"I mean, sir, what will happen to him? Will he and his family be sent to America?"

Our LT shook his head. "I doubt it. The Army promises such things, but I haven't heard of a single translator being moved."

"What if Al Queda kills him for helping? Is there something we can do, sir?"

"Like what? We can't issue visas."

"Write to somebody?"

"Who?"

"Sir, if the captain hadn't sent us on that stupid mission—"

"The captain—" His hand wiped the thought away. "Many things are out of our control. Just leave it at that."

We sat there, not saying anything for a while. I realized I'm the one injured, that I didn't have to think of anything to say. He looked past me as if seeing something. "I expected that jerk to confess that he stole our binoculars," he said, "not that he'd given them to another station. I wanted to throw it in the captain's face."

"What we get for helping, right, sir?"

"Yes." He looked at me as if realizing something. "Sometimes," he said, "I wish I was just a private."

I heard commotion out in the doorway, lots of laughing, and Hitch popped his head in. He grimaced when he saw the LT, then saluted.

"At ease," said the LT.

"No hurry, sir," Hitch said. "We'll be in the waiting room."

"No, no." The LT stood as if he'd run out of things to say anyway. "Get better, Rivera. We'll talk."

"Thanks, Lieutenant." He left, and as he did, in came Hitch, Styles, Jordan, and Yanni, all fresh from the barber shop. No long hair in the Army—two weeks, tops. Styles looked serious, but the others only pretended to be as if they needed straight faces to pass the lieutenant. While alcohol was hard to get, I suspected that Hitch had received another box of chocolates from his cousin, who had injected some small hollow chocolate bunnies with Everclear alcohol. Hitch had chocolate on the corner of his mouth.

Once I heard the LT's footsteps gone, I whispered loudly, "Are you guys bunnied out?"

They laughed, all except Styles. Styles said, "I wrote you a little something. These guys will help."

"What're you talking about?" I said.

Yanni whipped out a kazoo from his pocket and began to blow into it. Jordan and Hitch instantly hummed along, and Hitch beat a rhythm on my bed with his hands. Styles then sang,

Hey man, you're driving that car.
Hey man, it's blowing up far.
Hey man, you're flying toward the moon.
Whatever you say, just, just, just don't go away soon.

They then leaned in together toward me and sang in harmony like quartet of David Bowies:

Because, hey, man, we love you the way you are.

My God, that was terrible, but it was sweet, as unexpected as Paulino's kiss, and my emotions may have been in a bartender's martini maker, shaken not stirred. I didn't want them to see my watering eyes.

Hitch said, "How you hangin'?"

I pulled myself together. "You guys are great. Thanks."

If I could turn them into stamps and mail them off to the president, I would. "I get a few days off," I said. "Not bad for being blown up." I turned to Jordan and held my hand out. "Thanks for saving me, man. How'd you know?"

"I saw a sheet of paper on the road. Then when I saw a guy standing in a doorway with a cell phone, my stomach dropped—like the paper was X marks the spot—and I shouted."

"Did you get the guy?"

"Nope."

I turned to Yanni and said, "I still can't believe a sergeant is hanging around us regular guys."

"You'll be one, too, with the years."

"I don't want to be a lifer with more responsibility."

"More importantly," said Hitch, "we get to move into three-man CHUs soon. The LT said we get to decide who we want as roommates. I asked two women, but we can't go co-ed."

"Hey, you popped your cherry yet?" said Yanni.

"Fuck you," said Hitch. "I fell in love with Veronica Guzman."

"Guzman?" said Yanni, impressed.

"For a day," said Styles.

"So love is fickle," said Hitch, turning to me. "What do you say, Rivera? Will you be my CHUmate?

I looked at Styles, who said, "I'm tenting with a gunner from El Paso—you know, older guy."

"Real old, twenty-five," said Yanni, grinning.

"And a kid from Maine," said Styles. "Tracewski."

"Trace," I said. "I met him."

"Yeah, he's kind of a neat freak, unlike you slobs."

"I'm neat," said Hitch.

"I'm neat, too," I protested. I looked at Yanni.

"I'm bunkin' with two other sergeants," Yanni said. "No fraternizing, you know."

"How about you, Jordan? Would you like to be with Hitch and me?"

"With you fuckheads?" he asked. "A pleasure."

When I played high school baseball, our coach made us wear athletic cups. It seemed stupid at the time, but it came in handy when an errant pitch hit me right there. I now realized friends are like those things—protective and not talked about. They are just there.

Gonzalez with his acoustic guitar.

ouch, Gonzalez, and Emery in performance at FOB Warhorse.

amuel Gonzalez, Jr., a punk rocker turned soldier, created a band called Madison Avenue in 007. He and his fellow bandmates became the inspiration for this novel. Those inspirations ere (L-R) Brandon Couch, Kevin Ballanger, Samuel Gonzalez, Jr., Blair Emery, and Kyle Lussier.

Sam Gonzalez, center, with Corporal Bullock (left) and Specialist Richie (right)."

Drummer Kevin Ballanger performs.

Couch, Emery, Gonzalez, and Lussier perform.

Soldiers mosh in front of the band, Madison Avenue.

Florida, July 2005

The fucking Florida air was a wet wash cloth as usual, but when I exited the Orange County Booking and Release Center and saw the blue sky and the green trees on the edge of the parking lot, I felt as if I could be Jane Goodall, the monkey lady who went to Africa and wanted nothing to do with people. After I was given my clothes back, I tried calling my father collect and then my mother, but neither answered their cell phones. I had to find my way back to one of their houses. Whoever I chose, the other would then say I didn't love him or her. Sometimes it's hard to do the right thing for divorced parents.

I knew I needed to come up with a whole new life plan. I had no band, no home, no girlfriend, and no job. My car was still at the apartment, but I'd deal with it later. After jail, I needed to catch my breath—don't do anything rash or get in anyone's way. I just needed to "be" for a day.

I decided I was the adult here, and I couldn't rely on my parents just yet. One of my friends would surely let me stay on a couch tonight. My cell phone was a brick, out of juice, so I needed to just show up at someone's apartment. Yet it was morning. Every one of my friends who wasn't in college would be at work. Who would be the best candidate?

My friend Aaron, who had been a good bud in high school, found a job at the Lake Mary Cineplex 6, not far from my dad's place. Aaron or one of his coworkers always let me in for free because the owner, some chain-smoking lesbian lady in her forties, rarely was there, so kids my age ran the place. Ever since I'd quit UPS, I'd seen a lot of movies, and I'd even helped out at times, no charge. I wondered how the lady made money, but perhaps enough old people went to the movies that even with the senior discounts, she made a profit.

I only had eleven dollars on me. I had more in my bank, but without a car, I'd save that journey for later. I just needed to get to Lake Mary, and the bus system wasn't bad, or so one of my friends had once said. The exit guard had told me where to catch the bus and which ones to take. He used a little book to figure it out. Even though it was just over twenty miles away, I needed four buses and four hours to get to where I was going.

"You start with the 57 bus," he said, and when it started getting complicated, he wrote the directions down for me.

Buses would normally make me antsy. Once on my first one, though, it was like pure oxygen rushed through me, boosting me up. I wasn't behind bars, and the ability to be somewhere besides a concrete cell was a celebration. I could have broken into the spiritual "Free at Last." I loved watching the cars pass us, noticing that most cars were black, white, or shades of gray. I suppose everyone was trying to fit in, and a crazy color like my Geo Metro with its strange avocado hue just wasn't right. I loved watching people at upcoming bus stops standing eagerly as if the bus were a giant ticket to a lotto game. I loved staring at the hands and fingers of the old lady across from me, working her knitting needles like a smile. Everything around me seemed like roses bursting in air.

At one point, I realized I needed to keep this feeling and stay out of trouble. I had to change my life—but how?

Somewhere in the early afternoon, I arrived in Lake Mary. It's known for its upper-middle-class people living in tile-roofed McMansions on lawns as green as Irish moss. The crime rate is extremely low, and the number of chain restaurants, extremely high. My arrival from jail probably changed its ratios, but all I wanted to see was Aaron.

The theater stood in a pod mall like most stores in Lake Mary. There's no downtown per se. The town only incorporated in 1973, so everything was basically new and spread out. The McDonald's I usually hit when I had a car had a big grassy area and a parking lot. It's a suburb meant for driving, not walking.

The girl at the ticket counter said Aaron was there, and she called him on a phone. "Your name?" she asked. When she relayed the information, she told me, "He'll be right down."

I hadn't given her much notice until then. Blond and skinny, my age, she wore a baggy blue UCLA T-shirt and smiled with big, glossy lips. I put my hands on the counter and leaned close to the window that separated us. My tattooed arms reflected off the glass. She looked at my markings, smiling as if she liked them. "Live around here?" I asked.

She rolled her eyes. Okay, so maybe I was too obvious. I stepped back and looked at the titles of the films playing, such as *The Dukes of Hazard, Fantastic Four, The Wedding Crashers*. "These movies sound like corporate bullshit," I said. "Nothing good?"

"*Charlie and the Chocolate Factory* is good."

"The classic seventies flick? You have old movies here? Since when?"

"You're thinking of *Willy Wonka and the Chocolate Factory* with Gene Wilder. *Charlie* is the remake by Tim Burton with the original Roald Dahl book title. Johnny Depp kind of plays Michael Jackson as Willy Wonka. It's really cool."

I loved her enthusiasm. No one else was in line so early in the afternoon, so I felt no pressure to leave. "Do you know the films of Stanley Kubrick?"

Now she looked at me differently, more seriously. "*A Clockwork Orange, 2001, Full Metal Jacket*, to name a few. *Full Metal Jacket* is my favorite."

"You like a war movie?"

She leaned forward. "Not just any war movie."

"Exactly," I said. "A Kubrick film. He shot it over the course of nearly three years—and all in England. Palm trees were brought in to make it look authentic."

She looked impressed. "I heard the drill sergeant in the film was a real one," she said.

"My dad was similar, a staff sergeant."

"You must have had a strict childhood."

"Yeah, but he's not a bad guy. My mom's wonderful."

She nodded. "I hate my mom. She thinks she's my age, like we're friends—it's so annoying. I like your tats, by the way."

I held up my arms again. "Life lessons. I guess we all get a few."

Maybe it was because I had been an ugly kid, bullied, and no one liked me, that such compliments stirred me. Whether it was my tattoos, my confidence, or simply that I'd grown into better looks, something worked in my favor. These days, I had no problem attracting girls, and each girl I was into, I'd be convinced I could make her into my girlfriend—a true, hopeless romantic, I guess. The problem was, I usually got bored with a girl after I slept with her. Was something wrong with me? Still, I'd convince myself the next one was truly the one, and this girl here energized me. She seemed so wholesome—far different from my first girlfriend, Lynette.

"My name's Sophie." I'd seen it on her nametag. The way she dotted the "I" in her name with a skull and crossbones made me fall in love with her right there.

"A beautiful name. You like working here, Sophie?" I asked.

"I love movies. It's the perfect place for me," she said. I was about to mention the sex scene with Nicole Kidman and Tom Cruise in Kubrick's *Eyes Wide Shut*—I love that scene where they fuck—which would tell me if I had a chance. The fact I had no home or place to stay didn't bother me. Maybe I could stay with her.

That's when Aaron popped into her booth. "Max!" he said. He was a short, stocky Jewish guy, originally from Rochester, New York, and he kept in shape doing Tae Kwon Do. When he was fourteen, his dad got a job at Disneyland in charge of the costumed characters throughout the park, so his family moved here, and we hung around the same circles, anyway. "Great to see you, man. Come around to the door," he said.

I waved bye to Sophie, and she smiled. I hated to go—but then again, I had other things to figure out.

Aaron let me in, and we walked on the royal blue carpet up to the concession stand where a teenage guy was selling a senior-discount popcorn-and-Coke package to a gray-hair. We zipped around through a door, taking the narrow staircase up to the projection booth, passing posters of past great films such as *Rocky, Jaws,* and *Taxi Driver.*

"Booth" was really a misnomer. It was a huge twilight-lit room, much of the length and width of the whole building. That's because three of the movie theaters were to the left of the concession stand, and the other three were to the right. The projection booth thus had three Matterhorn-size 35mm projectors on one side of the room, and the other three were on the other side, all softly clacking away, creating the noise of a mechanical rain forest. There was a couch as well as a big splicing bench with a swan-necked light. Most feature films arrived in six parts, on six reels, and those reels then needed to be spliced together onto one monster reel for each projector. When a film's run was over, the movie had to be broken back down to the smaller reels and returned to the distributor.

I'd been up here many times, sometimes helping Aaron with the splicing or checking the films, and we'd do lines of coke or speed. Either was perfect for this job. Marijuana wasn't. One time I'd brought a joint of some great stuff. We smoked it, and it was only when we heard some shouts from one theater, and the phone was ringing, that we'd realized we hadn't set up the next movie. We fell on the floor laughing. You couldn't be laid back. Better was to be amped-up. One projectionist ran all six theaters at once, and Aaron was great at it. You had to be ready if something went wrong, such as a splice broke or the projector's gate jumped around or got clogged.

When we got up there, Aaron peeked through the small windows into each theater to make sure all was fine, then said, "How've you been, man? I never see you anymore. I thought you were on tour."

"I was," I said, and I explained about getting kicked out, getting into a fight the same night with my roommate, and now just getting out of jail. I still had to go to court.

"Oh, man, that's fucked," said Aaron, clicking on the swan-necked light at the splicing bench. "I have something you need. You deserve some." He immediately started pouring white powder from a glassine envelope onto a pocket mirror on the splicing bench. He used a one-sided razor blade to cut the tiny crystals smaller.

"Actually," I said, stepping over. "I don't do that anymore."

"You? The king of Kilimanjaro?"

"I know. But the last seventy-two hours really fucked me up. What the fuck am I doing? I'm doing myself in."

"You sound like your dad."

"He's right. It's physically wrecking me, and I'm angry all the time."

"That's just you."

"It can't be me anymore. I have to make big changes, and I'm not sure how just yet. I don't have an apartment anymore. Can I crash at your place tonight?"

He knelt down to his mirror, snorted, and smiled.

"Sorry, man. I've got two friends from college visiting." Aaron had spent two semesters at Arizona State University before he dropped out. He never seemed like the college type to me. He was happy projecting movies and would probably be there until the place closed or burned down.

"Shit," I said.

"Why didn't you call?"

"My cell phone died, and I'm low on money."

"How about you stay here? There's a couch." He pointed to the one near us, a funky orange thing he'd found on the street somewhere, and only now did the cat piss smell seem to be gone. What choice did I have?

"What about your boss?"

"She's in Italy for the month. Even if she weren't, she wouldn't mind as long as you *don't* eat the hot dogs. I'm the manager now."

I nodded, knowing he'd always eaten the hot dogs. This was an ominous start to my new life—living in a darkened room with no prospects for jobs. On the bus, I'd considered going back to UPS, but damn if I'd do that again. Making a change in my life didn't mean joining the bubble. I'd considered a new band—music had been my life—yet before I assembled one, I had to rethink how to find the right musicians and create a way of living that wasn't so destructive. After all, Same Old Story worked well in talent, but none of my band mates watched my back. Maybe no such kind of band existed. I had to consider that, too.

The movie projectors clacked like cards on bicycle spokes, spinning away lives that burned into light. My own life unspooled, too, and yet I could choose which projector I wanted to be. I could change. My lifestyle that had fueled much of my anger had led to my songs and their popularity. If I didn't live as I had, would my songs become about puppies and Jesus and apocryphal stories? Maybe I should give up performing on stage completely. There were other ways to be creative that didn't need me to be self-destructive.

I stood and looked through one of the projector's windows. Johnny Depp as Willy Wonka, in top hat and page-boy haircut, opened the door to his chocolate factory. I couldn't hear any sound, but I saw a neon-green-colored path into the land of candy. Maybe I was reading too much into everything, but the land of another candy could be mine. All six projectors sang to me. I could be a filmmaker.

"What's wrong with you?" said Aaron. He snapped his fingers.

"Nothing, man. I'm fine." I walked toward him. "In fact..."

I was about to ask Aaron if I might get a job there when a knock came on the door. Sophie walked in, nodded to me, and looked at Aaron. "That new girl, Ariel, came into work. She said you'd scheduled her for now." Sophie ran her finger down the schedule board by the door and tapped Ariel's name. "Yep."

"Shit."

"My shift?"

"How about you come back tonight?"

"Aaron," she said in a way that seemed more personal than a mere employee. "You can't waste my time, dude. I was in first."

"But she's been in the hospital with pneumonia. She needs the hours."

"And I don't?"

"How about I make it worth your while?" He pointed to his powder on the mirror.

"I can be persuaded." She went to the mirror, built herself a long line, and sniffed. She again smiled at me. She bounced over to the projector where I'd been standing, looked out the little window into the theater, and flipped a switch nearby. The sound to *Charlie and the Chocolate Factory* came on. She peered again through the window. Her shirt, too small for her long figure, showed a little skin. Damn, she was hot.

As if Charlie in the movie noticed the same skin, he said in the movie soundtrack, "It's beautiful," and Willy answered, "What? Oh, yeah. It's very beautiful."

"My employees tend to be very loyal," Aaron said proudly, his words snapping me back to him. "Part of it is meeting their needs." He looked over at the coke mirror, and said, "Sophie! You weren't supposed to take that much."

"It wasn't a lot. You're getting low."

He turned to me. "Would you mind running this place for about an hour? I want to pick up some more blow. Sophie doesn't know the projectors as well as you do."

"You need to go now?"

"I work all the time, like twelve hours a day. Now I have you—a Godsend. I can get a few things done."

"Okay," I said. He told Sophie he was going, and then he was gone. Part of me was excited to pursue Sophie—she wasn't working, and maybe we could chat and stuff.

I looked in her direction. "You enjoying it?"

Sophie flicked off the sound. She said walking toward me, "I'm sorry. You said something?"

"I was just wondering if it was a good part."

She smiled and sat next to me. "Did you get some of Aaron's treat? There's still some on the mirror."

"I'm fine."

"It's *really* good."

She swayed her body when she said it, and I glanced at her breasts. Because the T-shirt was baggy, I couldn't tell how big they were, maybe B's, but I was guessing she was self-conscious about them, which was why her T-shirt was baggy.

"My eyes are up here," she said.

She was astute. I liked that. "Caught me," I said.

"A sniff?"

I hesitated.

"I'm going down. See you later," she said as she headed toward the door.

Just like that?

"Maybe I'll try just a little?" I indicated the mirror. She turned, waiting to see what I'd do.

She said, "I don't use it often."

I went to the mirror. Coke made me horny, so maybe this wasn't a good idea, but maybe that's why she suggested it. I'd been in jail, after all.

I should relax a little—not be so tough on myself. I inhaled, and she was right. My spine and body tingled.

"I take it you didn't go to college," I said.

She looked offended and walked right over to me. "Why would you say that? You think I'm dumb?"

"Oh, no, no. I'm— I mean, I didn't go to college, either. I've been playing in a band on tour—yesterday in Orlando, actually."

"Where?"

"The fairgrounds."

"The Warped tour?" Her eyebrows moved up and she nodded.

"College wasn't for me, either," I said.

"I'm in college. Valencia College—which is why I'm pissed when Aaron gets my hours wrong."

"Community college?"

"Yeah. I want to get all my humanity and required stuff out of the way so that I might get into USC or UCLA. It'll be cheaper this way."

"California? What're you going to study?"

"I don't really know yet. Maybe something in the arts. I love film."

By now she was tracing lines around my knee with her index finger, and I was finding it hard to concentrate. "Uh huh," I said. "You know, you're really beautiful." I touched her hand with mine.

"You're saying that because you're coked up."

"Not really."

"You know exactly what to say."

She was probably right, but I said, "For the record, I thought you were beautiful when I first saw you downstairs."

She reached to the bottom of her shirt and pulled up until her shirt was off. I didn't expect this so quickly. She was very slender in that I could see the outlines of a couple of ribs. She was what I expected, nice firm B's. She was built like a model.

"Definitely gorgeous," I said, so in awe and stunned, I didn't know what to do with my hands. My heart pounded in my throat.

She smiled widely and moved on top of me, aiming her mouth toward mine. We kissed. This was so much better than jail. Neither of us seemed in a hurry, so we really kissed deeply until she stood and removed the rest of her clothes. I took off mine. Whoa. All systems go. This was happening. She pushed me onto the couch, retrieved a condom from her pants pocket, and fit it on me.

"You come prepared."

"Because I've learned guys never do," and she straddled me. We fucked, and it was good. We just kept going until the terrible sound of a broken film whacking itself against the projector reached my consciousness.

"Oh, no!" I blurted, and I pulled out. I turned to see which projector and promptly fell off the couch. Sophie laughed.

"It's *Charlie and the Chocolate Factory*," I said.

"Fix it!"

Rather than yank the huge heavy reels off the projector to bring to the splicing bench, I simply rethreaded the film from where it broke.

Sophie joined me, naked, and looked through one of the windows. "Hurry, hurry. The audience looks pissed," she said.

I couldn't get the gate closed properly. The faint noise of people grew louder. My erection softened until the condom fell to the ground. My fingers were like people in a crowd after someone yelled "fire!" They were banging into each other. Fuck.

"Come on," yelled Sophie.

With one final flick of a switch, the light pushed through the moving film. It worked. Relief swept over me.

As we stood there laughing, Sophie said, "I know where Aaron keeps tequila."

| | | |

I woke up as I felt liquid on my face and I gasped. Aaron stood above me, holding the tequila bottle, which he'd poured on me.

"You call sleeping being in charge?" he said.

It was near eleven p.m. according to the clock on the wall. Sophie was gone, and Aaron sat on the couch next to me.

"Hey, man," I said.

"She found my secret stash."

I looked at him with embarrassment.

"Sophie. Damn it."

He looked funny saying it, which made me laugh, which made my head pound. How was I going to have a new life if I couldn't make it through one day without the usual temptations? Being around friends, drugs, and liquor wasn't going to change me at all, and I'd be just another millennial going nowhere.

"I'm about to start the last movie of the night," he said. "Have you ever seen *Platoon*?"

"I know of it. When I was a kid, my dad had me sit for some of it on TV. You're showing that?"

He nodded.

"Why?"

"Its twentieth anniversary is coming up. I get to show old movies late at night sometimes, and this one deserves it. Come over here." He flipped the sound switch, and MGM's lion roared. I stuck my head in the window and saw the belly of a plane open up—I assumed in Vietnam—and a platoon's worth of young men—men my age—walked out. One of them was a very young Charlie Sheen.

Dust wafts up, and then two men lift a black body bag off a gurney onto the tarmac where other body bags are laid out. "Oh, man, is that what I think it is?" says one of the soldiers in the background. All the young men grimace as they walk by the bags.

It struck me then and there: how much was my seeing this movie coincidence, and how much was divine intervention? After all, I'd just learned how weak I was—not only with the jail experience but also with the last day. Then along comes this movie. I just had to take it in. Movies sometimes could be more than mere projections of light and sound. They could be a religious experience.

The movie showed a helicopter flying over the jungle and offered the title, "September 1967, Bravo Company, 25th Infantry, somewhere near the Cambodian Border." I became glued to that projector's window. The sound wasn't great, but it didn't matter. While I could have run down from the projection booth into the theater, I didn't want to miss a moment of it. It was perfect.

Nothing about this movie was "feel good." It wasn't a romanticized rendering of war, no John Wayne-type yelling, "Men, we'll show them what being an American means" as they plunge tough into battle. It wasn't anti-war or pro-war. It just was. I felt the mosquitoes and biting ants, the weight of the packs as the grunts carried themselves through the jungle, the need for sleep in the rain, and it was crazy how death came from standing in the wrong spot at a wrong moment. I loved the faith and hope in the movie hovering in pockets of air. The insanity and brutality grabbed my attention.

In short, no one would ever be likely to do anything after this movie other than feel bad. I was alone in the projection room afterwards, and all the other projectors had long stopped. When the final credits ran, I turned off the projector. No one was in the theater except a teenager who'd turned all the lights on and was collecting abandoned popcorn boxes and cups from the floor and chair handles. I sat on the orange couch, and a sense of what I had to do enveloped me. When everyone was gone, I ran the movie again for myself, this time sitting in the theater.

There's a moment about fifteen minutes into the film where the idealistic Chris Taylor, played by Charlie Sheen, writes his grandmother. Taylor had dropped out of college and volunteered for infantry combat in Vietnam because he felt the poor people of America shouldn't be the only ones fighting our battles. He's already endured heat and sleep fatigue and numerous pests, harassment for being a "greenie," endured long marches in the rain, and witnessed death. Yet he tells his grandmother, "Maybe I finally found it, way down here in the mud. Maybe from down here, I can start up again, be something I can be proud of without having to fake it, be a fake human being. Maybe I can see something I don't yet see or learn something I don't yet know."

This was it exactly. Taylor went in because he could not bear who he'd become. He'd been on a false path, one like mine, the one crushing me. He understood the irony that to have purpose, you have to plop yourself into a purposeless place, one without morals or logic or sensitivity or meaning. You had to face the monster of chaos head-on. Then and there in that theater, I had an inkling of what I needed to do. It was what Rheingold in the jail had said, unspoken. I knew we had two wars going on, in Iraq and Afghanistan, but ironically enough I had no idea why we were there particularly, other than it had to do with 9/11, a day that saved my life. I couldn't be afraid. I had to confront my demons. I wouldn't be doing this without help. This could give me the physical fitness I never had. It would teach me how to survive better than I'd been doing. This would be a good thing. Then I could pursue whatever I wanted.

Back up in the projection room, I found the *Yellow Pages,* and I looked up "Recruiting – Armed Forces." There was an ad for the Armed Forces Recruitment Center in Altamonte Springs. I knew where it was exactly, in that beautiful outdoor pod mall with the Outback Steakhouse about ten miles away. The center was open 9 to 5. I'd go there in the morning.

Aaron came in early the next day, just as I was pummeling down the stairs.

"Are you off?" he asked.

"Yeah," I said stopping, nodding.

"The couch okay?"

"Everything was great."

"Need another night?"

"Nope." I knew I'd be off to boot camp or something, and I was feeling great. "You really helped me more ways than you'll ever know." Little did I know this would be the last time I'd see him. Years later I'd return to this place to find it was an L.A. Fitness Center. He had settled down with a punk-rock princess and worked in real estate.

"You okay?" he asked.

"Absolutely!" It was as if life were as clear and perfect as the crystal Waterford vase my mother bought, refracting sun from its shelf to make rainbows. If you held the vase, you saw its flawless lines curving up toward heaven.

If life were only that simple.

Iraq, February 2007

The morning Paulino and I were getting out of the medical center, she came to my bed in her loose hospital gown, underwear showing underneath, with that ten-thousand-watt smile of hers. Her orthodontist should win an award. She jumped right on me, kissing like we'd been going out for weeks. "What's your first name, anyway?"

"It's Max. You know that."

"Right. And what's my first name?"

Shit. That was so strange. I knew I'd been chanting her first name in my mind as I fell asleep. "Lulu?"

"No."

"Letty?"

She made a double-buzz sound like the wrong answer on *Jeopardy,* then said, "Laurel."

"An L name—in the ballpark."

"Not good." Something was wrong with our memories. We were both having bad headaches, too. I'd feel as if I was in the end of *2001* with weird lights streaming past me while someone tapped a tiny ball-peen hammer inside my head.

Paulino and I did not go out on missions as we were allowed to recover. I missed the action. We each saw a doctor every few days to get assessed. Some days I was just fuzzy. Some days, I might not get out of bed right away, feeling down.

We'd moved into CHUs, and I kept forgetting where my CHU was.

The new CHU village had street names taken from the Monopoly board. My CHU was on Baltic Avenue, but I kept looking for Billy Avenue, which isn't even a Monopoly name. Paulino, on Park Place, seemed to have it worse than me.

With time on our hands, we worked out in the gym, played one-on-one basketball together in the air-conditioned court, and fucked like mad either in the gym's bathroom when no one else was around, or, to get away from our roommates, in one of the porta-potties at night. The blue plastic john was hot and smelly, but we didn't care.

Neither of us drank or did drugs—both were hard to come by anyway—so sex seemed a healthier way to get away from the war. Even in the confines of Warhorse, though, we couldn't get away from the violence. Bombs in the distance always rattled the sky, and helicopters zoomed in and out all day long and often at night. If a soldier died, his platoon if not his whole company would meet in formation on the tarmac to transfer his body to a waiting plane. Each time we did this, it reminded us we were waiting for the boom that would do us in. During one such formation to transfer a soldier killed by a sniper—he'd only looked over a wall for a mere second to see what was out there—word came in that a whole infantry squad had been blown up checking out what intel said might have been an IED factory. The place had been booby trapped with so many explosives, mostly only rubble remained. The houses on either side lost walls. It was amazing that four of our eight soldiers were still alive, whisked back to Warhorse and worked on. Soon Black Hawks from Balad came for them. The point: we were always close to death. You couldn't think about it, though. The trick was to stay occupied.

and I weren't always fucking. She liked to play videogames. A lot of guys played videogames on their laptops when they weren't watching porn, jerking off, or working out in the gym, but I never got into games because so many of them were about war, such as *Company of Heroes, Gears of War, Defcon,* and *Battlefield II.* My guess is that some of the guys who joined up thought the real thing was one step closer to the ultimate videogame. Paulino, though, liked playing *Atomic Battle Dragons,* which was about dragons jousting. She played it one time when we were in the MWR, the Morale, Welfare, and Recreation Center, where the gyms, ping pong tables, shops, and all the internet computers were. I sat in front of a monitor in one of the computer carrels, and she sat nearby on a folding chair with her laptop when I heard sounds of swordplay and dragon slaying. I was busy on an internet computer doing something fairly new for me: researching.

I wanted to know why we were driving Humvees and not something better, not something safer, like tanks or MRAPs, which were mine-resistant. I confirmed my suspicions—tanks and MRAPs were slower and more costly and not great in desert terrain. The Humvee had supplanted the Jeep. Humvees had a wider wheelbase, and in the Persian Gulf War, they'd negotiated the desert sand with ease. In Afghanistan after 9/11, Humvees proved valuable in the rough, mountainous terrain. It was only when IEDs started being used in Iraq that revealed the vehicles' vulnerability. The Army quickly brought in armor kits for the vehicles, but the added weight and strain on the chassis made them break down more. "Hey," I told Paulino. "In the first four months of 2006, sixty-seven U.S. soldiers died in Humvees."

"I'm busy," she said, moving her pointer finger along her built-in trackpad.

I left my computer to move next to her. I didn't want others to hear me, and this was important. "Don't you realize we're part of a numbers game? The Army knows so many will die in Humvees."

"Why are you focused on this shit?" she said. "We're alive. We're not on the memorial." There was a huge set of free-standing slabs near the Warhorse entrance where names of those who died in combat were remembered. It had started with a slab of slate against a blast wall and had become bigger over time. Benches had been added as if it were a place to sit and contemplate. What're we to think: some people had luck and others didn't?

"I'm just curious. Did you know anything about Iraq before we came here?" I asked.

"What's to know? Terrorists were trying to take over the world, so we had to fight them." She fixated back on the fiery blasts onscreen.

"Originally, Iraq was Mesopotamia, the cradle of civilization," I said, pulling out facts from my previous research. "Then, from the Sixteenth Century until World War One, it was a part of the Turkish Empire—also known as the Ottoman Empire."

"I never liked history," Paulino said.

"You're playing *Dragon Age*."

"And what year did we have dragons?"

"It's medieval."

"What're you on my case for?"

"All I'm saying, we have to realize where we almost got killed—in a civil war that's not ours."

"If someone shoots at me," she said, "I shoot back."

"If the U.S. had never got involved, the Shiites and Sunni would've just shot each other up instead of us."

"And then we'd have some crazy-ass dictatorship wanting to blow up more of the U.S."

"You call this a democracy?"

"You're sounding like your friend Styles."

"Styles makes sense."

"And I'm *not*?" she yelled.

"Relax. Lower your voice please."

She looked away, calmed herself, then looked back at me. "If the Army wanted us into politics, they'd have put it in the manual," she said, tapping the rules of engagement in her left breast pocket. That's where we all carried them. If we had doubts about something, we had the rules to look at.

"Don't you care *why* your life is on the line?" I said.

"Fuck it! Fuck *you*." She stood up.

"What's wrong? We're just talking."

She slammed her laptop shut and walked off without me. I watched her retreat to the Monopoly streets. I knew to let her be, yet so much of me said to run after her, say I'm sorry. But what was I sorry for?

My headaches went away over the next few days, but Paulino told me she wasn't sleeping well, and much of her body ached.

"We should get you checked out," I said in her CHU when her room-mates were out.

"I'm fine."

"No, you're not."

"That's not what you said the last time you came in me."

"Jeez."

"No. I'm a terrible soldier, a terrible person, a terrible excuse for a human being," she said.

"Why're you so hard on yourself? It wasn't your fault we were blown up."

"You want me to smile like some bimbo from Minnesota so you can fuck me some more?"

"You always initiate it," I said.

"I'm sorry," she said, touching my hand the way a lover should. "I'm a poor excuse for a woman."

Something sizzled in me, ready to slap some sense in her. I'd pulled my hand back to do so. Her eyes widened. This wasn't like me. What's going on?

I put my hand down. "I'm sorry," I said.

"I'm sorry, too." We hugged, but as we did, I wondered what the hell was happening to us.

The next day as we got a slice from Pizza Hut, she told me about where she grew up in International Falls, Minnesota, on the Rainy River across from Ontario, Canada. "It's the coldest city in the nation. In the winter, there're days where it's over forty below zero," she said.

"And here it's cool if it's a hundred degrees," I said.

"I like the heat a lot better. If we marry, I don't want to live in International Falls."

Marry? I stopped chewing. "I thought you were engaged."

"I'll have to fix that."

My heart pounded, and then I felt dizzy. Would the Army marry us? Could we stay together and fight together, married? I'd have to research this. I knew I was too young to marry, and it didn't make sense, but I didn't want to lose her.

Over the next day, I worried and wondered and stayed quiet, but Paulino didn't seem to notice. My stomach churned. At lunch in the chow hall, I finally said, "When and where do you want to get married?"

She said, "Marry? Are you crazy? We're just fucking. No one should marry me. You'd be miserable." She'd forgotten what she'd said the day before.

Still, we couldn't get enough of each other. Later that day, we pulled off each other's clothes in one of the gym bathrooms. At the time, no one was there—they were either on a mission or sleeping, so we had the tiled room to ourselves, and as she pulled off my T-shirt, tears fell from her eyes, which surprised me.

"We don't have to do this," I said.

"No, it's okay. I'm all right."

"What's wrong?"

She pulled off her T-shirt, and then went at me as if I were her oxygen line. Five minutes later, she shivered in orgasm and then lay on the gym bathroom floor, spacey looking, staring off.

The hardest thing for me was not being able to sleep with her through the night. Sometimes I woke up with a gasp, deep in sweat, after dreaming about being in the Humvee that was blowing up. I just wanted it out of my mind, but it wouldn't go. I could have used Paulino next to me. She would have understood. Hitch or Jordan rarely heard me wake up in terror, but if they did, they'd ask. "You all right?"

I'd say yes, and they'd say okay.

Some nights, I walked around the base with my flashlight, which helped clear my mind. It was a blacked-out camp because we were so close to the enemy, and we didn't want lights on poles to make targeting us easier. If it wasn't cloudy, I wouldn't use my flashlight. The stars felt as if God were sprinkling me with his blessing. I tried believing, at any rate.

I'd never seen so many stars, which covered everywhere except where the ash and smoke of the war-torn city would get in the way.

After one such night, I called home from the telephone tent. We soldiers would get wonderful packages from home, including calling cards, which we could use on the pay phones. My mother once sent a whole case of Twinkies, which made me a star for the day as I passed them out to everyone I saw. Now, it was just after eight at night, which meant in Florida is was just after noon. My mother answered on the first ring, but she seemed distracted with just a plain "Hello." Maybe she didn't see where the call was from.

"Hi, it's me, Mom. Max," I said in English. She'd grown up in Panama, and I'd grown up speaking Spanish with her, but in grade school, I announced I was only going to speak English because that was the way it worked in school. My parents went along with me. "Max! Oh my baby, how are you?" She still had a Spanish accent.

"I'm fine now. Did the Army call you?"

"For what?"

I would have thought they'd called. I told her about being blown up in the Humvee, and she kept saying, "Madre de Dios." Then she asked, "Are you okay? Do you have all your bones?"

"My arms and legs, yes. I'm fine." An automated voice on the phone announced I had four minutes left. Only I could hear it.

"I worry about you," my mother said.

"I know, I know. Something interesting's come up recently. There are women in the Army, over here, as you know."

"Oh, oh." I think she thought I'd gotten someone pregnant.

"No, no, everything's fine," I said, going on to explain how I was "fond of" one of the women, Private Laurel Paulino. Of course I didn't go into the many sexual positions this young woman introduced me to. I'd never tried it standing up until her, but in a porta-potty, it's a good position, farther from the stench.

"What about Sophie?"

"I never told you. We broke up when I was in boot camp."

"Why?" she said. "Why didn't you tell me?" It was Sophie and my mother together who had helped me get into the Army. My joining hadn't been as easy as signing up. I had to pass a physical, and when the recruiter had me run in the parking lot, he shook his head. Maybe it was all the smoking and drugs I'd been doing. He'd explained that after signing up, I'd have to go to MEPS, the military entrance processing station in Tampa, where I'd be tested in a variety of ways including physical tests for drugs and alcohol, tests for aptitude and intelligence, and physical exercise. Once in, there would be much physical training I'd have to endure, yet I was coughing and struggling in the recruiter's parking lot. He said to get in shape and come back. My mother became as tough as any trainer and kept me away from my friends except Sophie, who joined her and soon lived with me at my mother's house. They fed me, kept me on a regimen, and loved me, each in her own way. The two became friends with each other, too. Three months later, I made it into the Army.

"I don't want to talk about it now," I told my mother from Iraq. "She moved on. It's fucked up, I know, but I only have a few minutes."

"Language, Max." I could have had my legs blown off and said *fucked up*, and she would have told me *language*.

"Sorry, Mom."

"So Sophie stopped writing you?"

"She has a new boyfriend, Ralph—Ralph from my band."

"Aye! Ralph. What's wrong with her? Should I call her?"

"It's way too late, Mom. That was last year."

"I thought you two kept in contact," she said. "It's my fault. I'm too busy working."

"I'm now with Laurel Paulino. She's better. Really. Wait till you meet her."

She cleared her throat. "Where is this Laurel from?"

"Minnesota."

Because we'd lived in Orlando, my mother had met many a Minnesotan in the winter or who had retired there. "So cold there, right?"

"I guess. Maybe I'll see the place when we get out of the Army."

"Hmm," my mother said, always skeptical of my girlfriends. In response, I chatted on about Paulino as someone who took my best interests to heart. "I don't know where it's going, but, yeah…" The automated voice said I had two minutes left.

"You sound different—not like yourself," my mother said.

"I'm fine."

"Last night's news was talking about how soldiers are coming back very disturbed—needing special help."

"PTSD," I said.

"Yes. I imagine you're under a lot of pressure."

"I'm okay, Mom. They're giving me time off." I explained how Paulino kept me company, kept me from boredom. One minute left, said the voice.

"Now don't get this woman pregnant," chirped in my mother. "Rushing into something isn't a good idea."

"I'm fine. Be happy for me." I sensed she didn't like the idea of Paulino. "Minnesota's a good place. Listen, Mom, I gotta go—there's a line of people who want the phone, so I'll say good-bye." There wasn't a line, but I'd expected her to be all excited about my meeting someone new, and now—now I was shaking, and I didn't want to talk about it. I didn't want to think about Minnesota or any state except the state of love.

A helicopter zoomed overhead. Thirty seconds.

"Tell Dad what happened," I said. "I can't call him now."

She paused. "I will. Nothing broken?"

"Nothing," I said. "How are you? Is business good?" I heard nothing for seconds.

"I love you," she slipped in.

The phone clicked off, and to the dial tone I said, "I love you, too."

After my parents had divorced a few years earlier, they got along better. Even before I graduated high school, they fought often, my mother yelling in Spanish, my father swearing in English. When I left, however, the empty nest syndrome did not crush them. With my father's pension and my mother working as a banker, they stayed together. Then he fell into a string of affairs. When my mom found out, that was it. At this point, though, she was happy to live alone.

After talking with my mother, I was still shaking. Laurel and I were scheduled to rejoin the missions the next day, yet I knew I was still messed up somehow. I needed to find Paulino. She wasn't at the gym where she said to meet. She wasn't at her CHU. She wasn't in the chow hall. Maybe she was doing last-minute things like using the Internet. I had to calm down. I had to take a shower and listen to music.

The showers were in a narrow building like a mobile home, ten showers, each in its own booth. Men had one unit of showers, and the women, another. I often brought my iPod in with me. I could leave it on the chest-high ledge meant for soap and shampoo, and string my earbuds from it. I wouldn't get my head wet when listening to music. The shower and music would just relax me.

Before I undressed, I selected my music well. This called for something calming and instrumental. This is where my love for film came in. I collected soundtracks, and I chose Mark Isham's soundtrack to *October Sky*, a film from 1999 about a kid from a poor coal town in West Virginia, 1957. Russia was the first to enter the space race with its Sputnik, which frightened much of America. This kid was inspired to build small rockets, against his dad's wishes. The soundtrack starts with a lone cello, much like this lone kid, and an orchestra slowly comes in. It always relaxed me and made me feel better. I tried it out. The opening track did its job, and I quickly skipped to the fourth track where a violin and hammer dulcimer weaved together. Perfect.

At the time, I didn't analyze why my own music could be angry or aggressive, and yet I adored this stuff, music not meant to be noticed. I also didn't parse why I loved the film so much, but later I realized the story of a kid with dreams trying to get out of his hick town was my story.

I punched off the music to crank on my shower and get undressed. That's when I noticed the other shower running. Who else was here? My platoon and others were off on missions, and the ones who had the night shift were sleeping. I detected no variations of sounds coming from the other shower. Someone had just left it on. I trudged over to turn it off. When I opened the door, I found Paulino naked and curled up on the tile like an injured animal. Blood from under her wrists mixed with the shower water, two colored rivulets leading to the drain. Each heartbeat brought more of her closer to the dark hole.

"Laurel, Laurel, Laurel," I said placing my hands over where she was bleeding. "What are you doing!"

"I'm sorry," she said. "It's not you." She was crying.

I wrapped her in a towel and rushed her to the medical unit, shouting, "Help, help!" as I ran in.

| | |

As I stood outside, waiting for word on her, I fingered my iPod in my pocket but didn't pull it out. Rather, there were no helicopters flying, no bombs exploding, no boots hitting gravel. Rather, there was nothing. Wonderful nothing.

A day later, she was sent off. People, of course, soon heard of her slit wrists, and even though I expected rumors about why, I heard none. She was not unusual. In the five months I'd been in Iraq, I'd heard of three suicide attempts. We all knew the stress. I figured some people couldn't handle it—even if I figured I could. Now I knew differently. The doctor who helped Paulino didn't tell me where she went. "Home to Minnesota?" I asked.

"I can't say. She'll be fine."

He didn't offer anything more. I didn't ask more.

That night in the CHU, Jordan told me there's a psych ward in Germany that soldiers with extreme cases go to. She probably went there.

I had the option to take another day off to recover from this emotional shit. I protested, said I was fine, that I didn't want to bang around the camp anymore. The doc agreed, so as scheduled, I went back out beyond the wire, and it worked as I hoped. I was so worried about being blown up again, I couldn't think of Paulino. I only had to deal with the present.

More and more, our missions had to do with supporting the infantry in securing sectors. The infantry was rooting out the enemy.

More and more, they'd find Sunni insurgents or battle with renegade Shiites.

More and more, I was also seeing how this whole idea of the U.S. here was crazy. If we happened to take on a Sunni group and disarm them, the Shiites would rush in to overwhelm the remaining Sunnis, and then word would be on the street that we, the U.S. Army, hated Sunnis and supported the Shiites. Soon, both groups were fighting us. Many of those captured weren't even Iraqi but often from Iran and had come to fight us as well. We were in a civil war and were being killed and maimed daily. Styles had told me we were losing ten to twenty troops a day in Iraq, and the embalmers in the Dover Air Force Base mortuary in Delaware often had to work through the night. He always had these strange facts. What was true was the 5-20 had lost some soldiers my first week back.

At night, I'd stay awake late in my cot wondering how was Paulino? Where was she? I had her email address, but she never wrote back. I'd thought of her as a friend, my soul mate. Some things went together naturally, like birds and trees—that was supposed to be us. She and I had lived through a horror together. No one would ever match what I'd had with her. I knew, too, the blackness she'd felt. I'd been there as a teenager, ready to kill myself. That must have been like a vaccine because I didn't have a similar urge now, but to my surprise, I cried, there in the darkness of the CHU, and at one point, my need for air must have woken up Jordan because in the dark came his voice. "You okay, man?"

While I shook my head, which he couldn't see, I said, "Yeah. Just thinking of Paulino."

"She'll be okay." He had the kind of deep, reassuring voice you could believe, like a late-night radio DJ who talked straight to you.

"I messed her up," I said. "She was engaged to marry someone else, and then I came along."

"Max, it isn't your fault. Look around you. What did you expect? People aren't meant to live this way."

"But—"

"Don't go there," he said. "It's not your fault."

"You're married, right?" I said.

"Yeah. Kid on the way—a girl."

"And what if you fell in love with someone else here?"

"Won't happen. Doesn't mean it was wrong for you and Paulino."

"I'm thinking she'd have rather died in the Humvee than stay in love with me."

"Bullshit."

"She tried to kill herself rather than be with me."

"The human brain is flawed, quirky—like a Series III Jaguar V12."

"Sports car?"

"Yeah. She may have loved you but maybe she had survivor's guilt. It's unexplainable—but so is this war. Let's just make it, man. That's the most important thing."

I nodded. His voice in the dark just made so much sense to me. I told him "Yeah."

It occurred to me then—crazy thoughts I had—that Jordan must have swept in from the heavens. He'd saved my ass telling me to swerve, and now he reassured me things would be fine. I believed him. The problem was, the war didn't care.

| | | |

The next day, our mission pulled us near Old Baqubah, the old town center where some government offices were, but so were a lot of bombed-out apartment buildings with, out back, brown and injured palm trees that looked more like used Q-tips than something from paradise. The insurgents, we were told, lived among the impoverished citizens. The absolute ruination of the place made you wonder how anyone lived there. Blocks and blocks of bombed three-story apartment buildings barely stood, and with so many electric wires running above the streets, it made me think there was no building department. It seemed individual apartments had to find their own electricity.

One end of one apartment building must have been freshly bombed because amid the rubble stood a perfectly fine water heater, toys, a few mattresses, and furniture. They hadn't been taken yet to be reused. Around me, the streets lay littered with rubble and trash, and water ran curbside as if fire hydrants here or there had been opened. A donkey pulled a cart, and three boys under the age of ten ran behind it, teasing the kid who drove it. A clean white pickup truck filled with young, bored men looked at us without fear. They were squished in the open back. The word NISSAN in red gleamed from their tailgate. We didn't stop them. After all, we wanted the locals to see we weren't there to hurt them but to protect them. Our job that day was just to set up a perimeter for a certain sector.

I drove a Humvee again, and the LT was once again in the back. He directed which group stopped where. I noticed for the first time that that the gunner atop Jordan's Humvee was a thin woman I didn't recognize. I stopped, picked up the binoculars to my side, and aimed them her way.

Her nametag said "Helwani." Middle-Eastern? Her chin and cheekbones appeared sculptural. I didn't know her. I guess I stared because I still wasn't used to women doing the same jobs as the men.

"Take a right onto Tora Tora," said the LT, referring to the boulevard ahead of us.

I was tense, sure something was going to happen, but then the LT, probably looking at his screen, spoke into his mike. "Hey, everyone. We're going back. The 5-20 can't make it today."

I let out a big gasp. I was just so happy—everyone was.

However, once we were back safe under the wire, my stomach still churned. I didn't want to eat. I just needed to be alone. I walked past the sandbags that stacked up to cover half our CHU. I entered and didn't even turn on the lights. I flopped on my cot. After a few minutes, I realized I was too hyper to sleep. I thought I'd work on Photoshop—that always brought the swirl in my mind down. I could just focus on pixels.

Jordan and I were among the few who had Apple laptops in those days where everyone else had HPs, Dells, and Lenovos. He was trying to learn video editing using iMovie. I loved Photoshop. I brought up a photo from before the war, cropped it, and played with the color. In high school, I'd had darkroom experience with black-and-white film. It was the waning days of film and printing in the darkroom, and as I think back, I'm glad to have witnessed its magic, watched in amazement as an image came up on a pure white sheet in the developer. I may as well have been a gopher then for the time I'd spent in the dark. Photoshop used similar terms from the darkroom, so I knew what it meant to dodge and burn, to increase brightness and contrast, to crop, and more. Also with Photoshop, I'd learned how to clone areas, replace a distracting branch with blue sky and all sorts of tricks to get the image I'd intended.

On the screen in front of me, Sophie smiled on a beach, bending over, mugging for the photographer, me.

That's when Jordan and Hitch entered, Hitch punching Jordan's arm, saying, "You're fuckin' married. You forgot what it's like." With an easy smile, Jordan said, "Nah, you don't forget." To me, he said, "She's pretty. Your girlfriend before Paulino?"

"Yeah. Sophie." I sent out vibes for them to leave me alone. Couldn't the two just go away? It had been a hard mission for me, even though nothing happened. I didn't want to talk.

"You're a great photographer," said Jordan. "I never see you take your camera when we're on missions."

"Why would I want to remember that shit?"

"To show others the hell we go through."

"It's the hell that we volunteered to do," Hitch said, opening his laptop, probably to watch porn.

"When we were young and stupid," said Jordan. "It seemed like easy money, right? Joining the Army?"

I nodded.

"We wouldn't get hurt," said Jordan. "Someone else would." He looked at me, and tears, goddamn tears, came to my eyes. I was the one who'd gotten hurt. I turned back to the screen to wipe my eyes.

We didn't hug or anything, but Jordan patted my shoulder. I nodded. Hitch continued scrolling on his laptop. The sounds of mortars approached, and soon one explosion rattled our tin can. At this point, it barely fazed us anymore. Sophie continued smiling, and I worked on that photo for over twenty minutes. Good old Sophie.

Florida and Missouri, August-November 2005

Sophie quickly pulled off her T-shirt and short shorts on the sand near the sea oats of Playavista Beach, not far from where huge rockets flashed men to the moon. She stood in her pink bikini, her skin as tan as my Puerto Rican and Panamanian skin. That day, a kite festival papered the sky with flying purple crabs, yellow and orange squids, blue cones, multicolored butterflies, strings of traditional kites, and more. Other people played Frisbee on the beach. None of that held my attention more than Sophie, and I took a picture of her, smiling, leaning toward me. From that same spot as a teenager, I'd seen a space shuttle launched from adjacent Cape Canaveral. The shuttle's twin boosters had blasted while its three main engines fired, and the ground shook, eighty fucking million horsepower lighting the skies just before sunrise with awesome eye-candy plumes of smoke like dandelion dandruff. As beautiful and powerful as that was, it was minor compared to Sophie in that bikini. I'd never fallen for a person so deeply or as quickly before, and I couldn't tell her that—too early. We'd taken her Pontiac Aztec and shot straight down the 402 to the beach after I'd discovered the recruiting station was closed—Sunday.

After I took a few more pictures as she sat and I knelt, I said, "I watched *Platoon* twice at the theater last night, once just for me alone."

"Awesome movie."

"Yeah. Tomorrow I think I'm joining up."

"What?" she said, looking stunned.

"Yeah." After I said it, my mouth felt dry, so I grabbed us a couple beers from the cooler she brought. I handed her one.

She frowned. "Or am I misunderstanding. Join what?"

I nodded, excited, standing tall.

"The Army? Max, are you fucking stupid?"

A Frisbee at that very second bonked me in the head, and a mere moment later, a wayward kite swooped down and stabbed me in the back. I screamed and fell down.

"Max?" Sophie yelled. I lay in the sand, groaning, and she gently rolled me to the side to look at my back. "Hey, fuckers," she yelled to two guys in bathing suits running over.

One said, "You okay?" the other blurting, "Sorry, man. The wind."

I sat up, giving the OK sign, handing the maroon kite to one, and a black Frisbee with cartoon heads of the band Kiss on the top to the other guy. Sophie cradled me in the sand, pulling my head into the crook of her pink bottomed bikini. "See," she said. "That's what you get. Karma's telling you something."

"That's coincidence."

"Coincidence can kill you," she said. "You're joining because of a movie? Or where is this coming from?"

I paused. I wanted so badly for her to understand. "My last band and touring was killing me. I need purpose."

"Try college like a normal person."

"I don't have the discipline for it or anything yet. Another reason for the Army. Also it may get me out of the shit that threw me in jail."

"So you're just going to abandon everyone you know? Your friends and family?"

"I don't know what the Army will offer," I said. "But it's not like I'll be hauled off tomorrow or even soon."

"Just when I think I've met the right someone."

The fact she said that impressed me. "We have time. Things work out."

She ran one finger over one of my eyebrows. "Yeah. Work out. I'll be out of college and you'll be some fucking grunt." She pushed hard on the brow.

"Ouch," I said.

She stood, swiping the sand off her legs. She pulled on her shorts and T-shirt. She threw my own T-shirt at me.

"You mad?" I said.

"Of course not." She turned away.

"Look, can't we just—"

"Forget it, Max. It's your life, isn't it?"

I pulled on my T-shirt and carried my sandals. I reached for her hand, but she crossed her arms and walked ahead.

"Sophie, come on," I said. "I didn't mean to spoil anything. The movie made me think about my life." That was the truth. Maybe she needed more convincing, so I said, "Look. This is a chance to make a difference, right? My shot."

"Bullshit. It reminds me of what my professor talked about in philosophy class this week. Psychological egoism."

"Egoism?" We reached the hard part of the sand by the water.

"A person's every action is determined by his self-interest," she said.

I reached for her hand again. She hesitated, then took it.

While we walked, she stared at the sand as if reading notes. "Psychological egoism is about the conscious and unconscious motivation of all human actions."

"Like doing coke and making love with six projectors clacking away?"

She looked suddenly. "Yes, actually. That's a good example. But attraction and enjoying life was more on my mind."

"Me, too."

"I just don't think the Army is after your best interests. It's Bush grabbing a bunch of slogan-loving kids—rah, rah, America's best—and sending them off to war."

"Thanks," I said sarcastically. "Maybe I'm stupid, maybe I love slogans, but I know after I saw that movie and how raw and real it was… I don't know. I just—" I fumbled in my mind how to make it clearer, then said, "I just have to, Sophie. I just have to. Maybe I'm selfish, okay, but you didn't see what brought me here. I was lower than the crabs in the sea, lost as that seaweed over there," I said, pointing. "Until I met you. You've given me something to—"

She shook her head, pulled away, and stomped off.

I didn't know what else to say, but nothing was going to change my mind. I had to keep moving.

| | |

I had yet to call either of my parents. Dad knew I'd been in jail, and he probably told my mother, but my cell phone showed no calls from either of them. They were used to me not calling often, so I'd wait. I stayed with Sophie for two days in her shared apartment near Valencia College. Her roommate, a girl named Angel, said two days would be okay. The Valencia West Campus was on the other side of town from my apartment by UCF, about thirty minutes away. Sophie drove me to my apartment to collect my remaining things, acting as an intermediary, which I needed. We stuffed my clothes, guitars, and other things into my Geo Metro. Derby and Michaela stood watch, barely saying anything to me beyond Derby's "See you around," when I left with the last of my possessions.

Not long after that, on the highway, my car spewed steam and conked out. I rolled to a stop on the side. My Geo wouldn't start after that.

Sophie used her AAA card to tow it to a repair shop near her apartment, and a mechanic there guessed I might need a new head gasket—expensive. We pushed the car into a parking spot on the street. I'd deal with it in a day or two.

Sophie and I didn't talk anymore about my joining up, but we knew it was there like an upcoming operation. We just didn't talk about it. While Sophie was in class one day, I called a taxi to take me first to my bank for some cash, and then north to Altamonte Springs to the recruiting office, not far from where my mother lived.

The taxi dropped me off in the tree-filled parking lot just after noon, and with both apprehension and excitement, I hurried toward the Armed Forces Recruiting Center, whose red neon sign had a giant flickering "R." Inside, a wall with three doors surprised me. One door said "Marines." One had "Navy." The last showed "Army." Three different paths—my life would be different depending on which door I selected. Until that moment, I'd never thought of how I had such decisions often. There was the punk band or college decision. There were the lines of coke or stay straight decisions. And then there was randomness, like the Frisbee and kite crashing into me.

I went in the Army door.

The long, narrow room had what I expected: a flag, Polaroid headshots of happy recent recruits on a wall, a few framed action shots of battle, and a big banner saying "U.S. Army." Three recruiters—two pretty African-American women and one Hispanic man who looked like he was addicted to bench pressing—each had a desk and were talking with young guys. The Hispanic recruiter looked at me when I entered and said, "Please have a look around, and one of us will get to you shortly." He pointed to a rack of brochures.

As I waited, I looked at the Polaroids on the wall and couldn't help but overhear one of the women speak to a young man, high school age, who looked like Dracula. His skin was as white as his T-shirt. This was Florida—how did he not have color? Also, he had a lot of small black moles on his arm and face that made you want to connect the dots with a crayon.

She asked, "Have you been to college at all?"

"Just graduated high school," he said. "Didn't plan no college."

"Has any of your employment been something that could be used in an Army career?"

"Not unless washing dishes at a diner counts, but I don't want to wash no dishes. I want adventure."

"And adventure you will have. We just need to make the right career path for you. Can you read and write?"

"Real good."

Can you breathe? I was thinking.

She said, "The Army is looking for people we can train, such as driving a Humvee or operating a drone from remote control or even repairing equipment such as trucks or air conditioners. Do you have any mechanical aptitude?"

"I'm not sure what that means. I wouldn't mind blowing shit up, though."

She laughed. "Of course."

"Do I get money for signing up? Someone said I did."

"Five thousand dollars once you pass all the tests."

As I now looked at the Polaroids, I was looking at a yearbook of the black, tan, and white cousins to the kid answering. They were all off in some way. One guy had such big nostrils, they could be bat caves. One woman had ears the size of satellite dishes and wore a parka as if she stepped in from Antarctica. While truly beautiful people are in the minority, so were the oddballs—but not here. If I wanted to make a freaky movie, this was the place to find a cast. Was I one of the oddballs, too?

The Hispanic guy waved me over to his desk, and as I approached, he held out his hand. I shook it with a nice firm handshake as my dad always told me to do. "I'm Staff Sergeant Randy Gutierrez," he said, which sounded like a good upbeat name. "Have a seat. Are you curious about joining?" I noticed him glance at my tattoos.

"Yes, I'm curious," I said.

"Let me ask," he said with enthusiasm, "why the Army door and not either of the other two—or even IBM or a fast-food place? I know the Chick-fil-A across from here makes a mighty good chicken sandwich."

"I worked at Chipotle," I said, "and it sucked. Some people loved it there, but for me, no. I didn't belong there. I'm looking for something more."

"Good. I'm listening." He nodded, clearly wanting more.

"My dad was in the Army," I said, "an infantry guy stationed in Panama. He was a paratrooper in the reserves, too. I think he'd be proud of me in the Army."

"You have to be proud of you. Can't do it just for Dad."

"It's definitely for me. Seems to me that the Army needs the most people. The Army can help me into a career." *Career* sounded like a good word.

"You're right. You have a good attitude. Now as you may know, we have a number of minimum requirements. One is physical. How fast do you run the mile?"

"I have no idea." Why was he asking me this? I didn't hear the pasty kid get asked this.

"You have to run it in ten minutes, minimum. And have you taken drugs in the past year?"

Shit, I thought but tried to look cool. "Does cold medicine count?"

"I'm talking illegal drugs. Everyone who applies needs to take a written test, and we'll analyze your urine and/or blood. Certain chemicals will set it off, understand? We don't want drug users in the Army. We want soldiers at their best."

I nodded, still a little high from the speed from last night. Sophie used it for studying. I used it for fun. Could the sergeant see it in my eyes? Was I that obvious?

"First things first," he said. "I see you're wearing running shoes." He pointed to my New Balance. "Would you mind running right now?"

"Did the guy who just left run?"

"He'll get his chance. Everyone does if they want to apply."

I hadn't planned on running. "What's the record for the mile?" I asked. "Like five minutes or something?"

"It's under four minutes."

"And I get ten? That's got to be easy."

We stepped outside. He took me to the road beyond the parking lot. "See that red light down yonder?"

For the first time, I heard the guy's Southern accent. In the South, no matter what your last name was, you were likely to have a Southern accent. I didn't because I'd grown up in the Bronx. "Yes," I said.

"That's exactly a half mile from here. Run there and back, and you've got ten minutes. He pulled a stopwatch from his pocket.

I now realized how far it really was. "You see, Sergeant—"

"Ready?"

"Oh, shit."

"Go!"

And I dashed. I thought of all the great runners of the world: Jesse Owens from the 1936 Summer Olympics in Berlin with Hitler watching. Jackie Joyner-Kersee from the 1984 Summer Olympics in Los Angeles with *Playboy* Hugh Hefner watching. I was running that well—for about a hundred yards, and then my mouth started doing something funny as I tried to breathe better. Then I coughed. My sides started to ache. I could feel my form go out as I huffed.

Hmmm. Cigarettes? Drugs?

Halfway to the light, I was merely walking. Soon I was walking slower, holding my side. I coughed more. Man, if only I had some coke, I could probably do this. As my stomach started lurching, I bent down. I took a second and got back up. I could do this. The world started to spin.

I puked and collapsed.

A blue car, a Toyota Corolla, pulled up next to me, and the sergeant rolled down his window. "Hop in," he said. "You're not going to make the ten minutes.

I entered the car.

"Kid, you're not in good shape at all." I suspected he knew this all along.

"I just need some practice," I said, sweat falling into my eyes.

Back in the parking lot, as we parked outside the recruitment office, he said, "How much do you really want to get in?"

My eyes said everything.

He nodded. First, you're going to need to make it your job to get in shape. If you're doing drugs—and I'm guessing you are from the number of tattoos you have—"

"I can have tattoos, right?"

"There's no policy against them yet. But stop the drugs. You don't have to tell me you took any, but know if you did, it's going to take up to three months for your system to clean out. Join a gym or something, too. Stop smoking. Run. Do push-ups. Once you get accepted into the Army, boot camp is no cake walk, but you'll be a better person."

"That's what I want."

"Nearly all day for six weeks, you're going to take classes and do a lot of physical conditioning. They're going to make you one tough man. You up for that?"

"Yes, sir," I said so enthusiastically, I coughed again. "I'll be back."

We shook hands.

"For the record, I'm not a 'sir.' Only officers are sirs."

I called my mother. She answered, and when I told her I'd been kicked out of my apartment, was at the Army recruitment center, and needed a ride, she grunted and said okay.

| | | |

Most of my goodness comes from my mother, Ivanna. My mom was like a smaller and Latina version of Mrs. Weasley from the *Harry Potter* series. She was just so likeable and caring and knew what was needed at the right time. She could hang onto my every word. Around her, I felt special.

My mother learned English quickly after she arrived in America, and she worked hard to attend Boston College to earn her college degree while my dad stayed in the military. I was conceived eight years after they married. My mother eventually became a head banker at a large Citibank in New York City while my dad delivered packages for UPS. Sometimes he took me on his route, and I'd sit strapped in on the seat next to him in that brown truck. He was so friendly to everyone, and I'd help, carrying the smaller packages and feeling proud. Little did I know then that the projects were the most dangerous part of the Bronx. I felt safe with Dad. However, one time we went down a dark hallway, and I told him it seemed scary.

"Don't worry, Maxie," he said. He knocked on a door, and an old black woman opened it. As she signed for the package, I heard someone argue down the hall, and I moved from my father to look. A tall dark man took out a gun, unzipped his pants, and pointed the gun at a smaller man on his knees. The smaller man then leaned in and sucked the man's penis. I was confused and scared. I didn't understand what was going on.

My father said, "Let's go, guy," and I ran to his side. He hadn't seen what I did, and I knew better than to tell him.

One day we walked up the long staircase in a brownstone. He fell backward, zipping past me, down a whole flight after he slipped on wet paint at the top. He stayed in the hospital for weeks and had to have two open-back surgeries. He got permanent disability and found the New York winters too harsh for his back—which is why we moved to Florida. I was eight then. We drove from New York, and when we crossed the Florida State line, there was a fresh orange juice stand we stopped at. The OJ tasted sour to me then, and it has ever since.

In the Armed Forces Recruitment Center parking lot, my mother arrived in her baby Mercedes, a silver C230. The first words out of her mouth and in Spanish were basically, "Don't tell me you've joined the frigging Army!" The car was for her clients. She'd become a real estate agent before the divorce. I always spoke to her in English, but I could understand Spanish well, thanks to her.

"No, I can't join now," I said. "I'm out of shape, and to pass the drug test, I need to be clean for three months." I climbed into her car, feeling defeated.

"Oh, mijo." She looked at me as if, for the first time in her life, she couldn't understand me—never mind the long hair, the punk look, and the lifestyle. This seemed odder to her. We started off, even though I didn't say where. "Why the sudden interest in the Army?" Soon we passed the light that I couldn't run to.

"Dad knew who he was in the Army. Everyone does. I need to know what that feels like."

"So you're looking for identity?" she said with her accent.

"I don't know. What I've been doing hasn't gotten me much, has it?"

"This is a big decision. Have you thought it through?"

We passed a tall water tower, a big bulb at the top. It reminded me of that picture of the Hiroshima bomb going off.

"Maybe they'll put me in the Army band. That's what I'm good at." I could feel my mother's doubt.

"So, what's your plan? Are you staying with me? Where's your car?"

"Things aren't going well," I said.

"I work. You called me for a ride."

"I'm sorry, Mom."

She pulled the car into the nearest parking spot. When she put it in park, the locks automatically snapped open.

"And you've been in jail? Your father told me."

"Just a night after I got into a fight. The Army was my plan, and now that's out. My car's at a garage—probably needs a head gasket—but I don't have money for that. I don't have a band. I don't have a job."

She looked at me long and hard. "So you're, as they say, down and out." It was a statement.

I sighed. I nodded.

"I've changed my mind about the Army. If you want in, I'll help you get in shape to join."

"Really? How?"

"If you're serious, you have to follow my rules."

"What rules?"

"No car—no going out at night. You eat what I cook, and you run two miles a day to start. No more girlfriends. You'll do sit-ups and lift weights, and I'm going to get you to read, too. You'll be reading some biographies of people who got us into these wars, such as Bush and Cheney as well as some great writers you didn't get in school such as Isabel Allende, Gabriel Garcia-Marquez, and Sandra Cisneros, and we'll talk about them. Maybe I'll throw in *To Kill a Mockingbird*. It's all about healthy body and mind. Okay?"

"Yes, except for the girlfriend part. I've been staying with a girl named Sophie. She's different from anyone I've gone out with before. She's a college girl."

"And where did you meet Sophie?"

"At the Lake Mary movie theater. She works there."

"I've seen your girlfriends. They're not a good influence."

"I think I've fallen in love, though. Sophie's really great—strong like you. You'd love her."

"She can come for dinner—no spending the night."

"But, Mom—"

"No. This is just a three-month deal to get you in shape. If you don't like my rules, then go live with your father."

I knew my father wouldn't let her spend the night, either. "Can I think about it?"

"No. Decide right now."

She was offering a different type of jail. She'd be the warden. I nodded. "It's yes."

She smiled and started the car. The door automatically locked with a snap. "If you do well the first week, we'll get your car fixed and sell it. You can keep the money."

Her house was a small one in a nice part of Apopka, tract homes that favored arched windows, beige paint, and gray asphalt-shingles.

The three months wasn't easy, but it did pass quickly. I quit drugs right away, and after about a month, I'd completely quit smoking. After my car was fixed, I sold it. I did a hundred sit-ups each morning after rising, then a hundred pull-ups, ate one of my mother's incredible omelets, then ran through the tree-lined neighborhood, having worked my way up to six miles a day. I lifted weights in the garage, read a lot, watched DVDs at night with my mother, and on the evenings Sophie came for dinner, we had great discussions. Neither of them liked the military, but they didn't change my mind. Late at night, I'd watch Army videos online, watch war movies, read Army books. Sometimes, from outside, Sophie would knock on my window and stay with me until morning, until after my mother left for work.

The time had finally come. At the thirteen-week mark, my mother drove me to the recruitment center. My recruiting officer, Sergeant Gutierrez again, was impressed with how I looked. He had me run, and I ran the mile in seven and a half minutes. I answered all his other questions easily. He offered me five thousand dollars for committing to two years, ten thousand if I signed up for five. Ten thousand seemed like a lot, but I took the five thousand, which I'd get if I passed MEPS, my last hurdle.

| | | |

Two days after I joined up, Sergeant Gutierrez picked me up at my mother's house and drove me to MEPS, the Military Entrance Processing Station, in Tampa, an hour and a half away. In all the movies and war stories I'd seen or heard, no one ever told me about processing, and so I saw it as my first big test. Gutierrez explained that if I failed at any one of the four levels—aptitude tests, physical screen, job placement, and background check—I would be out.

"What about drugs?" I asked. "I'm clean and in great shape, but will they hold my past against me?"

"You don't have to make a big deal of it. Were you an addict of any sort?"

"No."

"Then you've tried a few things. No big deal."

I caught his drift, but still I was worried. My past could do me in. Also, would background checks find Ralph or anyone who hated me? How far would they go? Girlfriends? Not all ended well. I couldn't let these worries do me in, though. I needed to do well in everything and believe I'd get in. I needed to leave Disney World, dive into hell, and come out stronger.

MEPS exists because the military wants to determine if you're really qualified and ready for service. This is no mere rubber-stamp operation. I would be there for two days, put up in an Embassy Suites with two roommates on a floor of all military candidates. As Gutierrez explained it, "Not only do they want to make sure you're physically and mentally fit, they also want to find your interests or talents that can help them."

Okay—and if jumping up and down with a guitar and singing about my lost generation was a job, I'd be slotted in, but I knew they'd find something else for me. I was excited. I was on my way to leaving permanently the shithole of Orlando.

On the way there, the sergeant explained to me that I'd be talking with people of various ranks, and when I'm asked a question to put a "sir" behind it if it was an officer. Enlisted people didn't have "sir" but rather their rank.

I said, "Yes, Staff Sergeant."

"You got it," he said. "And if you have any questions that aren't answered, ask me, and if I don't know it, I'll get you the answer."

In Tampa, MEPS was a big white building with a green lawn, a big portico entrance, and a huge flag flying. The sergeant and I arrived early, and we were shown into a small conference room where I joined about twenty other people, a couple of them women. We were a crazy hodgepodge, a mixture of races and attitudes—light-skinned, dark-skinned, tall, short, thin, fat, self-assured, full-of doubts, anxious, cocky and more. I wondered how some of them thought they'd qualify.

The sergeant at the front said first thing, "You are enlisting in a time of war, which means you have far greater chance of fighting than in the past. Depending on your job, you could be directly in harm's way. Does everyone understand that?"

We all shouted, "Yes, Sergeant!"

"Does anyone have any questions, reservations, or reluctance to join up at this time? Now's your chance."

"No, Sergeant," everyone said. We didn't drive all the way down here just to turn around. I soon saw at MEPS, everyone had many chances to withdraw. The military truly wanted volunteers.

We followed the sergeant into a computer room where we each got our own keyboard and screen and took a battery of tests. It was like a super SAT thing that tested us in science, math, reading and writing ability, mechanical ability, and auto and electronics skills. One of the first questions was to write a short essay on "Why do I want to join the Army?" Oh, shit. It felt like a trick. I couldn't explain about not fitting in, about growing up with the local punks, about *Platoon*. What did they want to hear? At that point, my high school English teacher Mrs. Spivak's voice came to me: "Don't write what you think I want. Write your own truth. You will fail if you're just trying to please me."

Maybe there was a midpoint—something that wasn't so complex as my reality but something that also felt right.

I glanced around the room. Everyone looked focused and serious, their fingers working furiously, their keyboards clacking. They all seemed to know what to say. Fuck.

Then I remembered my teacher saying that a minimum essay was five paragraphs: an introduction, a conclusion, and three main points in between, a paragraph each. I now knew what to write, reciting much of what I told my mother and Sophie.

After that, the other tests didn't seem so hard. Mechanical knowledge included if a gear goes one direction, what direction does the 15th one go? Later in the afternoon, we worked with blocks to build a cabin. My roof kept falling in until I figured it out.

Even though we had lunch—which looked much like prison food in individualized packages—I was beat and was thankful that later that day would just be a physical exam where I didn't have to think about much.

After our meal, a group of men and I lined up in our underwear, the sergeant asking us to hold the folded exam gowns in our left arm before we changed into it. I whispered to the guy next to me who was holding his gown in the right arm. "Your other left arm," I said. He looked at me, confused. "You're supposed to hold the gown with this arm," I said, lifting my arm. He looked at it and switched. We then had to get down on our haunches and do a weird kind of duck walk—for balance, I soon learned, as I saw a few people fall over. We then stepped into our gowns, with the opening in the rear. Not everyone got that right, either.

My doctor gave me the kind of checkup I had before starting school each year, checking my eyes, ears, reflexes and more.

Afterwards, once we were all dressed and back in a line, the sergeant said, "Turn to the left," and I swear half my group turned to the right. This wasn't even a test, but it seems to me it should have been. That was the first day.

The next day, for the job search, my group and our recruiting officers sat in a white room with blue plastic chairs, waiting to meet with counselors who had the results of our tests. One by one, people were called, until I was nearly the last. So much of my time at MEPS seemed to be hurry-up-and-wait. I would find out later that was the Army's game. When a young woman announced my name, Sergeant Gutierrez and I followed her to a cubicle. The counselor, older, gray-haired, who probably did this a thousand times a week, nonetheless looked at us in a personal way that reminded me of my grandfather in New York. My grandpa always said my name with delight. "Well, son," said the counselor. "I'll make this simple for you. Based on your scores, we have openings for two things, infantry and military police." From the talk I heard at lunch, infantry was for the non-educated, the ones who had no other talent. They were human shields, the first ones sent into the shit.

"No language school like for interpreting? I'm great in Spanish. I can learn a new language."

"We're not going to be in the Mid-East that long. This is it."

"Or Army band? I play guitar, bass, and other instruments. You didn't test for that."

"There are no openings. Just these two things."

While I joined to see action, I didn't want to be machine gun fodder. Sergeant Gutierrez leaned toward me and whispered in my ear, "Military police."

"I can be a cop? Where?"

The counselor said, "Wherever they need you—on a base in Ohio or on the front in Iraq or Afghanistan."

Something told me I wouldn't be in Ohio.

A nearby clock struck twelve.

I took the MP job.

My background check proved fine, and before I knew it, I was standing back in the room I started with, ready to take my oath of enlistment with twelve other people.

Twelve of us, including two women, were grouped in a wood-paneled room with a red carpet, and a sergeant stood at a podium at the front. Welcoming us, he smiled as hard as we did. My energy could light up Manhattan. I did it, made it in. My troubles were over. A few people held up camcorders, and I realized they were parents of recruits. I should have called mine, but I didn't think that far ahead.

The sergeant at the front said, "We have amazing news for you proud people." His huge grin made it seem as if the President and the Pope were coming. "Your official oath ceremony will happen this evening in Raymond James Stadium during a monster truck rally. It's a big deal. You'll be on the news and in the papers. It's going to be amazin'!"

I glanced around. Everyone looked jazzed. Monster trucks? It sounded hokey. He said, "If you can't make it, I'll induct you right now, but tonight's worth it." I realized I could have my parents see the ceremony after all. I'd skip calling Sophie. I didn't want to push this stuff too hard.

That evening, I met my parents in the parking lot. They'd come in separate cars as my father brought his wife, Juanita, a short woman twenty years younger than he from El Salvador, and shy.

We met the sergeant at a particular entrance, who shuttled us into a meeting room under the stadium, which featured a large buffet. A few hours later we inductees gathered in a line, and an honorary squad in dress uniforms and rifles led us onto the dirt field. This was a modern football stadium with two tiers. Where did all this dirt come from? Monster trucks in red, white, and blue, and sporting huge black tires taller than most cars, sped around us. Some of the monster trucks raced up dirt mounds and flew off into the air. The crowd applauded.

We stepped up on a small platform where there stood an Army captain in a dark dress uniform, spangled with gold medals, gold braid, gold buttons, colorful bars, and a black bow tie. He smiled and moved to the microphone.

"Ladies and gentlemen," he blared. "I'm Army Captain Oliver Pedersen, and this evening I'm proud to induct a small group of volunteers who have agreed to fight for our country."

The place roared, and the audience—most of the men in cowboy hats and many women in Daisy Duke shorts—excitedly waved little flags while the jumbo screens around the stadium showed us with a giant flag unfurling.

"But first, let me introduce you, overhead, to the U.S. Special Operations Parachute Team." Spotlights like those in a Hollywood movie premiere clicked on and showed four soldiers under white parasails already gliding down, holding American flags in one hand and pink smoke coming from their feet, and again the crowd roared.

The monster trucks had stopped, as if to watch. The paratroopers curved right into the stadium, and landed expertly on the dirt field. More roaring and flag waving. While I should have been completely in awe, I mostly felt like I was a Roman peasant just led into the Coliseum to be gobbled by lions.

The captain turned to us and said into the microphone the same thing the sergeant had said to us when we first started at MEPS: "You are enlisting in a time of war, which means you have far greater chance of fighting than in the past. Depending on your job, you could be directly in harm's way. Does everyone understand that?"

We all shouted, "Yes, sir." The citizens shouted their praise.

"Does anyone have any questions, reservations, or reluctance to join up at this time?"

"No, sir," we shouted. Enthusiasm swirled.

He offered the oath, whose words became a blur to me, and then it was over.

Cheer, cheer, cheer.

It struck me that maybe America went to war because it seemed like a football game or a monster truck rally. Too late now, I thought.

Soon after in the parking lot, with the sounds of roaring engines still audible and my parents talking with each other how fun this had been, I called Sophie. Her pretty little voice said, "Hello."

"I did it," I said. "I'm in."

| | | |

Ten days later I received my orders. A few days after, I reported to my recruitment center where a bus stood in the misty morning to take me to Fort Leonard Wood, Missouri. Although it was six a.m., still completely dark out, there were enough lights in the parking lot to make it seem like a celebration. I hugged both of my parents, who didn't seem to have ill will for each other, and I kissed Sophie in front of them.

"Stay tight," said my dad, shaking my hand.

"I will." His wife Juanita gave me a little hug.

My mother stepped up. "Mijo, I just want you back, promise me," and she gave me a deep hug.

"I promise, Mom."

"I'll email you," said Sophie, "if you get the Internet."

"Not much in boot camp," I said, "But afterwards, the Internet is everywhere."

"Love you, man," she said.

"You don't have to wait for me if you don't want to. Like you said, I'm a grunt, you're a college student."

"Don't be silly. You know I didn't mean that," and we kissed again.

I was the only recruit from there that day, so I hopped on with my duffle bag. I was on my way.

I watched through the back window as my family and Sophie became smaller and smaller until the dark swallowed them.

I learned the trip would be over eighteen hours, and we'd arrive around midnight. I don't know how the driver was so relentless. We didn't stop at rest stops because there was a little closet with a toilet in the back. He never seemed to need it. The driver stopped at two Burger Kings on the way, one for lunch, one for dinner. I don't mean to criticize, but why not a Cora's Café or even a Stuckey's in place of a Burger King?

The bus kept going—through the flats of Florida, the hills of Alabama, some road construction in Tennessee, the shacks of Mississippi. I pulled out my iPod, chose a favorite playlist, and fell asleep as we passed a sign that said "Welcome to Missouri." Little did I know then, I was really entering the state of misery.

Iraq, March 2007

Near the start of spring, the LT spoke to us in our morning formation where it was a moderate 72 degrees—yet I felt hot and sweaty. "Today," the LT said, "we're going to support the 5-20 in an operation north of Combat Outpost Adam in Old Baqubah. We've been putting a lot of pressure on the AIF lately, disrupting their safe houses, raiding their supply networks, disabling their IEDs, and killing their IED emplacement teams. We're upping the pressure starting today."

I figured this was the mission that didn't happen last time, but with this speech, maybe it was something bigger.

"We'll join other MP units in securing a number of neighborhoods and sectors," he continued. "The 5-20 Strykers and other infantry units will charge in. There will be a special forces operational attachment. Hitch, you and other snipers will be trucked in to some buildings we've already secured. It'll give us some high ground."

I knew then, this would be no ordinary day.

"Baqubah has become a stronghold for the Islamic State, and we're here to break them," the LT ended.

This time, I didn't drive. I sat in the back with Hoogerheide, who reminded me of a spaniel. Styles drove with the LT next to him. Perhaps it was because the LT didn't want music today, but he could have just said something, and I wouldn't have used my iPod. Still, I was glad to have Styles in our Humvee. He was fast on his feet, and if we were getting into something unusual, he'd be on my team. I pulled my small Nikon Coolpix

7700, a camera my parents recently sent me after I mentioned the camera I had was too big to take with me everywhere. This one fit in my pocket. I showed the camera to the LT, saying, "It's okay if I use?"

He nodded. "If you get something good, maybe I can send it to *Stars and Stripes*."

Up close, he looked no different from us other than the lines above his brow, which made him appear older than he was.

I turned the mode dial on the camera for a landscape shot out the window, and snapped a shot of kids climbing a mountain of rubble at one end of an apartment building. The LT said, "How would you like to live here with kids? What kind of future do they have?"

"What kind of future do we have?" said Styles.

I focused farther down the street where I saw a huge line of Strykers already stopped. On either side of them stood M1 tanks, and then the whop-whop-whop of helicopters, a pod of Wolfpack attack helicopters, flew overhead.

"Holy Jeez," I muttered, trying to zoom in. "How big is this operation today?"

"Big," said the LT. "We're joining another company of MPs to secure the area. Zoom forward, Styles. We have the green light to go."

I noticed the letters "REC" blinking on the bottom of my screen, when I looked at my dial. I'd accidently been recording in movie mode. I'd never tried it before, but I switched it back to landscape mode and shot the standing Strykers, tanks, and helicopters.

The LT, getting directions from his radio, moved us past the gathering, and, as we'd done on other missions, we took positions at intersections to secure a particular neighborhood. Over our earpieces came the order for the Strykers and tanks to move in.

I snapped a couple of shots. "Great view, eh?" I said.

Our Humvee stood on a slight rise where a field met our city street, and the Strykers fanned out and ran across that field. The tanks stayed on the streets. If the sight of all these vehicles and, soon, troops didn't surprise and strike terror in the terrorists, nothing would. I captured images of this, too. I wanted to show their movement, so I switched back to REC.

As the line of Strykers approached the street we were on, loud shots from mortars began from behind a few houses.

"What the—" said the LT.

At the edge of the field, underneath one Styrker, a volcano exploded, thrusting the vehicle aloft, covering it in fire. I dropped my camera as it surprised me so. I started shooting again when another huge IED—must have been a deep anti-tank mine—shoved another Stryker over. The other Strykers stopped, and their back ends dropped. Soldiers poured out. Some ran toward the burning pair of Strykers, while other soldiers headed right toward the wall of the neighborhood. Machine gun fire from the wall knocked a few of our men down. Our own gunner began shooting his .50 at the wall, and puffs of stucco rose where the powerful bullets hit. We weren't surprising the insurgents. They'd anticipated we'd be coming, and they were prepared. They'd surprised us.

"Fall back! Fall back!" said my earpiece.

The LT shouted, "That guy over there!" He pointed to a squirming man on the ground. "Drive over," he told Styles who immediately put our vehicle in gear. We raced over, and Styles stopped near the fallen soldier, placing ourselves between the man and the wall. He was on my side, and without being told, I opened my door. A bullet slammed into its glass, but I wasn't thinking of anything other than saving him, so I still leaped out. Then it was like someone punched me in the chest. I fell. Was I bleeding? No blood. I hurt like hell, but my Kevlar vest had saved me from a bullet. I crawled to the guy on the ground. He was crying. I could see one of his fingers was gone and his bloody arm revealed a hole in the middle. He bled from his neck, too, but not an artery.

"I'm here," I said. "I'm pulling you to the truck, okay?

"Thank... you," he said, gurgling, barely speaking.

The gunner above me kept rattling away, the many shell cases of hot brass falling from the turret and streaming into our metal coffin. No one else shot at us. I yanked the soldier by his legs closer to our Humvee, and then I lifted him by his torso into our truck. Hoogerheide pulled the man in. She had more strength than I'd guessed.

I popped into my seat. By that point, more Strykers, taking the road, had come around closer to the wall, and dozens of our soldiers now climbed the barrier and hopped over, shooting the whole way. It seemed we'd regained control.

"Medic!" yelled the LT into his radio as Hoogerheide wrapped the man's hand with gauze from a medical kit. "We have a wounded man in our vehicle." We received instructions to drive a short ways to where a medevac helicopter, already in the area, had just landed. Remembering my camera, I pulled it out, this time purposely choosing the video mode. I recorded as we raced down the street and soon saw a whirl of dust where it was. We raced up to it. A pair of medics emerged with a stretcher and ran to us.

With all the noise, none of us said anything. The medics knew what they were doing and pulled the guy from our vehicle. I never even noticed the soldier's name.

It was only then that I once again felt the pain from my own chest. I could see a hole in my jacket above my heart. I didn't find a bullet. It must have dropped out. I wasn't going to disrobe here, but I was guessing I'd be black and blue, which turned out to be true.

It took a couple of hours for the infantry to go through each house in the area. We became inundated with people trying to drive out of the neighborhood. We let small families go on without searching, but if there were fighting-age young men in the car, we patted their bodies down and searched the car. One was full of assault rifles in the trunk. Had they not expected us to stop them? We turned them over to an Iraqi police van. No telling if the young men were let out several blocks later.

Nothing more happened near our position, but we heard two more huge explosions. I feared it was one booby trap or another. Humvees raced with the injured to the same helicopter area we'd gone to.

When we returned a few hours later to Warhorse, we cleared our barrels in a second test-fire range. When we thought all our ammunition had been removed, we aimed into the test-fire pit and pulled our triggers to make sure. That's when the loud sounds of a blade truck approached. The blades, the engineers, were in charge of retrieving inert vehicles, and the truck pulled in one of the burned Strykers from today's operation. The engineers, too, stopped to clear their guns, and while they did so, I walked up to the open back end of the Stryker. A hell of a lot of blood coated the inside. I could smell the flesh of soldiers.

I glanced back to my platoon, and as they stared at the burned vehicle, their long faces betrayed the wear-and-tear on their souls. This war, this meat grinder, devoured young soldiers by the day.

All night long, the battle continued. I awoke occasionally to helicopters landing or taking off and platoons roaring off or returning. The next day in the morning chow hall, everyone was quiet, none of the usual banter. While I sat with Hitch, Jordan, and Styles, none of us said anything. We all seemed to be thinking this might be our last meal, our last day here. Or might we lose our legs, eyesight, or something else today to live the rest of our lives as a half-person? Had World War Two soldiers felt something grander? Perhaps Nazis taking over the world felt so real that stopping Hitler was worth losing their lives for. In this place, who was I saving? Me, I suppose. I spooned bland Cream of Wheat into my mouth, skipping the usual granola and brown sugar, thinking how stupid and wasted my life had been. If I died today, I wouldn't know what it would be like to wake up next to my wife, my love, whomever she'd be, day after day for years. I wouldn't have children. How the hell had I ever thought war might be exciting and character-shaping? If I made it through this horror, I vowed not to waste another second of my life.

Just before we left, after we'd tested our guns in the test range, a huge multi-wheeled paddy wagon pulled up nearby, and a line of eight blindfolded black-haired terrorist suspects, all in their late teens and early twenties—our age—stumbled down some steps at the rear, their hands bound behind their backs. A pair of interpreters speaking to them, touching their shoulders, guided them down. We stared. The terrorists didn't wear uniforms of any kind, but, rather, colorful Polo and button-down shirts with jeans. Their hair, neatly trimmed whether curly or straight, appeared date worthy. They looked nothing like sheiks or some of the bearded religious types I'd seen in the streets. They could have been guys from a Florida mall, and they probably smooth-talked their way into Saturday night nightclubs to dance and drink with the more progressive and Westernized girls. Everyone wanted to be like Americans, yet these young men would have been happy to hack me down with an AK47.

Our convoy left the blast walls of the base to return to the same area as the day before. Sections of the neighborhood wall had been mowed down, probably by M1 tanks. Piles of rubble sat where houses had undoubtedly stood the day before.

After the LT set up positions for each Humvee around the neighborhood, he turned to us. "We have orders to secure a house where men had run from last night. The commander wanted to wait until the light of day, in case it's booby-trapped. I volunteered us," he said. "I'll take the lead because if anyone'll get hurt, it'll be me."

Who talks like this? Why was he volunteering for something the infantry should be doing? Was this where my life would end, all because he was going for a promotion? Only the day before, I'd rushed into danger, but today, none of it made sense.

"Okay?" said the LT.

"Yeah," said Hoogerheide, and I said, "Yeah, sure LT." We were too chickenshit to say anything else.

The house was a more upscale place than its neighbors, meaning it had two stories in white stucco with ornate iron gratings on its windows. A seven-foot wall surrounded the house, and two large steel doors in the wall appeared the only way in. One stood wide open onto a rich green lawn. The garden wall and the house walls betrayed a lacing of pockmarks as if a hell of a lot of .50 caliber ammunition had been focused on the place. Yet no artillery or bombs had been used.

The four of us, goggles on, M4's out, stepped toward the house. The LT indicated for us to stop while he stepped forward. His gun poked the door, another steel one, which opened with little force. He peered in, then gave the sign for us to move back while he walked in. My sense was if the place was going to blow up, he'd be the only one to die. But this was for the infantry, not MPs. Why were we here? This didn't feel right.

About four minutes later, he stumbled out, holding his head in one hand, his stomach with the other.

"You okay, sir?" I said as Hoogerheide and I ran to him. She grabbed his shoulders and said, "Are you okay?" He shook his head, and she told him to sit down.

"What's in there?" I asked. Even though he mumbled something, maybe "No," I stepped in. The smell was the first thing, like burnt and rotting carcasses. Dried blood and perhaps brain matter covered one wall.

In the living room, on a Persian rug, lay two dead men, Iraqis much like the captured men in casual clothes I saw at Warhorse earlier. One held a sign in his dead hands with what looked to be a phone number, suitable for photographing. The man's image was probably on the Internet now. The other had his shirt up and his pants down, as if in death he was being humiliated. I recognized the one with the phone number. He'd been one of our translators, missing for a few days.

I stepped into the next room. Fifteen faces stared at me from the ground, their heads neatly arranged on their necks to greet visitors. One wore a U.S. helmet—maybe one of our own. I don't know where their bodies were, but I, too, now felt light-headed, and I stumbled backwards and out. What kind of universe was this that people did this to each other?

I barged out, hyperventilating, and over my short breathes, the LT said into his radio, "We need CID on this, over," asking for investigators.

On the ride back, I said little. Hoogerheide stared at me; I could feel it even though I was looking out the window at a row of shot-up apartments. She touched my shoulder, "Maybe you two should get checked out at Combat Stress when you get back."

"Pointless," I said. Leave it to the military to cure us. Between the bullshit combat-stress appointments and the over-prescription of ibuprofen they shoved down our throats, we were better off on our own. I told her, "Give it another day or two, and we'll see something even worse."

Back in my CHU that night, I skipped dinner, listening instead to my iPod, my acoustic playlist, which included, "The Only Song" by Sherwood at 3:12 in length. As the first guitar chord struck, splices of gore and blood on the wall from the house kept flashing in my memory. Next came "Woe," by Say Anything at 4:07. With each vocal harmony, I closed my eyes to the sight of corpses steaming in the Iraqi heat and desert sand. Then there was "Jasey Rae" by All Time Low at 3:34. The snare drum of the song quickly converted to .50-caliber machine-gun fire.

Jordan touched me. I jumped. He held out a croissant breakfast sandwich, knowing I liked them. I pulled out my earbuds. "Thanks," I said. "Maybe I'll eat it later."

"Sorry, man," he said, clearly not knowing what else to say. He saw my camera on the cot and asked, "Did you grab photos today?"

"Yesterday," I said.

"Mind if I look at them on my computer?"

"Go ahead."

He took the memory card out and downloaded them onto his laptop. I returned to my music. As the next song came on with an epic cymbal crash, the sight of a Humvee flipping over with burning soldiers took over my mind.

Jordan said something, so I pulled out my earbuds again. "What!"

"You all right?"

"Of course not. But what'd you say?"

"You shot some video," he said.

"An accident at first, then I did some more on purpose."

"It's good. Mind if I use it? I'm learning iMovie."

"Go ahead. No skin off me."

"Apology" by Alesana played on my iPod, not the acoustic remix version but the full-heart-screaming you're-everything-to-me drum-and-guitar-pounding angry version. The footage of the day played on Jordan's screen—and there was a crazed gnashing-your-teeth beauty about the images and music together—everything I was feeling as if I, too, could show how everything was shit. Then I got curious. I took my earbuds out and put them in Jordan's ears. A smile grew on his face, and he nodded.

I didn't have to tell him anything more. Over the course of a couple of hours, he took my footage, cut it, moved it around, and then downloaded "Apology" and added it to what he had. As we watched it together, a weight lifted from me. It was as if what I'd been feeling wasn't secret—it was right here.With each shot, the music intensified. Each frame built an incredible nerve of war and drama. Then the screen went black. The images had ended as the song went on. I could see the possibilities, though. Jordan said what I was thinking: "You need more footage."

I nodded. This could be something really interesting.

Right then and there I ate my croissant. It tasted particularly great. I was hungry.

The next day, the LT didn't show up at formation. Another LT addressed us and said our LT had the flu and we'd get the day off today, considering how we'd been working so hard.

After we broke up, I grabbed Jordan and said, "How about we shoot a few things today? I have this cool shot in mind on the test range." He grabbed the people in his Humvee, and I grabbed mine and added Hitch.

Styles was wary. "What do you want to do?"

"Jordan and I are making a movie—putting footage to music."

"For what?"

"I don't know. Just come on."

"All right."

I jumped on the hood of a Humvee. "Hey, guys. I need you all for something quick, full combat gear. A movie I'm making."

Within the hour, I lined them up on the test range. Everyone was side-by-side, ready to shoot with their assault rifles. "Please don't put in any ammunition, and please do not pull the trigger," I told them. "I'm going to walk in front of you with my camera low. You'll just stare straight ahead as if I were invisible. Don't look at me. I just want a shot from the front." I didn't tell them I was really borrowing a tracking shot from Kubrick's *Paths of Glory*, his World War One film from the trenches.

I started my shot on Hoogerheide, her round face moving to look down the barrel of her gun. I slowly sailed down the line of soldiers, including Hitch with his sniper's rifle, and ended on Jordan's gunner, Kayla Helwani, wisps of her dark hair like ballerinas dancing from under her helmet in the breeze, her eyes, twin blue planets. I held on her for a moment.

Missouri, November 2005

Standing…I was standing…on a snowy ledge. High up at sunset. Winter in New York. Chrysler Building over there. An older woman shouted something from a nearby window. I didn't feel good. I looked down, and far below on the street, people stared at me with their mouths frozen. I felt younger, like I was in high school again. I didn't play my guitar well enough. I wasn't worthy. I looked away to the sky. The setting sun painted pink the wisps of clouds, and far opposite, the full moon rose—beautiful. Soon a sense of peace overcame me. A perfect time to go. The sounds of a song and the words "teenage wasteland" echoed past every skyscraper until it overtook my body. Just as a dot in the distance, deep in the sky, began to grow, the bricks under my feet began to jiggle. The song became louder, and the dot grew larger until it was a jet. It zoomed toward me, and I lost my footing. I fell and tumbled in the air.

I woke up in the near dark, shivering as the charter bus bounced. In the chilly air, the song "Baba O'Reilly" by the Who played in my earbuds, and I pulled the nubs out. None of the Army recruits in front of me moved or talked, as if they were frozen corpses. Must be sleeping. Outside appeared to be a black, foggy winterland. Where was I? Wasn't the nightmare over?

Next to me, a voice said, "You're awake."

I turned toward the person in the next seat, a young guy who hadn't been there before.

"I'm Whit Hitchcock. From Houston," he said, holding out his hand.

It took me a few seconds to realize I should shake it. In a dark hoodie, he looked as if he were in middle school.

"I'm Max Rivera. Orlando."

"Orlando—Disneyland!"

"Disney World, actually, but fuck that place."

"Y'all don't know what you got till it's gone," he said in a drawl. Definitely he was a Texan. "Nice to meet you, Max."

"Nice to meet you, too, Whit."

The bus lurched and came to a stop. Bright flood lights poured on outside the bus, betraying a flat, icy landscape with trees and white wooden bungalows. "Whoa. Army base," said my seatmate. That's how I met Hitch, as we arrived in Fort Leonard Wood on the bus for our first day of basic training.

"Firsts" are important moments in our lives—our first love, our first favorite band, our first day of high school. I've kept going back to my "firsts" in the Army, particularly my first encounters with Hitch and Styles. Nowadays, I focus like a dog nosing scents on these firsts, in no particular order, hoping I can find reason to why things arrowed off.

The driver clicked on the interior lights. He opened the door and started to exit. He peeked up from the little stairway and said, "Welcome to hell." I took it as humorous rather than something to worry about. I shouldn't have.

Although the lights were not particularly bright, it was enough to wake up at least some of the people. The black guy across the aisle from us had earbuds in his head, which made me wonder what music he fell asleep to.

Now with the light, Hitch's black hoodie showed, in huge white letters, the words, "Pray for the Soul of Betty." I knew of the hard-rock band—the band of *American Idol* heartthrob Constantine Maroulis, who younger kids liked. In fact, this kid Hitchcock was so baby-faced, I wondered and said, "You eighteen?"

"Yeah, just turned. You?"

"Twenty. So you like that band?" I pointed to his sweatshirt.

"Totally, Dog."

Everyone around me turned toward the windows on the right side of the bus. Their faces looked uncertain. Out of nowhere, six silhouetted figures with their flat shadow hats moved like sharks toward our bus and two other buses that had pulled in behind us.

As they got closer, we could see their faces. The one in the lead looked tall, black, and mean. He grimaced, and his teeth looked as square and big as bathroom tiles. I said, "Sure hope he's not our drill sergeant."

"Yeah," said Hitch. "Look at those eyes, like coal."

That's who stepped first on our bus, our point of no return. Some eager beaver recruit at the front already had his duffle over his shoulder and was ready to step outside. The drill sergeant grabbed him by the lapels and literally threw him down the stairs, only saved by another drill sergeant who caught him. Next was the black dude who had his earbuds still in his ears, smiling, apparently missing what just happened. The drill sergeant yanked the earbuds out of the kid's ears, grabbed his iPod, stepped to the door and threw the two things as far as he could toward the dark woods.

"Read the memos!" yelled the man, who we'd come to know as Drill Sergeant Starwood. "No music devices, no cell phones, no gizmos of any sort in basic training. Any found will be thrown away."

I slipped my iPod deep into my pocket and would hide it later.

"All right, recruits," the drill sergeant now yelled. "Let's move out!" We thundered out of the buses, crashed our duffle bags into a single pile directed by another drill sergeant, and gathered as a group on the icy ground as the uniformed men circled us as if in a shark attack.

They screamed at us as if we'd entered a maximum security prison. It was a long night before we got our uniforms, our 30-second haircuts, and bed.

| | | |

We awoke at five a.m. to reveille, a trumpet call, our wake-up song. Drill Sergeant Starwood stood in his flat-brimmed hat and his crisp, well-fitting uniform, with two assistants to his side. He shouted, "You flabby asses, get out of bed *now* and stand at atten*shun*. The last one out has to do pushups until I get tired."

We all stood at attention in seconds in our underwear. The room was so quiet, I heard rain, and it was fucking cold—maybe fifty. I shivered immediately. This was not like a scene from a 1950s movie, all white guys and maybe one black. We were a huge mixture of races with whites in the minority. Our ages ranged from eighteen to probably twenty-eight. Plenty of shitty tattoos were displayed as if both the wearer and the tattoo artist were drunk at the time. I could draw better peeing in the snow. My tattoos, such as a skeleton rising from a cemetery, reflected how I felt at the time after my band crashed.

One guy, who happened to sit near me on the bus and must have had indigestion because he'd been farting all the time, looked Alaskan Eskimo, and he was the last out of bed. Admittedly, he was on the pudgy side. The drill sergeant stomped over as if the guy had given him the finger. "What's your name, asshole?"

"Unicompt, Drill Sergeant."

"Are you calling me an unkempt drill sergeant?"

"No, Drill Sergeant. My last name is Unicompt."

"All right, Unicorn. Maybe you had a hard-on this morning and didn't want to embarrass yourself with your unicorn horn, but that made you late. Do pushups for me right here until Mary, mother of God, relieves you herself."

"Yes, Drill Sergeant!" and the fat kid immediately fell to a doggie position then put out his legs for pushups. Unicompt reminded me of me in junior high with a sway-backed pushup, his stomach hitting the ground before his chin.

"You are so blubbery and worthless that even as I speak, your parents are packing their trash and leaving town with no forwarding address. They don't want to see your fat fucking face again. The night after you left, they threw a big ass party. I was invited, but I had to stay here to make sure you didn't fuck up my Army."

While Unicompt continued his pushups, Drill Sergeant Starwood turned to us, and it was then that I realized the rain wasn't outside—too cold for that. The showers were on. "Girls," he said. "Welcome to the *terror* dome. Today starts your PT, your physical training. I'm going to PT you until your fricken little hearts burst. I am going to kill you… rebirth you… and kill you again."

He walked, smashing his boots on the floor to make as loud a sound as he could, glaring at each of us as he walked by. He stopped in front of me, glared at me. "What're you looking at, private?" he asked me.

"You, Drill Sergeant."

"Why?"

"Nowhere else to look, Drill Sergeant."

He smiled. "Fucking right. This soldier has it right. When I'm here, there is nowhere else to look." He walked on. "Now I am going to have you run through the showers, and when I say run through them, I mean walk fast. Don't slip. You slip and crack your head, well, goddamn, don't do me any fuckin' favors. Take off your underwear and zip into the showers—including you, Unicorn."

We made a naked single-file line into the showers. I was at the front. Four showers were running. Beside the first and third shower stood a uniformed sergeant with a large pump bottle. "Go!" shouted Drill Sergeant Starwood coming to the front of the line. I rushed in. The first shower was fucking *cold*. It felt like snowmelt, and I screamed. The man there slapped something on my head, and he yelled, "Lather!" I now understood it was shampoo, and I lathered. "Rinse in the next!" he yelled. I dashed into the next showerhead, which was blessedly hot but quickly it felt too hot, and the water became needles. Screaming again, I rinsed as fast as I could, and for a second, it felt as if I couldn't get enough air. This all blindsided me.

The next shower, fucking cold again, a man grabbed my hand and squirted something in it. "Your body!" he yelled. I lathered my body. I had to rinse under the fourth head, screamingly hot again. Drill Sergeant Starwood shouted, "I don't want to hear *screaming*, you girlie men. I want to hear the fucking Army song. Start *singing*." It was a song we were supposed to learn before arriving at camp.

"March along, sing our song, with the Army of the free," I chanted with the others, telling myself to hang in. Somehow I hadn't expected marching to be so painful. Around the next corner, a sergeant handed me a white towel. As I sang, I kept thinking to myself, "This is what I wanted. I will be better for it."

As the room filled with steam and screams, we continued singing. "Then it's Hi! Hi! Hey! The Army's on its way."

We continued back to our bunks, dressed, and kept singing: "For wherever we go, you will always know, the Army keeps rolling along." When we finished, Drill Sergeant Starwood said nothing. He walked among us standing at attention by our foot lockers, giving us the evil eye, until he shouted for us to hurry outside—where it was fucking cold again.

The sun had not risen yet, so floodlights on the buildings gave us long and deep shadows on the icy ground. We also practiced how to salute, how to stand at attention, and stand at parade rest. I could tell we were in the beginning stages of becoming robots. The sergeant marched us into a building with a red cross on it.

"Shit, we're going to get shots," Hitchcock whispered in line behind me.

My heart pounded. I hated shots. "Okay," I whispered back.

"Vaccinations," Hitch stressed the way someone might say "hellfire."

Someone behind me said a little louder, "No, thank you," but the drill sergeant didn't hear it.

Hitch whispered to me, "Haven't you heard vaccinations can make you stupid? I'm dumb enough as it is. I don't want no vaccinations."

"Do you want to ask if you have a choice?"

"I'm not good at pushups."

The drill sergeant yelled, "Next!"

Once inside, we faced a number of soldiers armed with hypodermic needles. Behind them were signs with the alphabet split up, A-D, E-H, etc.

An assistant drill said, "Get in the line appropriate for your last name. If your name is Unicorn, then you'd be in the S through V line."

When it was my turn, I sat and gave my last name. The medic, who looked younger than me, found my chart and gave me three shots, for flu and two other things.

Drill Sergeant Starwood stormed in, saying, "Who's the fucking soldier who said *no, thank you?*"

Everyone froze, but it wasn't long until a lone voice said, "I did, Drill Sergeant." It was a white guy to my left with blond stubble for hair. He apparently refused to sit for his shots. I'd noticed him on the bus in a polo shirt and leather jacket and could picture him behind the tiller of a sailboat. What was he doing here?

Starwood stomped over to him. "What's your name, soldier?"

"Blake Styles," he said.

"I think I'll call you Styleless," said the man. "Anyone ever call you that?"

"Only pot smokers, Drill Sergeant."

"You think I smoke pot, do you?"

"No, Drill Sergeant."

"And why don't you want to take your vaccinations?"

"Seventh-Day Adventist, Drill Sergeant."

"Well, this is the fucking eighth day, so you'll either take the shots or take a dishonorable discharge. I am not compromising the health of my unit. There are diseases over there we have to prevent catching. Do you understand?"

"Yes, Drill Sergeant."

"My stepfather was Seventh Day Adventist. You believe in one body. The human body serves as the perfect metaphor for the people of God on Earth. I believe that, too. The Army is one body, and that body needs to be vaccinated. You will take your vaccinations now."

"Yes, Drill Sergeant."

Starwood looked surprised, then he nodded.

"Very good, Private Styles. You may go far."

Starwood exited with no further ado. No pushups required. I looked at this Styles guy, amazed.

A moment later, I heard something akin to a bag of dirt hitting the floor. It was Unicompt, passed out on the ground. The medic, with his thumb still on a hypodermic, looked to the assistant drill. "He fainted, Sergeant."

| | | |

After the vaccinations that second day, we entered the mess hall, one big room with a buffet line. We couldn't say a word. Servers scooped the same food on metal plates: eggs, bacon, toast, and hash browns. For drinks, there was fucking milk, fucking OJ, fucking grape juice, and water. We were required to drink at least one juice and one water to stay hydrated through the day. For food, they did not skimp. These calories were to be muscles.

After we grabbed our food, I spotted Styles. Hitchcock and I sat down next to him. We filled up tables in order, so that was just lucky.

"Whit Hitchcock," said Hitchcock, whispering, holding out his hand. As privates, we weren't supposed to talk in the chow hall, but we were at the far end, away from where officers sat, and could talk. Styles shook Hitch's hand and whispered, "Blake Styles."

"I'm Max Rivera. That was brave of you." I shook his hand.

"It's not bravery. I can't stand fucking needles to save my life."

We all shared a quiet laugh.

"So you don't mind now?" whispered Hitchcock. "I thought no shots were part of your religion."

"I'm going to take a lot of shit for the next nine weeks, so I may as well go for the whole enchilada. Besides, he made a good point about one body. Also..." He bent his head down and whispered, "I'm not a strong believer in God. Shit. Take a look around you sometime, and you'll figure it out."

We learned he was married with a kid, and once out of basic, his family would join him in married soldier housing. "Until then, I'm a barracks dude with you fuckers," he said, giving that grin of his. I couldn't help but like the guy. Everything he said just made sense.

Right from then, Styles, Hitch, and I did a lot of stuff together. We watched out for each other. The weeks passed quickly, every day something new catching us off-guard, such as learning about grenades in the grenade pits, falling in the obstacle courses, trying new running drills. I later realized that's part of the training. Hell, that's the way life is.

| | | |

After breakfast and outside again, with the sun up but low on the horizon, we learned about formation. Formation was not like the lines in elementary school where you just stood in the first available space. The first and second lieutenants had their spots to the sides and backs. If there were higher-ranking officers, they were behind them. Each one of us, according to our jobs, stood still in a particular place like wax figures—and it was only ten degrees above zero. We were freezing, trying not to show it. Drill Sergeant Starwood stood before us and said, "Unicorn is out. We learned he has a history of fainting, which he forgot to tell his recruiter. We can't have fucking fainters. This Army is for fighters. Are you fighters?"

"Yes, Drill Sergeant," we yelled.

"Today you're going to learn to march. Before we do, I have a new marching song for you. After I say each line, you reply with the word 'Zero' and then a number. We'll start with *zero one*, then go to *zero two*. Got it?"

"Yes, Drill Sergeant."

He then sang out, "We are marching."

"Zero one."

"For Private Unicorn."

"Zero two."

"Because he's a pussy."

"Zero three."

"A big pink pussy"

"Zero four."

"Pussy pussy pussy."

"Zero five."

A long covered truck pulled up, the kind to haul horses.

"All right men," said Drill Sergeant Starwood. "We're now going to the marching field, but the road is rather icy, so you get this nice little truck. When I say it's little, it is. You have to fucking jam yourselves in. I'm going to ride with my assistants in a Cadillac. Too bad it's not pink in honor of Private Unicorn."

With our backpacks and rifles, we crowded into the truck more than shoulder-to-shoulder. I could feel the weight of people against me and smell their hashbrown breath. The inside was all scratched wood, the kind of cheap, aged, beaten-up wood that might come from Holocaust trains. Our breath froze in the air, so the place had a foggy quality to it, showing the beams of light through the few slits in the side. The truck drove, slipping here and there on the ice. We came to call the truck the cattle car. We were meat on ice.

We marched on the field. We marched down roads. We marched until I just wasn't thinking about marching, and my fingers froze and felt like hammers on the end, with sharp prickles deeper down. Marching was about endurance. In battle, you needed inner and outer strength to make it though. This I figured out later. That first day, where we hiked probably over twenty miles, we sang what the sergeant called cadences. We'd repeat what he barked out.

If I die in a combat zone,
Box me up and ship me home.

Put me in a set of dress blues,
Comb my hair, and shine my shoes.
Pin my medals upon my chest,
Tell my mama I did my best.

When we marched and didn't sing, I thought of Sophie. I thought about the night before when we'd been given our uniforms, and I'd gone through my pockets of my civilian clothes. I came across a folded slip of paper with a flower drawn on it. Sophie must have slipped it into my pants as I left. It said, "Love you, Max. Save the world! Love, Sophie."

Shit, I'd meant to call her at the Burger King in Mississippi. I knew soon, though, we'd get to use the phones to call home to say we were fine. I'd call Sophie then.

After the morning PT, we stood in three long lines in front of pay-phones in a breezeway between the barracks and where the sergeants had their offices. Snow had been cleared off the walk, but the frigid air bit into us. The sergeant told us to call home to tell our loved ones we were fine. "It's the only call you'll get to make for six weeks. Have your phone cards or money ready. You get just two minutes. Talk fast. Say you love your sergeant. Over the next weeks, you can send and receive mail. Otherwise you're your ass belongs to the Green Mean Machine." I hated such cheesy lines.

When it was my turn, I punched in the number for Sophie, though I couldn't feel the buttons as my fingers were so cold and numb. Her phone rang.

"Hello?" said Sophie's mother.

"Hi, Mrs. Kershaw," I said, "It's me, Max. Is Sophie in?"

"I thought you were off."

"I am. I only get two minutes for a phone call, so I was hoping Sophie was in."

"She's not. She's off early to try out for some band."

That was odd. She'd showed no interest in playing music before. "Playing what?"

"Singing, she said."

She sang? "What about her college?" I asked.

"Well, you know Sophie."

"Yeah. Can you tell her I called?"

"Yes."

"And I love her?"

"That's a question?"

"No, it's my feelings for you to tell her. Can you tell her?"

"Enjoy the Army, Max." From her tone, I realized she didn't like me. She hung up. Bitch.

I had part of a minute left. I turned around to see the long line of freezing recruits behind me. I quickly started pushing in the number for my mom. The sergeant standing next to the phone who had a stopwatch took away the handset. "You only get one call," he said, and thumbed me away, saying "Next" to the next person.

At the end of our first day of basic and all that marching, I wasn't sore or complaining like some of the others. If anything, I was feeling angry—not at the Army but at my previous life. The marching let me see things in a way I never had before. It was like I was watching a movie of me.

I headed back to the barracks, realizing I'd just have to write Sophie, my mother, and my father each. The snow crunched under my boots in a rhythm, singing to me like a cadence of worry, "Uh-oh, Uh-oh."

That night after everyone was sleeping, I pulled my iPod out from my pillow, and I stuck in the earbuds. The music was Santana, warm and inviting, as I imagined myself as a little kid again dancing with my mother. I only listened to two songs as I didn't want to fall asleep with them on. I then slipped the iPod into a sheet flap I'd found in one of the hospital corners.

| | | |

Styles soon became the guy in the bunk bed below me, and a few nights later, just before lights out when everyone was getting ready, someone said he thought we'd get our first pugil stick training in the morning. I asked Styles, "What the hell's a pugil stick?"

"It's a big padded stick for bayonet and rifle-butt training—close-contact stuff."

"You ever use one?"

"Hell no. We'll probably have to fight each other with them, like on *American Gladiators*."

"Shit."

"You notice how each day here is new?" He told me that a first time for anything essentially "threw us." Something can be so new that it'll throw you off your usual state of being, such as traveling to a new country for the first time. You're in the moment, seeing everything, hearing everything, trying to process it all. "You are present in the moment."

"I'm always present," I told him.

"No, you're not. In the last few minutes you probably worried about what's next—or thinking about your parents."

"Nope. Neither."

"Or your girlfriend."

Shit. I was. Sophie. Couldn't help it.

"The only way we can truly live is to be in the present."

"Not sure I want to be in this present," I said. Only later would I realize that Fort Lost-in-the-Woods in retrospect wasn't so bad—far better than Iraq was.

"What's wrong with thinking about good things?" I said.

"Nothing," he said, "but are you living?"

"I am when I'm playing music," I said. "I'm there. Playing. In the moment." And it was true. I'd never think about bills that had to be paid or what someone said to me last week or even my girlfriend. I was there for that song—for each note that slipped from my fingers and voice.

Styles smiled. "Same here, man."

In that moment, I knew we were brothers. Months and many battles later, I'd see him looking lost, helpless, stuck somewhere in his head. It's as if he didn't know how to take his own advice.

| | | |

My days in basic became routine quickly. We did a lot of physical training each morning, not only marching and performing sit-ups, pull-ups, scaling walls, learning marksmanship, rushing through obstacle courses, and snaking our way on our bellies under barbed wire. It was as if we were running on a treadmill twenty-three-and-a-half hours a day. One early morning we had to attach our bayonets to our rifles, and we charged at rubber men, screaming, yelling slurs, and stabbing them. All the high energy made me feel as if I were in a movie, and we acted brilliantly, some guys even spitting on the dummies. The few women in our platoon hung in there—a lot more rugged than I expected. It didn't make them dainty, but I wasn't dating them. They were warriors like the rest of us.

In the afternoons came the classes. There we learned first aid, gas mask use, rules of engagement, army core values, and our way around a map. The only thing that particularly came through in the classes for me were the many different videos of 9/11, made like infomercials, where we were reminded time and again that America had been attacked, and we were the Army, defending America. At the time, I accepted it, but it was like a scratch I kept itching. The terrorists on the planes were from Saudi Arabia, not Iraq or Afghanistan. The reason for going into Iraq, the weapons of mass destruction, never existed. Of course, this didn't come up in any army classes. We were in Iraq, ostensibly, to give Iraqis freedom.

In boot camp, we didn't get a lot of free time, and when we did, most people wrote letters—old-fashioned snail mail, the only form of communication we were allowed. I wrote Sophie most days. She wrote me back once a week in her block printing, telling me she was proud I was doing what

I wanted, then going on about what one girlfriend or another was doing. I wrote her the most when I was on fire guard. Each night, we'd take turns of an hour each to stay up and not just guard those who were sleeping, but also do some cleaning. I'd have to do it every two or three nights. Mopping would take about a half hour, and then I'd have a half hour to just stay awake, which could seem like hours. Some guys would go to the can and jerk off, the one and only moment of the day for privacy. I would write Sophie, give her the details of what I was up to, tell her my thoughts, until the next shift of fire guard would take over. Between thoughts of her and the music I secretly listened to at night on the iPod I kept hidden, I made it through the days. Music and love can take you through a lot of shit.

Before I knew it, it had been nine weeks. I felt trimmer and more in shape. I could run my mile in six minutes now.

On the last day of our basic training, we were given the afternoon off because the sergeant said we had one final test, which would happen that night. I didn't like the joy in his voice when he said it. He probably had some new, horrible way to humiliate us. He didn't tell us what the test would be, other than we had to be fully dressed for combat with our rifles and rucksacks. A bunch of us hung around the breezeway, chatting and joking. I knew Styles wrote his wife. Hitch read a comic book.

The test turned out to be a fifteen-mile hike to a night-time obstacle course with live rounds fired over our heads. When we reached the end of the course, stadium lights turned on to cheers in the stands. Soon we were surrounded by friends and family who came to support us on our final night. Both my parents came, hugged me, and my father looked at me in a way he never had before—very impressed with me.

Afterward, on the way to the barracks, we soldiers also got to make a phone call. I couldn't have been happier. Sophie answered on the first ring. I thought I heard some man laughing in the background.

"Max," she said right away. "I miss you. How are you?"

"Good—I miss you, too," I said. "Who's that with you?"

"The TV? Did you graduate?"

"No, not yet. Tomorrow." I thought I heard a man tell her something. "That's not the TV. Who's there?"

"Oh, that. It's the funniest thing," she said. "One of the guys I sold a ticket to a while back knew my name. I asked how he knew because I didn't have my nametag on, and he said he was a friend of yours."

I tried to guess which friend. I didn't really have any left after my band kicked me out. "Which friend?" I asked.

"Ralph," she said. "He seems like a really nice guy. He asked me to try out singing for his band, and I did. I sang in a paid gig for my first time last night. He has only good things to say about you. He misses you, too." Fucking Ralph was the guy who'd taken over my band. We hated each other, and now he was eating at my life again.

"No way," I said. How did he know about Sophie? She had come after the band. "What did he say about me?"

"He says you're a genius at lyrics. He said you both had a huge misunderstanding on the Warped Tour." At that instant, I felt my blood rush to my head. I was so angry. I didn't know how to contain myself, so I blurted, "Sophie, he hates my guts. I can't believe he's there! He's a manipulator. Can you go in another room, at least?" She honestly sounded confused but I didn't care.

"One sec," she said. I heard a door close, then she said, "Are you just jealous or something? He's such a nice guy. I wouldn't have told you about him if I knew you had such strong feelings."

"Are you going out with him?"

"It's not going out. I just sing in his band."

"My former band."

"Don't make a big deal out of it. I'm not sleeping with him, if that's what you think."

"Yet. I know Ralph."

I could picture Ralph playing her like a chess board. He'd done it with my band. He was probably saying how beautiful and brilliant she was. She was only nineteen. She'd eat it up like ice cream. I couldn't get the idea out of my mind of Ralph slowly pushing Sophie's head down on his cock while he praised her.

"What do you talk about?" I asked.

"We talk about you. We're both proud."

I could hear the door open, and then his voice in the background said, "Hey, man, you've got a great girl. Don't you see that I care?"

The last line, "Don't you see that I care," was a quote from one of my songs. The stanza ends with "that we make a good pair." He was telling me he will fuck her. I smashed the phone against the side of the box.

In the breezeway at that very moment, as if the stars lined up for this to happen, the captain of the company came to visit us. Everyone snapped to attention, but I didn't think about why. Sophie said, "What's that noise?"

A soldier yelled, "At ease!"

I quickly turned and shouted, "Shut the fuck up!" and only then did I see the captain.

"Max?" said Sophie.

I didn't respond. I saluted to the captain as if I could make up for my mistake.

"Miss you," said Sophie. I could hear in her voice she was trying to make herself believe it.

I wanted to say somethng so badly to get to the truth. Before I got there, the drill sergeant came over and pushed the receiver down. "Time's up," he said.

Sophie was gone—not just from the call but I knew right then and there I'd lost her to Ralph.

Hitch, standing nearby said, "What? What happened?"

I was so pissed, I could hardly see. I started running—running to I didn't know where, but then when the track came up, I headed there. I ran around it thinking if I could run fast enough, everything would go away. Why does life have to be so fucking hard so often?

I ran around four times before I stopped. I was out of breath. As I came upon the barracks, Hitch and Styles walked toward me.

"Shit," said Styles. "We were just coming to find you. That phone call must have been bad."

"Yeah," I mumbled.

Hitch said, "Like you needed this after our final test."

I told them about Ralph and all that happened. "Sophie'll soon send me a letter about her love for Ralph, and she'll say, 'Sorry about that.' Is God after me?" I asked. "Maybe I've done something horrible in a previous life, and so in this one, he's torturing me."

"I'm more into determinism," said Styles. "From the moment we're born, we set certain things in motion like one of those Rube Goldberg machines where a series of events happen, like marbles falling in a pail, frightening a parrot on a stick that flies off, pulling a string that shoots a gun. You see what I mean?"

I laughed.

"What's he talking about?" Hitch asked me, which made me laugh more.

Styles turned to Hitch. "Let's say a guy talks a girl into sex in the back of a car. She gets pregnant. He freaks out at the news and yells at his boss for some stupid thing, so he loses his job. With his unemployment, she leaves him and becomes an angry single mother who screams at the baby. He grows up feeling unloved. See what I mean?"

"That's called life," said Hitch. "God has his plans."

Maybe the Army would make me an atheist.

We still had ten minutes before 21:00, when it would be lights out and confined to quarters.

Soon we were in bed. As the clock struck the 2100 hour, the drill sergeant yelled, "Good night, privates!"

We said, "Good night, Drill Sergeant," in unison.

With his retreating footsteps, I heard the metallic crack of a beer can opening. Not long after, the lights blasted back on. Many beers appeared from under pillows and from foot lockers. One guy retrieved a beer wrapped in his socks.

Almost everyone was drinking—but there was an absence of women. "No chicks?"said Hitch.

"You know they can't be in our barracks," Styles said.

Hitch handed me a Heineken bottle that someone had given him.

"We're not supposed to drink on base, either," I said, astounded.

"Booze is easier to get in than women," said one guy.

"We learned this is a tradition," said another. "I mean what the fuck can the sergeant do? We're done with basic. He's done with us. This is boosting our morale, right?"

"All right," I said and yelled "Skol" loudly, as if I could get all my anger out of my skin, and I raised my bottle high. My comrades raised their beers and shouted "Skol"—certainly loud enough that the sergeants would probably hear us without their intercom on.

I suppose they knew that boys had to be boys to prepare us for all the shit we'd still have to do, including deployment. Before long, two drunk guys, one short the other tall, faced each other, fists in the air ready to fight, even if they could barely stand.

"She's my girlfriend," the short one babbled, referring most probably to one of the women in our platoon, housed in a different barracks.

"There are no girlfriends in the Army," said the other. "It's free for all."

They punched the air mostly, and the rest of us shouted and laughed because these guys could hardly swing, and they fell often. After they each landed a few punches and looked stunned, the tall one said, "I'm sorry, guy."

"I love you, too, man," and they hugged. We cheered.

Soon someone came up with a game called "ball bowling," where some guy would spread his legs wide, and people took turns bowling unopened beer cans across the room toward his balls. The closest person to reach his balls without hurting him would win. Of course, the fun was in hurting him.

I drank more than I should have over the next hour—call it determinism—and when someone brought in a guitar, I grabbed it and started singing a fast-paced punk rock version of "Yellow" from Coldplay. Normally, a popular band like Coldplay would be too mainstream for me, but after being bombarded enough with their melodic pop and searing guitar riffs, I accepted them as one might a new half-sibling—related enough to count. If nothing else, Coldplay could pull at the heartstrings, and mine needed pulling. I liked Chris Martin's earnestness and emotional truth. "Look at the stars, look how they shine for you," I shouted as I played, and Styles and Hitch raced over and joined in singing. "They were all yellow," we sang in harmony.

Man, our voices were perfect together. We all looked at each other in that instant as if we were the Wright Brothers finding Kitty Hawk. We had talent together.

We got the whole room singing, but it seemed to me that every room on all three floors needed to join in, and I grabbed Hitch and Styles and said, "Follow me!"

"Where?"

From the third floor, we raced downstairs and out the doors to the breezeway, past the phones, and into the building where the drill sergeants had their offices and where the intercom was, in a room by itself. A sergeant was walking by as we ran in, and he yelled, "Hey!" but we locked the door behind us and laughed.

The drill sergeant hammered on the door, shouting, "Back to your room, privates!" and "You men are in trouble!"

I then heard Drill Sergeant Starwood's voice from down the corridor. "Out of there now, privates!"

We laughed. I switched on the intercom and said, "This one's for the man of the hour, Sergeant No-First-Name Starwood. The stars are in this song, Sarge," and I strummed "Yellow" one more time, and the three of us sang. We sang as if our vocal chords were racing to the moon. Singing and cheering roared from all floors of the barracks.

Soon there was multiple hammering on the door and something about court martial, but we just kept singing. We knew they wouldn't court martial us. We were their men.

And as I sang, I could feel the tears run from my eyes because, damn it, Sophie had been the best damn girlfriend ever, and she was gone. My whole reason to be in the Army had just died. I sang, "They were all yellow."

Iraq, June 2007

In morning formation, already over a hundred degrees, our LT told us to stand at ease, and he looked from face to face. We were relaxed, despite the heat. Our presence patrols in Baqubah had been calm recently—no violent activity. In our off-hours, we watched movies, tried out video games, worked out in the gym, played basketball, slept, ate well, and did other things to unwind. In the evening, I often walked the camp, either to make video interviews for Jordan's and my project, or I took still photos of the camp. The only action we saw at this point were new Chuck Norris jokes in the shitter. I added one, taking a black Sharpie out of my pen pocket in my left sleeve. "Big Foot claims he saw Chuck Norris."

The LT strode back and forth at the front of the formation. Recently he received a distinguished service cross for his effective command back in March. "Today is a day you may remember," he said. "It's the first day of what's going to be a new operation. We're calling it Operation Arrowhead Ripper. Why? Because we're now going to shoot pointedly into the heart of Baqubah, the so-called capital of the Islamic state."

A couple of the guys, as if feeling the spirit of a football coach, shouted back, "Yeah!"

"We're going to *rip apart* the Islamic state, starting *today*," said the LT, raising his voice.

More shouts of support erupted, camaraderie building with every word he spoke.

The LT looked me right in the eyes. I nodded. He continued, "For the last two months, our fighting in Baqubah has had a positive effect. The Islamic State has been killing fewer citizens who don't bend to their wishes, and we've seen the marketplace come back. People feel freer. You may have noticed the difference."

We nodded.

"The command has been asking for more support, and we finally have it. Last night, the Third Stryker Brigade Combat Team, Second Infantry Division, along with members of the 1-505th 82nd Airborne Division, launched an offensive with a night-time air assault. Today, we're going to support the 1-12 Cav as they rush in. We're now part of the surge, and we hope to clear out the insurgents in Baqubah in short order. Any questions?"

None of us had any. We had been expecting the shit to get worse—even talked about it for a while. In fact, I got onto the subject the night before with Styles around a campfire he'd made at the edge of our CHU city. I'd caught him staring into the dark night as if he could see something. The cloud cover made everything black.

"Hey," I'd said.

He only nodded back. His isolation didn't seem unusual. For days, soldiers were all in their own spaces, and time seemed slower. It was as if we all knew what was coming. We knew we'd probably lose people in this operation. I sat down with him and stared off into the void, too. I didn't see what Styles saw.

"Did I ever tell you about the birth of my daughter?" he said, not looking at me.

"You mentioned it—I guess not really."

"Five years ago in New York City exactly on nine-eleven."

"Holy shit," said Hitch.

"Ann's water broke early in the morning—during rush hour, of course. I called our doctor, who was going to meet us at the Jersey City Medical Center, just on the other side of the Holland Tunnel. Not far away."

He paused, and we both stared at the fire, at the mini-vortex right in the center consuming the wood and sending black smoke to join the darkness.

"Well, once we hit the Avenue of the Americas, traffic absolutely stopped. Ann grit her teeth in a contraction. We didn't want the baby to come out in the car. We had to get through the tunnel, but traffic didn't move. Out on the sidewalks, a lot of people scurried all in the same direction toward lower Manhattan. I opened up my VW's window to talk to the couple on the sidewalk pushing the baby carriage. 'What's going on?'

I said. 'A parade this early?' 'No. The towers are on fire, didn't you hear?' said the woman, pointing behind us. I could now see a coil of thick, black smoke above."

"My God," I said.

"We were stuck—tunnels and bridges were closed—and Ann started going into labor. Cell phones didn't work because the circuits were overloaded. Luckily, I found a nurse a few cars down, trying to get to work. We moved to her car, a Volvo. We needed to drown out the chaos around us. The radio had mostly news, but we found a classical station. Our little girl was born to Beethoven and arrived just as the dust from the falling towers rolled over us like a tsunami."

"You came to Iraq because of nine-eleven?"

"Partly... I got laid off from my firefighter job—had no degree and my unemployment was coming to an end. Ann's job at a copy shop didn't cut it."

Beyond the campfire, a huge explosion came from the distance like thunder, but we couldn't see anything.

"Some shit's happening," he said, "The bombs are getting closer."

"Yeah." I rubbed my neck to avoid thinking about it.

"If I die, will you tell my wife and daughter I love them?" said Styles.

"We haven't lost anyone for a while," I said.

"It's only a matter of time."

As we prepared to move out for the operation, the LT assigned Styles as our gunner, and I drove with the LT next to me. I'd become his regular driver again, sensing that the LT surmised that lightning didn't strike twice in the same spot. Mohamed, our new translator, replaced Hoogerheide in the back. He had a dark face and easy smile. Before we left, I stepped out to talk with Styles, closing the door so the others wouldn't hear.

"You want to drive, and I can be the gunner?" I asked. "I'm sure it'll be okay with the LT."

"Drive?" he said.

"Yeah."

He paused as if it were some strange math calculation, multiplying destiny times action, reducing belief, dividing by pi.

"I'm fine as gunner—going with the flow."

"The flow works fine inside, too."

"Thanks, but I'm looking out for you, bro."

"I could say the same."

"I'm fine."

So I drove. I felt tense, as if I could guess the stars as well as he, and I worried. Was that scrap of paper on the road covering an IED? What about that stain on the asphalt? Pockmarks in the road showed where previous IEDs had blown up.

Once we got into town, I felt jumpy. Because we were in civilian traffic, IEDs were less likely, but many people's eyes were on us as if they were plotting. I followed a polluting, beat-up Corolla, white with a red door. The door must have been a junkyard replacement. Most of Iraq, you ask me, was like this car, abused but somehow moving.

At a stoplight, with people crossing the street, a loud bang came from the car—gunfire? The next few seconds changed everything. Styles tore into the vehicle with his .50 caliber gun rattling, cutting up the car and driver and passengers, red mist spraying the windshield before the glass burst apart. The people in the street danced as if they could miss the bullets and somehow did. The moment Styles stopped, the LT opened his door, and so did Mohamed. The people on the street shouted at us, pointing at the victim.

I jumped out, too, asking Styles, "Are you okay?"

"I didn't get hit," he said, looking shaken.

An Iraqi man in a white caftan strode purposely at us, shouting, unafraid, waving his finger at Styles. Mohamed came up, trying to calm the man down in his native tongue.

Meanwhile, Jordan, Hitch, and Yanni, who had been in the Humvee behind us, came running with their guns drawn, ready to protect us from what seemed to be a growing angry mob.

"What happened?" said Hitch before he got to us.

"Someone shot at us," I said.

"No," said Mohamed. "The man's car backfired. The fuckin' thing's old. These people want to know why we killed him."

"A backfire?" I said, now realizing what I'd seen.

"I didn't know," said Styles in a near whisper.

"Killed him, his wife and baby," said Mohamed.

"A baby?" said Styles, shaking, white.

"The cousin in the back seat is still alive." Some people pulled the young man out to his anguished screams and cries. With is face covered in blood, his chin looked to have a wound.

I walked closer to the car and could see the bloody baby carrier against the front seat. At least one bullet must have ricocheted to get it. The screaming in a language I didn't know grew and became oppressive white noise.

The LT came over. "Hey, guys, guns down. Don't make this worse." He turned to Mohamed. "Is everyone saying it's a backfire?"

"Most of them. They know the family. That old man there is saying, 'You don't care about us, only oil.' The man next to him is saying, 'The liberators are now our oppressors.' A woman over there is saying 'Americans hate Sunnis, and we should kill the Americans.'"

Everyone around us shouted and looked as if they'd murder us if they could. We were no longer the Army men pulling down the Saddam statue. I saw us through Iraqi eyes, our fingers on our guns, our sunglasses or goggles shielding our eyes, our ACUs with flak jackets, extra ammo, kneepads, thick boots. We looked like invaders.

"Tell them it's an accident. It sounded like gunfire," the LT said earnestly.

"Really?" asked Mohamed.

He turned to Styles. "I know it was a mistake, but this is just terrible."

"I'm sorry," said Styles. His face looked drained of blood.

"Get down from there. Hoogerheide will replace you. Jesus. We're going to be late for our mission." The whole convoy stopped while the LT radioed for the blades to come take away the car and the remains of the three people. Someone would fix this.

"What will be done of this?" said Mohamed, after listening to a few people. The LT was about to speak into his radio.

"I don't know," said the LT. "Tell them some people are coming. Say it's tragic, and we feel horrible. Say we're only trying to do good. This man's family will be compensated."

"You have this authority?" said Mohamed.

"A specialist coming down will have it." He turned to us. "Now let's move!"

What about Styles? I thought. Styles looked like he'd died on his feet. The lights in his eyes had gone black. "LT?" I asked.

"No time!" shouted the LT. "Get Styles moving."

What had I expected? The LT was really a kid like me, but he'd gone to college—and not in psychology.

We drove off.

Perhaps because we were late, we were assigned the far edge of a neighborhood where we created check points and stopped and searched people coming and going. Always Iraqis gave us suspicious eyes and attitudes. I now felt like we were the bad guys.

When idle, I shot video from where I stood. My first recording centered on Hoogerheide and Styles checking a young couple as tanks approached. Styles appeared tentative, as if he might do the wrong thing again, and that seemed to make the young man suspicious. Helicopters flew overhead. A dust cloud of Bradleys, Strykers, and other assorted trucks blew in. We were the surge. We were dying for them—didn't the Iraqis understand that? If we hadn't volunteered, we could have continued shopping at Krogers, bought furniture through Craigslist, and hooked up with girl-friends. We'd come here to help you. Had everyone forgotten Saddam? If you were Kurd, he would gas you. If you were Shiite, maybe he'd round up your household and torture you all. If he wanted to disappear you, you were gone. You should shout, "Thank God for the U.S."

Next, without thinking, I trained my camera on the sun through the trees on a single neighborhood street. Tan seven-foot block walls stood on either side of the dirt road, but huge branches of old-growth trees hung over those walls as if on the other side grew the Garden of Eden. A gentle breeze made the sun sparkle through the boughs. Sometimes something so beautiful just made me wonder—especially after what happened with Styles shooting up that family.

On the ride back to camp, I couldn't help but see beauty hiding every-where, like a Jackson Pollock painting: chaos but oh so wonderful.

That night, Jordan took my new footage and edited it with some of what we had had previously. I had also started doing interviews. I'd con-vinced Hoogerheide to be my first. On the monitor, in a steady tripod shot, looking slightly off screen at me, she said, "There's a notion that women can do anything in the Army except fight on the front lines. I fight on the front lines now. Something like fifteen percent of military police in War-horse are women. We received the same full training. Sure I'm short, but even before training, I could have probably taken out many of the guys."

"I'm sure you could," I said off-camera.

"Those of us here, we're the best. Women, too."

The screen cut to Hoogerheide running, crouching low, shooting—at which point the movie stopped, and Jordan gave a satisfied laugh. So what do you think?"

"Yeah," I said in our CHU, "but it doesn't really have a story yet, does it?"

"That's the way documentaries work," he said. "You just shoot a lot, but then you start focusing on certain people like Hoogerheide. She's kind of like a fox, don't you think? I'm not saying sexy, though there's some-thing there. I'm saying she's compact, fast, and sly. She's smart."

"Yeah, but not my type," I said.

"She doesn't have a waist or much in the tit department," said Hitch from the corner of the CHU. "But she has a cute face."

Hitch pulled out some drumsticks under his pillow. Recently, he'd started drumming on his legs as he listened to music. His mother had sent him the drumsticks and said she'd ship him a couple of his drums.

"She's like one of the guys," I said.

"She's still a girl," Hitch said with a smile. He was in the corner because that's where he liked to beat off, as if we wouldn't notice. What most women didn't understand about guys is that the need, the itch, the absolute desire for sex could become so overwhelming, we could barely think. Hitch told me a sniper buddy on one of his roofs had been going nuts in a sandstorm, pulled down his pants, and jerked off to the facing apartment building as if not concerned about being shot. Sex above safety. The desire needed to be addressed. There was a calm that arrived with ejaculation, too. How this was a great design for human beings, I didn't know, but then again, maybe that's why the earth had over six and a half billion people. What Hitch was saying was that Hoogerheide appeared to be a good option for his becoming calm.

Women didn't seem as driven that way, but from what I'd seen in Iraq, getting shot at changed a lot of things. The women's three-man CHUs often had that: three men with the three women. There were few virgins in Warhorse.

| | | |

Just before sunset, Jordan worked on his great new inventtion: the water balloon catapult. Weeks earlier, our CHU street, Baltic Avenue, took on another CHU street, St. James Place, in a game of our making—Water Fight. As I think back, God knows why we played a kind of war to avoid our thoughts of war, but getting wet in that way was a whole lot of fun, and getting the girls' T-shirts wet had other benefits, particularly if they purposely didn't wear bras. Jordan made a catapult that threw farther than any of us could throw. "My wife sent me the kind of giant rubber band I needed," Jordan said, showing off his latest improvement.

We gathered near sunset for a skirmish with the thermometer pushing over 120 degrees. We brought ten people, they arrived with ten people, and each side had a load of filled multicolored water balloons in cardboard boxes on a red Radio Flyer wagon. Jordan loaded up his catapult as he kneeled on the gravel expanse that stood between two CHU villages. We even had a small audience, guys and gals who sat in blow-up kiddy pools on top of their flat-roofed CHUs. Our opposing force was at least a hundred yards away in their dusty end of the space. It was like we were in the Old West at the O.K. Corral, ready for the shootout.

"Let the games begin!" shouted Jordan, letting loose his catapult. His bomb went far higher than I'd seen any go before. He didn't have his aim right, and it veered over into the CHUs, coming down hard onto the edge of a kiddy pool. For some reason, the force was enough to make the puffy pool burst, and the two guys in it fell out. The water drained over the edge, to shouts of delight.

"Charge!" a soldier shouted.

We ran toward our enemy like warriors in *Braveheart*, all of us armed with multiple balloons, as the other side did the same thing toward us, all of us shouting "Errr" or some other Viking-like sound. We threw balloons, hitting our targets, laughing, cheering, getting wet, reloading from the wagons. The catapults on each side zeroed in on the mass of people, hitting their own soldiers at times, which didn't matter.

The idea, in fact, was to get wet, and one of the guys who ran fastest—and had a good eye—leaped in the air toward a catapult bomb, and his head smashed the water balloon as if it were a soccer ball. He and those around him got splattered to their own huge cheers.

Hitch nailed Hoogerheide, and she returned fire, hitting him on the side of the head and then, accidentally in the crotch. "Man down!" she shouted, grabbing two more balloons as Hitch groaned face down in the red soil. She dropped two more on his back. He laughed and protested at the same time.

I aimed my balloon at Kayla Helwani and whacked her on the side of her beige T-shirt. She hurled a balloon back at me, smack in the chest.

"I love the smell of water balloons in the morning," Jordan shouted, sending off another balloon with the promise of rain.

It was over in minutes. If you left the balloon battle dry, you were doing something wrong. We loved the skirmish and made more balloons. However, it wasn't long before the sounds of real explosions in the distance took over. Reality set back in, but for those preceding few minutes, we'd been free.

At that point, we were so charged up, we hit the chow hall or, if we were lucky and had a partner, dived into sex. I'd never realized until then how food and sex were eerily similar in satisfaction when you were hungry for either. On this day, I had a thick BLT, no mayo but with cream cheese on sourdough. Maybe because you could not get pork out in Greater Iraq, what with an Islamic prohibition against eating pigs, I wanted such meat all the time, in strips, in chops, in roasts, in ribs, as Cuban-style, as Chinese sweet and sour, as ham, as crispy rinds, as nearly every way you could get except for consuming the squeal.

When I ate the last crispy bite of my BLT, relishing the squish of the roma tomato against the stiff bacon and the romaine, I saw Kayla sit down a few tables over, seeming preoccupied—even sad. After a few minutes considering what I should do, I moved and sat across from her, her T-shirt already dried, leaving me once again to my imagination.

"That was fun, huh?" I said.

She looked at me as if trying to remember who I was. "Hey, man," she said.

"You got a good arm," I said.

"And a few other things," she said, winking.

Aie yie yie. I told my imagination, *stop, stop, let me be.* Her tray held a hoagie sandwich with multiple meats. She had a side of raw veggies: broccoli, cauliflower, carrots. Girl food.

"You're that guy I heard about that got nearly blown up, right?" she said.

Is that what I was getting known for, surviving an explosion? I'm the boom guy? "That's what they keep telling me," I said. "Where're you from? How come I haven't noticed you until recently?"

"I transferred in from Fort Lewis, a replacement," she said, "though I grew up in California."

She took the place of Paulino, I realized. "Los Angeles?"

"Orange County."

"Orange County, California?" I said. "I'm from Orange County, Florida."

She grinned. "It must be beautiful there. I've never been."

"You're not missing much, believe me. Fucking flat and filled with old people and tourists."

"My Orange County is beautiful," she said. "Red tile roofs, malls of gold, high schools like scallops."

Whatever that meant. "You remind me of a guy in my squad, Blake Styles," I said. "Know him?"

For a flash, she showed surprise, then said, "I don't think so. Was he in the water balloon fight today?"

I pictured the teams again. "No, he wasn't. He's tall, smart, from a nice neighborhood on the East Coast."

"Educated, too," she said under her breath.

"So you know him?" I was taken aback.

With a shake of her head, she said, "I'm still new. I'm still getting to know people."

I wanted to know more of her. Best as I could tell, she had grown up rich. "So why'd you become an MP?"

"It's complicated. I needed out."

"Me, too. I hated Florida."

She smiled. "Didn't seeing that statue of Saddam come down make you wish you were here?"

Was she for real? No one joins for that.

"No," I replied. *Why* was she here? Her face was perfect, like a statue from an old Italian sculptor or someone. Why would she want to be a guy? On the whole, the rest of us were plain or worse in comparison. Granted, back at Camp Victory, when the women were in their bikinis, I was surprised how many had okay bodies. Some of them—the men too—had legs like tree trunks and pock-marked faces or even acne still. Almost every woman had short ugly hair. Some had cheesy tattoos, such as stars on the back of their necks, or the name "Nick" or some lover on their forearm. Kayla, though, stood out: beautiful skin, a taut body. *Why* was she here? Her smile, her cute nose—like rain after a drought.

"I saw *Platoon*, which inspired me," I said. "Ever see it?"

"No. Don't think so."

"About Vietnam. Best war movie ever."

"I'll have to check it out on DVD sometime."

"Yeah, haji vision." To her confused look, I said, "The haji store at the MWR can get about anything."

She bit into a hoagie sandwich, her teeth, her lips, her eyes taking it in and making it a part of her. There was that beauty again. I wish I could capture that single moment. It's why Stanley Kubrick became a photographer and filmmaker: to make people see what he saw.

| | | |

That night, with it still over a hundred degrees, I took her to a place at the edge of the camp near a blast wall, where we parked the Humvees. It wasn't near the CHUs, which is why I liked to go there if I wanted to be alone. Sitting on top of a truck on earlier evenings, where I could often catch a breeze, I could see the desert under a full moon, see the outline of some of the scrub and imagine being a scorpion or snake, calling it home. The twilight sky in Iraq sparkled like a beaded dress during a night of dancing—beautiful, I'd give it that. When I first arrived at Warhorse, I spotted the Pleiades in the night sky, just above Orion's left shoulder—follow Orion's belt to the right, and you'll bang into a cluster of six or seven stars. Pleiades. Now in June, it was gone.

As I pulled out the key for the Humvee that I sometimes drove, I pointed up to another sight for Kayla. "See the Big Dipper?"

"Yeah, that's the only thing I recognize in the sky besides the moon."

"How about the North Star? You can find it by going to the front of the Big Dipper's pan. If you follow the line up from those two stars—" I pointed. "That takes you to Polaris, the North Star. And Polaris is the end of the handle of the little dipper."

She nodded, and we entered the Humvee. I opened the door to the gunner's nest. This model did not have a lot of the armor for the gunner as the newest models did, but it was better than the ones we had from Kuwait. The stars twinkled through the round hole where the gunner would stand. "See, there's Polaris again," I said.

"How do you know this stuff?"

"When I was a kid, my dad showed me lots of the stars. He got me a telescope for my birthday. Those were good times." I paused, thinking about my dad. "He could be stern—but he loved me. He even found a way to put a camera on that telescope, and we took pictures of the moon. He blew one up and framed it—special for me. What about your dad?"

Her face turned instantly grim, but then she shrugged. "He's a lawyer. We're not close."

"A lawyer?"

"He's complicated," she said. "Not very interesting." Then she smiled as she looked out at the night sky. "Wouldn't it be cool if we could go to another planet where everyone was nice? No serial killers or perverts or even wars?"

I wondered why her dad let her join the Army. What would I know about problems in a rich family? "Everything we're seeing up there are things that people two thousand years ago saw. There were wars then and wars now. You'd think we'd have improved."

"You'd think," she said.

We said nothing after that as if we knew exactly what was on each other's mind. The night stood eerily quiet as if even the bad guys wanted a night at the casbah or away from death.

Inside the truck, with only starlight and a crescent moon, we could barely see each other, but we started kissing madly, deeply. The heat didn't matter. I was ready, of course, to go all the way, but if one hand became too eager, Kayla gently took it and held it.

"Slowly," she whispered. "Enjoy each moment." I had to smile because it reminded me of what Styles would say. This was a good case where the moment should be cherished. I listened to her and concentrated on her lips on mine.

I couldn't help but think how this was so different from my band days when on the road. It was weird, the road. Girls seemed to get naked easily—as if no clothes were a raincoat, utilitarian and no big deal. I'm not sure when average girls became as comfortable as porn stars, but the way I looked at it, in my band days, sex was just another drug. Smoking a joint was standard, and fucking some little punk rock princess on the road was, too. It's what we did.

Now was different. Kayla or I might not be whole or alive tomorrow. It mattered. Her attention was as if our nervous systems were connecting to become one "I." We wedged in the valley between the front and back seats. She kissed my neck. The stars above her head appeared like a glowing halo. There was nothing more beautiful.

I thought of how artists were lucky. They could focus on this rather than fighting. I saw a documentary on an artist once, and he created nudes every day. A young woman would sit in front of him naked for hours. He could watch all he wanted, and then, like God, he made small replicas, ripe, ready, fruit of the earth. There were better lives than I had, but at this moment, feeling Kayla on top of me for the first time, there was nothing better. I could hear John Lennon and Yoko sing. Give peace a chance.

"I just want to hear you breathing—just for a few minutes," she said, laying her head on my chest, "and hear your heart beat."

I listened to her breathe, too, the slightest silkiest sound of air entered her nose, and I pictured it going down into her neck and dividing to fill up two beautiful lungs. I then imagined the air filtering around the tiny blond hairs in her nose and sweeping out, drifting into the night, sailing over the wire and finding a tiny plant in the sand that took it in, finding new life.

Somewhere around there we fell asleep in each other's arms. Only when the sky was lightening, did we stir. I wanted her so much then, that I reached down and slipped my hand in her pants. She gently pulled it out.

"I love you," I said.

"That's nice, but I know boys. If it's too fast, it doesn't last."

"What? I mean it. I love you. You're the one."

She smiled and kissed me deeply. I moved my hand down to her pants again. She let me play down there a little bit before moving my hand again.

"It's time to go," she said.

"We are meant to be together," I said.

"In time." She stared at me with a wonderful, quizzical smile.

"What?" I said.

"You're a nice guy."

"Thanks."

"Someone'd told me that."

"Who?"

"Doesn't matter. It's just true."

I smiled—but then didn't. "Wait. Who told you that?"

She shrugged, then looked off as if recalling something. "Were you there when Blake Styles accidentally shot up a family in the city?" she asked.

Why would she ask me that now? "Yeah," I said.

"Seems like it's going to kill him."

"I thought you didn't know him."

"I never said that."

"How well do you know him?"

"What's it matter?"

"It matters."

"Come on. He's super depressed, and that's what we should worry about."

"He's my friend. I don't have sex with his girlfriends."

"You wanted to just now." She paused. "But I'm not his girlfriend exactly. You're not going to get all crazy on me, are you?"

"He's married!"

"So am I."

I sat up, grabbed my shirt. "Isn't anyone true to anyone around here?" I got dressed.

"Let's not make this what it isn't."

She could have pulled out a hammer and smashed me in my head. I wouldn't have cared. She opened the truck's door and jumped down. She looked back in. "Coming?"

I listened to our boots on the desert soil. We didn't speak anymore—or hold hands. It was as if our souls slipped back into two different, cracked coffee pots.

| | | |

When I got back to our CHU, Hitch was gone, and Jordon sat at our one-and-only desk, editing on his laptop. "There you are," he said. "I was wondering what you're up to."

"Just talkin' with Kayla Helwani."

He gazed up at me, his head rising above the computer, just staring at me disapprovingly, not even seeming to blink.

"What?" I said. "She's been your gunner. I thought you said she's great."

"She's a great gunner. But she's part of that bunch on Park Place—Yanni, Styles, and those guys."

"Styles?"

"Yeah, and the others. I never see her with women. I'd watch out for that one, if I were you."

"She likes me—is that okay?" His look softened, as if he understood I was already into her. I continued, "One thing I've learned from my band days is that the good-looking women intimidate guys. They don't date as much as plainer women because guys don't ask them out."

"Believe me, I'm not intimidated. But if you like her, who am I to say?"

His opinion meant a lot. Six years older than me, Jordan often acted like a concerned brother. A few times in formation, he'd seen something off in my uniform—a collar up once, and a Velcro pocket open another time. A great marksman with four marksmanship badges, he'd given tips to me and Trace, which helped us earn our own badges. We proudly wore them on our ACUs. Also, Hitch was a sniper in our platoon and had seven confirmed kills, crediting Jordan with the assist. Before the Army, Jordan worked as a guard at the San Onofre nuclear power plant, an hour south of Los Angeles, right near the Marine Corps base Camp Pendleton. In the power plant, he'd worn a security uniform and a handgun—protecting against possible terrorists. He made rounds at night, but he had so much free time, that was when he started learning Final Cut on the Mac for moviemaking.

"You gotta look at this footage," he said, getting away from Kayla. "Did you hear the captain's orders?"

"No. What?"

"We have an early mission."

"A few platoons or the whole company?"

"The LT didn't say, but it feels like some big last-minute change. I'm hoping you can shoot more video tomorrow."

"Definitely. I'm sure I can figure out when."

He then showed me what he'd been editing, his interview with Hitch, who looked like the goofy kid we all knew. Hitch spoke into the camera: "Frankly, I never quite understand the bigger picture. Someone tells me to sit behind a wall on a certain roof and shoot, and I do it. I'm a soldier, not an officer strategizing. I figure the brass knows what they're doing, and I have to trust them. I'm still not real clear what we're doing here—most of the Iraqis look at us with fear in their eyes. Still, like I say, I'm just a soldier."

Jordan's voice came on asking, "You think we're doing good here?"

As he sat on his cot, Hitch pulled out his drumsticks from under his pillow. He began drumming the air. "Yeah. I hope so—considering Americans are getting hurt, mangled, and dying. I like to think we're helping. This month we've been a big part of Operation Arrowhead Ripper, stopping our IP stuff," he said, referring to the Iraqi police training we used to do. Baqubah cops aren't watching our backs anyway. This is a surge—over ten thousand extra soldiers. We're making a difference. I'd love to clean up Iraq and get home." He silently drummed on his legs, smiling at the music that only he heard.

Wow. Maybe I don't give Hitch enough credit. Not only has he been a great friend, but in his own way, he's brilliant. Jordan, too: our documentary was coming together.

The next morning, just at dawn, we hurried outside for platoon formation. "Five months until we're home," said Jordan as we stepped out of our CHU with Hitch just behind.

"I wish it were tomorrow," said Hitch.

Kayla stood outside our CHU and said, "Hey, Jordan."

"Hey."

"Private Rivera," she said to me, professionally, not suggesting the intimacy we had had.

Jordan looked at me, away from her, with disapproving eyes.

"Private Helwani," I said, being just as professional. She signaled for me to come closer. I let Jordan and Hitch move ahead and stepped to Kayla. She smiled and said, "Good morning."

"Is it?" I said.

"Don't be that way. We'll have time together later."

Was she crazy? Was she fucking with my head? What was this?

We moved toward the meeting area. We stepped into a rough formation, Kayla and I, toward the back. She stood to my left, glancing seriously at me.

"All right, Mr. Perfect," she said. "Am I the first girl you've fallen for here?"

"Yes," I told her.

"Dress right–dress!" commanded First Sergeant Ichisada. We all moved to our exact positions exactly behind the person in front and held up our left arms to make sure we were one arm's length away from the next column. I was inches from touching Kayla.

"What about Paulino?" Kayla whispered.

"How do you know about her?" I gasped.

"You think there are secrets here? Now how can I trust you?"

The LT checked that each row was exact. When he was satisfied, he stepped to his position near the first sergeant, who said, "Ready – front." We put our arms down and faced forward.

"At ease," said the LT stepping forward. "Shortly, we'll be in a company-wide clearance operation as part of Arrowhead Ripper. The plan is to start from the southeastern corner of Old Baqubah and clear northward, using Trash Alley in the east as one boundary and Tora Tora as our western boundary. The MPs will be used in blocking positions."

He read from a list, assigning who would be in what team and Humvee. Kayla was gunner again with Jordan driving. I'd be gunner with Styles driving, Yanni as our team leader and navigator, and we'd have Iraqi interpreter Mohamed.

"Platoon dismissed," commanded the sergeant. Kayla and I eyed each other as we headed to our trucks.

"I'll never lie to you again," I said.

"I have to think about it."

Soon, I stood in my gunner hole, resting against the strap that made a good seat.

As we neared Baqubah's outskirts, I could see how grand this mission was, with tanks, Bradleys, and Strykers ready to move in. We moved to the front, ready to stop anyone but us entering or leaving the city sector. At this moment with my camera, I grabbed a great shot of the scene, ending on the rising sun.

I also captured the swoop of helicopters coming toward us, superseded by the sound of two approaching F-18s that, as they passed overhead, each sent off two smart bombs that guided themselves into two different tall buildings, exploding. Concrete clouds puffed in the air, with the booming sounds coming seconds later the way thunder comes after lightning. The clouds cleared to show holes in the still-standing buildings. In my earpiece, the LT said, "Move quickly to your positions," and we took off.

Once we hit our intersection and stopped, the Strykers zoomed in behind us, dropping their back doors, and troops poured out, guns ready. They approached a line of homes. Men would stand on either side of the door, knock, then with a ramming tool, bash the door in. Our soldiers entered quickly, one by one, holding up their guns, ready to fire if necessary. I pictured being part of a family living in one of these places, to be greeted by goggled, gun-toting, ammo-carrying Americans in camouflage uniforms—must be terrifying. We had to root out the enemy, though, and search for weapons.

Soon, I heard gunfire from one home. A second squad rushed to that house. Not long after, the LT called our squad by name over the radio, wanting us to go to that spot. "Your squad needs to collect two detainees. Mohammed, talk to them first, find out who the dead guy is, and see why there is medical equipment there. Also, there're sketches of city streets that look like plans of attack. Bring the men to the holding area."

"I've changed my name to Tommy," said Mohammed. "I don't want anyone to recognize me as I'm helping you."

"Whatever," said the LT. "Tommy."

I came down from my perch and sat next to the new Tommy, who pulled a silk stocking on his head as if he were going to rob a bank.

"Aren't you hot in that thing?"

"Better than dead. I can't be recognized anymore."

Styles drove over quickly. I hadn't really talked to him yet, and I sensed he didn't want to talk with me. He had barely glanced at me the whole morning, but now I couldn't hold back. I said, "I know about you and Kayla."

"She's a good girl—messed up, but good."

"What about your wife?"

"The affair was a mistake. I wasn't myself."

"Affair? She said—" Now I wasn't sure what she had said. Maybe I misunderstood. "Are you fine now?" I asked.

"Fine?"

"Blake. Talk to me. I'm not out to hurt you. I don't want to see Kayla if you are," I said.

"She wants you. She told me. I'm fine. Now *drop* it."

He slammed on the brakes near the house. We all hurried out, guns drawn. Outside the bashed-in front door, I yelled in, "We're here for the detainees."

"In here, y'all," said a voice with a Southern accent.

We entered, guns still up just to be safe. It was a house much like others I'd seen: woven rugs on a tile floor, ornate wooden chairs, and curtains made with a heavy cloth, this one showing pink roses. What was different was the giant framed poster, a copy of some painting of the Virgin Mary holding a baby Jesus. This couldn't have made the homeowners popular in their neighborhood. On a couch covered with a cheap Indian bedspread that Pier 1 Imports used to sell sat two young men, dark hair parted the same way on the left and having the same thin mustache. They looked like runaway Arabic silent film stars, brothers, their hands bound behind their backs in plastic tie handcuffs, the kind we all carried.

I waved over our robber-faced interpreter. "Hey, Tommy," I said.

"Yeah? You want me to find who the dead man is?" He pointed to the body in the kitchen. From our angle, we could only see his blue-jean legs and his Nike shoes, as if he were some kid asleep in a city park in America.

"Actually, first find out if they live here, and if they do," I said, "can you ask them about baby Jesus here?"

Tommy quickly spoke Arabic, and then one brother spoke up, then the other joined in and it was just a wall of words until they stopped. Tommy asked something else, and the conversation became spirited. I whistled for them to stop.

"Tommy, tell me something," I said. "I'm on edge here."

"Of course," he said. "They're saying the dead man took their wives and wasn't going to give them back until each brother killed three Americans apiece." He pointed to baby Jesus. "The dead man said they also had to convert to Islam or die."

"How were they going to kill three Americans each?"

Tommy asked and then the brothers started speaking real fast again. I waited for an answer.

"One brother was going to wear a suicide vest and kill six or more," said Tommy. "The other promised to care for the dead brother's wife when the women were returned."

"Is this a crazy place or what?" said Styles. "Sometimes I'm wondering if I'm dreaming this shit."

I wondered if the LT had noticed Styles had been acting out of it lately. I turned back to Tommy. "What do they know about where this guy came from?"

Tommy spoke to the two, and the brothers said the same couple words in harmony. Tommy asked something else, then nodded as the brothers spoke. Tommy told me in his sometimes fractured English, "They said he come from that tall building down the street, one of the one that just got bombed. There were more bad people there."

I turned to Styles and said, "I think we should call the sergeant about this."

"Roger that," Hitch said, grinning. He was the only guy in our platoon who seemed to like his job.

I relayed the information to the sergeant, who said he'd talk to the LT. Soon the LT got on the radio and said we had to take the two brothers to the holding area. I had Tommy explain to the brothers that we had to take them away but they should be back in a few hours. "Inshallah," they said, which I'd heard several times over the past few months. It meant "If God wills it."

After we dropped them off a few kilometers down the road to a large truck gathering suspects, the LT called and said, "The captain says all infantry troops are busy—so we need to clear the building the brothers mentioned."

"Infantry is supposed to do that, not MPs," said Styles into his mike. Until now, Styles had always been a can-do kind of guy. This again told me he was not quite right.

"They're short troops. It's a favor. You were trained for this stuff."

"The tall building closest to us?" said Styles.

"Roger that," said the LT. "I'm sending your whole squad," which meant our convoy of four Humvees would be involved. We'd only cleared one home before. Normally, we trained Iraqi police and patrolled—but this was the surge.

The building was easy to drive to, but its height made for a good vantage point for an ambush. The building, all concrete, painted white, was only six stories, but it looked larger because it wasn't particularly wide. I was ready on our gun, pointing it upward. Shortly after we got there, the other three Humvees arrived. Kayla, too, had her gun aimed up at the building. Rather than smile when she saw Styles and me together, her eyes widened.

"We'll take it one floor at a time," said Sergeant Gasparyan, Yanni, our squad leader. "Hitch and Styles, get the battering ram. Jordan, you watch the stairs when we find stairs. Everyone else, you know the drill." He turned to Kayla. "Helwani, you follow in a few minutes, once we're in the building."

We soon learned there were six apartments per floor, three on the west side, three on the east. Rather than a central hallway, each apartment was entered from an outside edge. The north side had an elevator and staircase, and the elevator was out—no electricity. My stomach did a somersault. I wished I had more experience clearing a building. We bashed in and inspected the apartments on the first three floors. No one seemed to live there as there was only minimal stuff, such as left-behind broken furniture and garbage. The fourth floor was a different matter—some of the apartments were fully occupied, but no one was home. The fourth and fifth floors were missing part of their walls leading into the apartments, thanks to our smart bombs earlier. The floors looked like a dollhouse, with the furniture exposed. One had a piano, perfectly black, but the top was covered in white concrete rubble and dust.

On the floor above us, we heard women's voices scream something in Arabic. Tommy wasn't with us. Yanni pointed to Styles, Hitch, Jordan, and me, and whispered loudly, "Follow me."

We ran up the stairs, guns pointed, taking each turn carefully. The voices came from one particular apartment. We stood on either side of it. Hitch and Styles used the battering ram to smash open the door, and the women screamed more. Styles gritted his teeth as if telling himself to just do his job. We rushed into what looked more like an office than an apartment. There were desks and file cabinets. Three women dressed fully in long black billowy clothes with the hijab, the head scarf, sat tied up against a wall. Styles ran to them first, kneeling and pulling out a knife, miming how he was going to cut the ropes. He looked crazed.

"Search this place," said Yanni, going down a hallway carefully toward the bedrooms. The women were screaming something in Arabic, though, and motioning their heads toward the wall. I turned. A gun appeared in the crack of a closet door. It fired and Styles screamed. To the side of the closet, I angled my M4 and clicked off a burst. An old man fell to the floor holding a small rifle. Styles held his shoulder in pain.

"Get Mohammed up here," Styles said.

"Tommy? He's not a medic."

"Get Tommy. I think we found the wives and one extra."

The women were all crying and muttering things we didn't understand. Yanni ran in, saw the dead man, then saw Styles holding his shoulder.

"Let me see," said Yanni. Using Styles' knife, he ripped open Styles' very bloody sleeve. "Lucky, lucky, lucky," he said.

"I deserved it," Styles said in a monotone.

"You're just grazed," I said. "Bleeding like a motherfucker, though. I'd fix it, but I don't have my medical kit on me. How'd we all forget ours?"

"Take mine," said Hitch from the kitchen. I ran in and took a bandage wrap from the first aid kit on his side.

Styles looked spacey, almost like a zombie. What the hell was he thinking?

I knelt down to the old dead man and turned him over. He wore a black T-shirt that said "Welcome to Miami Beach." Yanni stood and kicked the body hard. "Fucker," he said.

I should have looked in the closet first thing. A glint now caught my eye. A gun barrel rose at the back of the closet, an assault rifle I assumed, and I couldn't get mine up quickly enough. Yanni had his back to the closet. Shots rang out, not from my gun, and someone inside fell down. I turned. Jordan's gun still smoked.

"You gotta be careful, bro," he told me. Fuck. "Inshallah," I whispered.

Jordan dragged out a young man from the closet who held an AK-47, placing him next to the old man. Jordan's gun had done a number on the man's chest and face, but best I could tell, he was young, early twenties, wearing jeans and a UCLA T-shirt.

Styles looked utterly catatonic right then. Perhaps he realized he had been saved twice in a matter of a minute. Kayla stepped in, gun drawn, when she saw Styles. She gasped and ran to him. Styles started crying, shaking his head, whispering, "I'm sorry," again and again. She only said "Shh" in return and hugged him. She stood, teary-eyed, and ran from the room.

Washington, March 2006

After basic training, we plowed through advanced training, and then we received our duty station. When Styles, Hitch, and I were given Fort Lewis, I figured the war stuff wouldn't be bad because we'd be together.

When we arrived at Fort Lewis, just outside Tacoma, Washington, a giant snow-capped mountain, Mt. Rainier, stood in the distance, popping out of the flatlands like some giant burrito. Pine trees surrounded Fort Lewis, and even the grass seemed different from fucking Florida. After we grabbed our duffles, we stood in a long line. A desk sergeant went down the line, saying "Iraq" to the first person, "Afghanistan" to the next, and moved down the line switching back and forth. I was farther down the line from Hitch and Styles, who were separated by one person. Hitch and Styles got Iraq. I got Afghanistan. Fuck. We wouldn't even be in the same barracks.

"Couldn't you figure out to move one ahead and be with us?" said Styles.

"I thought I was," I said.

We then had to separate and meet our platoons. They put me in a group of soldiers who had just returned from Afghanistan, assigned to go back. I met them just outside our barracks, where we'd have rooms with just one roommate. We were replacements—for dead guys, I assumed. My roommate was a really tall guy. Out on the front lawn just before formation, Sergeant Murdock looked at both of us and shook his head. "You'll never be Gonzo or Frack," he said as if he instantly hated us. He looked up to the tall guy and said, "Private Rashidi, what kind of last name is that?"

169

"Moroccan, Sergeant."

"Are you Muslim like the fucks we're shooting in Afghanistan?"

"Christian, Sergeant. For many generations, even in Morocco."

The LT nodded as if thwarted by some planned slander. "You play basketball?"

"Yes, sir."

"What position?"

"I like center, Sergeant."

The Sarge grinned. "We need a good center. Welcome to the unit." He turned to me.

"And Private Rivera. Your family swim across the border?"

"No, Sergeant. Three generations American." I wouldn't tell him about my Panamanian mother.

"You play basketball?

"A little, Sergeant. Point guard."

"We don't need a damn point guard, and you say you only play a little?"

"I spend a lot of time playing my guitar. I'm more of a musician."

"Like that's what we fuckin' need, a musician? What's happening to today's Army?"

"I want to help in any way I can, Sergeant."

"Singing?" He turned to one of the corporals and said, "Give this guy the toothbrush."

The corporal grinned, went over to the wall, and grabbed a pink toothbrush from the shelf. As he approached me, I could see its bristles were worn. He handed it to me.

"This toothbrush is for cleaning the grout around the toilets tonight," said the sergeant. "You get fire watch first tonight, four hours. I want the grout spotless by the time your watch is over. Do you get me, private?"

I was already dreading this platoon. "Yes, Sergeant," I said.

"PT six a.m. Don't be fuckin' late."

For the rest of the afternoon, none of the others spoke to me unless I said something first, such as, "How was Afghanistan?" to one guy.

He said, "Better than Iraq. We had a few hairy missions, lost a few, but not like the constant shit in Iraq. Consider yourself lucky."

Otherwise, I seemed to be plutonium to those guys—no eye contact, even.

When we broke for dinner, I walked with Rashidi for part of the way. "What do you think of our unit?" I asked.

"The Army is bullshit," he said, "but it's the only bullshit we got."

"Why'd you join?"

"Blow the shit out of some terrorists like everyone else." He said he had to get to the PX, so I went on to the chow hall, where I found Styles and Hitch already there. Unlike basic training, we could sit anywhere and talk.

"About time," said Hitch. "How's your platoon?"

Styles was cutting his steak into even bite-size pieces and looking at me for the answer.

"Fucked," I said. "They've already been to Afghanistan, and everyone in my platoon moved up in rank. Me and another guy are the only privates, so we're getting bullshit from everyone. We're the outsiders. It's dangerous." I looked down at my cold rubber steak on my plate. I lost my appetite.

Styles smirked as if I were being crazy. "How's your sergeant?" he asked.

"Sergeant Murdock—the worst I've ever seen," I said. "He acts like a drill sergeant."

"Mare-dah," said Styles. "That means 'shit' in French. He's Sergeant Merde."

Hitch laughed, of course, and said, "Our sarge is great. An Asian guy. Our LT is really involved, too, Lieutenant Graver."

"That's not a good name," I said.

"He's a great guy," said Hitch.

"'Grave' can mean 'serious'," said Styles as if names were everything.

"Then I have grave doubts about my sarge," I said. "I don't know if I can fucking take this place."

"Merde will come to love you just like we do," said Styles.

Over the next weeks, though, it never happened. Sergeant Murdock made me and Rashidi do bullshit drills like carrying a pile of heavy logs from one place to another and back again. We took more night watch than anyone else, and I wasn't getting enough sleep. I became sloppy in everything, not by choice.

One night I woke up to the sounds of splashing and gurgling, and Rashidi's bed was empty. Out in the hallway, I heard laughter. I emerged. Sergeant Murdock stood over a corporal who scrubbed the floor with Rashidi's head while Rashidi kneeled, not resisting, just taking the hazing. The corporal would plunge Rashidi's head in the bucket, and then scrub some more.

"What the fuck are you doing!" I said without thinking. "Let him go."

Sergeant Murdock merely smiled and pointed to of a few of his trusted troops, who quickly grabbed me, pinning my arms behind my back.

"Let me go!" I screamed.

"Now we don't have to wake you up," said the sergeant. I fought as best I could, so it took three guys in contrast to the one for Rashidi.

"It's just part of our training," said Rashidi to me. "Go with it. Then we're one of them."

"I don't want to be one of them!" I said as hands pushed my face into the bucket. I squeezed my eyes shut and held my breath, but I tasted the pine of Pinesol. They didn't grind my head into the floor, so much as lightly drag it. I stopped resisting for a second and felt one of my arms go loose. I yanked it away, twisted around, and really punched whoever was there hard in the stomach. The guy doubled over, and the other two let me go. The corporal also let Rashidi go, who stood and spit on the floor.

I stood and said, "This is fucking shit!"

Sergeant Murdock stepped close to me, not worried. "We are a team," said the sergeant. "Our traditions make us so. You don't seem like a team member to me."

"Why did you have to do this?" I said.

"Why didn't you just go with it?" Rashidi interjected.

"I was helping you," I said to him.

"I didn't ask for any. Why do you think I didn't wake you?"

I couldn't answer. Our heads dripped with the stink of floor cleaner.

"Have a good sleep, ladies. PT at six," said the sergeant.

Back in the room, Rashidi fell into his bunk, turning his back to me. "You okay?" I asked. He said nothing. Soon I heard he was asleep. My blood boiled. I kept squeezing my hands into fists. I needed something, and I flashed on the bell-ringer-shaped Goldschläger bottle in Rashidi's duffle. He'd snuck the booze in, schnapps, telling me it was 107 proof with real gold flakes floating around in it. I'd never had schnapps before, but it was liquor, which is what I needed.

I found it, unscrewed its cap, and tipped it back. After I drank a big swallow, which felt like fire, I coughed immediately, getting the aftertaste of cinnamon. Rashidi didn't turn around. He really was asleep. I told myself just a little more. I drank at least half of it until I was really spinning. Shit. I hoped I wouldn't throw up.

Rashidi shook me awake. "It's PT, man!" he shouted into my face. "And my bottle was on the floor! You didn't even ask me!"

"Sleep, man," was all I could get out, meaning he'd been asleep, but he had to know I wouldn't have asked. My head now pounded.

"You can't sleep, man. The sarge will be here in a sec."

That was enough to motivate me. I yanked on my clothes quickly. I didn't have time to shave before we had to be down on the field.

We had to march with a platoon of newbies with our rifles in the early-morning fog across the base toward the forest edge, then down a forest road until we came to a huge green field. Where the hell were we? As we marched on the field, I wondered if we were we going to play football or soccer for PT. Yet there were no lines marked, and no goals or goal posts. We came to what appeared to be a sewer cover in the middle of the field. Sergeant Murdoch funneled us around it.

"As you know," said the sergeant, "Afghanistan can be hot as fuck. It's why you've been practicing giving each other IVs."

The week before, every afternoon in a classroom, we'd do that—find a partner's vein in the crook of his elbow, rub an area clean with a sterile alcohol towelette, insert a needle, tape it down, and connect it to an IV saline bag. In case a medic was lost or injured in combat, we could help each other. People could die of heat stroke over there. We also had to learn how to drink often—three times the amount we normally drank. Hydration was everything. It'd be an oven over there.

The sergeant continued, "It can also be dark as fuck in that shithole of a country. In a nighttime combat situation, things can get hairy." He pulled the manhole cover off with the help of a crowbar. "We have a whole tunnel system down there." He pointed. "It's like a sewer maze with no sewage. There are no lights. One of you will go hide someplace around a bend in the dark, and then shout out 'help!' when I give you the signal. Then another of you, with only one of these glow sticks—" He bent a glow stick until it gave off a green light. "—Will go down, find the asshole, administer an IV, and then drag him back to this entrance. Got it?"

We all shouted, "Yes, sergeant!"

Man, my head beat like a bad drum. How the hell was I going to do this? At least I wouldn't have to be first. The first two did it in what seemed no time. Next thing I heard was "Rivera, Rashidi!" We were second. He made Rashidi the guy to hide. I had to give the IV. The sarge thrust the bagged IV kit and saline solution into my hand and gave me the glow stick. I stared at the stick, trying to remember what to do. Shit, my head pounded.

The sergeant stepped up to me and shouted in my face, "Rivera, make it glow!" I was too slow. He grabbed the stick from my hand, bent it, and jammed it into my chest. I gasped.

"Get down there!" he shouted.

I did so. The hole was right above what looked like clean sewer pipe. I dropped down perhaps five feet. It wasn't enough to stand straight up in, but one could hunch over certainly.

"Rashidi, it's your cue!" yelled the sergeant into the hole.

I could hear a distant "Help, help!" I moved into the dark. The glow stick did little more than a handful of fireflies. I had to hold my hands in front of me so I could feel the curved edge of the wall and move forward.

From his voice, I was getting closer, but my headache worsened until Rashidi's voice changed into the laughter of Ralph, my old bandmate who'd stolen Sophie. "Ralph?" I asked.

I could hear the voice change into Sophie's "help!" What the fuck were my ears doing? "Sorry, Dude" came from what sounded like that stoner Wagonkenect. I had to sit for a minute and hold my head. When I felt better, I listened again. I could hear Rashidi's "Help" not far away.

"I'm almost there," I said.

"About time," he replied.

When I got to him, he said, "What took so long?"

The sergeant's voice came roaring at us. "Rivera? Are you shitting down there reading a newspaper?"

"I'm giving him the IV!" I shouted.

The glow stick barely showed Rashidi's crook of his elbow. I wiped it with the towelette and opened the needle. Rashidi screamed in pain when I stuck him. Wrong spot. I tried again and felt his blood spurt against my chin.

"This is fucking karma," Rashidi said with clenched teeth. "I should have never bought the schnapps."

He screamed two more times until I seemed to get it right. I had him hold the glow stick as I pulled him toward where I'd come from. "Jeez, you're heavy," I said. "You eat too much."

"Fuck you," he said. I kept hitting my helmet at the top of the tunnel as I huffed, puffed, and pulled. Would I ever find the entrance? Then I saw the morning light. At last.

I lifted Rashidi toward the surface, and a few pairs of hands grabbed him and pulled him away. I tried getting out of the hole, but I couldn't jump hard enough. After a few tries, I just wanted to lay down.

"What the fuck, Rivera," said the sergeant. "We're all going to get killed because of you someday. Someone lift him out."

Another two pair of hands grabbed me, and I rose.

The sergeant stood hunched over Rashidi and angrily pointed at me. "Rivera! Blood everywhere—and on you!" I looked down. My blouse was deeply spattered. "You didn't tape down the needle, either, fuck!" Before I knew what was happening, I saw his fist come at me and smash into my stomach. I gasped and bent over. It was all I could do to not throw up.

"How'd God fit three gallons of shit into your one-gallon head?" he yelled. He leaned close and smelled my breath.

"You've been drinking!"

"No, Sergeant," I shouted back. "Listerine, Sergeant."

"You're fucking playing that game. I have my eyes on you!"

The next day as we performed early morning jumping jacks, I was waiting for that day's hell. At this point, I knew the sergeant and none of these guys would ever have my back. I would be a dead man in Afghanistan.

As we worked out, a captain approached with our LT, Lieutenant Van Lowe, who'd I'd barely seen since I joined this platoon. The captain asked permission to speak to the troops. The LT gave him the nod, and the captain said, "The company across the way is looking for volunteers to go to Iraq. They're leaving sooner than you're going to Afghanistan, which means you'll get back earlier. That maybe the only benefit. They need volunteers. It's what I have to ask."

My heart beat quickly. That was Styles' and Hitch's company. I wanted to raise my hand instantly. But if I raised my hand and for any reason did not get transferred, my life, whatever was left of it, would become even more miserable.

"Any volunteers?" I made sure to read his name on his uniform. Littman.

I kept my arm down. I figured the sergeant would volunteer me and Rashidi anyway. Everyone around me looked down. No one wanted to say a thing.

Captain Littman said, "Okay. Thank you. I'll try the next platoon." The man walked off. The LT said to Sergeant Murdock, "Carry on," and he, too, left. I glanced to the sergeant, who looked at me in surprise as if mystified. My heart crashed. Did I just do a dumb thing?

At lunch, rather than zip to the chow hall, I asked around and found Captain Littman's office. He was just leaving when I got there. I saluted. "Permission to speak, Captain?"

He looked at my uniform for my name.

"Yes, Private Rivera."

"Do you still need a volunteer for Iraq?"

"I do."

"I'd like to volunteer."

"Whose platoon are you in?"

"Sergeant Murdock's, sir." I almost said *Merde*. Words do have power.

"That's Lieutenant Van Lowe's. Why didn't you volunteer earlier?"

I didn't want to get into the truth as I was the new guy. "I want to help my country, sir," I said, figuring it's what he wanted to hear.

He bought it, nodded, and returned to his desk. He quickly filled out a form, which he gave me. "Clear out from your barracks and bring your duffle to this building." He circled a building on a base map. "Report to Lieutenant Graver and give him this." He handed me my papers.

I wanted to hug the guy, or scream, or do something wild, but I just smiled and said, "Thank you, sir." Later in Iraq, Styles and I would get into how much power a person really has in life, and I would say I changed my own fate by going to the captain.

Styles would disagree and say, "Actions were in motion for you to see the captain. It was your destiny, don't you see?"

I didn't agree.

I packed up my shit into the duffle, and as I left the barracks with duffle and guitar, my old platoon stood in formation out front. Sergeant Murdock's back was to me, but as a couple guys shouted to me, "Chicken-shit," Sergeant Murdock turned.

"Fucking princess, you are," he said. "No fucking fortitude." Rashidi even shook his head.

Hell, I just smiled and walked with my head high.

Minutes later, I arrived at the new company and found Lieutenant Graver, the beefy LT I would come to love. "Welcome," he said, and I saluted. "At ease." He shook my hand and showed me my new room where I had a roommate who was out. "Get situated. Change into your PT gear. Everyone's out front," he said. "Go ahead and join them."

As I walked outside and the door closed behind me, a sense of relief washed over me. On the green front lawn, everyone kneeled, and I joined in quickly. Styles, leading, directed us to get down on our haunches and put our fists on the ground like a gorilla. "I call this the monkey fucker," he said, sort of bouncing up and out. "Do it," he said, and everyone did so gleefully. Hitch was there, too, laughing and lurching. My new sergeant joined along. Even though we were all about to deploy to a desert war where some of us wouldn't make it back, morale was high—what a difference.

That night, Hitch walked me around the barracks, introducing me to everyone, floor by floor—a diverse bunch, including hou-rah go-go-Army types, a few geeky-looking guys and women, a few serious ones, but I didn't get the kill-or-be-killed vibe from any of them. They accepted me as one of their own. My new platoon gave me a little party in the hallway that night, with cold Pabst and salty chips. Someone played on his laptop the song "If You Want to Sing Out, Sing Out," a cover by Death by Chocolate.

"If you want to say yes, say yes!" we sang and shouted.

|　　|　　|

The last "first" I often think about was back in basic, when a half hour before sunset Drill Sergeant Starwood came storming into the barracks, crashing a baton against a steel garbage can. While on most days we were done by five p.m., this evening in early March with the bite of winter gone and it drizzling, we were told to dress warmly in rain gear and get in groups of three of our own choosing. Hitch, Styles, and I chose each other. The whole platoon crowded in front of the cattle car, where we had to tie blindfolds on.

"What the fuck is this all about?" someone said softly near me. The sergeant made him do pushups right in the mud. Drill sergeants hear everything.

Once we couldn't see, he shoved us into the cattle car. We drove for about thirty minutes, and came to a stop. I was thinking this was some kind of prisoner-of-war thing, and maybe we'd be tortured to see if we'd talk. I may have seen that in a movie once. The back end opened, and the drill sergeant said, "Remove your blindfolds and exit."

A thick, mostly leafless forest surrounded us, colder than camp, wetter than shit, and a bunch of jeeps, each with drivers, seemed to be waiting for us among the trees.

Drill Sergeant Starwood said, "Each group gets a compass, a map, and one combat flashlight."

He handed out thirteen sets. The combat flashlights only gave a dull red light, so if the enemy were watching, they couldn't see the glow.

"We're going to drop each group off at a different spot. I want you to pretend you're behind enemy lines, and you have to get to a safe house, which is our base. Get there by following the map and not getting help from anyone else. Any questions?"

I wanted to ask where we were on the map, but I wasn't in the mood to kiss mud at the moment. I vaguely remembered some compass-and-map stuff we learned in class, but, truthfully, I hadn't been great at paying attention. All the physical stuff in the morning usually left me exhausted in the afternoon, and now I felt fucked.

Hitch, Styles, and I were assigned a Jeep, which drove us into the woods. The driver stopped and said, "Here. Good luck, ladies. You've got twenty hours." We stepped out onto wet brown leaves, and we scanned around us. Giant gray-armed trees everywhere. A few showed buds, but it felt mostly like dead wood there. You couldn't see hills or much of the sky. Our driver left driving straight rather than turning around.

At this point, the sun had set, but we still had twilight. I had the topographic map and opened it. In the middle stood Fort Leonard Wood, and the map showed the surrounding countryside for about forty miles, with altitude and terrain. We couldn't have driven forty miles.

"Where do we think we are?" said Styles, on one side of me.

"We didn't drive that long. I'm thinking fifteen miles," I said.

"Sounds right. The cattle car isn't that fast," said Hitch.

"Not a horrible walk, fifteen miles," said Styles.

"Yes, but if we walk in the wrong direction ten miles, then we'll have twenty-five," I added.

"What do we do?" said Hitch, who looked anxious.

"Calm down," said Styles.

"I'm fucking calm!" Birds in the trees flew into the cold sky as scattered silhouettes.

Maybe he was just exhausted with everything, as I was.

The light was dimming, making it harder to read the map. "I say, we draw a circle fifteen miles outside of the fort, then memorize the landmarks on either side of that circle. Once we come across a landmark, then we'll know where we are."

"Great idea," said Styles, and we got to work.

All I saw at first were a lot of forest areas and rivers. "It seems to me," I said right away, "no matter where we walk, we should hit a river of some sort."

"What good will that do us?" said Styles, "We won't know which river or which bend. Did either of you notice where the sun set?"

We looked around, but it was hard to see for all the trees. I said, "No," and Hitch added, "It's cold and getting colder. We're going to freeze to death if we don't hurry."

"We need to find a clearing *fast*," Styles said.

They each took a different direction, but I yelled, "What for?"

"You'll see," shouted Styles.

"Wait! Shouldn't we take note of which direction we're going? What if we lose each other?"

"Don't go far," said Styles. "We just have to get our bearing."

I went a different direction than either of them, and soon came to a clearing. "Over here," I shouted. "Here!"

They soon came running, and we could now see the horizon over the trees.

"Where did the sun set?" said Styles.

"Over that way," I said, pointing to where it was still lightest.

"That way is west," said Styles. "This time of year, closer to southwest."

"Our compass could have showed us that," I said.

"Oh," said Styles. "True."

The clearing gave us a little more light, though, so we took note of such things on the map as a set of caves, a radio antenna, and a river bluff. There weren't a lot of landmarks on the map.

"I say we choose one direction to walk," I said, "and stick with it until we hit a river or a landmark."

"What if we hit a river?" said Hitchcock.

"I don't know what they said in class, but in Cub Scouts we were told to follow it downriver until you hit a town or road," I said.

"That's our plan," said Styles.

"Because most of the housing and city stuff is east of the fort, we're probably west of the fort," I said. "Therefore, I say let's walk due east toward the town."

We walked east, following the compass. About five minutes in, Hitchcock shouted, "There! A radio antenna. See the red blinking light on top?" He pointed, started running as if it were the Emerald City, and I was about to shout "there!" when I noticed the red light was moving.

Styles yelled, "That's a jet, dipshit."

Hitch, still running, shouted "Shit" and seemed to trip, falling out of sight. Styles and I ran, and we came to the edge of a steep hill on which Hitch rolled below us.

"Hitch!" I yelled.

He came to a stop with a thud and a grunt against a tree. Styles and I slid down feet first toward him.

When we arrived, he was groaning, rubbing a knee.

"You okay?" I said.

Styles pulled him up and said, "Can you walk?"

He did with a limp.

"Fuck," I said.

"I'm okay," Hitch protested. "I can walk. Leave me be." He had his pride.

"Put three boys in the forest, and look what happens," said Styles.

"Enough, Brainiac," said Hitch. "Could happen to anyone."

It started to rain, and Styles suggested we huddle under some trees. "Better yet," Styles said. "Let's tie up a poncho, make us a tent. We did that in Cub Scouts."

"Cub Scouts is for pretty boys," said Hitch.

"I appreciate that, asshole," said Styles.

I strung up my poncho, saying nothing, worried that the darkness and the cold rain were going to lead to something worse. These guys didn't take things seriously enough.

As we huddled under my poncho, I asked, "Have either of you two regretted joining?"

"I had no choice," said Styles. "I have a wife and daughter to feed, and college didn't get me shit."

"You have a degree?" said Hitch. "Then why aren't you an officer?"

"Actually, I was a few classes shy of a degree. My mass-comm law professor wouldn't accept my final project, and I said fuck it. I had enough college credit to become a New York City firefighter, so I applied, got in, and that was fine until the cutback last year."

I shook my head. "Man, one small thing can change your life."

"You ever think about why Jesus came to save us?" said Hitch.

"No, no, no," said Styles. "Why do you always have to bring religion into this?"

"Because of one small thing. Jesus sacrificed himself for us."

"That's small?" I asked.

"Jesus was infinite," Hitch said. "He gave that up to pay for the punishment we deserved."

"Why did we deserve it?" I asked.

"If you have to ask, you'll never know."

"Bullshit," said Styles. "Sin is a design flaw. If God designed us to have sin, then he's to blame."

The rain picked up. It was as if God were trying to interact with us.

"I'm a believer. I'm not ashamed," said Hitchcock.

"That's fine," said Styles. "It makes you who you are. I accept that."

"Me, too," I said as I could feel the sharp fingers of cold moving into my muscles.

"And just accept that death is inevitable," said Styles. "Heidegger said confronting death leads to the affirmation of life. If you confront death, as I guess we're doing here in the Army, then it's a way to feel good. Feeling good?"

"Enough religion talk," I said. "Anyone know any good tunes to sing?" I hoped to push off the terrible pit in my stomach. Without an answer, I started to sing the Army song: "March along, sing our song, with the Army of the free."

The guys looked at me strangely, then Styles joined in, then Hitch. We bellowed, "Count the brave, count the true, who have fought to victory!"

The rain started to let up. I spotted another red light of a jet. I sat still as we continued singing. The red light wasn't moving.

"What?" said Styles.

"The radio tower," I said, pointing. From there, using our flashlight, we saw the line to the base. Styles had paid attention in class, and made a more precise measurement: fourteen miles southeast, setting the compass correctly. We didn't have to swim across any rivers but had to navigate through dark woods. We made it back before the sun rose. We felt great. We felt like the Three Musketeers. That's the feeling I wanted to keep. Unfortunately, that's not what I experienced at the end of Iraq.

Iraq, June 2007

We investigated the whole floor, and there had only been the one apartment with people in it. The dead men had been low-level soldiers, we guessed. The filing cabinets had been cleaned out, and we found no plans, but a desk drawer had been filled with propaganda—leaflets that were anti-U.S.

Tommy the translator explained one to me. It showed a woman crying over a dead man and two dead children. He read it, translating the Arabic: "America does not care for our citizens. While we were grateful they got rid of Saddam, the U.S. then disbanded our army, leaving us unprotected. American bombs now kill innocent civilians, and they call it *indirect damages*." Tommy paused. "I think they tried to translate "collateral damage." He then continued to read. "They kill us from the sky with their drones. They smash into our homes and kill our families. All they want is our oil. The U.S. must go."

"We're here to help everyone," I told Tommy, who'd taken off his mask. "Can't your people see this? Today we saved three women, and they can go back to their husbands. Doesn't that count for anything?"

"You don't have to sell me, boss," said Tommy. "But will you take me to America when you leave? No, I expect you abandon me."

I was going to protest, but I knew he was right. The Army would eventually forget this place, leaving him to fend for himself. I could do nothing.

"Still have your camera?" Jordan asked me as we left the apartment. He pointed to the helicopter approaching. I recorded it, and then moved back into the apartment to show the two dead men. What a viewer couldn't see was the terror we'd felt, how the hidden could kill, how luck and timing leaned this time in our favor. What I photographed explained everything and nothing. Our lives had just changed, but we weren't certain how. How much longer would our luck hold? Would we get back to America alive and whole? How would we explain what we'd seen to our families and friends?

The LT arrived in another convoy and sent Styles to the helicopters to fly back to Balad to be looked at, even if his wound might not be life-threatening. As I exited the building, I noticed in the rubble the neck of a guitar. I cleared away the debris around it and pulled out a perfectly fine acoustic guitar, barely scratched, just really dusty. I wiped some of it away and strummed it—out of tune. I used my voice to mock an E note, using it to tune the guitar. I lost myself there for a moment as I started playing chords.

The LT, seeing I'd found the guitar, said it was okay to keep. He added, "Styles wants you to fly off with him, if that's okay. Keep him company."

"Sure."

"Get going," he said pointing to the medevac helicopters.

Before I left, I nodded to Kayla, who stood nearby at her Humvee. She offered me a half-smile, which really didn't explain anything. With a small turn of her head, she glanced at Jordan, who approached. Jordan looked at me, shaking his head as if to say, *See what I mean?*

"Thanks, Dad," I said, adding a sarcastic smile. The guy was always looking out for me, but he was wrong about Kayla.

The LT seemed to see this exchange because he frowned.

I ran toward the helicopter emblazoned with red crosses, its rotor blades already turning. Inside, I was given a set of headphones to keep the noise down, and I could speak into a protruding microphone to talk with anyone on the helicopter. I swapped my helmet for the headphones.

Styles sat strapped into an aluminum chair rather than in one of the stretchers. He cocked his head as if trying to recognize me. Then he nodded. The paper napkins on his arm had been replaced with a large sterile pad and lots of medical tape. He held a small smile as he looked up at the ceiling. I figured he just had a morphine shot and felt extra great.

"Hey," I said.

"Sorry, Dude," he replied.

"About what? I'm here for you."

"I should have died."

I couldn't tell if he was thankful he wasn't dead or was he saying he wished he'd died. "You'll be okay," I said. "Rest. Take it easy."

"When I realized I almost died," he said slowly, "I asked myself what did I wish I'd do if I had more time?" He paused.

I said, "Well?"

He stared at me. "What would you do if your life were given back. Say a bullet was zooming for your head, and you wished it away? What would you do with your life then?"

"I don't know." I tried to imagine. I thought joining the Army was what I wanted to do, but now I wondered.

"My problem," Styles said, "is I know what I should do and what I really should do."

"And what's that?" I asked.

He smiled a deeply mysterious smile and said nothing else for a while. Then: "I'd always pictured myself dying in a soccer game, just after kicking the winning score."

On the other side of him sat two medics, who, I'm guessing, were thankful Styles wasn't a big medical problem. I realized that Styles might be able to go home with this. Sometimes even with minor wounds, a soldier would be sent home—just simpler. I strapped myself next to him, putting down my guitar. I looked up front and saw that the pilot was a young woman.

She placed her feet on some pedals, flicked a few buttons, and worked the lever to her left and the joystick in front of her. The helicopter revved and lifted up—an odd feeling, especially with the doors open. We weren't airborne long, when we headed back downward. The pilot turned to us and over our headphones she said, "We have to pick up another injured soldier."

Perhaps only twenty meters high, we travelled down a street until we came to a burning Humvee, landing on the other side of it. Four men on four corners rushed a stretcher in, and a young woman my age had a tourniquet above her knee. Below her knee was nothing. She wasn't conscious. The medics instantly leaped to work, closing the doors, and I looked away. I'd recognized the woman as an MP from a different platoon. I remember her playing foosball with Hitch the other day in the rec center. I tried to imagine my life without a leg. Did the unconscious woman have a boyfriend or husband? Was she a mother? Can she still be?

"Sucks, don't it?" said Styles.

"It makes me mad," I said. "Iraqis don't know us."

Styles, lighting a cigarette, said, "We don't know them."

Looking outside, I noticed green fields like quilt patches. I hadn't thought about it before, but people were growing things amid war. A little canal fed the patches. Palm trees edged one field where the desert rammed into agriculture, nothingness meeting somethingness. Growing things seemed so positive, life continuing. Yet not far from the fields, sections of road blew up all the time the way popcorn did when meeting hot oil. In the midst of it all were civilians. How people could live with so much violence didn't make sense. I felt too dumb to understand it. That dumbness was perhaps why I was here—why would I otherwise join during war? It occurred to me then, rising in the sky, that if I made it out alive, perhaps the best thing to do with my life was go to college. I wasn't brave enough to try it before. Now I had the guts.

"What do you want to do when you get out of here?" I asked Styles.

He took a long drag on his cigarette as if he could see his life through a squint, then he flicked the butt out the door. "I don't know anymore."

"You have a family."

He paused as if thinking about it and said, "I should call home more."

"And Kayla?"

He paused again. "What about her?"

"The problem is I like Kayla, too," I said.

"She's yours."

"Like she's a baseball card?"

"Just be true to her."

"Like you two are true to your spouses?"

"It's not a black-and-white universe here. Don't you get that?"

We said nothing after that. I pulled out my camera and recorded video through the front windshield. The landscape like a terrarium appeared dry and rocky, with scrub brush and the occasional hut with a goat or some skinny farm animal running around. Then I saw a cow. I swore it was a cow, even though I hadn't seen one in Iraq until this point. It was so thin, I could see its bones, and as we swept over it, it fell right down. It probably died. The animals and the people here had it worse than us.

| | | |

The E.R. doctors saw the young woman amputee and a couple of others first. We had to wait, and Styles didn't look so good—head down most of the time.

Soon, Styles was called, and I went in with him. "Lay down here," said the doc, a guy older than my dad, a grizzled captain. Styles did, appearing ashen and shaky. The doctor briefly examined the wound and ordered Styles a unit of blood immediately.

"I thought he was just grazed," I said from a chair.

"A bit more than that," said the doc. I wondered why would a doctor his age come here. As a male nurse connected Styles to an IV, the doctor irrigated the wound. "No bones were hit, thankfully," he said, "but there're a lot of blood vessels in the shoulder, as well as delicate nerves. If all goes well, he can be out tomorrow. Up for going home?" he said to Styles.

His eyes said he wanted to go home. Styles knew, as did I, that a wound such as this could earn him an honorable discharge immediately. Yet I sensed there was some unfinished business keeping him here.

"Take it, man," I said. "I would. You don't owe us or the Army anything."

He shook his head. "I'm staying."

I wondered what his wife would think in hearing this.

"Well," I said, standing up to say good-bye. Styles waved me over and held up his hand to low-five me. He had some blood on his hand, and so did I. I slapped his hand, then shook it. "My blood brother!"

"You're a better friend than I am," he said.

"Hardly. We'll see you tomorrow. Get some rest, okay?"

As I walked out, I had the terrible thought that if he died, I wouldn't be so jealous of Kayla anymore. I felt rotten for even thinking it.

Before I left the building, a drawing of a guitar caught my eye. It came on a poster that also featured a juggler and and a female acrobat with the headline, TALENT SHOW! An upcoming talent show at Warhorse would be for all to attend for a fun and relaxed evening. I could use one of those. It also gave details who to see to be a part of the show. Hmmm. Except I had no band.

I was able to catch a medevac back to Warhorse, and after I landed, Kayla ran from the medical facility to me.

"How'd you know I was coming?" I asked.

"I heard over the radio. They said Styles is staying at Balad. Is he okay?" she asked.

"He needed more blood and observation."

"I'm sorry about everything," she said.

"Are you?" I turned to walk away from her, but she stopped me.

"Don't be that way," she said. "You can see he's hurting—and not just from the bullet he took."

I nodded.

"I really like you," she said.

"Do you?"

She looked around, saw we were alone, and whispered, "My CHU. Eight o'clock."

My god, my god, I thought. She does like me. This would be it.

| | |

When I stepped into my place, I heard the words, "Can you go back to being normal?" which came from Jordan's laptop. Jordan hunched over his screen, running an interview I did from the other day with one of the engineers who caught me recording different angles of a burned-up Humvee. The man had asked me why was I always shooting video. I'd said I'm just trying to understand things. I then asked if I could interview him, and that's what Jordan ran now:

"Do you like it in Iraq?" I ask the engineer.

"The adrenaline rush can't be beat at times," he says. "Nothing like this. How do I explain? The rush is because you're really celebrating. You're alive! Me and the people in my team—they're my family away from my family."

"Are we doing good things here?" I ask.

"We're the world's cops, aren't we?"

Jordan closed his laptop and said, "I really think we're making something here. With your visuals and my editing, we make a good team."

"It's looking good."

"Bah bah bah," said Hitch on his cot, wearing headphones, and beating along to music with his drumsticks. He noticed me and waved. I waved back.

"How about if I scrounge up a video projector and we show this on the basketball court?" said Jordan. "We can make it a movie night. The place is big, air conditioned. It'll be great!"

His enthusiasm blasted at me, but I couldn't reciprocate. "Believe me," I said. "People here want to get away from the war, not see more of it. This needs to get out in the world. It's not the shit that CNN shows."

"Maybe we can get it to Sundance," said Jordan.

"Sundance?" asked Hitch.

"A film festival. The best."

"It would need to be a feature then," I said. "A documentary."

"And with original music," said Jordan.

"What music?" said Hitch.

I picked up the guitar from its spot on the white wall, where it hung next to the mounted .50 caliber machine gun from my Humvee. When I was gunner, I was in charge of keeping the weapon clean and calibrated. I liked that my guitar was the better instrument. I strummed a riff that had been banging around my head. "See." I had started making lyrics for my song earlier, but now I needed to write it all down. I played my riff again to make me remember. Jordan waved me off, opened his laptop, and plugged in headphones so he could keep working on his video. I started writing. It felt good, like the old days.

Something came over me.
I couldn't stop it.
I never thought I could escape it.
This fuckin' country!

Even if I have great friends
fighting in blood and sand
I never thought I'd find a woman
Who could help me forget this path.

Then you came here, you say,
from Orange County,
and we lay together in the wire
under the red sky. We are fighters!

I played the riff again on my guitar and began singing. Hitch looked over, pulled off his headphones and smiled. I didn't have any more words for my song yet, so I just started over. Hitch started slapping his drumsticks against his leg and singing along with me, and we did it two more times, getting louder each time. Jordan pulled off his headphones to watch and listen.

"You can't use her real name, can you?" asked Jordan.

"Maybe I can change it to Layla," I said.

"Layla, you've got me on my knees," Hitch sang, quoting Eric Clapton's classic song. "Layla, I'm begging, darling please."

Jordan laughed. "It has a similar theme, I see."

Right then, a knock came from our CHU's door.

"Come in," yelled Jordan.

The LT and Yanni entered. Yanni wasn't the LT's usual sergeant.

"Sir!" we said in unison, standing.

"It's cool. Relax guys," said the LT.

Yanni said, "I told the LT what a great job you guys did today. After all, clearing buildings isn't our usual job."

The LT nodded. "I wanted to thank you personally for what you did—and I'm thankful you're all okay."

"Thanks, sir," we each said, not at the same moment. We were a mutual admiration society.

"I asked the commander for a lighter load for you for a day or two," said the LT, "and he offered something. Would you mind convoying a *New York Times* reporter to Camp Normandy?"

"When?"

"This evening. Then you'll have tomorrow off."

"Forty-two kilometers each way," said Jordan. "But it avoids the heart of Baqubah."

"That's right," said the LT.

"I'm up for it, sir," said Jordan.

"Me, too," I said.

"Me, three," said Hitch.

"The reporter's name is Barbara Bivins. How about we meet at eighteen thirty hours? Sun doesn't set for about forty-five minutes after that. You'll have light the whole way there, dusk on the way back if you hurry."

"Sounds good, sir," I said.

Any driving outside of the camp could be dangerous, but as far as missions go and avoiding Baqubah, it was great. I glanced at my watch, which made me realize that if we were going to convoy the reporter at six-thirty p.m., I wouldn't be back by eight for Kayla. Maybe she'd be in our convoy, though.

"Excuse me, Lieutenant," I said, interrupting Jordan's conversation. "Have you told others in our convoy about this yet?"

"You're the first. I'll tell them all and thank them personally."

I bolted out of there.

As I left, the LT left just behind me and called, "Private Rivera?"

I stopped on the dirt path, and he came up. "I have a quick question, if you don't mind," he said. "Do you know Private Kayla Helwani well?"

My heart leaped. Did he know? While coupling was forbidden, it wasn't enforced. Given our stress levels, men and women pairing up brought more relief than problems. Gay sex was don't ask, don't tell, but men and women, it was the American way. Still, we weren't supposed to flaunt it. I worried it showed all over my face.

"I know her a little—why, sir?" I said.

"At the end of the mission today, I saw the look Jordan gave her. Is there animosity there?"

"What? No. They get along fine, sir."

"I think I'll swap her out anyway. I want each team working well."

"She's a great gunner."

"I'll swap her with another gunner," he said. "Carry on, Rivera," and he took off right toward her CHU.

| | | |

At 18:30, the reporter Barbara Bivens couldn't be missed when we met at the memorial wall in Warhorse. The memorial started in 2004 with a

slab of slate propped up against a blast wall, listing the names of twenty-seven soldiers who died that year and the previous one. Each new rotation brought more names of the newly fallen, stenciled in carefully with a black Sharpie. You had to look closely to see the names weren't chiseled. I saw there was a whole new slab for names. We passed it every time we went to and from the chow hall, hoping we wouldn't end up on that wall.

Bivens didn't dress like us but wore a long-sleeved tan shirt with a dark blue Kevlar vest, and she held her blue helmet under her arm. In her early thirties, her dark hair, parted on the right, spilled around her shoulders. She was tall and grinning like a soldier who was told he could spend his leave in the Caribbean, sipping down margaritas. Few people had enthusiasm for this place. I guessed that coming here was a trophy for a reporter. The LT stood next to her, starting to introduce her around—a casual gathering rather than formation. I came with Trace, Styles' CHU-mate, who I'd run into on the way.

As he and I approached, Trace told me, "The Army was damn smart to embed reporters, unlike Vietnam. Now we protect journalists. They're thankful and write well. This war's going to just keep on going." He seemed pissed, as if he hated his part in promoting a positive image for the Army.

I shrugged. Nothing we could do.

"This is Private Rivera and Private Tracewski," said the LT as we joined the circle.

"Nice to meet you," I said and shook Ms. Bivens' hand.

"And this is Specialist Carlos De Jesus, who's replacing one of our team leaders who's in the hospital tonight." That made me hope Styles would get some leave time. He needed it.

Bivens and De Jesus shook hands. I didn't know De Jesus, but I knew he was from another platoon.

"Where're you from?" Bivens asked us. I said Florida, Trace said Maine, and De Jesus said Denver.

"I know the theme park there—Elitch Gardens," she said to De Jesus.

"I'm from what you might call a rougher part of town. We couldn't afford Elitch."

"Maybe when you get back," she said with a smile.

"Yeah, maybe."

"Ms. Bivens and a new medic will be in your Humvee, Rivera." I nodded. Our last medic would soon be on the memorial wall, I realized, lost a week ago, shot by a sniper. "De Jesus will be team leader and navigator. You'll be gunner, and Private Hitchcock will drive."

Jordan, Yanni, a new gunner named Macy, whose lack of neck reminded me of a gerbil, and a big and brand new civilian contractor named Brad Hankshaw would be in the lead Humvee. Kayla and others would be right behind me in the third and fourth Humvees. The LT wouldn't be going as he'd be joining two other squads on missions outside of Baqubah. Yanni remained squad leader.

Hankshaw was a brawny guy in his thirties who looked like he served in an earlier war for his gung-ho attitude. Contractors were being spread into our company more and more as there weren't enough recruits. Essentially soldiers for hire, contractors were paid more than us, and they could also go home anytime they wanted to. Our interpreters were contractors, too.

Hankshaw shook the reporter's hand. "Why're they sending a pretty woman like you to be in a dangerous place like this?" he said as if he were picking her up in a bar.

"Because I can write," she said. "I can look at you and pick on the subtleties that you emanate."

"Emanate," he said, laughing. "I love to do that."

"My guess is you were in the Gulf War, which was the best time of your life, and the wife and kids probably didn't work out, so you're back trying to be young again."

His face fell, and I swore he wanted to punch her. Was he going to have a blowout in front of the LT? Instead, he smiled and winked. "Never said I was hidin' anything. I'm defendin' America, that's for sure. This is a way to help keep terrorists from crashing into more buildings."

"Then I thank you," she said.

"You're welcome."

"All right," said the LT. "Move out." The Humvees started, creating a joint rumbling. As we headed to our vehicles, I passed near Kayla and we pounded fists. I smiled. I jumped in the back of my Humvee and wedged a few empty Gatorade bottles near my gun in case I had to piss. Could I do so in front of our guest? I then calibrated the gun, put on my headset and helmet, and was ready to go. Ms. Bivens sat just below me in the back. The medic on the other side was a woman, too, but I didn't catch her name— not sure when we got her.

We pulled out of the camp.

"Ms. Bivens, you like it here?" I asked, mostly just to be polite.

"It's god-awful hot in here," she said into her headset. "How do you stand it?"

"You get used to it. It's not pleasant. It just is."

"Today in Warhorse," she said, "I felt wiped out walking just ten minutes to the dining hall. The insects, too, are a daily battle even if you dip your clothes in bug spray."

"That's true."

"The fleas, I hear, even carry an incurable disease."

"Guess you don't like it here, then," I said. "If you're worried about this road, it's perfectly safe."

"I know better than that," she said. "In fact, I met a soldier with a head wound at the hospital in Balad. He'd been on this road when a car bomb exploded fifty meters from his Humvee. He was the gunner, knocked out cold when they came to a fast stop to avoid hitting the suicide bomber in a car when it came into their lane. The car then exploded."

"You're never short on things to write about, I expect."

"You're right."

"Maybe you can explain this place to me."

She looked out the window at a beige block hut and two barefoot kids running around in some kind of mud—probably sewage. We hadn't yet crossed the Diyala River, which had green scrub bushes, long grass, and palm trees on either side. We were on the outskirts of Baqubah.

"I suspect if I wrote from now until doomsday, I'd never really get across what you all do here. Everyone back home is busy with their lives, their football games, their saving two dollars on a gallon of paint."

Soon, as we approached a bridge that we'd cross under at the edge of the city, Ms. Bivens said, "Oh, my God." Instantly, I was on the lookout for something moving, my finger on the gun. I saw nothing.

"Up there," she said. A fully clothed man hanged with a rope around his neck off the top of the bridge, which we now passed under.

"He's an Islamic State militant," said our team leader, De Jesus. "It's one way the police show they're at work." In that moment, I realized I was used to such things.

We arrived at Normandy without incident. I liked the look of the place better than Warhorse, which was flat and mostly treeless. Here, there were trees and hills and layered rock formations worthy of a national park. Styles had told me another time that Normandy used to be an Iraqi Army base, but the place was looted after we disbanded Saddam's Army. The place got renovated, and instead of tents and boxy CHUs, soldiers lived in concrete structures, solid buildings. Still, the place was much smaller than Warhorse.

We came to a stop near headquarters, and the base commander, a new captain named Carpentier, in his early thirties, with his sergeant, appeared at the door for Ms. Bivens. I ran around and opened the door for her and said, "Nice meeting you. Good luck."

She stepped out, unsnapping her helmet, and said, "May I get a picture of you all?" We agreed and stood by our Humvee like happy tourists at Disneyland.

She took her picture with a small camera then said, "Let's all have luck."

I nodded, not wanting to say anything more about luck—it'd be unlucky.

After Ms. Bivens and the camp commander walked off, Yanni said to all of us standing in one area, "What do you say for a quick bite here?"

"It'll be dark soon," said Hitch, "but I'm famished."

"*Famished*?" said Jordan. "You're using that vocabulary builder I gave you."

Hitch grinned. "Yeah. Let's *mastercate*."

Jordan laughed, and said, "Sorry. You mixed up masticate and masturbate. You can't eat and fuck at the same time."

"I can try," said Hitch, not the least embarrassed.

While we ate cabbage and burritos, we got caught up in watching a grainy TV, a show from America called *Project Greenlight*. I hated reality shows, but this one, which I'd never heard of, grabbed me. It wasn't about whispering to dogs or watching Orange County housewives. It focused on first-time filmmakers being given the chance to direct a feature film. I could see Jordan and me doing it. Why not—two Army vets trying to make it big—that could play, right? "Absolutely," said Jordan after I suggested it. "We should apply now." I always loved his optimism.

I was so focused on this, I forgot about Kayla. I looked around. She wasn't far away, laughing, standing with Hitch, Yanni, and a couple of others who weren't watching TV. She didn't hang with me probably because she sensed Jordan wasn't her top supporter. In fact, Jordan nodded toward Kayla. "You can see how she never has any women friends, right? She's always with guys."

"Whatever. If you looked like her, wouldn't you be with guys?"

"But how can you relax then? There's something to be said for plain-looking girls who are just into you."

"That's not *true*," I said, slapping his arm. "I've seen pictures of your wife. You're the luckiest guy alive. And with your kid just born?"

He pulled out his small Velcro wallet from his vest and showed me a photo of his baby girl.

"I get to meet her on my R&R," he said. "Hey, I'm a dad! Maybe we can make a movie with her as our little actress."

I grinned big. Who knew that a trip to another camp would give me a new goal? I'd been so into music, I'd forgotten about film—but Jordan and I, we could make films.

Just before that week's winner was announced on *Project Greenlight*, Yanni turned off the TV. "All right. Move it. We're outta here," he said.

"Sarge," said Trace, Style's CHUmate, "can't we see the end?"

"Nope. Outta here."

It was coal-mine dark when we returned to the Humvees. We needed our flashlights to find our vehicles. We should have left earlier. As we walked, I asked Jordan, "You think the LT will be mad we're getting back late?"

"He didn't give us a time table. This is a reward. Why not relax?" he said rhetorically.

For once, the night cooled. We opened some of our windows more than a crack, and Hoogerheide told jokes over our headsets. "Why did the game warden arrest the ghost? Because she didn't have a haunting license.... Why did the blonde put lipstick on her forehead? Because she was trying to make up her mind."

Sure, they were stupid, but we laughed and wanted more. It made the time pass. At one point, I remembered looking out the window at the rising moon, just a crescent, a rising smile framed by the hills. That, then, reminded me of Kayla, behind me.

I opened up the hole to the topside, to stand with the gun. In the minimal moonlight, I nonetheless could see Kayla at the ready—or I guessed that had to be her. Our convoy purred down the quiet desert dirt road.

Over the earpieces, Jordan said, "We're coming to the edge of the city."

"Which city?" I asked.

"Outskirts of Baqubah, held by us. It should be okay, but be on guard," he said. My hands rested on the gun.

One street over, a Stryker brigade had parked, and in the moonlight, I could see the infantry in silhouette. None of the buildings had lights on—the electricity was out.

As we came up to two buildings, Hitch blurted out, "Phew, who ate the beans!" I couldn't believe he'd say such a thing with team leader De Jesus, new to us, in our Humvee. I started laughing and said, "I shouldn't have eaten the beans. Sorry everyone." Hitch coughed with exaggeration, and I said into my radio, "Jordan, you ate the beans, too."

He said, "Open up the topside. I feel like a rocket, ready to take off."

"Oh, no wonder!" said one of his teammates. Yanni maybe—and exaggerated coughs came from over there, too. We became quiet.

Outside I didn't hear a sound, either. I took off my headphones to listen better.

A bright light appeared. At first it didn't register, but then the light lifted up Jordan's Humvee. *Odd* was my first thought. The truck ascended higher and higher as if a giant's hand from underground shoved it aloft—but the hand was all made of light. A fraction of a second later, a shock wave hit me and shoved me back until I hit my head and arm against the armor plate behind me. The sound of the explosion slammed into me, and I watched as the Humvee, surrounded by fire, came slamming down so hard, all four wheels broke off. I instantly screamed "No!" Hitch jammed on our brakes, and I then jerked forward, hitting my helmeted head again. Jordan's Humvee swirled in a ball of fire, and I gasped for air. This couldn't be.

"Jordan!" I yelled. I burst out from above through the turret just as gunfire erupted all around me. A few rounds hit our truck, but miraculously not me. Kayla and the gunner behind her hammered with their guns at the roofs of the two buildings from where we were being ambushed. I should have been shooting, too, but I had to get to Jordan. I wanted nothing more.

I'd probably only taken two steps when De Jesus grabbed me. I hadn't even seen his door open.

"Get back in!" he shouted. "That's an order."

"No way! I'm not letting him burn." I smashed him with my right fist in the face so he'd let go, which he did. I only cared about Jordan. I abandoned my post and ran.

So much happened at the same time. Two doors burst open on Jordan's Humvee, and the contractor from the rear and Yanni from the front raced out of the fire ball. The flames followed them. Their clothes burned. The gunner, Macy, on his knees on the ground, wasn't burning, but his legs splayed at odd angles. He'd been blown from the truck. He screamed in pain and at the same time shot his automatic rifle in a three-round burst into the air without aiming.

Gunfire penetrated the road all around us as Kayla shouted, "Max! Get back." She continued firing.

I continued racing toward Jordan's Humvee. "Jordan?" I yelled. "Are you in there?"

An RPG launched at that moment from the side somewhere and smashed into Hankshaw, the contractor, still running, still on fire, and he exploded. Parts of the man went flying, and something mostly soft bashed into my leg. I couldn't see anyone in the Humvee, totally ablaze. I couldn't get closer. I had to hope Jordan had escaped when I fought with De Jesus.

Yanni lay burning in the street, and I hurried over to him instead.

"Grab sand, put him out," yelled De Jesus, now at my side. In moments, we quenched the fire, and we each grabbed one of Yanni's arms. "Into the empty building here," said De Jesus. The building, all concrete, had no doors or windows, and we dragged Yanni in.

De Jesus whispered something to the sergeant as I raced toward the open door to see if I could spot Jordan. I stopped myself as ammo and grenades exploded in Jordan's Humvee. Bullets were still flying, mostly from Jordan's gunner, Macy. He was in shock. His legs looked like a mosquito's after you hit it with your hand. I shouted, "Stop firing, so the enemy can't see you!" Every shot showed a muzzle flash. "Play dead, play dead," I said.

Macy was out of ammo anyway, and he lay there, breathing heavily. In my earpiece, someone called for the infantry and Strykers. "IED! Our lead Humvee is still on fire, and we're in an ambush—taking lots of fire."

I heard only whimpers from Macy and the sound of the flames. The ambushers had probably run off. We never saw their faces, anyway. They were just flashes of light, a uniformless enemy.

Another pocket of fire came from the contractor, whose torso and legs still burned.

Within a minute, it seemed, Strykers raced in. Soldiers with fire extinguishers raced to the Humvee and the contractor. They blew out the contractor's parts in seconds, while it took a minute for the Humvee. Other soldiers, guns drawn, headed into the buildings to clear them. Without the light from the fire, and with the moon behind a cloud or something, the world turned pitch black. Flashlights snapped on, and they scanned the smoking Humvee. There was no more gunfire, and for a moment, the night stood eerily quiet. I had to hope that Jordan had exited.

I ran toward the lights, but I quickly tripped on someone who groaned, and I came crashing down. Jordan? I had hope. I grabbed my small flashlight from my vest, and when I turned it on, Hitch, flat on the ground, stared at me. I didn't see him bleeding anywhere.

"Hitch, what's wrong?"

"I tripped, and now my left foot..."

I aimed my flashlight at it, and I could see a hole in his boot and some blood oozed around it. "Stay there," I said, "Lay quiet now." Jordan was the only thing on my mind.

I moved my flashlight from Hitch to the Humvee. Three men pulled on Jordan's door. One of the soldiers, Trace, said, "Rivera!" They needed help, and I hurried. We strained at the door, the bottom of which dripped blood as if the Humvee itself were bleeding. A dark puddle grew underneath it.

"Pull!" said Trace, his thick fingers wedged inside the door. Mine were on the handle. I yanked, and the door started to loosen. We were able to creak open the door. Smoke and ash filled the inside. Once it cleared, I pushed into the strong smell of burnt oil. A body lay on the bottom, but it was mostly a skeleton with pieces of meat here and there. "Jordan?" I blurted, starting to cry.

His face, mostly a skull, peered upward. Most of his face and bones were blackened. Still, I could tell it was him, and I screamed his name.

Two men had to pull me out. As they yanked me, I noticed Jordan's eye sockets were just jelly. How could a person be a person and then so quickly not? My cries and screams overshadowed everything else. A few more soldiers had to hold me down until I didn't fight it anymore.

Kayla found me sitting on the ground, and I could only shake my head.

Soon, a medevac helicopter landed nearby, and soldiers leaped out with stretchers. They loaded up Hitch, Yanni, and Macy.

"Fucking Jordan's gone," I said. My head throbbed.

She nodded. "I'm sorry."

Tears came to my eyes.

Three men lifted the remains of Jordan into a body bag. Soon the engineers came and put wheels under Jordan's Humvee and carted the wreckage off.

| | | |

In Warhorse's medical facility, as I heard the sound of two helicopters taking off close by—probably medevac helicopters—I waited in an exam room. The same doctor who looked at me the first time strolled in and said, "We had to get a guy to Balad…." He was already lost in his clipboard as if purposely trying to keep his distance.

I nodded as he looked at his paperwork—then he looked at me more closely, saying, "You again. Were you in that ambush in town tonight?"

I nodded.

He said, "I heard we lost a couple."

I looked down at the ground, thinking again about Jordan's face, the jelly in his eye sockets. I realized his nose had been sizzled away—just crust around a hole in the skull.

He glanced at his clipboard and then pointed to what triage wrote. "Possible concussion," the doctor said. I thought about it, and as I was thinking, he added, "Do you have ringing in your ears?"

Now that he mentioned it, I did. I nodded. "I also have a killer headache."

He looked in my eyes with a flashlight. "A concussion again—not a good thing."

A few seconds floated by like a bee on the wind. "It doesn't feel as bad as last time," I said.

"You need rest. We can observe you overnight, if you like—a couple rooms over."

"I'd rather sleep in my own cot."

He let me.

As I stood to leave, a nurse knocked on the door, popped her head in, and said to the doctor, "He passed. Didn't make the whole flight."

The doctor looked sad, and I watched them both, wondering who else died. My face must have looked horrible because the doctor said, "Oh, no—not Baqubah. Here."

"What happened here?"

"Just before sunset, a car bomb exploded two hundred meters in front of the entrance. A huge cloud of chlorine gas floated through here, sickening sixty-two—chemical warfare now. Once that was done..." He paused, trying to absorb it. "I'd read somewhere there's been like ninety suicides by active-duty soldiers here and in Afghanistan this year."

"Someone killed himself?"

"Yeah."

He looked away. "Some days are just harder than others."

I nodded and stepped off.

It was still night, and I slinked toward my CHU. It was the longest walk of my life. Jordan or Hitch wouldn't be there. I'd be alone. That made me stop at Styles' and Trace's CHU, where I knocked. No one there, either. The Monopoly streets were all quiet. Maybe there was a meeting of some sort with the brass and the troops. Maybe they were analyzing. I reconsidered walking back to stay overnight in a hospital bed. There at least I wouldn't be alone. My boots crunched the soil as I walked, sounding like someone eating cereal. Each step drained me more. Images of Jordan before and after tumbled within me. There he was playing basketball. There he was warning me about Kayla. There he was burnt as a skeleton. I gasped.

When I turned the corner, a number of dark figures stood in front of my CHU. Was I hallucinating? I was ready to run back to the medical facility. Then I heard "Max?" It was Hoogerheide.

Then "Max?" in Kayla's voice.

Then "Max!" from Trace and everyone uninjured in our team and more from our platoon. They encircled me, hugged me, and all I could do was cry. I went limp. They picked me up and carried me into my CHU. God damn these people. I loved them.

At some point, someone brought in bottled water and sodas and watermelon. Where did they find watermelon in Iraq near midnight? It tasted so sweet. We told fun stories of Jordan. At different points, different people started crying. Jordan seemed to affect us all. Someone said they'd heard from Balad that Yanni and Hitch would be back the next day. Hitch had a bandaged foot, and Yanni, despite the fire, only had second-degree burns on his face and hands, and a few other places—very little on his torso. We'd put him out quickly enough.

After everyone left, Kayla stayed with me. She said nothing, just turned out the lights and slipped off her clothes. Her form like starlight shimmered in the dark, approaching me. She gently removed my clothes.

I wasn't me. The normal me would've jumped in, conscious of my goal to do it, climax, and consider it a victory—another entry on my sexual resume. After what happened with Jordan and the events since then, not only didn't I expect this to be happening, but I felt so happy and sad at the same time. My tears fell on my cheeks. Kayla kissed them off.

Soon, we kissed deeply, urgently. She seemed as needy as me and directed me to my cot, where she pulled herself on top of me. She teased me the way she rocked and rolled on me. I laughed, loving her so much, and I held her face, amazed at this person. Her soul felt part of my nervous system, and I cried more. What was happening with my feelings? I didn't know what the hell to think, but just let it all be. She reached down for my lower self. Then I was in. It was like the core of the earth pulsed right there. Nothing mattered but this moment.

She moved herself first up and down, then side to side, and I watched the crescent of her face and held her sides.

When Kayla gasped, so did I, and we came together. Then I thought about nothing, which was a blessing. In the distance, just above a whisper, a helicopter fluttered and disappeared. A muezzin called out to prayer. Maybe my mind was making it up because what Kayla and I just did was a religious experience, a Middle-Eastern consummation, worthy of God.

Kayla fell asleep, but I didn't because I heard a knock on the door. Who would be there at that hour? I didn't move, just held Kayla. Jordan walked in, his face obscured. He stepped over to the corner, where he used to edit at his desk, and then I saw his face was scorched off, his jaw gone. He calmly said, 'Why would you leave me?'"

I couldn't breathe. Maybe there were such things as ghosts. In high school, my English teacher had us read Shakespeare's *Hamlet* and then showed us the movie version with Mel Gibson as Hamlet and Glenn Close as his mother. Hamlet's father's ghost made sense. He was a soul stuck on earth. Maybe Jordan stuck around to help us. But how was he helping us?

Someone or something was shaking me, and then, next thing I knew, Kayla's face was before me? "Are you okay?" she asked, worried.

"Holy shit,"I said. "I thought you were alseep, not me, and Jordan came in here, wondering why I left him.

"Powerful stuff," she said.

After a while, she found her panties and T-shirt. I didn't move. "I guess I should go," she said.

"Yeah." I reached for my underwear and pulled them on. Kayla seemed to stare. Maybe there was more light from her angle. Maybe there was something to see.

| | | |

In a rare company formation, our four platoons stood the next day on the hot tarmac with a corridor down the middle. In our permapress camo uniforms, we did not carry weapons, body armor, or helmets, but wore our billed caps. In the merciless sun, most of us wore sunglasses. I stood in the wide space between the two groups, joining three other people, ready for the Warhorse version of what we called the Patriot Ceremony. We pulled Jordan's flag-draped silver transfer case off a flatbed truck, the flag-and-case a colorful contrast to the rusted bed and the brown and tan of the nearby soil. Normally, Hitch and Yanni might be part of the four, but they hadn't returned from Balad yet. Just released from the hospital, Styles stood next to me on the other front corner, looking surprisingly upbeat. Or was he twisted and damaged?

"You okay?" I whispered.

"Who we have in our hands has nothing to do with authenticity," he whispered back.

I didn't understand.

"We are finite. That's what counts." Then he stared across the tarmac to the plane stone-faced.

The case wasn't very heavy. Had they put Jordan's bones in a uniform? I hadn't dared to ask about that.

The First Sergeant said, "Turn in," and the troops turned in unison to face inward to us, creating a passageway. They all saluted as we walked slowly.

I spotted Kayla at the back of our platoon even though I couldn't gaze at her face. Styles did not look in the same direction. A lone bugler blew something ceremonial that I didn't recognize, and my group moved forward toward the waiting helicopter. Jordan's body would be returned to his wife—to Fort Lewis in Washington? I wasn't sure where. He'd at last meet his daughter, Newshell. His wife wanted to name her Michelle, but Jordan wanted something new, thus the amalgam name. Newshell would never meet his live self.

Once we placed him in the helicopter, we stood back, and we saluted. The whole company turned toward the helicopter and saluted anew. The helicopter rose, throwing dust all around us like so many Tinkerbells, and the whirlybird became smaller and smaller until it seemed we dreamed it all. Captain Carpentier then dismissed the company.

As I walked off, I spotted Kayla, and she saw me.

"Hey," she said.

"Hey," and it looked like she wanted to hug me, but with other soldiers passing us, she resisted and nodded to them. "That was a nice send-off," I said.

She nodded. "The Army actually does good stuff every now and then. Where will his funeral be?"

"I don't know. He's from San Diego, but his wife and daughter still live at Fort Lewis. What's Blake Styles say about Jordan?"

"Why're you asking me?"

I felt I needed to say what I hadn't the previous night. "You just have a lot of men in your life, not a lot of women."

"That's a really fucked thing to say, you know?" Hot wind pulled strands of her dark hair across her face.

"I'm sorry. I'm not accusing you of anything. Just saying what I noticed. Jordan noticed it, too."

"Why're you spoiling everything?" She stared hard at me.

"I'm trying to be honest."

"And I'm honestly saying I'm with you."

I toyed with a stone on the beige earth with my right boot. "There're just things I can't forget, like you and Styles together."

"Not this again. Are you really that insecure?"

"I am." What could she say to that?

"If Blake is really your friend, you have to see he's fucked up right now. Is he going to do something stupid and get himself killed? Around here, suicide can look a lot like killed in action. You should be helping him, not off being fucking jealous."

I probably nodded, but guys like Styles always had everything. He had a family and was handsome and smart. Kayla was attractive and brainy. What did either like about me? I couldn't keep up. After Iraq, they'd probably each land on their feet well. Me, I had my doubts.

"What is it that I have to prove for you?" she said.

"There's probably nothing."

"Then while you're alone in your CHU tonight, ponder what it might be like with us not being friends." She scowled and stepped off angrily.

"Kayla," I said, but that didn't stop her. Fuck it. I had too much on my mind with Jordan. I went to my empty CHU. Instantly, I realized how well she knew me. The place was an empty aluminum can. I didn't want to be in it alone. I should go to the gym or grab something more at the chow hall.

I spotted my guitar. I knew what to do. I grabbed it, and I sat on the floor, leaning against Jordan's cot, and I started to play—nothing specific, just chords. Moving my fingers on her neck and feeling the strings press into my fingers felt reassuring. C, G, D, C—so good, especially D with my third finger hitting the sweet spot of the second string, third fret. So good. D, D, D. Like a blackbird singing in the dead of night. I tried d minor instead, and it felt more right, more sad. That was it, and I kept playing them over and over until other minor chords came along, and I couldn't stop sniffling until I started humming—and I kept playing and playing. Then louder but not faster. I kept thinking about Jordan, how I'd never had a friend in high school like him—no one like him, ever—but he was easy to hang with. He pushed me, watched out for me, showed me I had talent for making movies. He understood my humor. I could be his friend without thinking about it. Unlike a lot of people I came to know in the Army, he hadn't done anything terrible in his past. He was just good. His wife, his baby, all good. How was his death fair?

The light inside the CHU changed for a moment, and I looked over. Hitch stood at the door, watching, nodding. I nodded. There was so much I wanted to say, but not now. I couldn't interrupt my sounds. As if Hitch knew, he moved to his cot and pulled out his drumsticks from underneath his pillow—and took the pillow, too. He sat next to me, and as I played, he drummed on his pillow. I still didn't have a song—just making up ever-changing chords and a rhythm, and Hitch kept up with me.

Several minutes later, Yanni popped his head in. He looked great, and I was glad to see he was okay. I waved him in. He stepped forward with a portable Korg keyboard, which had built-in speakers. I knew he played, but I hadn't realized he had one in camp. He unraveled its long cord, plugged it into the wall, and then sat the keyboard on a single-X keyboard stand. He plunked himself on my cot and pulled his keyboard closer. He watched us a little bit, then started playing chords to match my pattern. It sounded a lot like an orchestral piano. I nodded. They nodded. Our music started to fall into sync as if we were a staged symphony. What was happening?

My guitar became more forceful, and my voice, instead of humming became more *errr* and *ahhh*, as if the pain I was feeling for Jordan's loss was finding sound. These two guys sailed with me, channeling their pain, too. I can't explain it, but it was as if we became a group of monks chanting into the cosmos, headed to outer space, traveling on notes of the spheres. I supposed people could hear us, but I didn't care.

I stared at where Jordan's cot used to be. Someone had come in and taken all of his stuff including his bedding and cot. You could see scotch tape residue where photos of his wife and baby once hung.His computer and desk were gone. It's as if a mess were cleaned and he never existed.

The light changed in the CHU once more. At the door stood Styles with a black guitar case in hand as well as a small amp. He looked worse than me, hunched, sad, as if needing the very thing we had going here. Behind him entered his roommate Trace with an uncased electric guitar in hand. My head nodded them over. They sat and Styles pulled out a bass guitar and plugged into the same amp. Trace played rhythm—not that he was particularly good at it, but he had enthusiasm. I showed them the chords I played, which now had a pattern—a song I'd made up. Once they followed what I was doing, I then improvised with high, forlorn notes, notes that shot to the heavens. My singing—not words but groans—became more urgent. Our pace quickened. Hitch, slapping the pillow and his legs for different sounds, reminded me of gunfire and the scene where we'd lost Jordan. I gasped. We all built to a crescendo and just stopped at exactly the right moment.

I was breathing hard. So were they.

I looked at my watch. Its face was cracked, and the second-hand didn't move. The time showed 8:32. Shit. That's when Jordan died.

Continuing: Iraq, June 2007

The five of us headed to the chow hall for dinner. Styles looked much improved, standing taller, and whatever jealousy I had over him had disappeared. He was like us all, crazed in his own way, but his heart was true. I felt lucky to know him and the others. They were the best of the best.

Just as I was clearing my 9mm Beretta into the clearing barrel outside the dining tent, Styles turned to me and said, "Come with me the haji souk. I need to get my father a watch. They have Rolexes there for like twenty-five bucks."

My heart took a leap as I thought how I needed a watch, too—did he know? "Rolexes?" I said.

"Yeah, normally super expensive. Of course, I don't expect it's real, but what is in that place? Those soccer shirts and DVDs aren't exactly genuine, either."

As we walked into the bazaar in the MWR Center, a young man at the watch table, wearing his official concessionaire security badge with his name, Rafik, dropped a watch on the floor. When he kneeled to pick it up, he looked up at us as we walked toward him. He looked flustered again, dropping the watch once more. Dark-skinned, he sported a U-shaped mustache that appeared thicker than his young thin face could grow. He also wore a scar in a dent on his chin.

"I'm not going to buy that one," said Styles, walking up.

Rafik laughed, stood, and stared intently at Styles. "I sell only the finest watches."

"Do you have a Rolex with a picture of Saddam on it?"

"Certainly, sir. We also have Saddam t-shirts, caps, and sunglasses, too," he said, moving his hand toward his display, accidently knocking over a plastic bust of Saddam with a white baseball cap on his head.

"You're kind of clumsy," said Styles, now looking at the young man more closely. "Have we met?"

I helped the young man by picking up the bust. Only then did I notice the baseball cap showed Saddam pointing up, and words next to him said, "I'm gonna drop from up there?"

"I don't think so, sir," said Rafik. Here's the Saddam watch. Rolex. Fifty dollars."

"Fifty?" said Styles. "I heard they were twenty-five."

The young man looked amused. "No, not Saddam watch. It's best-seller. Forty for you."

"Thirty-five," said Styles.

"Thirty-five?" The young man stared at it as if selling it at that price would be painful. "Real gold band," said Rafik.

"That's bullshit, but that's okay. Thirty-five."

"Okay, sir."

I held out the Saddam baseball cap, saying, "And I'll take this and a Saddam watch, too."

After our purchases, as we walked back toward the chow tent, Sergeant Ichisada hurried up to me and said, "There you are, Private Rivera. May I speak with you?"

This was a highly unusual thing for him to say. Sergeants don't ask. They talk.

"Yes, Sergeant," I said. He waved me over, away from Styles, clearly not wanting him to hear.

"I'll meet you inside," said Styles.

"Am I in trouble?" I asked. the sergeant. Something was up.

"Private Jordan's widow asked the Sergeant Major if you could attend the funeral in San Diego in a few days," he said. "The request was granted." That meant I'd be given leave.

"I—San Diego?" That answered where he'd be buried. And I could leave the war? "Of course," I said. "It'd be an honor. When do I go?"

"We've arranged everything. You leave at sunup tomorrow. Check in at the flight line at oh-five-hundred hours. You'll need to be back here in seven days."

I was so stunned, I clasped his shoulder as if he were a good friend and said, "Thank you, Sergeant."

He looked on my hand on his shoulder, smiled, and said, "We all loved Jordan. Do us proud."

This would be no paid vacation. There would be no welcome-home party for me in the States. Instead, I'd watch my friend be buried. My smile faded.

"Roger, Sergeant," I said.

The night felt long. I couldn't keep my eyes shut.

I also felt bad I couldn't find Kayla before I left. I wanted to apologize. I wrote I was sorry in a note that I left in her CHU and admitted I was out of it lately. I just missed Jordan.

To leave, I joined a convoy to Camp Victory. I felt pleased as I left, but you'd think I'd be outright giddy to get out. Rather, once I headed out of Victory by helicopter, I felt a pain in my chest. I hoped it was acid reflux and not a heart attack—but I felt like shit all over, and I thought if it were my time to go, it may as well be this. The helicopter from Victory brought me to Kuwait. I then grabbed a military transport out of country.

Part of my feeling poorly, I guessed, was guilt. I hadn't saved Jordan. Added to that, once I landed in Amsterdam, was I didn't fit in. In Amsterdam's modern airport, people around me laughed, chatted, smiled, read, ate, shopped and, unlike me, didn't worry that someone would shoot them around the next corner. I wasn't in Baqubah, but that feeling didn't disappear. I looked up at a TV, and CNN had a story about a mass shooting at Virginia Tech three months earlier. Was the war also at home?

I bought two bottles of tequila in a duty-free shop as a gift to Jordan's widow. Was liquor a good thing to bring to a funeral? I didn't know, other than wanting some. In one hand, I carried the sealed carry-on pack of tequila, and in the other, my guitar. I'd be alone in the hotel often. The guitar was my friend.

Even though it was early morning, I ordered a Heineken at an airport bar. It didn't taste as good as I remembered, but I drank it fast and ordered a second. Was the guy across from me staring at me? No, he waved his hand at a woman behind me in a white dress and multicolored top, who I saw when I turned. There should be a special chamber for people in my situation, the type divers use if they zip to the surface too quickly. Maybe a day or two on an Army base in Germany would have made me realize it was okay not to be paranoid, that people who looked at me in my uniform in the airport weren't going to pull out a gun.

Finally on my commercial flight to the States, I felt my stomach hit my throat when the airplane soon fought a heavy wind. I drank a rum-and-Coke to numb the experience.

It wasn't long before I awoke with my face on the little drop-down table. I wiped the drool from the corner of my mouth. I had the window seat and needed to pee badly. I unbuckled my seat belt and folded up my table, and started to stand in the hunch-back way by the window. My seatmates got the signal. A well-dressed teenage girl, white blouse, sensible slacks, and a gold cross around her neck, and her librarian-looking mother had to step out for me to go. "Are we getting close to Minneapolis?" I asked the woman, referring to where I had to grab my flight to San Diego.

"We left only an hour ago," she said.

"About eight hours left," said the girl, whose long auburn hair framed an innocuous face that could launch a thousand painters. I could picture her as a heartbreaker someday. Her first boyfriend would prey on her innocence, but then she'd get it. Women had the power. They didn't realize how lucky they were.

God, this would be a long flight. The pee did me good, as did walking the aisle.

I'd flown little in my life, and when I had, there were no free meals or free beers, but here on KLM, the attendants offered both—free Heineken, no less. First we got lunch. The mother turned to me. "Thank you for your service," she said. "Where are you stationed?"

"Iraq."

"How is it?" I didn't want to say my best friend was fried before my eyes, and so many young Americans, men and women from mostly poor or rural families lost their lives, limbs, or their sanity. Instantly, I felt queasy.

"Are you all right?"

She probably could see the war in my eyes. "Just a little airplane jitters," I said.

I don't think she bought it.

"Well, thank you," said the daughter.

I needed to lose myself in mindless drama, and I selected from the generous movie menu something called *300*, where 300 Spartans confronted the Persian army in the mountain pass of Thermopylae. Why I watched a war movie, I can't say other than it took place in 480 BC, and there were no IEDs or RPGs or other groups of devastating acronyms. Also, the visuals were amazing. This filmmaker could really deliver. As I watched, the young woman next to me said, "Oh, *300*—awesome."

"You've seen this?" I asked.

"Yeah. The director went to Art Center."

"Art Center?"

"It's an art school in Pasadena."

"Film program?" I said.

"Yeah, but I'm an illustrator. There's a great car design program, too."

I nodded politely, wanting to get back to *300*.

She pulled out earbuds from her purse and ordered the same movie on her screen.

After *300*, I selected the James Bond film *Casino Royale*. The Bond story with Daniel Craig offered great twists, surprising me in that most Bond films were predictable. In this Bond, he actually felt open to love. What's the world coming to?

Six hours after breakfast came lunch. I could get used to this system. This was the life.

We finally landed, and it was still the morning. It's weird how you lose so little time flying west—like getting part of your life back. In Minneapolis, with an hour and a moose coffee cup from a gift stand, I boarded the next flight.

I knew nothing of California except what I saw on TV and the movies: shots over glass skyscrapers at night, the Hollywood sign, people at the beach, and the Mamas and the Papas' song, "California Dreamin'". Once we landed, maybe I'd see movie stars—except where I was going was a couple hours south of L.A. As the airplane approached San Diego, we dropped down, gliding over industrial parks, malls, homes, freeways, and narrow belts of trees like green paint fallen from a bucket. Large homes with red-tile roofs impressed me, then a golf course, and a freeway carved into a canyon.

I yearned for the ocean, and I knew the Pacific was here. I wondered if I'd have time for a swim? I was tired of the desert and the dry sand. Give me waves and water.

Before I'd left Iraq, I'd received an email from Jillian, Jordan's widow, who said she'd arranged a hotel for me, Humphreys Half Moon Inn. It's where most of the funeral party would be staying. She explained while Jordan hadn't lived in San Diego since joining the Army, he had thought they'd live there once he got out. That's where a lot of his friends still lived. We were part of Fort Lewis, up near Seattle, so it's where Jillian and the baby had been living, waiting for Jordan's return. She thought it best for him to be buried there, in the Fort Rosecrans National Cemetery on Point Loma. She said it wasn't far from the airport, so just grab a cab and then call her from the hotel once I arrived. She'd come find me.

My bearded cab driver knew exactly where my hotel was, and he raced down a wide street called North Harbor Drive in the very late-afternoon light. I could see the ocean, the blessed ocean. I'd almost forgotten what it looked like.

As the driver drove toward the front entrance of Humphreys Half Moon Inn and Suites, I gazed at tranquil water on either side of me. We glided on an isthmus in a quiet bay, and sailboats like sleepy soldiers stood with stick masts into the yellowing light. Humphreys Half Moon

Inn was about as far from living in an aluminum can in the desert as it could be.

The hotel felt Hawaiian, palm and banana trees everywhere, bright orange and blue trim in the lobby of light wood—a tiki-type place. The restaurant, white tables in a glass room that overlooked the sailboats, grabbed my breath. When I saw the swimming pool on my way to my room, I forgot about calling Jillian. I had to swim. This place was the exact opposite of Iraq—no rubble, no shooting, no one dying. Palm trees and low-level ferns acted like a giant hedge, a green shield, lush, verdant. Once poolside and in a suit I'd only used at Camp Victory, the bar with two women drinking something pink with orange slices looked good, so I ordered that, slugged it down, swam, then settled back into the hot tub. I became so drowsy, I felt weak. I pushed myself back to my room.

My Army-booted feet crunched against a gravel path in a strange, tall-hedge maze, like in Kubrick's movie *The Shining*. I don't know where it was or why I was there, but I could hear women laughing seductively. All I remember doing was running ahead with no plan or no sense of direction and feeling lost. A rat could have done better than me.

A phone rang. I blinked awake to find myself on top of the bed in my swimsuit. This is where I must have fallen asleep, not the hot tub.

"Hello?"

"Max?" said a woman. "It's Jillian."

"Oh, man," I said. "Sorry I didn't call. After all that flying, I crashed right on the bed in my clothes." I was freezing in my now-dry swimsuit, actually. "What time is it?"

"Almost nine."

I heard a baby crying, and she told me to hold on a sec. The crying soon stopped, and she said, "You still there?"

"Yep. How'd you stop your baby crying so fast?"

"A breast. I'm like one of those *Seattle Weekly* ads for topless housemaids. That's me, walkin' around the place with my breasts at the ready."

The image made me wince. I couldn't be thinking of the widow's breasts. I quickly said, "Thank you for the hotel. It's beautiful."

"It's the least I could do. Did you have a good flight?"

"Yes.

"Sorry we had to meet this way," she said somberly. "We're having a little gathering tomorrow night," she said, "and then the funeral is the day after tomorrow, on Saturday."

I was glad I was here, but I worried about all those people. I'd be the face of the Army to them, the face that took away their boy. I could only say, "I'm sorry about Jordan."

"It's not your fault," she said, now sounding more down. "He arrives tomorrow."

I wanted to say if only I got to him faster, maybe I could have grabbed him. I'd spent hours wondering if I could have done things differently. Thirty seconds faster to the Humvee probably wouldn't have done it. What if we'd left Camp Normandy earlier? What if I had suggested another route to Jordan? What if I hadn't been joking at the time?

"He was a good, good man," I said. "My best friend."

"He talked about you a lot—you and your girlfriends."

"Girlfriends? I didn't have that many."

"Yeah?"

"Two is all this year, not at the same time." That made me think of Kayla. Was there something more I could say in an email that would make things right? Would it sound better coming from thousands of miles away? I'd tell her I was thinking of her, and that California was amazing. Her hometown in Orange County wasn't far away. Would I ever get to visit her there?

"Jordan said he was glad you were his friend," Jillian said.

"He only said great things about you. Made me envious." Jordan had figured out love. If only I could.

"Want to come over?" she said. "I have a suite, and there're a few people here. I'll introduce you."

I didn't feel like seeing people now, but I said, "Of course," and she gave me her room number. "Give me ten minutes to freshen up," I said.

I quickly dressed into jeans and a T-shirt, splashed water on my face, and brushed my teeth. But I couldn't go just yet. I worked on a song I'd been composing in my head about Jordan. For lack of anything better, I called it "Jordan's Song." I pulled the guitar out of its case, found a pick, and created an opening sound, a kind of overture heavy on the bass. Then I tried out the lines, which I'd written down in my notebook.

Ever see two puppies wrestle and play?
They prance and they paw in affectionate display.
They're friends without thinking—we were that way.
Amid the bombs and the bullets, I could say:

In you I had a friend, water balloons, crazy tunes,
run around the room. It ended too soon.
Even before we could make our movies.
Oh, man, what am I going to do?

That's the way it is,
but your absence is biting.
The truth always stings,
and I don't want to be fighting.

I don't know what to do.
This song's for you.

I stopped because I also thought of Kayla. Her absence was biting, too. What was wrong with me? Jordan was gone, and thoughts of Kayla buzzed in like flies.

Write honestly, I told myself, and my pencil began scribbling.

The stars above Iraq
Told me all I need to know
We're two little specks on the fall
Looking for meaning if I could be anything at all.

This is my truth. It's all I have to say,
I can't stop loving you. I can't stop thinking of you.
I can't stop wanting you.
I just can't stop needing you.

The stars above Iraq
Told me all I need to know
We're two little specks on the fall
Looking for meaning if I could be anything at all.

The music echoed through the room. I looked down at my fingers—cracked fingertips lined with blood. The clock on the desk showed it was almost nine-thirty. I'd better go.

| | | |

I soon knocked on Jillian's door. The door opened, and in the background, someone laughed amid the sounds of "Clocks" by Coldplay. While the song was a little too mainstream for me, the solo piano meeting the driving beat of the drum and guitar brought tears to my eyes. It was one of Jordan's favorites, and in that instant, I realized I was an emotional mess.

With a sleeping baby swaddled in pink in her arms, Jillian smiled, her face an Ivory Soap commercial, her blue eyes radiant. She seemed a lot younger than I expected, maybe because I thought of mothers as older. She was probably nineteen or twenty, younger than me.

"Max!" she said as if she knew me.

I hugged her with one arm and looked closely at the little girl. I touched her sleeping cheek. "Newshell," I said.

Jillian smiled wide. "You remembered. Almost no one gets it right."

"She's new." She looks just like him, I realized.

She waved me in. A hubbub of chatter grew.

This wasn't the usual hotel room, but a huge living room with thick beige carpeting, two leather couches, smaller easy chairs, ocean art on the white walls, and a raised sloping wooden ceiling—with people everywhere. On one couch sat an older couple with beers, talking with a young woman, a younger clone of Jillian, perched on the end. A huge circular table for eating stood near the galley-style kitchen, and all eight seats were taken. Mostly young people stood, talking animatedly.

Confusion never stops, sang Coldplay's Chris Martin, *Closing walls and ticking clocks.*

"Max, this is Jordan's parents," Jillian said, giving their names. "And my sister."

I'm often terrible with names, and right now, they didn't even come through.

"Hi," I said.

"Max from Iraq?" said Jordan's mother.

"Yes."

"I've heard so much about you," she said. Her eyes glistened as if she'd been crying recently.

The sister said something to me, and it appeared to be earnest, and I nodded, hoping that response would do.

"And here," said Jillian, moving to four people about my age, introducing me.

"Hey-O," I said, generic enough.

They laughed, and I wasn't sure why.

"Are you hungry? asked Jillian. "We have leftover take-out Thai."

"A little," I said, even though I was starving. She handed the baby to her father, a funeral director who oversaw Jordan's burial.

"Nice to meet you," he said.

In the kitchen, Jillian grabbed a plate from a cupboard and said something, pointing at the boxes.

"I'm sorry, what was the question?" I asked.

"Pad Thai or seafood fried rice?"

I nodded, and she loaded me up from the white take-out boxes, adding some yellow curry thing and what looked to be mint-covered beef. She threw the plate in the microwave and zapped it, and I nodded or felt like I was.

She looked at me, concerned. "Are you okay?"

"Sure," I said. "Why?"

"You look like I'm feeling, as if my guts had been yanked through my belly button." Tears came to her eyes. "I miss him!"

I hugged her, no thinking required.

"It's okay," I said, "even if I'm probably your worst guest ever."

"Why would you say that?"

"I don't know what to do... to just be. Jordan has all these other friends, and really, who am I?"

"You're more. You helped him in such a difficult time."

"Not as much as he helped me, believe me."

"He said you made him laugh so much."

"That's me, a goof-off."

"No. Come on. Don't be so hard on yourself."

It was as if I'd known her forever. I see why Jordan found her. The microwave dinged, and she handed me my steaming meal.

"I'm hoping you can say something at the funeral," she said.

"I'd like to but—" My palms went clammy. Even though I'd played in front of over a thousand people, this idea of speaking without music terrified me more than anything else. "Maybe you should get someone who's known him longer." I scooped Pad Thai into my mouth, which instantly burned my tongue.

"No. You," she said.

| | | |

On Saturday afternoon, headstones like white teeth fell in neat rows on Irish grass down the hillside to the sea. Live oaks toward the bottom framed a destroyer in the bay. A naval base wasn't far from here. This cemetery, I'd learned that morning using Google, had originally been a coastal artillery station, last manned in World War II when we worried about a Japanese invasion.

Jillian, her family, Jordan's family, his and her friends, stood around a neat oblong hole, edged cleanly with a green mat. Earlier, one of Jordan's cousins mentioned that this national burial ground normally was closed to new interments, but someone in Warhorse had pulled some strings, and a space had opened up.

Rosecrans National Cemetery seemed so quiet, all these soldiers from the mid-nineteenth century and up, veterans all. That's a lot of people protecting this country in one spot. They deserved a sunny, postcard place. Jordan did for sure.

A military chaplain said something about being called home. Jordan's home wasn't anywhere but a hole six feet down. I hadn't really been listening closely, mainly because I was waiting for my name to be called. I'd told Jillian that morning before the funeral that I just couldn't do it. I wasn't a good speaker, and Jordan deserved someone more eloquent than me.

She'd said, "But Jordan always talked about the songs you wrote, how they were so emotional."

"Really? He said that?"

"So do a song."

Why hadn't I thought of that? The idea set me free. In fact, I wrote a new song that morning. It wasn't perfect, but it was from the heart. My name was called. I reached behind me, picked up my guitar, and stepped next to the minister.

"Thank you for having me. I'm Max Rivera. I was in Iraq with Jordan, and I witnessed him ... leave us. It was a very difficult thing, but seeing you all here makes me realize even more how many lives he's touched. I wrote this song for him."

I started to play, and I sang:

When I was young, my love left me,
I hurried to a tall roof and almost took the dive.
Now I've joined a war across the sea
where men and women fight to stay free
As my friends and I try to help each other stay alive
in one battle, my best friend has died.

As I looked out, turning to each and every one there, some people nodded at me, and others started to cry. The sky never felt bluer. I continued.

The night after in Baquabah,
on a car seat under the sky,
I looked into the starfield, and I kept asking why.
Why was it you, why you and not I?

But no answer comes, what can I say?
You had such humor, I wished you could stay.

I sing this with love, with prayer and with feeling
May your soul dance with us amid the heavenly ceiling.

Then quiet.

I didn't expect it. I don't know what I expected at a funeral. I didn't get any applause, but I saw their faces, some crushed, some smiling, others crying. They felt very much like me.

An honor guard of three soldiers shot into the air three times. A lone bugler played "Taps," and afterwards, people came to the chaplain to thank him and tell him it was a good service. A number of people approached me, too. One man, unusually thin, perhaps forty with a gaunt face that reminded me of a holocaust survivor, came up and held out his hand and said, "Wes Besko."

I shook his hand. "Nice to meet you, Wes. Max." His thinning hair looked electric.

"Your song made me think—and feel. Thank you." He smiled, revealing a few missing teeth.

"You a friend of Jordan's?"

"Oh, no. I'm a vet, though. Gulf war—the first one, nineteen ninety."

"Oh." What the hell was he here for?

Perhaps my question showed on my face, as he said, "I like to go to funerals. Kind of imagine, you know?"

"Not really. I hope I don't have to go to another for a long time. What do you do?"

"I teach pottery to adults. It used to mean a lot to me."

"Not anymore?"

He held up one hand, which shook slightly. "Parkinson's. Some days better than others. I don't know what I believe anymore. A pot should be as true as a woman, I used to say," he said, which made him laugh and made me look for Jillian. She was walking over and waved.

"It's not karma," Wes added. "Karma says bad things come because you did something bad in a previous life. Fuck that." He held his two middle fingers up in a fuck-you to the sun. "Stars explode. Cars crash on the Coronado Bridge just over this hill. Bad things happen just because. Am I right?"

"It's all chaos," I said.

"It didn't used to be," he said, and turned to the ocean and pointed. "When I was a kid, the ocean was really something." He stared at it.

I felt bad for Wes, so I shook his hand again and said, "I hope your clay gives you pleasure again. Thanks for coming."

He nodded and muttered something I didn't quite hear as he walked off. I stared after him. Sometimes people are like a hot pocket of fire. He unnerved me.

Jillian arrived and said, "Who's that?"

"Wes Besko, Army vet. Makes me realize no one gets out of a war unchanged."

She stared at me, then hugged me. "What you did was a poem—for me, for everyone. Thanks."

I nodded.

"Jordan said how great you are in film, but you're a talented musician, too."

"Wish I could have a career in either."

"Art is everything," she said. "Follow it."

I looked back to see Wes walking toward the hillside until his silhouette faded.

| | | |

The rest of the time in San Diego floated by. At the hotel pool, I stared at the sky for the longest time, watching a jet create a white cigarette contrail. It must have been a fighter because high in the sky, it cut the blue in two. The trick was just to be, and I was being, but then Jillian and the others left that afternoon, and I felt deeply alone. I stayed the extra day because I could. The morning I had to leave, my stomach knotted. I ordered a huge breakfast in the hotel so the time would last longer, and I read the paper, the *San Diego Union-Tribune*. I never read newspapers because they're so full of made-up shit. Still, I picked up a paper because I always admired how people in the movies used to sit with their breakfast at a hotel and sip their coffee, eat their eggs, and read a newspaper. That's what I did.

Funny what you see on a printed page. I paused at the article on the Bush administration's negotiations with Iran over its nuclear power program. Iran might be building a nuclear bomb, and the U.S. needed to slow Iran down or stop it. Iran was next door to Iraq. Bush didn't appear to be serious in dealing with meaningful long-term restraints. Didn't matter. I would be long out of the region by the time this was settled or not.

Apple was going to start selling full-length movies on iTunes. Good. About time.

On page fourteen, I stopped at a picture of a man with crazy hair. The caption said, "Artist Wes Besko." It was under a headline that said, "Artist Identified as Man who Jumped from Coronado Bridge." The paper said the bridge, a suicide magnet, had over 225 people jump from its 200-foot span since 1969. While Besko hit the water faster than forty miles per hour, broken bones and devastating injuries didn't kill him. Drowning did. The county Medical Examiner's Office put an identification bracelet on his right ankle, gave him a case number, and noted his place of death as "San Diego Bay, N. of Pylon 19."

I shook. Did my song inspire him to jump? He must have been planning it. The man probably attended to see his final resting place.

I checked out at a quarter after noon, grabbed a cab out front, and ziplined it straight to the airport.

On the flight to Amsterdam, I couldn't sleep. I drank two Heinekens and still couldn't sleep. I sensed I was like Besko, on my way to my death. Iraq was a lump in my throat that I couldn't wash away.

I had a four-hour layover in Amsterdam. I was to show up for a military transport back to Iraq. I stood in one of the airport's wide, modern halls, and everyone zipped around me toward one of the signs: retail to the left. Liquor and tobacco stores to the right. Lounge 2 just ahead. Baggage claim was down an escalator, restaurants and gates were up. Everyone had a clear purpose and hurried. Was mine to die? If anxiety were a guitar string, I'd be a very high note.

I knew what to do. I hurried and found the sign for money conversion. I handed the woman behind the window three hundred dollars, which she turned into about two hundred Euros. I ran to the front of the airport and found a taxi. I jumped in and said in English, "Take me to freedom."

"Freedom. No problem."

It was just after seven in the morning. I hadn't explored Amsterdam the first time, and the place just looked different than America. Everything was jammed together, the buildings like old banks. The streets didn't go straight because of the canals, and motorboats jammed the waterways. The city seemed complicated. A tiny café with two small tables on the sidewalk stood next to a narrow cellphone store next to a store that only sold men's shirts. One place said "Coffeehouse Smokey." I remembered hearing that some coffeeshops in Amsterdam also sold hash to smoke—all legal. That might be helpful.

He dropped me off in front of a building that had tall windows on the first and second floors with red curtains drawn. Part way down, a sign in neon said, "Moulin Rouge."

"How is this freedom?" I asked the driver.

"Red light district," and he told me the price of the ride in Euros. It seemed reasonable, but I wasn't used to Euros being about a third more valuable than dollars. When I handed him the money with a generous tip, he said, "Enjoy freedom."

As the exhaust from the cab dissipated, the world seemed light years away from the sunny beaches of California. I stood on the sidewalk with my duffle bag on my shoulder. I wasn't wearing my full uniform but a black T-shirt that said San Diego, and my uniform's camo pants. I walked around and found a narrow street where more closed curtains hailed me from either side.

One place had no curtain. In its window box sat a young woman with striking cheekbones wearing a white bikini, reading a newspaper in a chair—this early in the morning. Did the paper have a picture of Wes Besko? I found myself staring at her not because I was interested but more because a underwear-clad girl in a window reading a paper seemed so unusual. I walked closer. I didn't sleep much on the plane. Flying eastward, with skipping over time zones and causing major jet lag, had made me a zombie, one who needed sleep or an injection of caffeine. All I remember was she looked up and smiled as if I were her long lost boyfriend, super happy as if recognizing me. Did I know her? She tossed down the paper, skipped to a side door, which I stood near, and met me, slipping her hand inside my shirt, skin on skin.

"Do I know you?" I said.

"English. Goot. I'm Katrina."

"Like the hurricane?"

"Yes, like de storm." She kissed my cheek and whispered, "Come, my man." She pulled me inside. It felt like a dream—and like Alice in a rabbit hole, I wondered what would happen next.

She guided me through another curtain at the back, which led to a softly lit room with a double bed and a couple of stuffed bears on it, as if it were a kid's room. She sat on the bed and cupped her hands on her breasts, smooshing them, circling them around.

Was this what I really wanted, sex with a stranger after a long flight?

She pulled off her bra to reveal beautiful medium-sized breasts with large areolas. I placed my duffle bag on the floor.

"You like?"

My erection instantly felt painful because in my underwear, it was at a wrong angle, pointed downward, and it was making me embarrassed and bend at the waist. I didn't want to be there.

"Sorry, I'm … tired. I didn't mean..."

She patted the bed. "Fifty-five Euro, yes?"

She tugged on my pants, and I plopped down next to her.

"Don't be shy," she said and gently took one of my hands and placed it on her naked breast. It did feel good. I'd never been with a prostitute. It could be a story. I was here for freedom, after all.

I pulled out my wallet, found three colorful 20 Euro notes with arched windows on them—much better than the dull green money America had—and gave them to her. She didn't make change but smiled and put the money in a drawer, where she pulled out a condom.

The sound of my zipper surprised me as she pulled it down. She yanked down my pants, stripped me naked, slipped on the condom, laid me on the bed, removed her panties, oiled her pussy, and inserted me in her. We could have been actors in a movie that explained how the human race continued.

"You're so *beg*," she said in her accent. "You're my man."

"Sometimes I wonder about this life. Is this what we're here for?" I said.

She paused. "Life? Our price of admission wasn't much. What were you expecting?"

I don't know what I was expecting. With her gyrating on top of me, I thought of Kayla's smile—not her outrage but how she appeared when I first met her. She was pure. Everything inside my head now screamed stop. My being in this room, on this bed, I was out of control here, like I was some inanimate object. I was a billiard ball, bouncing from bumper to bumper.

I pulled out. "I'm sorry, Katrina," I said. "With all this craziness in the world, I have to find some sanity."

"It be all right. More people do this, the better."

"I'm just— I can't."

Her hand massaged my penis, which had quickly become soft. "No worry," she said. "I help."

Funny how cartoons rule our lives. I thought of the devil Bugs Bunny on my left shoulder saying, "Feels good, no? She's an expert. Let her give you head, too. She needs you. Be her man. Beautiful tits." Then the angel Bugs Bunny, who would be on the other shoulder, said, "You think this is erotic? This is mechanical. It's robot sex. She doesn't love you. Kayla does."

I took the girl's wrist and guided her off me. I stood to go. "You can keep the money."

"I know those pants. And your big soft bag. You're a soldier, yes? Instead of killing people, fuck me."

It wasn't a bad sentiment, but I couldn't. "Sorry. This was a mistake."

"I am goot. I be your girlfriend all day. Three hundred Euro."

"No." I knew in that moment I couldn't just react to situations anymore. I had to claim my life, make my life. I threw the condom in an empty wastebasket and pulled on my pants.

"You are like House—selfish!" she suddenly spit.

"I'm a house?"

"House, U.S. TV show. Man who treats people as if—how you say?—they are like sheet."

"Pardon?"

"Stront. Caca. Mierda." She hit her butt.

"Oh."

"You Americans export sheet. Your stupid TV shows, your wars, your butter from peanuts." She grimaced at the last. She scavenged the bed, looking for something—and found it, her cotton bra, which she pulled back on like Kleenex on grapefruit halves. "You stay Amsterdam night?"

"Why would you care?"

"Ah," she said, smiling. "I help. Discount for you," and, bottomless, shaved clean, she went to a different drawer in her nightstand. She pulled out a card and handed it to me. It said, "Sofitel - The Grand." It had a picture of an expensive-looking hotel, exactly what I wanted. I needed to hang out in a place that would take care of me. Still, I looked at the card warily.

"No, really," she said, now pulling on her panties. "You like, and then maybe you come back here."

"No, Katrina," I said, stepping toward the exit curtain. "I just need to sleep."

"Come back tonight?" She looked hopeful, like a car salesman.

"Where's the Grand?" I asked.

She took me outside and pointed me in the right direction. I ambled down the narrow street, a street that had no shred of rubble nor did the buildings have their sides blasted off. I showed the card when I felt lost, first to a waiter at a café, then to a hot-dog-cart guy. They pointed, and I walked until I saw it. Grand.

Checking in, I was so tired that when I spoke to someone, I felt in slow motion. "A room?" I told the young woman in a crisp burgundy top at the front desk.

"How long?" said the woman, and I had to look away because I was imagining her behind a window near the Moulin Rouge. "How long would you like to stay?" she said again in perfect English.

I felt like saying "forever," but I said, "Two days." By then I hoped to know what to do.

The woman typed on her computer and gave me a price. I gave her my debit card. I had the money. Fighting in Iraq, I'd been getting a salary plus hazard pay, and no way to spend it. I had over twenty grand in savings, more than I ever had. She returned my card and also handed me an electronic key. I followed a bellhop and fell asleep on his baggage cart with my duffle. He shook me awake after wheeling me into my room. I gave him a tip of ten. I fell asleep on top of the huge king-size bed with its extra-thick comforter. I awoke when it was dark out.

I felt strangely peaceful and rejuvenated. The bedside clock said it was just after 10:30. Outside my window, the lights of the city glimmered like fireflies. I stood and gazed out. Better than fireflies. The hotel stood next to a canal, and the lights from globed street lights across the waterway reflected on the ribbed surface like tiny light sabers. The canal-side trees glowed from underneath, and the illumination from the four-story buildings on the other side looked friendly, as did the people walking on the street. Rowboats and small-engine motor boats lashed to the sides hugged the canal. American cities should have such channels—they were serene, assuredly going where they've always gone.

I thought of Jordan. I'd just been dreaming of him, I remembered. I'd been standing in formation in really bright sunlight, waiting for the LT to say something. Then I realized there was no LT, no sergeant, no anyone up front. I looked at Jordan, who shrugged. I looked at other soldiers. Wilhelm, the first soldier I saw die, shrugged his shoulders, too, but stared straight ahead, ready for someone to tell him what to do. There was the dead Iraqi who Styles had shot, holding his dead baby. Everyone in formation was dead, I realized. In the back, just behind me, stood Laurel Paulino. My stomach fell. "What are you doing here?" I said.

"Things didn't go well after Germany. They called it an accidental overdose."

Jordan turned to me, breaking formation, and came over. "You're not a part of this group," he said. "Get out of here."

"Where do I go?"

"You know. You always have," he said.

"Isn't that a line from the *Wizard of Oz?*"

"No. You're thinking of 'Follow the yellow brick road.'"

"No, I'm not."

"Maybe you should follow the yellow brick road, then," he said, clapping me on shoulders. He shoved me forward, saying, 'You'll be all right.'"

That's when I'd awakened.

I continued staring at the canal, which glimmered. I wouldn't be officially absent without leave until the morning. I stayed up all night, drinking from my minibar. Shortly after sunrise, I fell asleep. I awoke and saw the sun. I was officially AWOL. The LT would know that, too.

| | |

I enjoyed the hotel's restaurant for lunch, choosing its outdoor garden seating. That morning, I'd strolled along the canal until I came to a men's clothing store. I wanted to treat myself to cool clothes, so I bought an expensive designer hoodie, black pants, new black-and-white Chuck Taylors, classic Wayfarer sunglasses, and a studded belt. I had the money. I sat at my elegant table with its heavy silverware and wine glasses. This was the life.

I spent part of the afternoon on a tour of the Heineken factory, filled with tourists. I sat at a table with an older Danish couple who'd taken the night train down.

"Are you an American soldier?" the man said in a mostly British accent.

"Why would you think that?" I wasn't wearing anything from the Army.

"You walk like an American."

"In Iraq," I said, not prefacing with "I was" or "I am."

"Denmark is fighting there too. Big mistake."

"Saddam was a bad guy."

"Americans never think things through. Who will take Hussein's place? Someone worse—or more likely, the whole country will be fractured and erupt in civil war. Hussein had kept the place together. He was a mosquito to the world. Why swat him?"

"What if he'd had weapons of mass destruction?"

"But he didn't. Whatever the spies had found was wrong."

His wife leaned in and said, "Please excuse my husband. He likes to talk." She had a perfect Meryl Streep accent from *Out of Africa*. I loved those old films. She turned to her husband and said, "The boy is young. He's not a politician. He just does what his country asks of him." She looked back at me. "Am I not right?" she said.

"Actually, I'm not in the Army anymore," instantly feeling the guilt. It probably radiated all over my face.

"Good for you," she said back—if nothing else, being kind.

I wondered what everyone was doing back on Baltic Avenue.

I rented a bike and pedaled to Vondelpark at the suggestion of the rental place. I fell in love with all the green lawns, tall trees, and ponds. It was so peaceful. I lay with my bike by a pond and took a short nap there. The beer must have done me in. Thankfully, my bike was still there when I awoke.

One of the great things I'd heard about Europe was its nightlife, and I was set to find it.

That night out on the street, I heard a distant pounding of music. I walked toward it, curious, loving its heavy bass line. I passed mostly people my age, smiling when they saw me. Maybe they thought I was someone. The kids my age were better dressed than in America. I didn't see many jeans or hear any English.

I considered then what the Army might be doing about me. My name was certainly on an AWOL list, and I would have been reported to the Military Police. I wondered what fellow MPs made of my going AWOL?

I knew from my training as an MP that it would take thirty days of being AWOL to be officially charged as a deserter, and an arrest warrant would then be issued. My guess was my friends and others were probably emailing me at this point, so I just wouldn't look at my email. I didn't want to know anyone else's thoughts. Maybe the Army had contacted the MP unit in Amsterdam, and maybe they'd alerted the Amsterdam police. That part I wasn't sure of. I had to put these thoughts out of my mind.

A little over a block later, the sound I followed clearly came from a church with a tall steeple. I walked up its steps and arrived at a heavyset guy at the closed front door.

"What's going on?" I asked loudly to overcome the music.

"It's a rave," he said in British English. "Twenty Euro. Pay inside."

The massive door brought me into the vestibule where a young woman my age took money and stamped my hand with a picture of an owl. The sound hammered from the nave with techno music and a light show that filled the vestibule with flashes of light in changing colors. A young woman sang repeatedly, "Let's do it. Let's do it."

As I stepped toward the party, joy surged through me. The bass notes, the lights, everyone dancing whirled before me in a kaleidoscope of exultation. The moment I stepped in, a pair of hands fell in front of me. They belonged to a beautiful dark-skinned young woman dressed in black tights with a bright red-and-white crocheted sweater, who smiled. She said something like "Latin we dancen?"

"You mean dance?" I said into her ear.

"Oh, you English," she shouted and smiled.

"American, actually."

She grabbed my hand, and we moved to the edge of the huge, undulating crowd. Computerized lights from two corners turned their heads in sync to the music, matching its intensity to the beat. They swept all around. There were no pews in the place, and a DJ stood with her equipment in the sanctuary, slightly above the crowd, pumping one fist to the music and laughing. This wasn't like the churches I knew.

The young woman in front of me looked exotic—long wavy dark hair, thick lips, a cute nose, and much shorter than me, moving like a professional dancer. She inspired me, and I twisted in new ways, keeping up with her as best I could, starting to laugh, too. Like some damn old man, I understood in that moment that this is what the people in Iraq could use—no bombs, no bullets, just the sheer joy of living. Then again, from what I saw of the religious propaganda there, the Shiites and the Sunni equally hated the West, and they wouldn't know what to do with a dance floor like this if they came upon it. They'd probably want to shoot everyone dead here. Why couldn't people around the world just get into the music, any music, and forget people's differences? We weren't hurting anyone else, just let us be.

Be.

Be.

Oh, man, this was great.

About five minutes in, I pulled her close, and she wrapped her arms around me. I said into her ear, "What's your name?"

"Nerkava."

"Nerkava—nice."

"Yours?"

"Max."

"Dance to the Max—yes?"

"Yes!"

The disco dance song probably went fifteen minutes, and the whole time, she kept eye contact with me. When it ended, two other couples approached and spoke seemingly all at once to Nerkava in what I assumed was Dutch. She said in English, "This is Max from America."

"Max from America," said a very tall man with short blond hair and only black clothes and black boots. "You want to accompany us outside for some air and a smoke?"

"I could use some air," I said.

He mimed a joint. "You toke?"

I instantly felt paranoid and shook my head. He asked nothing more.

Out front, we stood near the sign to the church that had some quote in Dutch ascribed to William James. That's funny, I thought. His last name was a first name, like Jordan's. Jordan Frank.

With the steady nighttime light of the city so I could see them better, I asked the other man in the group, who was black and wore a white jacket, for his name.

"Yan," he said. "Spelled with a J."

"Jan," I said, using the J sound.

"No, 'Yan.' And this lovely lady here," he said pointing to his girlfriend, who could have been from Scandinavia—tall, blond hair, blue eyes, not thin but voluptuous—and wearing a black sweater with a plunging neckline, "is Gerty."

"Are you enjoying Amsterdam?" said Gerty in what sounded to be British English.

"I am. I've been here just over a day, but what a city."

"For people our age, it's better than Paris," said the man with the short blonde hair in an accent that I guessed was German. "I'm Gunter," he said. His girlfriend nodded, wearing what looked like a dress made of rope, stiff rope with many openings, revealing what seemed to be a one-piece swimsuit underneath. "This is Betty," said Gunter, pronouncing it sternly like "Bet-TEA."

In that moment, I realized we all looked like kids dressed up as adults. We were masking ourselves.

Gunter offered cigarettes from a pack all around. Everyone except Nerkava and I took one. I'd given up smoking the day Jordan died. To make conversation, I pointed to the James homily on the sign. "What's that translate to?"

"William James?" said Gunter. "He's an American philosopher. He's called the father of American psychology."

"Yes, but what's it say?"

"It says, 'It comes down to faith or fear. Choose faith.'"

That was rather religious for a psychologist, I thought. I spotted a bar across the street, a bustling, tidy, well-lighted place, and said, "How about a drink? First round is on me."

That brought smiles and yeses.

We soon sat inside in a booth near the window, steins of beer all around. I considered at that second how great it was to be here with these people. It reminded me of something in Kurt Vonnegut's *Sirens of Titan*. The main character, Winston Niles Rumfoord, spends most of the novel bouncing around the universe, and, back on earth for a short time, he tells everyone we're all just part of a series of accidents. Here in Amsterdam, I loved this accidental gathering of people.

"George W. Bush," said Yan, glaring at me. "What kind of a wanker you got running your country?"

"Bush needs brains," said Gerty.

"He has them in Dick Cheney, who needs a heart—and some facts," said Betty.

My mouth probably dropped open. I was the one buying, and they were criticizing me? I shrugged, not wanting to get into it. "We're getting by," I said.

"What do you think of Bush?" said Nerkava.

"He's my president," I said, stating the obvious. The fact was all my friends in Iraq and I said angry things about the prez, but hearing these people in this safe, fly-over country talk about him, annoyed me.

Before I could say anything more, Yan asked, "What do you know about the Netherlands? Do you know who's the prime minister here?"

"That's sort of like a president, right?" I vaguely remembered an overview of European parliaments in high school. The prime minister thing seemed complicated, having to make deals with different parties. Two parties made it easier, seemed to me.

Gunter rolled his eyes. I didn't have to take this shit. "What're you guys doing for terrorism?" I asked. "The U.S. has to take care of every hot spot? You like to watch, and we have to send in our troops, who die. My best friend died last week. I just went to his funeral."

That stopped things for a moment. Betty leaned in, "The Netherlands sent over a thousand soldiers to Iraq to help fight."

"But are you there now?" I knew to ask this because I'd learned that many countries in the multi-national force in Iraq had pulled out. The Netherlands, if I remembered right, was no longer in it. Betty leaned back, saying nothing more. I added, "The Mideast has been a powder keg, and Saddam Hussein was lighting the fuse. He had to be dealt with. Bush found him. Bush isn't entirely bad."

"Bush didn't find him," said Gunter. "Some soldiers did."

"Semantics," I said.

"Are you a soldier?" Gerty asked. All stared at me.

"Yes, I am." I didn't tell them that I had just stopped being one.

"You in Afghanistan?" asked Gerty.

"Iraq, actually."

Gerty giggled and pointed to Nerkava. "That's where she's from!"

"Why are you here?" I asked.

"I'm a student. My country needs rebuilding, not more war."

"That's what we're trying to do. We're pumping billions of dollars to bring you to the twenty-first century."

"No," she said. "Billions of dollars go to the corrupt rich. Very little is getting to the people."

"That's for sure," I said. Still, I felt a twinge of guilt as if I were being anti-American. I wasn't.

"Are you on vacation or something?" said Gunter.

I shook my head. "Thinking about heading back, actually." I hadn't planned on saying this, but the words felt right. I didn't have to be ruled by confusion. Rather, this, my new path, was clear. As free as I'd felt earlier this night, I felt even better now. Of course, my AWOL status was a problem, but maybe I could say I lost my way. I had, in truth.

"Why would you go back now?" said Nerkava.

"The Kurds, the Shiites, the Sunni—isn't it all crazy?" said Betty.

"It is," I said. "But the people there deserve freedom—like the rest of us."

Yan laughed, choking on the swallow of beer he just took. "Freedom? Those people know nothing of it. They aren't educated. The mullahs, the jihadists, the militias—it'll be a power grab forever."

225

"The place is hopeless," said Gunter.

"It's not hopeless," said Nerkava. "It's my country."

"Sorry," said Gunter. "How about I call it backwards?"

"It is that," she said. Turning to me, she added, "You should stay here. Don't contribute another death—which may be you."

"Yes, you can stay with us. We share a flat. You can stay a while."

I considered. Could I live here? Would it mean giving up my American citizenship? Would this country have me? No, this was crazy.

I shook my head. "I only have a few months to go. I can't leave my friends there in the lurch."

"You Americans want to control everything, yes?" said Gerty.

"I've never understood the politics," I said, "but Americans are good people. Most of us chose to go—we weren't drafted, we joined."

"Tell me, Max," said Yan. "Why are you really going back?"

This seemed an odd question. "You don't have friends? Aren't these your friends here? Would you let them bake in the sun or burn alive in a Humvee so you could get your jollies in Amsterdam?" Yan looked stunned. Rather than say anything more, I held up my beer and said, "Cheers." They responded holding their mugs up and saying "Proost."

We shared a few more beers—many—to the point where I swore I was speaking Dutch, and I no longer felt angry. I came to really like these people. We hugged goodnight, and I stumbled back to the hotel. I didn't want the night to end, so I picked up my guitar and started playing. I went louder and harder. No one bothered me for a while, and when I sang particularly loud, I heard knocks from the wall on one side. I stopped, spent.

Check-out time was noon. I was up and showered by 8:00 a.m.—out the door by 8:30. In full uniform, I swaggered down the crowded Amsterdam street, guitar in one hand, duffle in the other, smiling to the older woman carrying a small bag with a baguette popping out, to the young man zipping by on a bicycle, to the young woman in hot shorts, to the people in the sidewalk café drinking their espressos. Before I knew it, I'd be strutting on Iraqi sand. I don't know where that sureness came from, knowing going AWOL wasn't taken lightly, but knock knock knock, hello I was here, I said to myself. At the airport, I simply told the Army transport person I'd missed my earlier plane, and he gave me the next transport to Baghdad.

As the plane took off, I couldn't help but wonder for a flash if I was doing the right thing. The William James' saying came back. "It's about fear or faith. Choose faith." I realized James could have been talking more than just religious faith. It was about believing things would work out. I had faith in my brothers. I had faith I could work it out with Kayla, too.

There might not be a good reason things would work out, but it seemed to me if you *felt* that, that's better than fear. And I felt great—certainly better than when I had landed in Amsterdam.

I realized there was one more element—a sense of purpose. Faith in anything alone wouldn't do it. You needed something pushing you. For me, music was once it, but if I were honest with myself, I hadn't been clear what I wanted in a band. To be famous? Maybe. Music was fun for a while—but the infighting, the lack of money, the difficulties getting anything done just sucked. Yet the jam session in my CHU after Jordan died reminded me of the healing power of music. Also at Jordan's funeral, my song gave people insight and feeling. I loved that. Music again—or something beyond this Army—had to give me purpose.

For now, all I really wanted to do was play with my buddies in the sandbox. What would I say when I saw them all? I couldn't say they were parts of God moving around in my blood, but I felt that my friends gave me oxygen. I was eager, but I had to be patient.

Oh, Kayla. Have you moved on, maybe with Styles? Could I win you back? Could I be patient?

The movement of the plane cradled me. My mind drifted toward sleep. Yes I can, yes to the mountains yes to the sea yes to my baby my baby my baby and me.

I powered up my iPod and selected my upbeat list, which I always used to keep my spirits up. The first song was "Suspension" by Mae.

I was once again looking from above at the brown landscape of Iraq, below. A big puff of smoke showed me an explosion.

17

Continuing: Iraq, July 2007

My helicopter from Kuwait arrived. Before long, I was back at Warhorse. I removed my headphones and stared at the black shit tarmac. Still, this is where I'd wanted to be. Beneath it all, this felt right. This was where I had to see things through.

As I stepped off the helicopter, I smelled the familiar scent of the whole region—a mixture of cooking bread, burning leaves, and sewer gas. Sergeant Ichisada met me, looking mad and disappointed like my mother when she'd first be angry then understanding. He made me piss in a cup to prove I hadn't taken drugs. On some level, I must have known I'd come back. After all, I hadn't gone into any of Amsterdam's hash bars. Next came the LT one-on-one, where I told him I'd been tired and confused after the flight from the funeral, and I'd just needed sleep, sorry about that. He let me return to duty.

As I approached my CHU, duffle bag and guitar in hand, sweat dripping down my back, my feet crunching on the gravel, I looked on our sand-bagged pathetic little village of box hovels, this shit storm. I thought *no place like home.*

I turned on Baltic Avenue. It seemed untouched, as if I'd never left. Then came the distinct sounds of rhythmic beating. When I walked through my door, Hitch madly played upon a full set of drums—and he was good. He stopped when he saw me.

"About time," he said. "I'm going nuts here."

"Doesn't sound like it."

"Amazing what mail order will bring you." He smashed one cymbal. I flipped open the locks of my guitar case. Lyrics that I wrote on hotel stationery lay under the guitar neck. I strapped the guitar across me and started to play, and Hitch joined me with his drums. We didn't play any particular songs, just things I made up on the spot, keeping in time to the rhythm he gave. It felt great to be back. When we were done, I placed my guitar back on the wall where I had a spot for it, next to where our rifles hung, locked and loaded.

After California, I knew I'd changed. In the Army and before Jordan's death, like everyone else, I'd just tried to survive. My future was not a thing to contemplate. Now I had purpose. I had this weird notion that what was about to happen would be good. I just didn't know what.

Later that day, I started shooting video using Jordan's VHS-C camcorder he'd lent me and which I'd forgotten about when the soldiers who specialized in gathering a dead soldier's things came and took his stuff away. I figured I'd send it to his widow eventually. In the meantime, I needed to capture the place. After all, we only had five months left to serve, and it'd be all over in a flash.

Perhaps it was Jordan's influence on me in making short videos, but I knew if I shot more of Warhorse and Baqubah, maybe I'd understand it better. Rather than play Xbox or basketball with friends, I shot them playing. I was the observer. I wanted to get this down, life as we knew it. I also brought my camera on patrol. I still found it odd that women were in this war. I didn't get how they thought or what they wanted, and I hoped this would, in part, help me understand. I was obsessed with Kayla in particular, though she was the most difficult to shoot. My lens was attracted to her.

The day I had arrived back, I spotted her in the chow hall. She eyed me as if I were a stranger. After I got my food, she was already gone. Shit. This was a deeper problem than I'd imagined. I had so much to say. I looked for her everywhere I went. When she was gunner in our convoy, I often shot video of her in her nest. Where she looked, what she did gripped me. I didn't see her with Styles ever, and I didn't shoot Styles at all. At night in my CHU, I'd play back and edit what I shot, and I'd watch the Kayla stuff over and over. That's when I saw one shot where she chatted and laughed with Corporal Asswipe. His real name was Asswynn, but he was a team leader who had ridden with me a few times, a cocky SOB. Was she sleeping with him? I slammed my laptop shut and hit the cot.

That very night, after everyone had gone to bed, I couldn't get the image of the two out of my mind. Before long, I stood outside his CHU, my ear on aluminum listening for her voice. Every little sound fueled my imagination. I could hear footsteps—two sets? Then springs. Were they having sex? I must have been there an hour. When I heard him snore, and no clear evidence of her, I left.

The next day, I left on her cot the moose coffee cup I'd bought in Minnesota. I included a little note that said, "I've been moosing you." I didn't hear back.

After that, I kept myself busy. I became particularly interested in the behind-the-scenes people, the fobbits. I'd shoot video of them working and sometimes interview them. These were people who never left our forward operating base, never were in the enemy's scope. The Humvees we drove daily had to be serviced, and a huge team of mechanics kept up all the machinery. Fobbits kept the Internet that we took for granted running and the computers in the MWR Center in tune. Many of the staff and officers in the camp's administration also never left the base. That included the military intelligence analysts. What did fobbits tell their friends back home? That they were fighting? I wanted to understand them. Why go to the front line and not fight? They felt the danger but could do nothing about it.

Over the next few days, I carried my video camera strapped next to my rifle. I'd search out fobbits to speak to. I interviewed anyone I could. I always asked, "Did you expect to join the Army and only do what you do?" Usually they told me how much they felt part of a team. They also felt that they were in danger, too— from the mortar fire that made it over the wire and from traveling to and from the airport. One time when I walked to the laundry, I could hear a mortar approach, but my ears were trained for the distance. It wouldn't hit us, so I didn't flinch, yet the fobbits in front of me scrambled for the concrete shelters we had. They were good people—just different from those of us who fought beyond the wire.

I also asked in my interviews of all soldiers, "What're you going to do when you get out of the Army?" Probably the most common answer, was, "Fuck, get drunk." I couldn't always tell when "fuck" was a swear word or just what they wanted to do before drinking. They also said, "I just want to go home." They had such pain in their eyes. Many had seen so much death, had experienced so much loss. Somehow the camera comforted them. Their desires rarely traveled beyond a day. When I asked about getting a job, they hadn't thought about it much. "I'm sure I'll find one."

"Doing what?"

"I don't know. Something better than before."

It always surprised me when the women spoke this way, too. I also had many people, unasked, talk about what disturbed them, such as some of the things they had to do outside the wire. "We failed to secure the streets and make things stable, man. We'd rush in and find a house or two with the enemy, kill or round them up, then leave. Then more Iraqi pieces of shit would come back," said one soldier. Another said, "I don't think this country wants democracy. Most people aren't educated. They don't get it. Who the fuck are we to force them to have it? I say we blow up the whole fucking country, cement it over, and build a Walmart right in the middle."

I felt that anger, too. When my friends and I came over as soldiers, perhaps we hadn't understood how our own lives were valuable, and we were giving all or part of it up. Back home, kids our age worked, studied, texted, got laid, maxed out their credit cards, did everything except understand who was fighting their wars. They didn't care about the military, or politics, or that Bush had flown onto an aircraft carrier near San Diego with a banner misstating "Mission Accomplished." They cared about Kim Kardashian, whose sex tape had leaked onto the Internet that year.

As I shot my Camp Warhorse video, though, I thought there could be something beautiful that would come out of all this. I had a purpose.

After I was back more than a week, we were called for a company formation—probably some announcement. Because our missions were lighter, I hoped for good news. The day, mostly cloudy, wasn't even as hot as usual, the high nineties. Amazing what you can get used to.

I looked around while standing at attention. These were my friends and colleagues. We'd survived so far. I felt optimistic that everyone there would make it—just five short months left. These were my brothers and sisters. Shit. I was fucking getting misty-eyed right there. Thank god I'd returned.

"Troops, hair check!" said the command sergeant-major, a short grizzled man named Rappaport, in his fifties, with mostly gray hair beneath his cap.

You gotta be fucking kidding me. Hair? We put our lives on the line, and they call us in company formation for this?

The sergeant-major walked behind the troops, looking to see if hair fell beneath anyone's cap. I knew mine would as I hadn't had a haircut since before I left for California—three weeks growth at best.

The sergeant-major stopped at Hitch nearby, rubbing his thumb on his neck. "You pass."

He approached another soldier, nearer me. He passed. I could only laugh to myself, knowing I'd be the focus of his anger.

The sergeant-major stood behind me just as the sun popped out from behind a cloud. The heat on my skin made me feel like a raw chicken in a rotisserie. Those near me laughed before he said anything to me. People whistled.

"Everyone, cut it out!" said the sergeant-major.

"I'll get a haircut, Sergeant-Major," I said.

"Oh, I believe you will." The sergeant-major removed his Gerber scissors from his pocket, as if he was going to cut my hair or make me do it.

"All right, Sergeant-Major, that's enough," said the captain. "In this Easy Bake Oven, I want to be quick and brief."

Captain Carpentier stepped forward and said, "You people are the backbone of America. You weren't drafted. You elected to help your country."

The sergeant-major whispered to me, "You lucked out. Get your hair cut." He stepped somberly to the front of assembly.

"You may be wondering why I called you here today," said the captain. "Your president is asking you to help just a little more. I'm really sorry to say this, but your specialty code has been issued what's called a stop-loss order."

We were not supposed to say anything, yet everyone groaned. Bush had rescinded our return home.

"Stop-loss means none of you have a date to return. As you may have seen, the tide has turned here in Baqubah. We now control the city, but we cannot lose our advantage. We need to fight in Iraq indefinitely."

My heart dropped. We might be here another year or more? Had my return been yet another stupid thing I'd done?

A banter of chatter grew around me. Everyone was surprised, frustrated. We may have volunteered for the Army, but it was clear this was a slave camp.

"Atten-SHUN," yelled the sergeant-major.

The captain continued, "I'm not happy about it either, but with the surge continuing—and without enough Army personnel or civilian contractors—we have to stay and do this thing—and do it well."

I looked around and saw Styles, Hitch, and Kayla most immediately. Hitch shrugged. Styles only stared at the ground. Kayla had been looking at me but turned away. She still wasn't talking with me. Yet I was even happier I was back. These were my kin. I can't tell you why I felt sure, but I did.

|　　|　　|

Our next mission was a short patrol through sections of Baqubah, and things were quiet—no skirmishes, no IEDs, and people on the street even waved at us, which surprised me after the usual wariness or hatred. Styles told me this had been the way it's been since I left. The surge seemed to have worked.

We returned to Warhorse after dark with no incident. As I walked down the gravel street of my CHU village, a few soldiers stood around an oil drum that had logs inside, burning. The nights would eventually start to get chilly, but the drums now were more like what campfires were, meant as a friendly place to congregate outside of our hovels. When I arrived at my CHU, I heard the sound of an approaching car on the gravel. The sergeant-major and Captain Carpentier pulled up in a Humvee. "Private Rivera," shouted the sergeant-major. I stood at attention. "The captain needs to speak to you inside," he said.

"Yes, Sergeant-Major."

I held the door open, and the captain and his sergeant entered.

"Private Rivera, Sergeant Nolan came to me yesterday to tell me about your video." How did Nolan know? I instantly remembered the sergeant who came with a few other soldiers from another platoon to look at the short video I'd edited down. Jordan had done most of the editing, and my recent interviews only added to it. I'd used one of the soldiers from the other platoon in an interview, and after I showed him, he wanted to show a few friends. The sergeant was part of that group. The video was something I'd hoped to send to the Sundance Film Festival, which Jordan had pushed for.

"Is there a problem, sir?" I asked the captain.

"Can you show me the video?"

I brought them over to my desk and laptop. I brought it up and started showing them.

"Turn it up, please," said the captain.

On screen, a soldier said, "We failed to secure the streets and make things stable, man; these kinds of mistakes happen all the time." Next to me, the captain said, "Stop. That's enough. How many copies of this do you have?"

"What's on my hard disk and a backup on a videotape." I held up the VHS-C copy.

"I'm confiscating your computer so a tech guy can erase it completely."

"Sir?" My heart pounded. "I don't understand why. This is a good film, pro-Army, sir." This made no sense.

"Not with complaints on it. The sergeant said there were more soldiers griping."

"I wouldn't call it griping. It's just real."

"You have your orders." He held out his hand for the tape and laptop, which I gave him.

"Come outside," he said. We walked to the nearby oil drum, burning. He handed me the tape. "Put it in there."

I hesitated. My heart cracked. I dropped it in and watched it melt, then burn., burn the way I was feeling inside. Fuck this Army.

"I don't want you making any more of these movies. Understood?"

I nodded. He didn't know I still had all the footage and that I could recreate the film some other time when I got out—whenever that would be.

"Thank you, sir," I said, saluting. God knows what I was thanking him for. My stuff wasn't court-martial material, but it was still fucked all around.

At the chow hall, I grabbed a pork chop and baked potato and ate alone, thinking more about what just happened. Styles walked right by me and out as if he didn't see me. Perhaps he didn't. He looked lost in thought. Maybe it was just lost. As bad as I felt about the film, Styles started to worry me. Even before stop-loss, Styles lacked his usual spark. Before Jordan had died, I'd had a short conversation with him about how I thought we should both go to college after we got out of the Army. Styles acted as if I were talking about flavors of yogurt. He dispassionately said, "I have a family. I'm not going to college. I'll need a job." I didn't know what else to say. We weren't the closest after I started seeing Kayla. I sensed now he had no faith or purpose. Was that something I or anyone could give him?

I knew I had to help myself first, much the way on the airplane, the flight attendants said in case of an emergency to take your own oxygen mask first before helping your children or others. You can't help anyone if you're gone. What could I do to help myself and then Styles?

When I returned to the CHU, two big boxes with my name on them stood in the middle of the floor. I ripped them open. One was a new white Fender Stratocaster electric guitar, and the other was a small amplifier. A letter was taped to the amp.

"Dear Max," it said. "Thank you so much for all you did at Jordan's funeral. Lots of people since have asked where I found you, and I've told them how great a friend you were to Jordan. I'm getting his life insurance, so please don't think of this as extravagant. You're incredibly talented, and I just want you to make more music over there. Jordan would approve. Your friend, Jillian." In that moment, I realized music was my oxygen mask.

I plugged everything in, attached the rainbow-colored guitar strap with the word "California" on it, and soon felt the new strings against my fingers. I loved the narrow neck, which I knew would let me play faster. Someone with stubby fingers might have a hard time with these frets, but I don't have big hands, so this was perfect. I tuned the guitar and began riffing away. With an electric guitar, I couldn't help but show off. I love the power of the sound, including the feedback I could get. It's why I got into punk—to let my teen-angst out.

With this electric guitar, everything felt right. I didn't hate my acoustic guitar, but it brought out a different, more mellow side of me. I was more introspective on acoustic. I'd forgotten until this moment how an electric guitar made my inner voice so much more direct. I started playing Green Day's song "Boulevard of Broken Dreams," starting to sing right out loud, "I walk a lonely road, the only one I've ever known."

Some of my nearby neighbors opened my CHU door, and I waved them in. Shortly thereafter, Hitch entered and moved to his drums as if we'd had this planned. He joined me, playing the song perfectly. When we were done, we had six people in there, and they clapped. Yanni stood at the door with his keyboards. He said, "Why didn't you tell me about this?"

Yanni plugged himself in, soon adding melodic chords to our sound that now drowned out the distant gunfire. I started playing my new song.

I said to our little audience, "This is for all the soldiers whose voices have been silenced." Tears came to my eyes. "This is something I wrote and played at Jordan's funeral."

While the song, composed on acoustic guitar, was soft in its lead-in, I created a new, yearning opening, bringing in the melody in short order, and I sang. Hitch created a great beat. He understood the song quickly.

When I was young, my love left me,
I hurried to a tall roof and almost took the dive.

Soon everyone was clapping in rhythm. We now had an audience of at least a dozen. People squeezed together on our cots or stood. I tore through the song in a much faster rhythm than at Jordan's graveside service. We drew in soldiers like onlookers to a car crash. It was turning into an underground punk rock show.

As if sensing my need for "more," Yanni stopped playing and quickly set a mike he'd brought, placing it on a stand before me. He jumped back to the keyboards.

Kayla entered. She caught my eye as my lips approached the microphone. The lyrics reverberated through the tin can room and out the door. When I finished that song, I said, "This next one is for a girl I once knew." As I started playing, I looked right at Kayla.

The stars above Iraq
Told me all I need to know
We're two little specks on the fall
Looking for meaning if I could be ANYTHING AT ALL.

When we hit the last chord and drumbeat, Kayla stood at the back and appeared stunned. I felt dizzy. She nodded, then smiled. Maybe I would get her back. As more people entered, I lost her after a while, but I kept playing.

Hitch said, "How about we do 'I'm Not Okay' – My Chemical Romance. I love the drumming in it."

"Yeah, and the guitar solo is sick," I said. "Everyone know the song?"

"Yes," said Yanni, "but let's get Styles and Trace in here—we could use the extra guitars on that one."

"Can anyone find Styles and Trace?" I said. Hoogerheide near the door held up her hand and dashed out into the evening air.

I told everyone the basics of Jordan's funeral with the pretty view, the chaplain's great service, and how Jillian and the baby looked. Hoogerheide soon ran in holding a guitar and said, "They can't make it."

"Did they say why?" I asked.

"Styles is on mission. Trace said he sucks, and he lent me his guitar. I'm pretty good. I know 'I'm Not Okay.'"

I looked at Yanni, who looked surprised, but he nodded. Hitch eagerly agreed and grinned. He always had a thing for her. I don't know why he never acted on it.

I said to her, "Okay then." She plugged into my amp.

Yanni, with his electronic keyboard in the piano mode, started the slow opening with Hitch making *tsk* noises with his mouth to recreate the song's background sounds. The moment the first lyric came in, Hoogerheide started singing in harmony with me. We hadn't agreed to that—but within a few words, I could see she had a great voice and energy.

In the refrain part, Hoogerheide started blasting away on her guitar, amazing me and everyone with her fret work. Trace had played the rhythm parts, and yet she was playing lead. Where did she come from? Who knew she could play like this? Hitch, Yanni, Hoogerheide, and I pushed our way through the song. When we hit the refrain again, Hoogerheide took off once more. Both Hitch and I played hard to match her. What we mumbled in lyrics, we made up for in instrumentation. Soon the people watching were dancing—moshing.

After we finished, everyone cheered. "More!" came from outside our CHU, too. Feet pounded on our roof. People were up there. Our door had been left open, and now that I looked, there was a crowd deep into the graveled street. I could hear boots crunching on Baltic Avenue, which led toward us. This was amazing.

"Wow," I said, placing my guitar down. I stood at the door, and people cheered. I waved the rest of our group over. When Hoogerheide joined us, the women in particular cheered. I ran my fingers against my metal guitar strings, which sent sound through us. "All right," I said. "One more." I turned to them, "'Dammit' by Blink 182?"

"I can fake it," said Yanni, "I've probably heard it."

I sang the opening line for him: "*It's all right / to tell me / what you think / about me.*"

"Oh yeah, yeah," he said now, remembering, and he played some chords on his keyboard. C – G – D – E.

"Yeah, you got it!" I yelled. "Let's go for it then," and my fingers tore into the opening solo notes of the song. Hitch's drums smashed in and pounded right on cue, and Hoogerheide, wouldn't you know it, knew the lyrics as well as me. Everyone in the CHU, on the CHU, and outside the CHU moshed as if their nervous systems had to dance and bump full throttle, knowing it was the last song.

Fuck, fuck, I didn't expect this, and I laughed, surprised. It was as if I were back on the Warped Tour, but playing with people I loved—and we'd never practiced. Okay, I can't say it was perfect in that every note was right. It wasn't, and we weren't even perfectly tuned, but every note meant well.

We sang the last two words, "Growing up," and struck the last note and let it fade. The cheering grew instantly. We took our bows, and headed outside. Hands reached out from above and latched onto Hoogerheide. She zipped up and out of sight.

What the fuck? I peered my head out to see what happened, while the cheering grew louder. Hoogerheide stood on top of the flat roof of my CHU with three muscular guys up there clapping for her. She raised her arms in the air like Sylvester Stallone dancing at the top of the stairs in that old movie, *Rocky.* Laughing, she then twirled and twirled as if she had too much adrenaline, which caused people to cheer anew. She spun a bit too much and, clearly dizzy, she fell from the CHU as simply and surely as the moon setting. For a moment, she seemed held in the air as if invisible strings kept her up. I ran toward her as my arms and other people reached out. I thought she'd smashed into the ground, but soon she floated on hands above people—the ultimate crowd surf. Before long, hands guided her back down, and she ran over. Seeing me, Hoogerheide hugged me, saying "Thanks!"

"Are you all right?" I asked.

"This is the best night of my life!" she said. She rubbed her wrists together, looking in pain. "I think I did something to my hands."

Soon the other guys joined us outside, and people swarmed around us as if we were superstars. We weren't, of course, but it showed just how pent up everyone's needs were to get out of the war even for a few minutes. Some people said, "Encore! Encore! Encore!"

I thanked them, feeling drained but incredibly good. The experience had been freeing.

Soon enough, everyone dispersed, and from a distance came the sounds of bombs. The war had returned. We cleaned up the CHU. Hoogerheide, however, couldn't hold a thing. Her wrists now really hurt. She showed me how they were black-and-blue. "I smashed them when I fell."

"Jesus. I'm taking you to the medical center," I said.

"I'll take her," Hitch instantly said. Good idea, I thought. He was sweet on her.

"You know, you guys might want to play at the talent show," said Hoogerheide.

"Talent show?" I asked, and then remembered the flyer from the hospital.

"Oh, yeah, I've heard of it," Yanni said.

Hoogerheide took a crumpled flyer out of her pocket and handed it to us. It was the kind that usually hung at the entrances to all seven CHU villages. It explained how the show was open to all sorts of talent: knife-throwing, stand-up comedy, dance skits, and music—"anything that will entertain people."

"It's in three days," I said. "Not enough time."

"Let's go for it," said Yanni. "The talent show will include the whole camp. And what if we dedicated it to Jordan? It'd be great, wouldn't it?"

"Three days," I said. "Hoogerheide's too injured."

"You can get Styles and Trace back," she said. "Bass and rhythm. You can teach Trace a few things. He'll be fine."

"Do you think we can convince Styles?" I asked. "He's taking the stop-loss pretty hard."

"We all are," said Yanni. "The talent show will keep our minds off of how fucked we really are."

"I don't see how," I said.

Hoogerheide shrugged at jammed the poster back into her pocket. Hitch took her out.

"Really," was all Yanni said.

I walked outside, troubled. Maybe it was my feeling Jordan's loss so deeply still, but as Yanni said, our playing could be for Jordan.

I spotted the bulletin board on our avenue, and it drew me toward it. A fresh, uncrumpled poster for the talent show said, "Come to the show— or apply to perform."

This evening had been helpful. It'd been fun, too. I touched the poster. We had to do it.

The next day out on mission, our orders brought us to a local hospital for a routine walk-through to offer a sense of safety. I didn't expect how much the hospital looked like an American one, rooms off of wide halls and good lighting. The nurses wore blue and the doctors sported white lab coats. Nurses and doctors, though, were always men.

In one hallway, three bloody women each lay on gurneys, their eyes open. Dead. A deceased young boy had his eye blown out and many scratches on his face. A blood-spattered dead young man missed an arm. Nearby, a young doctor walking concentrated on a clipboard.

I said, "Excuse me, doctor. Do you speak English?"

He turned, looked me up and down, and nodded. "Yes. What may I do for you?" He had a British accent.

"Just curious what happened to these people," I said. "On our patrol, everything has seemed unusually quiet."

"Actually, things are calmer. Few shootings or bombs lately. We've been mostly getting people who have what you might call 'normal' needs—fevers, kidney stones, car accidents. I had my doubts you Americans would get serious, but you did. Baqubah is much safer. I thank you."

I didn't expect that. "So what happened here?" I said.

"A suicide bomber rode his bicycle up to a café in a Shiite neighborhood and exploded—back to our religious war. I'm hoping it's not a growing trend."

I nodded. Right then, Kayla came up to me from behind. She was in the convoy but not in my Humvee.

"We have to talk," she said.

I motioned to her and moved away from the doctor. She looked upset and puzzled.

"You didn't write me at all when you were gone," she said. "And then you went AWOL. You were just going to leave me here? And why aren't you talking to me?"

"You said we were over. I don't believe it, but you said it."

"I didn't say that. I said think about what it might be like if we *were* over. You don't fight for what you want?"

"I seemed to upset you all the time. Like now."

"Because you drive me crazy!" Her eyes crinkled as if she were ready to cry, and yet I felt incredibly light and happy. She wrapped her arms around me—with the feeling she'd never let go. Both of us wore full battle gear with locked-and-loaded rifles to our side.

I poked my head into the nearby room. No one in it. I pulled her in, and we immediately kissed. How I missed her. We only stopped when I heard someone clearing his throat. The young doctor stood in the doorway. I offered a polite laugh.

"I always wondered the effect of women soldiers in an army," he said.

Kayla said, "Do you need the room?"

"I do," he said.

Kayla swung her arm around me. We walked out, laughing.

Back in the empty hallway, she said, "I hope you've stopped with your obsession about Styles and me. I don't think of you and Paulino. If you haven't noticed, Styles is even more withdrawn. I think he should have a psych evaluation."

"Really?" I said.

"Guys never see these things."

Around the next corner, Styles stood just outside the front door by our vehicle. I hoped he hadn't heard. I was the driver that day, and Trace, the navigator. Styles, our team leader, would man the gun if needed.

Styles watched Kayla walk off.

"You back together?" he asked.

"I don't know. I thought you two would be back together when I was gone."

"This isn't high school. And I'm married."

"That didn't stop you before."

He shrugged. "There are reasons."

I said, "Are you okay? Kayla suggests maybe you're down."

"Of course I'm down!" he said, looking pissed. "We've got to stay in fucking Iraq for God knows how long. I should have taken the discharge."

"You should have."

"Buddy, we're looking at our own last chapter, beauty and brawn brought down, the lamb and the lion sleeping together and then slaughtered, the finest wine and the flimsiest gowns, the curl of smoke and the wonder of women come crashing down on Highway 61."

"What?" I said.

He kept going: "Birthday cakes and banana boats and pumpkins carved with care. Sesame Street and all the books you won't remember. Wealth and fame, frailty and shame, leave no trace like yesterday's beer. Nothing to cheer about. It don't mean a thing if you ain't got that swing."

"What're you talking about?"

"We're dead," he said.

"No, we're not. Things are better here now. A doctor inside said the whole city's better. Maybe we'll go home on time."

"Maybe unicorns will sing us to sleep."

I needed to make him feel better. "We really should jam together again. That was fun before I left. We should do it."

"Not really," he said.

Trace stepped toward us, and this clearly wasn't the time to bring up the talent show. I'd have to save it for later. Styles moved into the back.

After we returned and I ate in the chow hall, I thought more about Styles. Kayla was right. I needed to do more. I walked to his CHU, but he wasn't there. I found him at the Pizza Hut shack. He never ate pizza. He hated the stuff. He pulled a Pepperoni slice from his mouth, with strings of cheese dangling between face and food the way you get those lines of spittle when you have to rinse at the dentist's office.

"Hey," I said, sitting down.

"What the hell you up to, Max?"

"What do you mean?"

"What's that serious look on your face? Leave me alone. I'm not some fucking kid in Africa you send five dollars to every month."

"Something's come up."

"Besides fighting this shitty-ass war?"

"More than just jamming," I said. "Talent show."

He looked at me as if I had arrived from the planet Naptha. "Yes, let's get some tap shoes," he said, "and we'll do a duet of 'Singin' in the Rain.' Maybe we can even make it rain here. That'd be something." That's the Styles I knew.

I said, "Hoogerheide joined Yanni, Hitch, and me yesterday, and she's awesome, but as you heard, she hurt her hands, and she doesn't want to sing. I liked how you and Trace jammed with us before. We thought we could be a thing if we had you. Win the show, maybe."

"And what's that get us? A couple of T-shirts that say something about freedom?"

"It'd be for Jordan. Our send off for him."

"You had to use the Jordan card, didn't you?" he said.

"It's not a card. It's affection. What's wrong with that?"

"He's already sent off."

"But not musically.""

"What about Trace?" he asked.

"He's in once I said I'd teach him a few things."

He sighed. "Fuck." He looked ready to strangle me. "Okay, just the talent show and that's it. For Jordan." He looked down.

I jumped up, pushing my fist in the air. "Okay! Thank you!"

"Yeah, yeah." He nodded but didn't look at me. I wanted to hug him, yet I could read his body language, so I just patted him on the shoulder and left with one more "Thanks."

| | | |

I held Kayla that night tucked into her like a spoon long after we'd made love. It was as if we just needed to say nothing and hear each other just breathe. Her two roommates, Yolanda and Germaine, were off with their boyfriends. That fact gave me hope for humanity. After all, Yolanda was on the short side and plump with short butch hair, and Germaine stood far taller than me at six-foot-six and gawky. For not being Army poster people, it's amazing how all of us found love or at least lust—well, mostly lust.

Then Styles came to my mind as I thought about how alone he really was. He could have been back in New York with a dishonorable discharge, but he'd told me his destiny was here. "Styles said he'll do it, the talent show," I said.

"Styles said he'll do it," Kayla repeated as if amazed, turning toward me. "Maybe the talent show will help him."

"Yeah. Styles would probably say, 'That and a grenade will get you an explosion.' I wish he'd see a shrink."

She froze a second, looked away, and said, "Yeah."

"What?"

"I talked to, you know, one in the medical unit."

"A shrink?"

She nodded.

"For what?"

"When you went AWOL, I had issues."

"I don't follow."

"Trust issues. It started with my father."

"The lawyer?"

"He's not a lawyer. We had a family gas station in San Bernadino, far from Orange County in a poor part of town. My mother left him and me when I was three—or so he said. Now I wonder. He bought the place next to the gas station—once been a barn. Turned it into a strip club called The Booby Trap. Course, Norton Air Force Base soon closed after that, so his place wasn't popular for long."

"You didn't grow up rich?"

"Far from it."

"Trust issues?"

"He fondled me often as a teenager. At sixteen, he put me on the stage

n the family business, dancing topless. Never fucked me if that's what
ou're wondering. Some of the patrons did, though."

"Why're you telling me this?"

"Shrink said I should be honest. I always wished to live in Orange
County, if you want to know."

"I see."

"Plus you're always asking why I joined. I married to get out of the
house. I joined the Army to get away from my husband."

"Yikes," is all I could say. I held her closer.

"What made you think of going AWOL in the first place?" she asked.
"I still don't get that."

"The States were good. It was hard to leave that."

"Yes, but you didn't stay in the States. You fled in Amsterdam. Why
here?"

"After Katrina—" I realized my mistake the instant I said it. I probably sounded guilty—I'm not great at lying. "It was just a moment where
realized I had a choice."

"Katrina?"

"I was thinking of the hurricane."

"No, you weren't. I was being honest, so should you. Who's Katrina?"

"You have to realize, I thought we were broken up and that you were sleeping with Styles again even though you weren't. I know now, but I thought—"

"What the—"

"No, it's not as bad as you think. I shouldn't have prefaced it. Katrina
was a Dutch prostitute—no love—no sex even. I stopped it before, you
know, anything happened. I was messed up, and then I got better."

"Explain."

I began with how lonely and lost I'd felt after the funeral, and the
driver took me unasked to the red light district. The place seemed so opposite of romance. I thought of how Jordan had had a great wife, and I'd
like to marry someday, and I thought of her, Kayla. "But you're already
married, so really, in the end, this isn't going to work, is it?"

I hadn't planned on pushing it this far, but as I considered the situation, the best defense was an offense.

"I filed for divorce while you were gone," she said. "I realized what I
wanted, which was you."

"And you didn't bother telling me that? Emailing me, for instance?"

"You didn't write me, either, you know. I thought we had something—
but you went AWOL."

"I thought we were *done*," I emphasized. "I was lost. I didn't want to
come back if I couldn't have you."

For a moment she softened. *"Really?"* I was going to say yes, when she blurted, "Hold it! Just a couple of days after an argument, and you had to go buy sex? You couldn't call and work it out with me? This is really disgusting."

"Katrina and I didn't get very far."

"You guys fuck?"

How honest should I be I wondered. "When I thought of you, I pulled out."

"Christ!" She threw off her covers, stood, and started pulling on her camo pants. "I should feel happy because you thought of me while having sex with a prostitute?"

"Where are you going?" I asked.

"I can feel my period starting. See what you made me do?"

"But where are you going?"

"I'm out of tampons, okay? Don't go have sex with someone else while I'm gone. I have to think this through."

"Hold it. You don't understand the biggest part. It's not so much why I went to her or why I went AWOL, but why I came back. I felt so sure. I just knew if I chose something, this something, good things would happen. I wanted you."

"You say it like I'm a responsibility."

"No," I laughed. She didn't get it, but if she could feel what I felt, she would. "It's hard to put into words. I just feel sure about things. I feel sure about you now. I feel sure about us."

"You didn't before?" she asked, fully dressed and tying her boots.

"Are you out to just ruin something perfectly good?" I said. "As much as I want to help you, help Styles, help my country, maybe it won't work out. All I can do is try. Be with me if you have hope."

"Your logic eludes me. Stay here."

And she left.

I dressed after that and ran to the showers. While I wasn't happy about the argument, I told myself as in a mantra, it'll work. It'll work. .

| | | |

On the evening before the talent show, I learned we'd be last because we were the last to sign up. "That's good," I told my bandmates. "When it comes to voting, we'll be on everyone's minds the most." We only had time to practice three songs.

The show would take place outside in the large courtyard, on a night hot as fuck. Now I had my doubts, but I kept them to myself. As the five us of gathered in my CHU, we were all nervous. "We didn't practice enough," said Trace, the least experienced musically. He was absolutely right, though. I wanted to have another day, but we didn't have it.

"We've done well," I said, even though we hadn't really nailed one of our three songs yet. My stomach spun, mainly because the last time I played on stage, I battled with Ralph, and I didn't feel I ever needed the stage again. What if it goes wrong, and these guys blame me?

"It's too hot for uniforms," said Styles, holding up some jeans and a T-shirt. We all had civvies in our duffles for R&R.

"Can't say as I feel like we're rock n' roll in these," said Hitch, pointing to his digies and cap.

Sweat had already run down my back, even though the CHU was air conditioned. "We're not allowed to play except in uniform," I said.

Yanni, our lifer, jumped in, saying, "We could get a dishonorable discharge for not being in uniform," he said. "It's about the music, not how we look."

"What'll they do, send us back home?" Hitch said. "This is a talent show."

"We're fine in uniforms," I said. "Let's go."

Just as we walked out, instruments and equipment in hand, a Humvee with the sergeant-major driving the captain drove near us. When Captain Carpentier saw me, he said, "Stop!", and the sergeant major stopped. The captain flagged us over.

"What're you up to, men?"

"Headed to the talent show, sir, where's we're playing."

"No you're not," he said. "I have a job for you. A new shipping container needs to be inventoried." We had shipping containers arrive all the time, big metal behemoths that fit on trains and ships with supplies. Inventory was a suck job out in the sun, yanking out everything and counting it. At that moment, I sensed the captain didn't like me. What did I do? I'd burned the tapes as he wanted.

"Sir?" I said.

"Say nothing," said the captain. "The sergeant-major will give you directions." The man did and we returned our equipment to my CHU.

Minutes later, after we stared at the fucking container and we opened the white beast, Yanni said, "This isn't right. He knew we're playing. Did you piss him off, Rivera?"

At that moment, the crowd under the tent at the nearby talent show cheered.

"Fuck him," I said, slamming the door hard on the container. "I say it's all just wind in the sails! Are we not men?"

"We are devo!" yelled Hitch, catching my reference to the famous Devo song.

"We should be in the talent show, not here," I said. "People are waiting for us. Fuck, I'm not wearing this uniform now," I said yanking off my blouse. "Let's go get ready."

They looked at me, astonished. "We can't," said Yanni.

"Think about it," said Styles. "They're not going to get rid of us when they need every available soldier. Dishonorable discharge for keeping the troops happy? No way."

"Exactly!" I said.

We whooped and ran back to my CHU.

Once inside, we stripped off our uniforms and changed into shorts and T-shirts. I yanked on my studded belt from near my ammo belt. Using some gel, we spiked up our hair, the little we had. I grabbed my guitar next to the rifle rack. We were preparing for a different kind of war.

We marched out of there with our equipment, proud.

A stage had been built for the show, and because we were the only band, our instruments and amps stood at the back of the stage. Everyone shared the two microphones on stands if they needed them. For videographers, I'd corralled Kayla's two CHUmates, I wanted to send the show to Jordan's widow. Yolanda and Germaine ran up to us.

"Where've you been?" said Yolanda. "You had us worried."

"We were detained," was all I said. Yolanda had my still camera. Germaine held the camcorder I'd inherited from Jordan.

"The important thing," I explained, "is not to cut. Keep your cameras going, and just move around. You can zoom or pull back if you want to, but be as steady as you can. I'll cut back and forth between you. Keep shooting."

The stage had a curtain at the back, and behind it, all the talent was to gather and zip on stage when the stage manager gave us our cue. The five of us gathered just as the audience started arriving. Over three hundred white folding chairs stood in neat rows before the stage. Where they found so many white folding chairs, I have no idea, but with the Army's billions of dollars per tank or plane, what're some chairs? My guess, too, was this talent show thing jumped from camp to camp—something to keep the soldiers occupied during the time of Stop-Loss.

"I didn't know they were expecting this many people," Trace said, clearly nervous, as he peeked from back stage.

"You'll be fine," I said. "We do what we practiced."

It took forever to get to us. Two women sang a cappella together, but one couldn't stay on key. "Amazing Grace" sounded more like Grace walked down an alley and was jumped. Then there was the comedian who perhaps thought he was Jerry Seinfeld or at least stole from him. "What's the deal with weddings?" he said. "If I'm the best man, then why's she marrying him? And you ever notice how dating is so differnt than marriage? My girlfriend loved to go camping with me, loved my cooking around the campfire. When we got married, she wouldn't go anymore. 'The ground is so hard,' she said, 'and your steaks are so burnt.'"

We had not one but two tap-dancing duos, then a pair of modern dancers, a man and a woman in black camo tights, and they wore Army boots, so it was funny, purposely. After all, one of the rules was that everyone had to wear their uniforms in the talent show. We were about to break that rule big time.

Then came some guy reciting poetry, but I couldn't tell if it was his or someone else's poems. He liked to speak dramatically, but he seemed to love big words such as "suspension" and "detention, "freedom" and "shedom," whatever the hell shedom was.

Then came a knife thrower, a juggler, and a woman who sang "Somewhere Over the Rainbow" while playing hopscotch.

Finally us.

We looked at each other back stage, all of us nervous. "Group hug," I said, and in one big ball of brotherhood, we did. Then I said, "Let's do it."

We stepped onto the stage, and my walk toward the front felt slow and long, yet with each step, I felt more confident as I looked at the people watching us curiously in their chairs—some people standing to the sides.

Instantly, people stood and cheered, chairs snapped to their folded positions. We all moved our amps forward and plugged in. Hitch sat at his drums and tested them all, bashing his cymbals, twirling his sticks in his fingers. With his foot, he hammered the bass drum.

Yanni adjusted his stand, plugged his keyboard into a bigger amp, and tried a few keys—nice and loud. Trace, with his wonderful Maine lobsterman fingers, practiced the chords G, A, and B the way I taught him. Styles stepped over to me and whispered, "You know what you're doing, right?"

I hadn't been on stage in years at this point, but when Styles said that to me, I felt the strings slide under my fingers, and I said, "Oh, yeah. Follow me. Watch me for any changes."

I took my position at the center, my mouth inches from the microphone. I peered into the crowd and felt right at home. I was free. I said, "A one, a two. One, two, three, four," and that first note to "Work" by Jimmy Eat World blasted from all four of us. Quickly people launched into dance. Some moshed hard, slamming into each other repeatedly. Kayla danced with Jenny Brown, Hoogerheide, and two other women. Hitch pounded his drums ferociously, winking probably to Hoogerheide with her two bandaged wrists. Styles, to my surprise, seemed consumed, pounding out the deep notes. His bass's amp pounded into the audience. Yanni worked the keyboards, and Trace on rhythm really felt the beat. We were tight. We were a group.

I sang, jumped in the air, and made my strings fly like RPGs. Trace and Styles started leaping into the air, too. Now they got it: pure fucking rock and roll.

In unison, we struck the last note, which reverberated into the night sky. The crowd cheered in explosive chaos. I turned to my band members. They all grinned as if they'd experienced a corkscrew roller coaster and felt better than expected.

"We did it, guys," I said, feeling as if I'd had the adrenaline rush of a bungy jump. When I turned back to the audience, I saw Captain Carpenterier speaking to two MPs. Shit. I couldn't think about him.

I asked the audience, "How're you doin'?" and they cheered, some fanning themselves. "All right, we got another." The audience moved the chairs out of the way.

We moved into one of my songs. Hitch puffed and thrashed, intensely physical, gritting his teeth but playing as if nearly every muscle in his body had to get out the music. Trace, my lobsterman, did nothing complex, yet his rhythm and intensity fit in with his jumping around. He was becoming a showman.

Yanni, bless him, perhaps had the deepest musical background of the four, and his rockabilly roots had him do a glissando, hitting all the white keys from the top on down with his thumb. Our audience ate it up.

Styles I couldn't be more proud of. Where he'd been lost in doubt and self-recrimination, he plucked his notes, jutting out his chin sometimes in rhythm to what he was playing. He was in the moment.

I turned back to the audience, thrilled at how everyone, even most of the shy ones standing alone on the edge, were now rocking out. They fueled me, and I sang and soared like I've never done. It wasn't about winning. It wasn't about surviving. It was about letting people lose themselves.

We ended with Patti Smith's "Gone Pie," from her *Gung Ho* album with its great driving rhythm and heavy bass line. I did her justice, and these soldiers danced hard. The music grabbed all of us. With more men than women on base, Kayla, Jenny Brown, and the other women soon moshed with multiple guys, but that was fine. I glanced at the captain and his MPs. They were clapping and nodding.

When it came time for everyone to vote on the show, the announcer, some sergeant I didn't know, asked us the name of our band. Yanni said, "The Max Rivera Band," but I said, "No. It's Baltic Avenue, the street where Jordan Frank's CHU was. Our performance is in honor of Jordan."

"Clap if you're voting for Baltic Avenue," he said. The whole place seemed to cheer. Other acts, when named, had clapping, but nothing like ours. In short, we won.

We jumped up and down to more applause, and I shouted into the air, "This is for you, Jordan!"

| | |

The next morning in the chow hall, the guys and I toasted each other with Rip-It drinks. I felt the way the air does after lightning strikes through it—fresh and alive. I stopped in at the souk, the indoor Arab bazaar inside the Morale, Welfare, and Recreation Center. All camps had MWRs—a center of activity with gyms, pools, shopping, whatever. I needed to get Kayla a little gift to show her I cared. As my dad told me, it's what you do that counts more than what you say.

I found Kayla after that in the chow hall. She sat with her roommates: so focused on talking, she didn't see me. Her oatmeal was half-eaten, and so was her fruit salad. I went up to her and said, "Can we talk? Outside?" Her roommates Yolanda and Germaine smirked as if I'd been the focus of their discussion, but I knew women did that—sliced and diced and dissected and analyzed and inspected relationships so thoroughly, that even if I were the perfect crystal glass, I would come out chipped and yellowed. Still, women were far better at this love thing than guys. I needed to prove myself to her.

"Great concert!" said Yolanda and "Absolutely" said Germaine. I thanked them—and thanked them again for their videoshoot.

Outside, she looked better in her digies than any other woman. I pulled her around the corner so anyone coming in wouldn't see us. "Are we okay?" I asked.

"Yes," she said. "Are you trying to make me crazy?"

"No. Maybe I'm confused at times, but I'm good." I wanted it to sound positive.

"What do you mean you're confused?"

"It's like we don't trust each other completely."

"How can I trust you?" she said, "when you run off to a prostitute after being away from me a couple days? Is your dick like a gun that has to shoot off a few times a week or it doesn't work?"

"Listen," I said, trying to wipe it all away. "I'm sorry. I'm not trying to start an argument. You're my best friend now." I looked down, rubbing my foot in the red dust, feeling my gift in my pocket. "You said you've filed for divorce?"

"Yes. I told you. You don't trust that, either?"

I pulled out the brown wrapped gift the size of a cigarette pack. She took the wrapping paper off it to find a little carved wooden box. It's the best I could do.

"I don't understand," she said. "I don't smoke."

"Open it."

When she did, I fell to one knee, which made her look at me curiously. She opened to find the little wrought-iron ring that the hajji had.

"It's just a stand-in until we get to the States," I said. "Then you can choose something you want. Will you marry me?"

"You're asking … me? You're a crazy person!" She looked aghast at first. Was I seeing wrong? Then she pulled me up as if realizing what I'd asked and hugged me.

"Will you?" I said.

"Fuck, yeah," she said.

"A kiss?" My eyebrows inched higher.

"Sure." We both looked around to make sure no one saw us. We kissed. She said, "You're the best."

"Thanks. You are, too."

She hugged me again, then suddenly looked worried. "You can't tell anyone. Soldiers on the front aren't allowed to marry."

"Actually, that's not true," I said. "I looked it up at the Army site on the Internet. This year, married soldiers on the front can have their own CHU."

"That's not going to happen if I'm still married, is it?"

"No."

"I don't want either of us to get transferred to a different platoon. You didn't tell anyone yet, did you?"

"No, not yet," I said, thinking she was overly paranoid. "I don't think our friends would—"

"No, promise me! I don't want to lose you. Loose lips sink ships."

"Okay," I said.

"I'll push for my divorce to go through, okay?"

I was about to kiss her again when I heard footsteps. The LT was walking by and we saluted immediately.

He glanced at us quizzically. "Is everything all right?"

In tandem, we said, "Yes, sir."

"Hmm," he said. He stepped away toward the chow hall.

"I won't tell anyone," I told her.

"I love you," she whispered.

With another set of approaching footsteps, I dared not say anything more. On the way back to my CHU, I ran into Styles, and I was so charged, I wanted to tell him, but I didn't. I merely said. "I've got to thank you. If it weren't for you giving me the okay with Kayla, I probably wouldn't feel this good."

He smiled. "Good for you, man." And he walked off whistling. Maybe this whole thing was a turn-of-the-corner for both of us. Where he was headed, I didn't know—toward the front gate. It wasn't toward the chow hall or his CHU.

Back at my CHU, I told Hitch something similar, too—I was just so fucking happy—when a loud knock came at the door.

"Yeah?" I shouted.

Sergeant-Major Rappaport, who worked with the captain, entered and said, "Private Rivera?"

"Yes, Sergeant-Major?" I said with a question because it's rare the sergeant-major would seek out a private.

"You played last night in the talent show."

"Yes, Sergeant-Major?" I said again.

"Colonel Baker is in Captain Carpentier's office and wants to speak with you and your bandmates. Can you all be there ASAP?"

My heart pounded. This wasn't good. We'd be cooked for disobeying orders about the shipping container after all. Yet was that enough to bring a colonel from Camp Victory? This had to be more serious than I'd ever considered.

"Yes, Sergeant-Major," I said. Hitch did not volunteer he was in the band.

Four of us soon headed toward the captain office, pushing through the wind and sandstorm that had come up. We hadn't found Styles. Trace said he had no idea, and because I saw him walk off toward the front gate, that didn't make any sense. It was short notice, so maybe the colonel would understand.

"Whatever happens," I said, "I'll take full responsibility."

"I should have never listened to you," said Yanni. "But it was the right call. I'm not putting the blame on you."

"Me, neither," said Hitch

"We should pretend we did nothing wrong. Let's just walk in clueless."

Trace laughed and said, "We are fucking clueless. Are you kidding me?"

We passed a couple people that I didn't recognize, a male and female private, but when they saw us, the woman said, "Incredible concert last night! Thank you so much."

"The guy said, "The best day of this fucking war. Thanks."

We all thanked them, adding a bounce to our step. If we were going down for this, at least it was in bright flames. I smiled. "Let's go."

Captain Carpentier's office was nothing grand: one small room in a prefab rectangle, much like a longer CHU. Inside was tight, with cheap blond paneling, a round battery clock on the wall, a long bare flourescent tube on the ceiling, and an American flag hanging behind the desk.

Colonel Baker sat at the desk, waiting for us. We saluted, and he said, "At ease, boys." No one questioned where Styles was, and I didn't volunteer it. The captain wasn't there, but the sergeant-major was. "I hear you guys gave a musical concert last night," said the colonel."

"Yes, I'm sorry,"I said.

"Sorry about what? It was a raging success." He laid out a copy of that day's *Stars and Stripes* with our picture on it with the headline "Winners!"

We weren't in trouble? "Yes," I said. "It was incredibly great." I wondered did the winner of the talent show get a visit from a colonel? I said, "People danced, had a great time." I gulped. "Sir," I added.

"That's why I'm here. This whole stop-loss order, while it's needed, has had a devastating effect on morale. As you know, Iraq is not an easy place."

"Yes, sir," we said in unison.

"A few of the higher-ups and I had this crazy idea—but it's not really crazy. What would you say if I could get you and your band to play at different camps around Iraq? You'd still have to do your missions when you're in Warhorse, of course, but playing in camps would count as mission work, too."

We could hardly breathe.

"What d'you say?" asked the colonel.

Hitch mouthed *What?* The sergeant-major looked astonished, too. The others looked ready to say, "What the fuck?" Playing in a band sounded much better than being an IED magnet.

With everyone nodding, I said, "We'd be honored, sir."

The colonel said, "Wonderful. We'll get you a list of events you'll play soon. Good luck, guys. Make it rain."

"Hoo-rah," we said, saluting.

"Of course, you'll have to wear your uniforms. That's not a problem is it? I heard it was, yesterday."

"No, sir, not a problem," I piped up. "Thank you, sir.

Continuing: Iraq, July 2007

We had a week to practice. At our first meeting, I said "We should have at least ten more songs down for the first show. We'll learn more later."

"This is what you think, do you?" said Yanni.

"Yes." I didn't want to get into an argument with him. At that moment, the door opened. Styles walked in with his bass. He wore sunglasses. He didn't look happy.

I had found him in his CHU after we saw the colonel, and when I told Styles about the offer, he immediately said, "Not me."

"Why? Isn't playing better than being shot at?"

"You can't fool destiny."

"Destiny! When'd you become so stupid? This is you choosing your fate. Music is better than war."

"And when has music been your friend? It threw you on your ass. That's why you're in the Army."

"Styles, wake up. You're so fucking negative lately. Yes, I'm sorry you mistakenly shot into that car and killed that family, but shit happens— you've said so yourself. Me and the band love you. Play with us."

"Negative?" He stood there as if thinking of clever ways to throw that back in my face, when he said, "When's the first practice?"

Now, as he strode in with his sunglasses and guitar, I said, "Nice to see you."

"Don't fucking say a thing more," said Styles, "And I won't try to be negative."

"This is positive?" said Yanni, testing the volume levels on his keyboard.

"Welcome," said Trace and Hitch at the same time.

"Let's try it, then," Styles said. We began with the Get Up Kids' song "Long Goodnight." I had to show Trace the chord progressions and even how to hold his fingers. At least he had enthusiasm.

"May I make a song suggestion," said Trace. "I love anything Mariah Carey."

"What the fuck?" said Yanni.

"Two words: boobs," said Hitch.

"That's one word, knucklehead," said Yanni. "But two boobs."

"How about 'Say Something' or 'Get Your Number'?" said Trace, ignoring Yanni.

"I got her number," said Hitch. "Number one!"

"Yes!" said Trace, and they high-fived each other.

"None of us have a voice like hers, so we're not doing Mariah Carey," I said.

"The voice of God has spoken again," said Yanni.

Right from the start of our practice sessions in Hitch's and my CHU, I liked the stuff I knew well, which were my songs, mostly about love, as well as rebel-filled punk. These days, it was as if I needed to pour out anger in such anthems such as NOFX's "Linoleum," The Vandals' "My Girlfriend's Dead," and Green Day's "Welcome to Paradise." Yanni, in contrast, liked the classic rock stuff, things like The Who's "My Generation," and Jethro Tull's "Locomotive Breath," and Led Zeppelin's "Kashmir." Sure, they had the punk spirit, but, really, Yanni wasn't that old. When he suggested Cat Stevens' "Peace Train," I had had it.

"You gotta be kidding me," I told Yanni. "It's not the kind of music we're doing."

"You don't want a peace train?" he said sarcastically. "What the hell're we fighting for in Iraq, then?"

"I want a peace train, but I'm not singing it."

"Hitch can."

"I don't know Cat Stevens," Hitch said. "Was he famous?"

"Fuck this," said Yanni, and yanked out the power plug to his keyboard.

Styles yanked off his sunglasses, upset, and instantly I worried they were going to punch it out.

"What's the big deal about Cat Fucking Stevens?"

Yanni glared at him. "Before I joined the Army, I was a policeman in Seattle."

"Am I supposed to be scared?" said Styles.

"I have another point," said Yanni. "One rainy night after midnight as was driving I-5 with my partner, we came across skid marks that fell off the highway and down a hill. I slipped down the hill to see, and I found a young woman with her neck broken, dead—a neighbor. I knew her since she was a little girl." He paused. "I loved the Cat Stevens song played at her funeral. Stevens has spirit."

None of us spoke. I thought maybe we should hug Yanni. Styles nodded, taking it in. Styles said, "Was it this Stevens' tune?" He played us a few bars of Stevens' "Where Do the Children Play?"

Yanni nodded and started to look near tears while Styles continued to play. The rest of us hugged Yanni until he pushed us back, saying, "Okay, okay."

Trace then tried, "How about Mariah Carey's 'Fly Like a Bird?'

"Are you fucked up?" said Yanni.

"What's your problem?" said Trace. "You don't like birds?"

Yanni looked surprised, then started laughing. "No, I don't like flying." We all laughed.

Luckily, our missions remained light that week. It was if Baqubah itself decided it was better off not banging our beehive. We made our patrols without incident. Maybe the bad guys had fled.

Because I'd had a band, I was obsessive about practicing. "You want to get better, don't you? It takes work."

If we wanted to play well, we had to be perfect. I pushed us deep into the night. Everyone but Styles tried hard, even if they got testy when I'd say, "Let's do it again." Styles, in contrast, seemed as if he were back in a haze. I was hoping our practice sessions would grab his spirit, but his playing felt uninspired. The next day, he arrived late and left early.

"What the hell do we have him for if he's not into it?" said Yanni. Styles had said he had to call his family.

"He needs our help," I said. "I was hoping music would do it."

"And we're not fucked up from the war? We're not upset we have to stay in his shit hole," said Trace.

"He's a downer," said Hitch. "It's like he's a zombie guitar player."

"Just give him time," I said. "We can help him. I'll talk with him."

But talk with him where? It would take a time when his emotional defenses were down, when he might listen. The next day when we were on patrol wasn't the time. He was the gunner in the Humvee I drove and was also the squad and team leader. The LT had given him this promotion. Hoogerheide was the navigator.

When we passed a playing field where a bunch of young Iraqi men played soccer on dead grass and dirt, he said, "Stop."

Shit. These were fighting-age men, probably hot heads. In their shorts or pants and many of them shirtless, they stopped to stare at us. Was this going to turn into bloodshed? They turned to us face-on, as if to say they weren't intimidated. In the yellowing sunlight, an hour before sunset their shadows stood long. Styles opened his door to get out.

"Don't say anything to get them mad," I said.

"You the squad leader suddenly?" said Styles, stepping out. Probably for the Iraqi's benefit, Styles clearly placed his rifle back into the back seat then shut his door.

The gunners on our other three vehicles had to be tense as they aimed their guns at the soccer field.

"Turn the guns away," commanded Styles. "In fact, stand down. Get out of your nests."

This was not smart. Styles had lost his mind. If anything happened here, this was a court-martial-worthy error. I opened my door and said, "Styles, what're you doing?"

"Get back in the vehicle," he ordered, and then, gunless, he walked across the field, his feet creating clouds of dust highlighted by the low sun. My heart was in my throat. He marched right into the group of young men who soon surrounded him. I opened my door. I pulled my M4 to my lap, ready to use it. All I could hear were mumbles. Styles said something, and a few English words from one of the young men flew my way, such as "Challenge" and "your arses." Then there was laughter. Styles laughed, too. He held his hand aloft, and said loudly, "High five."

Apparently several of the men knew the expression, and they held their own hands aloft and high-fived him. Styles came running back to our trucks, smiling innocently like some kid given a gold star. "Hey," he shouted. "They agreed to scrimmage with us. Anyone want to play soccer? We can show them we got this game."

No one moved. My heart suddenly raced. I'd remembered how he pictured he'd die in a soccer game.

"This isn't a good idea," I said.

"Come on, people," he said to everyone. "I'm not going to make you, but don't you want to mingle with the people we're protecting? What's the point, really, otherwise?"

I stepped out. I realized I could prevent him from kicking the winning score and he'd live. Was I thinking like him now, dementedly? Yet I'd returned to Iraq to go with the flow, and this was the flow. As crazy as it was, it seemed right. "Sure," I said. "I'll play. But in boots?"

"That's what we're wearing," he said.

Hoogerheide came out, too, her wrists still in Ace bandages, but she was back on duty. "Me, too?"

"Of course," said Styles.

With that, the other men and women in the other trucks got out. Of course, the other men weren't going to let the women show them up. One guy sat out, though, and I could imagine him thinking he'd be the lone survivor to explain how eleven troops were lost in a stupid game. I prayed it wasn't going to happen. There were no guns.

The Iraqi men drew down to eleven, leaving a handful to stand on the sidelines. I noticed all the Iraqis had fairly new Nike shoes with the swoosh, and bright yellow socks. A few had shin guards. The nets at either end looked official and substantial. Someone had funded these guys. They'd neglected to water the field, though. Then again, things like electricity and water remained problematic in Baqubah. The edges of the field were marked in a ghostly chalk.

At mid-field, Styles spoke with their leader, who pulled out a coin and flipped it. "Heads" said Styles before the coin hit the dirt. They both looked, and Styles jammed his hands in the air. "We'll kick off toward that goal," and he pointed.

"Can I be goalie?" said Hitch.

"Sure," said Styles, who placed the ball in the circle mid-field and took the position to kick it off. He punched it to me. I kicked it to another guy who slammed it to Hoogerheide. Damn, she was good at soccer, too, driving in toward the goal, deftly faking and moving past each opponent. She kicked hard, aiming to the right of the opposing goalie. The man leaped, caught the ball, and with a few steps, kicked it hard toward one of the Iraqi players downfield. That man bounced it off his chest, then charged toward Hitch and kicked. Hitch missed.

Goal!

We played hard. Even though we were losing, I wasn't afraid of our opponents—they were great players, and they seemed to be impressed with us, too. Plus I loved this because there was no way Styles would kick the winning goal and die.

In the end, we lost big time, just as the sun was setting, seven goals to our one, scored by Hoogerheide. Of course, they had replacement players to put in, and we didn't, and we were stiff in our boots. Afterwards, as they poured chai tea in paper cups for us, I couldn't help but think some of these guys, surely, had fought against American troops, yet here, with their smiles, the occasional comments such as "America good," and whatever they said about us to make each other laugh, they enjoyed us. We all high-fived each member of the other side before we left, and we walked back toward our trucks, spent and full of life..

On the edge of the field, I did a double-take at a young man talking seriously to one of the happy Iraqi players. The young man had a thin face and a dent on his chin and seemed familiar. When he looked our way, I waved, but he didn't respond. Maybe I didn't know him after all.

"I didn't expect that," I told Styles back at the truck.

"You didn't think it'd work, did you?" he said.

"This was great. I wish I could see some of this energy in you in band practice."

"I'm playing well."

"Not like you did here, full force. I'm not giving you news. You must know it yourself."

He grinned at me. "Yeah. I guess I've been preoccupied. My family. I've been toying with a song about my wife, though. Can I play it next time? Maybe you'll like it."

"That's why we're a band. Everyone contributes."

He seemed to think about that, then nodded. "Okay. Thanks," he said.

That evening at band practice, he was hot. He gave us the chord progressions for his song, which was on the quiet side and full of desire. He said the name of the song was "Our Destiny."

I saw her dressed in white.
She was an incredible sight,
And the way she walked, I knew I had to ask her.
It felt so right and I knew I might
Just fall in love and find my destiny.

She said her name was Lucy,
and the way she laughed moved me.
and we danced and twirled, and I fell right into her.
It felt so right and I knew I might
Just fall in love and find my destiny.

Well my heart beat fast
When we left that bash
And I could feel her soul mix with mine.

When we walked, the bells on her ears talked,
And she whispered to me, which is in my memory.
She said it felt right, and she knew she just might
Fall in love and find her destiny.

The chords were simple yet sweet. I really liked Styles' song and melody. It was interesting, too, in that he was using "destiny" in a positive way. It occurred to me, though, something was off. "I thought your wife was named Ann," I said.

"It didn't have the right rhyme," said Styles.

"How will she know it's about her?"

"Oh, she'll know," he said with a smile.

"I like it," said Yanni.

The three of us practiced Styles' song again, not the words but the melody. My mind was so much on the music, I invented a blues riff full of rage for the song. It could be a solo bit that would contrast the lyrics. My notion was that love soothed the savage beast, so the song needed some beast in it to stand in relief to the love-song lyrics.

We played so late, I didn't go to Kayla's CHU afterwards. Besides, her roommates were back and wouldn't appreciate the intrusion.

| | | |

Over the week, we became better, tighter. The first show of our tour was at in a hanger at Camp Normandy, the place for our last meal with Jordan when we'd watched *Project Greenlight*. A convoy not from our platoon drove us there, which felt weird, as we were treated like visiting dignitaries. The five of us and our equipment were in a large truck, and everyone in the convoy wished us the best and urged us to play at Warhorse again soon. We asked if we could bring a few friends from our camp, which the LT approved. He came along with Kayla, her CHUmates, and most people in our platoon in other trucks.

On a stage built with six-by-sixes and thick plywood, we started our show with the three songs we did for the talent show, then went on with our new hard-hitting version of "Where Do the Children Play?" After that, Styles said to me, "My song?" as a question, but I told him, "In a few." This audience needed to get their adrenaline pumping more, and we did our Green Day hit and one of my older songs—fast-paced love ballads.

At last I said, "This is a song that Blake Styles wrote, and he's going to sing it, too." I offered the mike to him, and he thanked me.

Sometimes I'm very slow on the uptake. Styles looked at Kayla when he started, but I didn't think it really meant anything. I focused on my guitar solo early in the song, the rage riff. When he got to the first refrain, "It felt so right, and I knew I might just fall in love and find my destiny," he was outright singing it to her. She looked uncomfortable. By the second refrain, when he hit the word "destiny," it was as if it were a special code to her, and she wiped a tear from her cheek. Now she was looking exclusively at him. But this song was about his wife. Did she want Styles back? Didn't she want to be engaged to me?

That old-time furor boiled inside of me. I felt like grabbing the mike from Styles. My chords became sloppy, and I didn't care. Then I purposely shredded the riff, but that didn't faze Styles. When it came to the line, "When we walked, the bells on her ears talked," I remembered Kayla had a set of tiny earrings that she sometimes wore on base that looked like little bells. This wasn't a song for Styles' wife. It was for Kayla, who now glanced at me fully crying, as if she were torn up and didn't know what to do. She ran out of the hanger.

When Styles was done, I glared at him and, raging inside, smashed my guitar on stage as if I were Pete Townsend from The Who. The audience was crying for more songs. I said into the mike, "A minute," and I ran out, looking for Kayla. I found her crying to the side of the chow hall.

"What's going on?" I said.

"I'm sorry." She wiped her eyes.

At that moment, Trace said into the mike, "This is another Green Day song we know." They started playing, but I didn't hear a bass guitar there. That's because Styles spoke behind me.

"I love you, Kayla." He stepped closer, but she backed up as if afraid of either him or her own emotions.

"Why?" she said. "I thought you loved your wife."

"I was hoping I did. It'd make it easier."

"I— I— " she said but found no verb to connect with.

I said to her, "I thought you loved me."

"I do," she said. "And I love Blake, too."

"Sorry, Max," Styles said. "I've tried to keep it inside, but you two kept pushing to fix myself, express myself, and so this is what you get."

"What about your family?" I said, trying to deflect him.

"If the war hasn't shown me anything else," he said to Kayla, "there is no good. There is no evil. Children fly apart from a bomb their parents created. Innocent people die, and there's no God to stop it. You get this, Kayla. We're alike. I can't help but feel we're meant to be together—destiny."

"Bullshit," I said. "You fling destiny about to suit your whim."

"Yeah—9/11 was my whim, right?"

"Anyway, Kayla and I are engaged."

Her tears rolled.

"Is that true, Kayla?" Styles said.

She nodded as if admitting to doing drugs. "You're ripping my heart, Blake," she said. She'd called him Blake and not Styles.

"You with me?" he said to her.

"And you're my friend?" I said to him.

"What's friendship or love in war except a way to feel something not dead."

"I don't need philosophy right now," I shouted. "I need her."

"Me, too," he said.

"Stay away from me—both of you," she said, now angry. "I need time to think. Just leave me alone to think." Then she ran off. We did not follow.

I walked the opposite way, back toward the gymnasium where the band was still into the Green Day song.

Styles ran up behind me and said, "Do you hate me?"

"I'm fuckin' pissed, Styles! What do you think?"

I turned around, and he looked so much smaller than he seemed a moment ago. He looked at me, though, not with anger but with hope.

"Believe it or not," I said, "I don't hate you. I'm trying to 'go with the flow,' and it's damn hard. You've fucked things up for Kayla, you, and me. Maybe war is this way—no one gets through it without some extra little twist of the knife ripping through your organs."

I didn't wait for a response. I walked back in, picked up the pieces of my guitar, grabbed my acoustic guitar, and joined the other four musicians. Styles snatched up his bass and walked out the back door. I played with so much need and passion that at least temporarily I could forget about things.

| | |

Hitch woke me up with his snoring. Normally, he didn't. A loud knock resonated from our door shortly after, at which point Sergeant Ichsada walked in, followed by the LT.

"Lieutenant Graver wishes to speak with you both," said the sergeant.

Hitch and I both stood in our underwear by our cots and saluted.

"At ease, you two," said the LT.

"Permission to leave, sir," said Ichisada.

"Granted," said the LT. To us, he said, "Sit, sit." I grabbed a nearby desk chair and offered it to the LT. He took it. Hitch and I sat on our cots.

"We have a situation," he began.

Hitch looked at me, puzzled.

"Situation?" I said.

The LT looked at me straight on. "I'm talking about Private Kayla Helwani. She told me that you two are engaged. Is that true?"

I felt lightheaded instantly, with my heart in my throat. I wasn't sorry or ashamed, but she had wanted me to keep it a secret. Since Kayla told him, I assumed she didn't expect me to lie.

"Yes, sir," I said. "However, we weren't going to make it official until we got back stateside."

Hitch looked surprised, though he didn't say anything.

"You're aware Helwani is married?" the LT said to me.

"Yes, sir."

"You're aware there are to be no sexual relations on this base?"

There was so much sex on this base, I thought that if it were chocolate frosting, we could cover a cake the size of Warhorse. The commanding officers were well aware of it and let it happen. Still I said, "Yes, sir, I'm aware."

"The problem is when it becomes rape or sexual harassment."

"No, no, no, there's nothing like— Are you saying—"

"She's trying to keep her marriage together, and she said you and Styles were harassing her?"

"She said this?" I could not believe it for a second.

"More or less. She's troubled, and this is what we made of it. I had to go to my superiors, who transferred her to another company. We had to nip this in the bud."

"What!" This made no sense. "If I was the problem, why didn't you come to me?"

"Private Helwani's situation forced my superiors to look at other possible inappropriate relationships going on. Our little platoon seems to have a lot of diversion. Thus, a few other women have been reassigned, such as Privates Jones and Hoogerheide."

"Hoogerheide!" said Hitch.

"I'm afraid so."

"This sucks," said Hitch.

The LT gave him a sharp look.

"Sorry, sir," Hitch said.

"I guess it does," said the LT. "I learned only today that a third of women in the armed services are sexually assaulted by fellow soldiers. Have you witnessed any of that in our platoon?"

"Not in our platoon, sir," said Hitch. "Everyone's good."

The LT looked at me.

"I was not aware of that, and I haven't seen any of that. So where did the women go?"

"I won't say. They were asked not to communicate with anyone from this camp for a while."

I stared at the ground, at our Iraqi rugs on the linoleum of our CHU. Why would Kayla complain to the LT about my proposal? She said yes, right?

"There must be some mistake," I said. "Why would Private Helwani go to you?"

"At first it was because she couldn't get a hold of her husband."

"He's probably upset. She filed for divorce to marry me."

"Incorrect," said the LT.

I said, "That's not true, sir."

"I agree, sir," said Hitch. "Privates Rivera and Helwani seemed very espectful with each other and... you know."

"No, I don't," said the LT.

"I don't want to get anyone in trouble, but they liked each other a lot."

"At the formation tomorrow, I'll remind everyone of the rules. good lay, privates."

The CHU and camp seemed unusually quiet. Hitch and I stared at each other.

"War is hell," I said.

"Fucked."

We zipped over to the MWR to use the computers and Internet. I brought up Kayla's email address and paused at the keyboard. Then I wrote, "What the fuck? What happened? Are you coming back to me?" The sounds of the keyboard were like little bullets.

| | |

Two days later, we had our second big gig, at Camp Anaconda in Balad, the camp with the trauma center. We had a similar convoy as before.

We got to Anaconda in the afternoon and the sergeant who met us said, "I thought you'd like to relax before tonight, so you have your choice, one of our two swimming pools, built before the war—thank you, Saddam—or our movie theater, where we show three free movies each day in thirty-five-millimeter. It's in one of our most hardened structures on base, so we go there during mortar attacks. It's where you'll be playing tonight after our last film."

"Pool," said Yanni, Styles, and Trace.

"Movies," said Hitch and me.

I didn't particularly care what the movie was, just so I wasn't with Styles. He didn't drop out. In fact, on the truck over he had said, "Sorry about all that," as if he hadn't just ruined my life. I said nothing back.

The film happened to be *Walk the Line*, a movie about Johnny Cash.

Talk about a God-damned metaphor: I was walking the line. I had my deep doubts that this band thing would work for long. First of all, Hitch and I looked and felt lost and depressed. We had not received emails back from our women. Add to that, Styles was a complete stranger to me now, and Yanni kept trying to run the band as if it were his, trying to shape the playlist to his way, but most of our audience would be five years younger than he was.

Yet that night, once the lights went down and I introduced us, and we hit that first hard chord of Blink-182's "Anthem, Part Two," everyone shouted. They were ready to mosh and scream. Pure chaos.

The front of the theater was free of seats, and that's where an instant mosh pit formed. This camp was strict on everyone bringing their weapons at all times, so all the moshers were in their uniforms, boots, and rifles slung over their shoulders, slamming against each other, screaming, hitting hard. A weird sight, and I pictured a battle scene in my mind from *Braveheart*.

Best I could tell, the theater held about eight hundred, and everyone seemed to be on their feet the whole time.

Basically, we only had a play list of about fifteen songs, and it could be divided into two groups: anti-establishment songs and relationship songs. Relationship songs were mostly what I wrote and Blink's "I Miss You." While we could not sing anti-Army songs, which people might welcome if I had one, we could get away with anti-establishment songs, such as anything by Rage Against the Machine. These days with stop-loss, everyone felt angry, and I certainly boiled even more now that Kayla was gone.

I didn't let Styles sing his Kayla song, and he didn't ask to play it.

After a few encores, we finally left the stage, shaking the hands of many of our audience members on the way out. Lots of people snapped photos of us, too, with their flashes. I knew someone from *Stars and Stripes* was there. That morning we'd been on the front page of the Army newspaper, touting us as great entertainment. We were the new sliced cheese.

Styles walked near me when we got outside, and I couldn't help myself. I asked, "Have you heard from Kayla?"

"No, but I didn't expect to."

"Why do you say that? She said she loved you."

"I don't think you really get her. She was never going to leave her husband." A flash went off right in front of me, disorienting me for a moment.

Styles walked ahead of me. I probably had fifty more questions. To his back, I said, "And you don't feel anything?"

He turned. "It's a dingo world. The baby always gets eaten."

Then he stepped off.

Over the next few weeks, we played at four other places: Camp Victory, Camp Ashraf, Camp Justice, and Camp Boom. We practiced in between, and we also had to go on a couple of missions with our platoon. While Baqubah remained eerily calm, I couldn't help but feel it would not stay that way for long. The pressure was also building in my frustration in not hearing from or finding Kayla. Hitch heard from Hoogerheide often now. She'd been redeployed to Camp Victory in Baghdad, but she hadn't been there yet when we played. They wrote and talked to each other all the time. I asked people I met in each camp we played if they'd heard of a Kayla Helwani. No one had any information—that is, until the guy in the chow hall line at the Warhorse mentioned he was visiting from Camp Hope.

I said, "That's where we're playing next. My band, Baltic Avenue, we'll be there Friday."

"I'll be back by then."

"You don't happen to know of a soldier named Kayla Helwani, do you?"

"She's that new chick, right?" he said. "Really good lookin'?"

I dropped my Rip-It drink, and it exploded.

| | | |

At Camp Hope, before our concert, I found her room. A helpful staff sergeant in the front office gave it to me. I knocked on the door.

"Come in," she said. It was her voice, the one I missed.

I entered. It was a small room, one small cot, and very spartan, light green. She was stuffing her clothes into her duffle bag. The wooden box I'd given her lay to its side on the cot with piles of neatly folded clothes. She saw me, sighed, and stared at me as if this was absolutely the worst time.

"Hello to you, too, my love," I said sarcastically. Did she miss me? Did she have nothing to say?

After staring at her duffle bag a few seconds, she said, "I'm sorry what happened—but I can't do this now. I have bigger things on my mind. I'll write you later."

"The way you wrote me over the last few weeks?"

"Max, please," she said, and she looked so vulnerable in that moment.

"You're not coming to see us play?"

"Wouldn't you know it'd be tonight? What was the Army thinking?"

"What'd you mean?"

"Such is my luck."

"Good luck has followed you all your life, I bet."

She said nothing.

"What am I supposed to think or feel?" I said. "We had a great thing. Now you're just trying to fuck with me—after we fucked?"

She still said nothing.

"Perhaps," I said, "I did something wrong, but I'm not sure what because I loved you. You made me feel like—"

"Did you ever get beyond me and Styles?"

"Yes! That's why I asked you to marry me. Then he had to do that stupid song."

"It wasn't stupid. That's part of the problem."

"If I've learned anything outside of how horrible this war is," I said, "it's that I've misunderstood you—but I'm trying to understand. I wasn't being crazy asking you to marry me. I thought we'd have our lives together."

She shook her head. "What was your plan? You'd get a job doing what after the war?"

"I'm planning to go to college and start a career."

"Doing what?"

"Film director."

She smiled. "I'll give it to you—you're an optimistic guy. And then we'd have kids and live in the suburbs and, I don't know, go to film festivals?"

"Move to Orange County, California. I'm fine with that."

"God, no. You know your problem? You're a love junkie. You think what we had was love, but it wasn't. Did you ever ask me more about my husband? He's a Marine vet, urged me to join up, gain skills and thought I'd understand what he'd been through. It's stupid, but at least he asked me what I wanted in life, and you've never done that. You really don't know me."

"I thought you were trying to escape him."

She said nothing.

"So my trying and caring didn't count?"

She leaned her head back as if looking to God for strength. Then she looked right at me. "My husband is in the hospital. That's why I'm packing. The Army is sending me back with an honorable discharge."

"You're leaving the Army?"

"Clearly they want what happened with you and me to go away."

"I don't want what we had to go away."

"I get that."

"So your husband, he's a manipulator, right?"

"He tried to commit suicide, okay?"

"Ain't I the fucking asshole. I'm sorry." That came automatically. Was I sorry? I said, "Was it because you asked for a divorce?"

"I never did that. How could I when I could tell he was so fragile? We're all just stupid."

"I don't agree."

"I mean we're not smart. Otherwise, why would we join a war? Do you see anyone reading around here or talking about, I don't know, bird migration? We're just doing the shitty details that our country wants done. Very few of us leave as normal, would you say?"

It was my turn to say nothing.

"My husband knows a few people in the service, and word got back to him about me—you and me or Styles, I don't know, but it wasn't good."

I held up my pointer finger. "Seems to me, we can have a say in this. We think. We feel. We love each other. We don't need other people to dictate to us or have fucking destiny to take over. We can be smart."

"For you and me, the world thumbs us into the ground. I can't change."

"My guitar gently weeps," I said. I thought of how George Harrison was dead. Yet he showed me how music could drive us forward. He was more alive than ever.

She stepped up to me and hugged me. I kissed the top of her head. Her hair smelled acrid, like apples left too long in the sun.

"Bye."

"Good-bye."

I left.

|　　|　　|

Later that night after I stepped on stage, I didn't expect such pain. Playing in front of people has always magnified things for me, and so this night, I played harder than I ever had. I even broke three strings. The other three did the job. I changed our song order around so that all the fast-paced rage-filled songs came first, and it was as if the audience was with me, singing, moshing, smashing more than any previous audience. At one point after a song, Yanni stepped up to me and whispered, "Slow down, man. We're wearing out. Time for a few slower numbers."

"I have to go to the bathroom," I said. "You take over."

Back at his keyboard, Yanni said into his mike, "This is a slower piece, a little piece we like from Cat Stevens."

It was after that, the world spun, and I collapsed on stage.

19

Continuing: Iraq and California, July–November 2007

We didn't have another gig for a week, so we were back on missions. I brought my camera with me everywhere, still wanting to capture Iraq, even as bad as I felt. I shot more landscapes now rather than people. In my free time editing, I noticed there was a beauty I'd never noticed before. We had the early evening missions, so I was often shooting near sunset. The clouds in Iraq could be spectacular, particularly near sunset. For instance, one day, Styles, Trace, and I were walking along a wall somewhere on the edge of the city, and at the end of the wall, this weird circular-tiered tower rose like a wedding cake. The setting sun hit the wall, the tower, and the clouds billowing above it to make everything seem rich and golden like we were in some picture book. I shot it from the other side of the street to get the whole thing.

Another time, out past Baqubah, in the desert where it was hilly and bone dry, nothing but rocks and a little scrub, a remnant of some building stood at the top of a hill. The structure appeared to be a stone wall about waist high and looked a thousand years old. A huge tree had grown in the middle of it—in an area where there were no other trees at all. Yet this big tree, growing in the middle of someone's rock house or yard, had become so old and dead, it had fallen over. What remained was just the trunk and a few fingers of its giant branches. It looked like a giant hand scraping at the rubble. That's what Iraq needed overall when we left, a giant hand from Mt. Olympus just getting rid of all that was ruined.

Supposedly civilization started around here. As I'd learned earlier, Iraq had been called Mesopotamia, which means in Greek, "in the midst of rivers." With the Tigris and Euphrates rivers, life began. It was the cradle of civilization. We and those who lived here were doing our best to blow it all up, baby with the bathwater, but if you looked closely, the cradle could still be found.

I found it once near a river. It was a tank destroyed, turned upside down and burned to shit. With the damp breath of the water and the setting sun bouncing off its treads, it was gorgeous.

I found another cradle near a temple and a minaret. First came the call for prayer, but I saw no one. Just the sound. The setting sun amid the palm trees looked like a ball of coconut ice cream sitting on mint leaves. My eyes ached, it was so beautiful.

One day when I was driving, thick puffy clouds like biscuits opened up, and a staircase of light came down as if God ordered it and shone on a set of U.S. helicopters flying by. "God Bless America," I thought, as if that's all God cared about—not Iraq or Iran or any place where people dressed funny—just America.

The last time I found the cradle was with Styles next to me. Trace sat in the back as gunner, and I drove down a city street. We were in the lead, and Styles peered closely at a map. "Take the next right," he said. In that moment, the way sun came through the window on his side, he looked content, as if he knew exactly what he was doing, as if this were the place to be.

I turned right.

"Keep going straight for a kilometer," Styles said."

This seemed like the right moment to ask what had been hammering at me, so I finally said, "Why did you write Kayla that song? For wanting her so much, you don't seem surprised at what happened."

"Most relationships end."

"But why did you write it?"

"Sometimes you seem like you're ten."

"What're you saying?"

"Exactly."

Trace in the back said nothing. I let a block go by, then said, "What you did deeply hurt, and I didn't appreciate it."

"Maybe you will someday."

"Are you saying what you did helped me? Because—"

"Sorry about that."

"Then explain yourself or Kayla." I could feel my anger building, but I knew I had to rein it in.

"Kayla has her destiny, and I have mine," he said. "Yours—yours is still up in the air."

"Can you stop talking this new-agey shit and just tell me what missed about Kayla or you!" I stopped the Humvee, screeching the convoy to a halt.

"Here's the truth for you," he said with a snap, but as he was about to say something else, he looked more closely on his map. We were right next to a narrow street with a lot of people near it, many of them robed. The crowd made me tense. Also, we'd never driven here before. This was an unvisited piece of road.

"We don't have permission for this," I said.

"Let's get out and walk. It's here." He looked out the front as if recognizing something.

"We can't walk here. We've never been here."

Near the edge of the street stood a half-dozen young men, huddled talking with each other. I thought I recognized a few, particularly a thin one with a dented chin.

"What?" I said. "We're not—"

"Just give me a second." He stepped out and walked up to the young men, his M4 at the ready. He started talking. One of the young men bolted and the rest ran with him. It was then I saw that a few of the young men wore Nike shoes and yellow socks. Styles shouted "Hey!" and charged after them. They ran down between buildings, too narrow for the Humvee. "Shit!" I said to Trace. "Let's go!"

We bolted out of there. The three Humvees behind us had just caught up with us. I didn't see anyone getting out, but as we ran down the alley I could hear Humvee doors slam. Why would Styles go off alone? Was he out of his damn mind?

Our weapons in hand, we ran where Styles and the young men had run, and we bashed into people, others stepping out of the way like Moses splitting the sea. I could tell where they all had gone by the way the people seemed displaced. Soon, though, I couldn't tell where Styles and the others had disappeared.

I was out of breath. I looked to my left. Nothing. To my right, nothing. This was a labyrinth of a city. We waited for support. Eight other soldiers soon joined us. We had a choice of three alleys, so we split into three groups. Trace came with me as did our latest translator, Habib, who preferred the name Joe. We ran a block before I held out my hand to stop. "Joe, can you ask if people ran this way?"

He asked a kid of about twelve dressed in white.

"Yes," said Joe. "They went this way, taking a right at the next corner." At that moment, a burst of gunfire erupted a block away, and then a few shouts. We ran.

We followed the directions and came to an unusually beautiful area with rose bushes and deep red blooms that edged a stucco wall. A bunch of women and kids encircled something. Joe yelled in Arabic, and the people ran off. Styles lay splayed on gray slate, dark areas pooling on his chest, and a red pool of blood growing by his head. I saw a hole in his neck. He appeared dead with his eyes open.

Next to him lay the young man with the dented chin. He had committed suicide, his black handgun in his hand by his head. I now recognized the guy, Rafik, who had sold us the watches. I also now realized where the young man got the scar on his chin. He was the surviving cousin of the family that Styles had accidently killed.

"Shit," said Trace, and he spoke into his radio. "We found Styles," and he gave our position.

Then Styles blinked, and his lips moved. I quickly knelt down, saying, "Hold on, Styles. Help's on the way." I could hear Trace saying, "He's shot but alive."

I put my ear near Styles' mouth, and he gasped out the word, "Goal!"

"No! Styles! Blake, hold on."

He gurgled, "You ... the right ... one." Then came his death rattle.

I gave him CPR instantly, but that just made his blood leak out more. He had too many wounds.

After a few minutes, Trace said, "He's gone, Rivera. Stop."

Styles' face did not look shocked. If anything, he looked peaceful, which didn't make sense. I looked down at Styles' hands. He held no gun. Stolen. He was probably shot with his own gun. Why did he talk to the young men? Why did they run, and why did Styles give chase? Why had he seemed so calm?

Something buzzed right in front of my face and made me jump. A hummingbird hovered over a rose bloom, sipping from it. The tiny bird had a red throat. I jerked at it to smash it, but it flew away.

Trace was crying, and I hugged him.

More of our platoon ran in, including a medic, who pronounced Styles dead.

We never found any of the Iraqi young men.

Years later, too, I learned there are no hummingbirds in Iraq. They only live in the Western Hemisphere, and a ruby-throated hummingbird, mostly in the Eastern United States. A bird specialist I found said I may have seen a sunbird, which is small, drinks nectar, and hovers like hummingbird. However, that bird is black with an iridescent purple at it throat. Had I misperceived?

And what did Styles last words mean? Was I the right one? The right what? Or was I right about something? To this day, I don't have answer to any of these questions. I'd like to think I was the right person for hin He was for me. He's part of me.

| | | |

A few days after Styles died, our specialty code was released fron stop-loss. Apparently, the Army had our replacements. We were to retur as originally scheduled. Once again, our company met in formation, and acted as a pallbearer, carrying with five others Styles' body and his silve transport coffin to a waiting plane. Again, a bugler bugled. The notio hit me that Styles sacrificed himself for us, but I didn't know why or hov exactly. I just had that feeling—and still have it to this day.

I never saw Kayla again. Somehow Hoogerheide returned to our pla toon. Apparently she protested and got results. She and Hitch became thing again, but much less overt. They later married and had two chil dren. They named the boy Blake.

After Styles' death, the remainder of the band gave Styles a memo rial concert in the same courtyard area where we had won the talen show. Trace had asked if he could play Styles' bass—"We need bass part right?" and I told him sure.

The audience started arriving about an hour before the show as the sun was setting. This time, there were no chairs provided, but soldier brought their own foldable ones or blankets for the hard ground. The weather was forgiving, too—not too hot, not too cold. Most of the FO was there. A majority of them probably didn't know him, but they knev of him—and everyone there had lost people.

The four of us, Yanni, Trace, Hitch, and I, gathered in a circle backstage and we put arms around each other's shoulders. The sound of cheering the anticipation, could be heard through the concrete block walls. I wa feeling that I was supposed to lead, and I wanted to lead, yet I couldn' help but think of Styles now as nothingness. He didn't exist except in ou minds. Animals didn't know they'd die, but we did—more than ever ir this moment. He'd once told me, "A dog might smell really well, but he doesn't think about, say, how one dog's butt is better than a rancid stick of butter. He doesn't think about the sweetness of a rose, or a rose by any other name. And dogs don't think about death, but we do. Because I know it can happen at any time, it's a possibility over everything I do."

I couldn't think about that. I had to say something to these guys. Something positive. Cliché was fine.

I said, "We're a little smaller today without our friend Styles, but let's make some noise for him to hear."

Hitch spoke up. "Even if the guy didn't believe in God, I bet God is making him laugh his ass off."

Yanni smiled and said, "He'd probably knuckle your head for that." We all laughed. That's what we have to do when we feel bad, no? Laugh.

"The fucker played a mean bass," said Trace. "Somehow I think he'd have made a good fisherman, too."

"Let's plug in," I said, and I led us to the stage. The cheers grew louder. I turned back to see the guys staring at me. "Start," said Yanni.

I stepped up to my microphone. "Blake Styles was like no other," I said. Hearing my voice each over all these people, I now knew what to say. "He wrote a song called 'Our Destiny,' which I don't think he'd want me to play or explain. Still, it was an important song as it showed me differences in our outlook. He was the philosopher, not me. Maybe that was his cross to bear. I hate to argue with the guy, but I don't think there's destiny other than what comes from that initial spark when you meet someone you know you like, who becomes your good friend forever. Styles was my friend, remains my friend, and I thank him for everything he gave me. I was going to begin with one song for him, but last month after we'd lost Jordan, I'd been writing another song. Right now I realize it's really right for our friend Blake Styles. I'm going to try to finish it for you right in this moment. Appropriately, it's called 'Present in the Moment.'"

I turned to my bandmates. "I'll start, and once you see what I'm doing, feel free to join in."

I began with my acoustic guitar.

Styles, you traveled with us for miles.
We're on the shore, wishing you could stay.
Moving like a sailboat in a gentle breeze,
All your dreams glide on their way.

At that point, Yanni approached his keyboard, and he started playing. I had played him parts of this song once, so he knew it a little, and Yanni came up with a great piano intro combining lush chords with a simple melody. I sang.

You have us wondering.
You somehow came to see
We're all in this crazy business
You called destiny.
What is that? Do our coins always land on tails?
Do our feet always step on bombs?

Trace now walked on, and soon his bass notes blasted into the audience.
You were my philosopher.
And the only way we can truly live
Is if each of us give a beat to this instant.
You were so insistent that we just had to be.
It's not destiny. We were meant to be
Just present in the moment.

Last, Hitch sat before his drums, and his beat centered us. We repeated the motif that Yanni had created.

No one danced but rather raptly listened.

I launched into a fast guitar solo, heavy on the high notes, bending the strings. We rocketed the song to a high-paced end.

After the cheers and applause, I switched to my electric guitar. We played six more songs. The soldiers danced hard. After that concert, we never played again. We weren't the same without Styles. The war had finished us.

| | |

With my end date in sight, I applied to film schools. I'd realized I'd dodged the proverbial bullet, and I had my life back. I could do anything. I had choice. I wanted to create—creation spoke to me—and I wanted to go to college.

In two months, I heard back that I'd been accepted to the Art Center College of Design in Pasadena in their film directing program. I could start in the Spring Semester, which would begin in January.

Weeks later, the morning that we were to convoy to the airport to return to the States, it began snowing in Baqubah. It came down in big white flakes, though the beige earth swallowed them up. Around me, the concertina wire still gleamed, the blast walls still stood, and those I worked with from Fort Lewis, still alive and in one piece, stepped onto the buses. After I threw my duffle into the belly of my troop bus, I leaned my head back and let the flakes fall on my face. I felt like ten. I wished that feeling could have lasted longer.

The buses drove out. Everyone seemed too exhausted to cheer.

Sometimes at night as I sleep alone, I'm a drone flying over Baqubah, looking for those young men in yellow socks. I move from snowy bank, to muddy rubble-filled streets, to a green field that stands empty. As I get closer, the bright field shimmers like surf on an ocean, and instead of grass, it's covered in green iridescent hummingbirds, hovering. Closer yet, I can pick out individual birds—one with a spray of red on its throat, others with lavender or pink. Their fast wings wave to me in a blur—and their varied pitch sounds like music.

Acknowledgments

Thank you to Lynn Hightower, who edited our initial chapters when we started out and set us on our course. Thank to also to our initial readers including Preston Rose, Ann Pibel, David Pibel, Mark Hughes, Peter Seed, George Meeks, Laura Meeks, Russ Kremer, and Sandi Holden. In the end, editor Carol Fuchs dove in and helped shape the final draft. We love the design Deborah Daly did for this book and cover, and for agent Toni Lopopolo's thumbs up. Thank you to Vroman's Bookstore in Pasadena for hosting the publication party, and our appreciation in advance goes to those who help us promote this book. It's difficult to get heard in the tsunami of media and social network outlets.

From Mr. Meeks:

After I finished writing my last novel, *A Death in Vegas,* I wanted to try something new, as I often do. Each novel brings its own challenges. At that time, I had lunch with my former Art Center College of Design student, Samuel Gonzalez, who ended up telling me he'd sold his life rights about his experiences in Iraq to a movie producer. Samuel's lawyers had retained the novel rights to his story for some reason, so he asked, "Would you like to write my story as a novel?"

I did—and for a few reasons.

I had developed the inner strength to write novels in the first place after I read and then taught Tim O'Brien's *The Things They Carried,* stories of the Vietnam war. The book resonated on many levels. The first was I was a Minnesota high school senior when the last draft lottery of the Vietnam war was drawn. My future lay in the order of the 366 ping-pong balls pulled, each ball having a birth date. I might have to go to Vietnam. My number was high, ever-so-thankfully, but I always wondered what my life would have been if I'd gone. Mr. O'Brien's book showed me.

O'Brien also wrote in that book about writing fiction itself, how story-truth was as rich or richer than what he called "happening-truth," the way events occurred in real life. Story-truth can hone in on the feelings and experiences one had felt by writing and changing things, editing out moments, exaggerating events, all to get at the deeper truth.

That's what I wanted in this novel. While I couldn't live the war, my magination has always been strong, and with Sam, I had my protagonist n front of me. I could ask him questions every day, and he'd answer, even f it was so tough, he would break down. I made it clear this was a novel ve'd be diving into, not a memoir. I wrote and he read, corrected, and of-ered incredible suggestions of where the story could go, events that could have happened, even if they did not to him. After all, he's a screenwriter and an amazing director (see his short he made for me for *A Death in Vegas* on YouTube), so he, too, believed in story-truth.

I also taught for two semesters at CalArts a class I designed, "Vietnam Through Literature," where we read Mr. O'Brien's book and others. I've since read a number of Iraq and Afghanistan war fiction, including Matt Gallagher's *Youngblood*, Phil Klay's *Redeployment*, Jesse Goolsby's *I'd Walk With My Friends If I Could Find Them*, and Katey Schultz's *Flashes of War*. The genre speaks to me, perhaps starting with Ernest Hemingway's *A Farewell to Arms*. Life, its absurdities and possible meanings, are condensed in war. I wish we could avoid it, but human beings are crazy—and mean and vis-cous, loving and musical, and many other great and terrible states of mind. I hoped to get at these things in this novel.

From Mr. Gonzalez:

Today is June 12th, 2017...and as I sit at my desk staring out the window at the City of Angels' skyline, a cup of flat ginger ale beside me, and the text cur-sor blinking slowly on my laptop screen, I can't help but remember the events that took place ten years ago today when I lost my best friend and battle buddy to an anti-tank mine on the blacked-out streets of Baqubah, Iraq. My life was and never has been the same since. Not a day goes by that I don't think about him and the young men and women that strapped on that M-4 rifle, helmet, and heavy Kevlar vest every day to fight against an invisible enemy without a real purpose or understanding of why we were even there in the first place.

I've had a lot of time to think about it, and in the end, what I did under-stand was that we did it for each other, for our families, and for the hope of a better future. Although my memory throughout those tough years has be-gun to fade, the power of the music we played on those stages over there still echoes in my dreams—and always will.

I would like to thank first and foremost every brother and sister in arms that marched on the desert sand and hot sun with me during those days. To the ones who came back and for the ones we had to carry back, your bravery and sacrifice are for forever and will be my inspiration in every step I take.

For Damon, who always believed I would one day get to higher ground, this book is a tribute to you. I know the angels above are laughing with your contagious sense of humor and the joy that you always shared with us.

Many more thanks to my collaborator and co-writer, Christopher Meeks who opened the doors to his life and home to help me gather my memories and pave the way for the book you have all read. His love for stories, literature, and characters reflects on every page, and he truly respected my vision for the war I experienced through young eyes, and for that I am eternally grateful.

Thanks to my mother and my father for being my copilots in life and for never allowing me to fail. They are my motivation to always express and be true to myself, and I couldn't have asked for better parents. I love you always. A special shout out to my brother from another mother, Christopher Lang—a true friend who has been through the low and high tides with me. You have been there during bright lights and dark nights, brother, and when I didn't have a flashlight to get me back home, you were always there to make sure you had an extra one. Thank you for all your support and friendship. And of course, to Emily Trosclair for your unwaning love during all those restless days and sleepless nights while trudging through the emotional roller coaster while writing the book. You listened time and time again to every chapter, every memory, and every story while encouraging me to keep going and pushing through. I am forever thankful for your presence in my life. You have been a true rock and a strong woman in my life.

Finally, I would like to thank music and to all those who create it, for you are the artists who saved my life and brought us home. Our ears were overtaken by distant explosions and passing bullets every single day, and my only escape were the words and melodies of some of rock-and-roll's greatest musicians. Thank you for guiding me home with the sounds of your chords, the truth of your lyrics and the soul of your vocals.

My experience in the Iraq War was different as it was for most of my generation. We were kids, with blinders to the world, playing in a playground with buried bombs. We are no closer to understanding our days there now, than back when we were dodging bullets in the sandbox. My goal in writing this semi-autobiographical book is that we will finally be able call this our final mission and rest easy—for all of us who have returned, for all those still out there, and for those to return to it. I hope this will remind us all that although we have been at war for as long as we can remember, that through the thick dark smoke, there is actually a small glimmer of light. For me, it was the MUSIC. May this book lead you to yours.

For all those who have supported me throughout the years on my climb up this mountain, and you know who you are, please know that you are always with me, as it wouldn't have been the same without any of you by my side. Here's to the next climb. Thank you all—HOO-RAH!

About the Authors

Christopher Meeks has had stories published in several literary journals, and he has two collections of stories, *Months and Seasons* and *The Middle-Aged Man and the Sea*. His novel *The Brightest Moon of the Century* made the list of three book critics' Ten Best Books of 2009. His novel *Love at Absolute Zero,* also made three Best Books lists of 2011, as well as earning a *ForeWord Reviews* Book of the Year Finalist award. His two crime novels, *Blood Drama* and *A Death in Vegas* have earned much praise. He has had three full-length plays mounted in Los Angeles, and one, *Who Lives?* was nominated for five Ovation Awards, Los Angeles' top theatre prize. Mr. Meeks teaches English and fiction writing at Santa Monica College, and Children's Literature at the Art Center College of Design. To read more of his books visit his website at: www.chrismeeks.com

Samuel Gonzalez Jr. is an Emmy-nominated and award-winning filmmaker who was born in the Bronx, New York, and raised in South Florida. He joined the United States Army in 2006 and was quickly deployed overseas during the height of the Iraq War as a military police officer. While there, in response to the stop-loss, he formed a punk rock band at Camp Warhorse, who then played several shows that raised morale for their fellow soldiers during the time of the surge. In 2007, he was awarded the Army Commendation Medal with "V" device for combat heroism. Since his return to the States, Gonzalez has received his B.F.A in Film from the Art Center College of Design and his M.F.A. in Screenwriting from the New York Film Academy. His feature film directorial debut *Railway Spine*, a coming-of-age period war and crime drama about the real psychological disease that is PTSD won the Golden Eagle Award for "Best Military Film" at the 2016 San Diego International Film Festival and several other awards including "Best Screenplay". He lives in Los Angeles where he is currently in development on "The Chords of War" as an eight-part television mini-series. To see more of his work visit www.vimeo.com/samuelgonzalezjr.

Made in the USA
Middletown, DE
29 November 2021

53778478R00168